Caiseal Mór was born into a rich tradition of Irish story-telling and music. As a child he learned to play the brass-strung harp, carrying on a long family tradition. He spent several years collecting stories, songs and music of the Celtic lands during many visits to Ireland, Scotland and Brittany. He has a degree in Performing Arts from the University of Western Sydney and has worked as an actor, a teacher and as a musician. Caiseal's family is from Youghal, County Cork.

ALSO BY CAISEAL MÓR FOR EARTHLIGHT

The Wanderers Series
The Circle and the Cross
The Song of the Earth
The Water of Life

CAROLAN'S
CONCERTO

A TOAST TO THE THREE SACRED PASTIMES OF OLD IRELAND:
MUSIC, STORYTELLING AND WHISKEY

CAISEAL MÓR

EARTHLIGHT

SIMON & SCHUSTER

London • New York • Sydney • Tokyo • Singapore • Toronto • Dublin

First published in Great Britain by Earthlight, 2002
An imprint of Simon & Schuster UK Ltd
A Viacom Company

1 3 5 7 9 10 8 6 4 2

Simon & Schuster UK Ltd
Africa House
64-78 Kingsway
London WC2B 6AH

www.simonsays.co.uk

Simon & Schuster Australia
Sydney

A CIP catalogue record for this book is available from the British
Library

ISBN 0-7434-2901-X

Printed and bound in Great Britain by
Omnia Books Ltd, Glasgow

ACKNOWLEDGEMENTS

I would like to thank Selwa Anthony, Julia Stiles and Linda Funnell for all their help, support, hard work, kind words and occasional encouraging laughter. I seem to have fallen in with a fantastic team.

My heartfelt thanks also to everyone at Random House Australia for their support. I hope this story gives you all a bit of a giggle.

To all those readers who have visited my web site at www.caiseal.net and who have dropped me a line, I would also like to give my special thanks. Writing a novel can be a very isolating experience so it is wonderful to receive such positive letters from all over the world.

Finally, thanks to all my understanding friends. They have grown accustomed to me disappearing for months at a time only to emerge from seclusion with another bulging manuscript under my arm. This time it was a bottle of whiskey.

Slainté.

Caiseal Mór
Sydney, May 1999

Toirdhealbhach
Ó Cearbhalláin

Turlough O'Carolan

1670-1738

ONE

Breath came hard and painful. The young man bent over, his hands on his knees, straining to draw air, chest fit to burst with the agony of the run. At the top of the bare, treeless hill, face dripping wet from the drizzle, he cursed his aching legs.

The effort to stand up straight made him gasp. He looked quickly about the grassy knoll and then leaned forward again to ease the cramp in his lungs. He was overburdened. The fashionable long dark grey coat-tails made running difficult. The wide button-back cuffs restricted the movement of his arms.

The young man considered discarding his coat there and then, but the soldiers would surely find it and track him down. Besides, he would need it in Dublin.

He glanced behind him down the green hill, smoothed by wind, weather and the passing centuries.

'Edward,' he berated himself, 'you are a bloody fool.'

Drops of water gathered at his chin and spattered onto his long black waistcoat. His throat was dry, his hands swollen, his heart beating rapidly. In his hand he still held the blood-spattered pistol.

Edward looked at the flintlock and made an effort to calm himself. But he was too elated and frightened to be cool-headed. He stood up straight, raised his head to the sky, defying the rain, and held the pistol out in front of his face.

He had not expected that there would be so much blood. He had never shot a man before. He had never even seen a man shot.

'I killed the bastard,' he gasped triumphantly, waving the pistol at the clouds. He took the weapon and threw it with all his might down the hill toward the fields. And then he coughed violently, clearing his lungs. 'Ireland forever,' he sputtered, bending over again.

Edward touched the other pistol in his belt, making sure it was safe. On this bare hill he felt like a king who had just won himself a kingdom.

'Jesus!' he cried hoarsely, lifting his voice to the heavens in exultation. 'I'm a bloody hero!'

He turned around, his arms flung out, to yell his defiance in every direction. But he had not had the chance to open his mouth again when he caught a glimpse of a bright scarlet flash not a hundred yards behind him. He felt a sharp stab of fear in his chest.

Soldiers.

He blinked, hoping that he had imagined the red-coated devils in their black cocked hats. But after he rubbed his eyes the Englishmen were still there. And now the three of them were steadily making their way up the hill toward him, the primed frizzen pans of their muskets carefully covered by grubby fingers to keep flint and powder dry in the rain.

Edward knew he was a dead man if he let them get close enough to shoot at him. He quickly scoured the sky for clouds, hoping for a heavier downpour. Then he removed the pistol from his belt, checked the powder in the pan and tucked the weapon back under his coat.

Before another breath was wasted on curses or congratulations, he turned away from danger and fled as fast as his feet could carry him down the other side of the hill. A fine felt three-cornered hat, acquired in Dublin at great expense, flew off his head and landed upside down on the wet ground. In his desperate haste the young rebel barely noticed.

With his hat gone, the black ribbon which held his straight

mousy blond hair tight behind his head loosened a little. The delicate strands fell about his face, obscuring his vision so that he could hardly see the ground in front of him. He brushed the hair away and ran on as the rain began to fall again, heavy, drenching and welcome.

He did not care that his fine clothes would be ruined. Damp was the scourge of all musket-men. As long as the rain fell steady and hard, the redcoats would not raise their firelocks. They would not risk a soaked powder charge or a misfire from a dampened flint.

The young man stumbled quickly down the slope, making for the stream at its foot. A cow was drinking on the far side, ignorant of all the fuss. She did not even look up as the young man came charging down her hill.

Edward's legs carried him over the clumps of grass and stones. But shoes of finest English leather are fashioned for the streets of London, Bath or Dublin. They are an extravagant liability in the wild Irish countryside. This well-dressed rebel had not gone very far before his polished soles betrayed him to the sodden ground and he slipped backwards to land hard on the soaked earth.

As he lay winded the shower passed away on the breeze. By the time he stood up and rubbed his bruised backside, the rain was gone completely. He shook the muck from his coat-tails, stared skyward and then dared to peer back toward the redcoats. No sign of them. It crossed his mind that his footwear would be the death of him, as sure as any ounce of lead shot, but he had no time to remove the shoes before a harsh voice addressed him by name.

'Edward Sutler, halt in the King's name!'

Edward did not look around. The redcoats must have reached the summit of the hill. He fixed his eyes on the cow drinking calmly at the stream and made straight for her. He stumbled again and had barely regained his footing when a wild whistling sound cut through the air. It was such a strange noise that it stopped him in his tracks.

Edward half turned toward the source of the whining shriek. In the next instant the ground not ten feet to his right exploded, spattering his stockings with soil. A sharp cracking noise followed a split second later. The loud retort of a military musket.

'Jesus!' he spat, feeling his guts churn with fear.

Halfway down the hill two English soldiers were kneeling to take their aim. The third man's face was lost in white smoke. From the muzzle of his weapon more thick clouds spewed forth. As Edward watched, the sky above the redcoats cleared and the sun shone down as if it were a sudden ally to their cause.

'Now I'm surely a dead man,' the young rebel groaned. 'They do not care whether they take me alive.'

Edward turned to flee once more as a second hissing musket ball raced toward him. He could not outrun the deadly lump of lead and so he prayed these men were not as well trained as they were blessed by the weather.

A hanging would be worse, he told himself, than a musket ball in the back. Both ends were gruesome. But hangmen were not always as skilled as some folk imagined.

The cow looked up from her drink, disturbed by the young man's sudden appearance so close. She could smell Edward's fear and it was a scent she was unaccustomed to. The cow bellowed loudly to warn him off.

The rebel saw the woods at the other side of the water and his hopes rose. Once he made it to that cover he would be safe. By the time the redcoats searched it thoroughly, he could be long gone.

He stepped out into the stream, the water rising about his knees, and struggled against the current to reach the other side. But it was hard going with his fine shoes and his long coat dragging in the torrent. And the water was so cold it made his teeth chatter.

Halfway across the stream the young rebel turned to look behind him. One soldier was already at the foot of the hill, reloading his musket. Edward drew the pistol from his belt, knowing that he was an easy target. He held the weapon up, arm straight as he had been taught, tipping it to the left a little so the powder did not run out of the pan. He breathed deeply, aimed true and pulled the trigger.

Nothing happened.

Edward swore then pulled back on the flint hammer until it clicked into position. In his nervous haste he had forgotten to cock the weapon. He levelled the pistol again as the soldier on the opposite bank finished with his ramrod and began to prime his pan with powder.

Edward took careful aim and gently squeezed the trigger. The hammer swung down toward the powder pan. The flint crashed against the palm of the frizzen plate. Sparks flew, the powder in the pan ignited and smoke billowed out in a tiny cloud of white. But then there was absolute silence. The charge in the barrel had not caught and exploded.

'Jesus!' Edward swore as he tossed the useless weapon in the stream and turned to run.

Just as he did so he again heard the steady high-pitched whistling of a musket ball. But he did not turn this time. He was determined to reach the other side of the water and the fear of English lead was not going to stop him now.

In that moment he placed his foot down upon a submerged stone. Edward felt the rock give way gently beneath him. The current pulled him harder, determinedly tearing at his coat. Suddenly his ankle twisted sharply. In the next second the young rebel was toppling forward to fall face first in the rushing water.

As Edward tumbled over he heard the loud crack of another musket. His heart missed a beat and he lay still, face down in the water, holding his breath. The stream took him along with it for a few seconds and then he placed his feet on the bottom again, surprised that he felt no pain.

Am I dead? he wondered as he raised himself up to brush the sodden strands of hair out of his eyes.

Then he noticed the water all about him was bright red. He raised a hand to his face and it was covered in blood as scarlet as any soldier's jacket.

'I'm done,' he muttered as he struggled to keep his footing against the weight of his drenched coat. 'They hit me.'

'Are you some breed of simpleton?' a stranger's voice barked in a thick Irish accent. 'Or did you damage your head when you fell?'

Edward looked up and saw a tall man with shoulder-length red hair standing on the far side of the stream. The stranger was dressed in a black mud-spattered overcoat that had seen better days. The tattered coat gave the man the look of a poor farmer. He was staring down sternly at Edward, his hands on his hips.

'Who are you?' the rebel asked, confused.

'Daniel McHugh is my name,' the stranger replied. 'And you are trespassing on my family's land. Who are you?'

'Edward,' the young rebel began but before he finished speaking a pitiful groan distracted him.

Not ten feet away on the pebbled shore lay the great brown cow that had earlier been drinking calmly from the stream. There was a vicious wound in her neck which was pumping blood into the water. It was a few seconds before Edward could make any sense of this horrendous scene. Then the penny dropped and he sighed with deep relief. The blood in the water was not his.

No sooner had the young rebel come to the conclusion that he was not mortally wounded than a movement at the edge of the woods caught his eye. Two more red-haired men dressed in black coats bounded out of the bushes, brandishing their walking sticks ready for a fight.

Edward quickly judged the three men to be brothers. Their resemblance to one another was stark and obvious. The youngest of the three immediately knelt down by the dying cow and stroked her head softly, speaking soothingly under his breath. The other man stood behind the animal and shook his head in disbelief. All three had bright green eyes that now burned with anger.

The tall brother who had been first on the scene strode purposefully to the water's edge. His face was bright with rage and Edward was certain there was murder in his heart.

'What's your name, boy?' Daniel McHugh demanded. 'Where are you from?'

'Edward Sutler of Dublin,' the rebel replied, straining to stand and bow at the same time. 'I beg your help, sir, for I seem to have fallen in with robbers.' Then the current grabbed him again and he fell over in the stream, struggling to keep his head above water.

Daniel's expression changed as he focused on something behind Edward. The red-haired farmer turned his head around and spoke a few words to one of his brothers, which Edward did not catch. Then he put his stick down on the pebbles and walked directly into the stream, offering his hand to the young rebel.

'Thieves indeed they are, but they are born of a race of brigands who have defiled the sacred earth with their warfare and their wily ways. Can you expect any better of them but robbery?'

Daniel's eyes narrowed. 'What have you got that the red-backs would want?'

'I have nothing,' Edward protested. 'I may have said some hasty words in the marketplace, which upon reflection, I concede, may have caused some offence. And now I am paying the price for sharing my wit.'

The red-haired man snorted. Clearly he didn't believe a word of this explanation. 'If you had any wit, you would not have been hanging about with redcoats in the first place.'

The farmer smiled a little as Edward got to his feet and the young rebel knew instinctively that, though this man did not swallow his tale, he probably sympathised with his plight.

'Have no fear, they will not touch you on this land,' Daniel assured him with a quiet confidence. 'My grandfather would have their hides if the soldiers laid a finger on you. Stand behind me and I'll see them off. My brothers and I will make sure you are not harmed.'

No sooner had the stranger spoken those words than the other two soldiers arrived to stand beside their comrade, puffing and panting, at the foot of the hill. The redcoat who had fired the last shot was already reloading. He had three broad white stripes on his sleeve and he was nimble-fingered at the task.

'Don't just stand there gawping,' the sergeant bellowed at the other two soldiers, 'reload your muskets and be quick about it!'

In a few seconds the sergeant's pan was primed again. The old soldier raised his weapon, pulled back the hammer with his thumb and levelled his weapon directly at Edward. The other two stood on the bank at a safe distance, painstakingly preparing their charges.

The young rebel stumbled backwards out of the water and stood behind Daniel as he had been instructed.

'In the name of His Majesty King George, the third of that name,' the sergeant called, holding his musket tight into his shoulder in anticipation of firing, 'surrender quietly or I'll blow a hole in you as big as the one in that cow.'

'Greetings to you,' Daniel offered, ignoring the order and stepping in front of the muzzle. He held out his hand to the soldier as if they had all met at a harvest fair and might be about to spend the afternoon swilling ales.

The sergeant grunted and moved forward into the middle of the stream to seek out Edward again. All while he kept his musket high and dry.

'What has this boy done that it deserves a sergeant and two private sentinels to bring him to heel?' Daniel asked innocently, a half smile on his face.

'He is a traitor, a murderer and a rebel,' the sergeant barked. 'He shot Major D'Arcy down in cold blood after the changing of the dawn watch this morning. Colonel Cumberland has put ten pounds reward upon his head. Dead or alive. I have been tracking the scoundrel most of the day.'

Daniel raised his eyebrows as he turned to retrieve his walking stick. As he bent to pick it up he bowed his head slightly to Edward in a gesture that could have been read as either congratulations or mockery.

'Ten pounds, is it?' the red-haired man exclaimed, touching a hand to his chin thoughtfully. 'Dead or alive?'

'Dead or alive,' the old soldier confirmed. 'And I mean to get the bounty for myself.'

'Well, sergeant,' Daniel replied with a gentle shake of his head, 'I am afraid I cannot let you take this lad back to your colonel. He is a guest of my grandfather's and it would be remiss of me to let him fall into your hands. Such an unwarranted action on my behalf would surely ruin my family's reputation for hospitality.'

'And who in God's holy name do you think you are?' the soldier snarled, letting the musket drop a little.

'Squire Daniel Connor McHugh. You may address me simply as Daniel if you wish. These are my brothers Finbar and Francis,' he added politely, sweeping an arm around to indicate the two other men.

The sergeant stepped forward, moved the muzzle of his musket away from the rebel and pointed it directly at the tall man's chest.

'You're no bloody squire,' the soldier laughed. 'You're nothing but a peasant farmer out cutting turf for his family.'

'This is McHugh land you're standing on,' Daniel informed him. 'And whether we be peasant farmers or squires, I'll thank you to pay some respect to our rights.'

'Your rights?' the sergeant smirked. 'What rights? You're Irish, remember?'

'You may not come onto our land without our permission,' Daniel explained. 'That is the law. I don't care how many white stripes you have on your arm or how many muskets you point at us. You are subject to the law the same as I am.'

'I am the law, McHugh,' the soldier laughed and then his expression suddenly changed.

'McHugh,' the sergeant repeated with a frown. 'Now I remember where I've heard of your family. You're Patrick McHugh's son. I saw your father placed in chains upon a prison hulk last year. He was a murdering renegade. A bloodthirsty blackguard if ever there was one.

'I've stumbled on a bloody nest of rebels,' the sergeant whispered in disbelief. 'This'll be worth more to me than ten piddling pounds.'

'My father was an honest man who fell in with thieves,' Daniel explained, careful not to let any emotion show in his voice. He stepped forward coolly, challenging the soldier to fire at him, until at last the muzzle of the sergeant's musket was pressing firmly against his chest. The Englishman was a good deal shorter than Daniel and he swallowed hard as the man came close.

'Your father'll meet a few more outlaws where he's bound,' the soldier quipped nervously, struggling to retain the upper hand. 'Botany Bay is full of highwaymen, murderers and pickpockets.'

'And that's just the guards,' the youngest of the brothers cut in.

'Be quiet, Finbar!' Daniel snapped. 'Show some respect for the gentlemen in red. They are only trying to do their duty.

'I have no quarrel with you,' he insisted in a quiet steady voice, staring the sergeant in the eye. He raised his stick and pointed back toward Edward. 'This lad is a guest of my grandfather. Let him be. Go on your way and you won't have any cause for regret.'

'Step out of my way and let me take the boy or I'll put an ounce of lead ball through your rebel head,' the sergeant growled.

'Will you now?' Daniel exclaimed, eyes flashing at the challenge. In a second he had reached forward with his free hand, grabbed the muzzle of the soldier's flintlock and pushed it high in the air, catching the sergeant by surprise. Then, with an easy grace, Daniel swung his stick around and knocked the soldier's black three-cornered hat into the stream, revealing a bald head underneath.

The redcoat was outraged. 'That is the property of King

George,' he fumed as his hat was snatched away by the current and carried quickly out of sight.

'Let King George come and claim it then,' Daniel smiled.

The sergeant strained to aim his musket back at Daniel's chest but the tall Irishman was too strong for him.

'Let go of my firearm!' the soldier demanded. 'Well don't just stand there,' he bellowed, half turning to the other two redcoats, 'help me!'

The two soldiers looked at each other but made no move to do as they were commanded.

By this time Daniel had already turned his stick around in his free hand and plunged the handle under the water. Moving it swiftly through the water, he aimed the knobby handle and brought it up hard between the sergeant's legs.

The redcoat's eyes widened until it seemed they might pop out of his head. He tried to gasp but the pain was so excruciating that all he could manage was to turn pale, gurgle and fall to his knees in the middle of the stream.

As the old soldier collapsed, his trigger finger jerked and his musket discharged harmlessly skywards. Daniel wrested the weapon from the soldier's grip and let it fall into the deepest part of the stream.

The other two soldiers were still fumbling nervously with their ramrods and charges. When they heard the musket discharge and saw their sergeant so easily overcome, they both took a few steps back and stood in confusion. Daniel strode toward them, the water splashing about his thighs as he did so.

'Go home, lads,' he advised in a calm and reasonable tone. 'Unless you want a scrap you'll remember for the rest of your days.' Finbar and Francis came forward to the water's edge, ready to lend weight to their brother's argument.

'Stand your ground, you bloody cowards,' the sergeant gasped, his strained voice barely audible, his face still purple with pain.

'Your pans are not primed,' Daniel noted. 'Your muskets are

useless. Whereas we have three stout blackthorn sticks that do not need reloading after each blow. Go home and take this pitiful excuse for a warrior with you.' He nodded toward the sergeant who was still on his knees in the stream, clutching at the pain in his lower gut.

'And God help us if the French invade us this year,' Daniel sighed. 'If all the sergeants are like him, we'd be better off sending an open invitation to the citizens of Paris to come and save us from ourselves.'

The two soldiers looked at one another and silently decided it would be best to retire with some dignity and no broken bones.

'You had better go with them,' Francis told the sergeant. 'You killed my grandfather's cow and he does not look kindly on any man who removes his only source of fresh milk and butter.'

The old soldier made a brave attempt to stand but Daniel lifted his boot and effortlessly pushed him backwards into the water.

'Before you go on your way you will compensate us for the loss of that animal.'

'I haven't any money,' the sergeant objected, spitting out water and shaking his head.

'I think you do have a few guineas about you,' Daniel said. 'And if you don't, we are going to take the cost of that cow out of your hide.'

'I have a warrant from Colonel Cumberland. I am on the King's business. And you are interfering with the execution of the law. Cumberland will have you all hanged for harbouring a rebel and assaulting an officer of the Crown.'

'The good colonel is a personal friend of my grandfather,' Daniel smiled. 'And if he had been commander of the garrison when the last blustering sergeant came storming onto this land, perhaps my father would still have his liberty. I am sure that as a gentleman, Colonel Cumberland would take a very dim view of the unwarranted slaughter of my grandfather's cow.' Daniel sighed as he glanced at the carcass of the animal.

'Enough injustice has been visited upon us in the last year,' he declared, his voice hardening. 'I will not allow any more intrusions on our liberty. My entire family relied on that animal for milk. What will we do for cheese and butter now? Have we not suffered enough brutality in the name of good King George?'

'There's a month's meat in that corpse,' the sergeant protested.

'It was worth more to us alive than it is sporting English lead in its neck. The meat will be all but gone in two weeks and we will still have no butter.'

'Thieves!' the redcoat hissed. 'Bloody rebellious Irish brigands.'

'Beat it out of him, lads,' Daniel told his brothers with resignation.

Finbar and Francis did not need to be told twice. They immediately made for the redcoat, thrashing the water all about them in their enthusiasm. They had not even raised their sticks before the sergeant found his leather purse and threw it in the stream at Daniel's feet.

'There's two guineas of gold coin in that pocket,' the redcoat told him. 'And every penny of it belongs to Colonel Cumberland. It was meant for the paying of informants.'

Daniel picked up the purse and tossed it in his hand to weigh the contents.

'It will do to be starting with,' the tall red-haired man said softly. 'Now remove yourself from this land before I change my mind about letting you off so easy.'

One of the private soldiers put his weapon down and ventured forward to help the sergeant to his feet. The other redcoat retrieved the old soldier's musket from the stream. Daniel and his brothers stood firm, the water rushing around their knees, until the redcoats had retreated up the hill a short way.

'You'll bloody well pay for this, Daniel McHugh,' the sergeant called back. 'I'll see you dangle from a rope for what you've done.'

'Go back to your barracks, and if you dare show your face on these lands again, you'll get another beating,' Finbar yelled.

Daniel smiled, satisfied the soldiers would not return for at least a little while. 'Francis,' he called, as the redcoats reached the top of the hill, 'go and tell Grandfather everything that happened here. And inform our sister Mhairgead that we're expecting a guest for supper.'

The younger man nodded and without a word went bounding off through the stream and into the woods.

'And then come back for the carcass!' Daniel yelled after him, but he could not be sure if his brother had heard him.

'Finbar,' Daniel said, 'I want you to take a jug of the finest over to Colonel Cumberland with my compliments. Let him know that one of his sergeants was caught poaching on our land and that Grandfather would see it as a personal favour if the man was brought to account.'

'Yes, Daniel,' his brother replied smirking.

'And if the colonel asks you about young Edward here,' Daniel added as an afterthought, 'tell him you never saw him. You know nothing about any rebels. We don't want that sergeant stirring up his whole regiment. With luck Cumberland will interpret the sergeant's version of events as an elaborate tale to hide his own misbehaviour. I'll see our hero back to the house, so I leave it to you and your brother to butcher this beast.'

'You have it,' the youngest brother replied and then he was off to find his horse.

Edward stood motionless beside the cow, his mouth slightly open in shock. 'How can I ever repay you?' he stammered, rousing himself. 'You must be true patriots to make such a stand for your country in her time of need.'

'What are you blathering about?' Daniel asked, shaking his head and walking back through the stream.

'You have saved me from certain death upon the scaffold,' Edward explained.

'Did you murder Major D'Arcy?'

'I did,' the young man answered proudly. 'I shot him in the back of the head as he was going into the tavern.'

'Well, no redcoat ever had more opportunities to have his brains blown out than that bastard,' Daniel nodded as he stepped closer to the rebel. 'But I did not save your life because I hold any patriotic ideals. And I did not drive those soldiers away because I was disturbed at the thought of your young body dangling at the gibbet.'

'Then why did you intervene?'

Daniel shrugged and threw his hands in the air. 'There's ten pounds on your head, young Edward.'

Before the rebel could raise a hand to defend himself, the tall red-haired man thumped him square in the jaw. Edward fell backwards, hit his head against a stone and in moments he was motionless on the ground.

'I simply have no intention of sharing the bounty with those red-backed gentlemen,' Daniel continued to himself. He knelt down to empty the rebel's pockets, relieved him of his second pistol and ran his fingers over the cloth of Edward's coat.

'You're a fine rebel then,' he whispered. 'Never done a day's work in your life,' he muttered in disgust after he'd examined the young man's hands. 'You might be worth more than ten pounds to us in the long run, Edward. Now don't be waking up or I'll have to batter you senseless again.'

Then Daniel grabbed the young man by the arms and effortlessly threw him over his shoulders. When he stood up he checked he had not left anything behind, took a last glance at the dead cow and walked off purposefully toward home.

And it brought a smile to the face of Daniel Connor McHugh to think he was carrying ten pounds' worth of Irish rebel home for what might prove to be the lad's last decent meal.

TWO

It was dark when Edward became aware of a stinging pain in his head. He stirred a little then winced in agony. His hands found his face and he gently touched the back of his skull, searching for damage. There was a damp patch in his hair which he guessed was blood.

The young rebel opened his eyes but he could not see anything at all. 'Am I blind?' he muttered to himself.

In what seemed answer to his question there was a burst of raucous laughter. Edward squinted and the sharp pain in his skull suddenly became a dull headache. He shut his eyes again and moaned. His heart was thumping loud across his forehead but at least he could move. Each beat made him wince with discomfort.

Once again he groaned aloud, clenching his eyes shut as he did so and massaging his forehead to soothe the ache.

'He's awake,' a woman's sweet voice declared. Edward could tell she was nearby so he lay still for a few seconds to hear what was said.

'Well get him to the fire then,' a man replied in a gruff tone.

Edward tentatively opened one eye and tried to focus. His vision was blurred and he could not distinguish anything in the room. All he could make out was a bright orange glow about fifteen paces away to his right.

'Oh God!' the rebel whispered to himself. 'I am blind.'

'You'd be in good company if you were,' the woman softly retorted. Edward felt a cup touch his lips. 'Drink this,' she told him, 'it will help your head to heal.'

Edward stared at the shape hovering above him and gradually the woman's features came into focus. Her eyes were sparkling dark orbs and her long curly hair was black. Edward thought she had the reddest lips he had ever seen and they were smiling at him in a strange way.

'Who are you?' he mumbled.

'Mhairgead is my name,' the woman replied and there was a warmth in her voice that was both comforting and motherly. 'Now drink this,' she went on. 'It will cure whatever ails you.'

Edward took a mouthful of the strong-smelling concoction and swallowed it straight down. Suddenly his tongue was on fire, burning intensely as if the drink had stripped away all the flesh from his mouth. His throat felt like he had swallowed molten lead. The liquid had barely passed into his stomach before he was coughing violently.

'Christ Jesus!' Edward shrieked as he tried to clear his mouth of the vile substance.

'Don't waste that stuff!' the woman exclaimed. 'It's precious and pure. And don't get it on your fine breeches unless you want the cloth to stain permanently.'

She saw the look of worry on the young man's face. 'Do not fear,' she cooed, putting her hand on his shoulder as if she were talking to a child. 'Like all good liquor, it may burn holes in your trousers but it is much better for your stomach.'

'You're trying to kill me!' the rebel choked.

Mhairgead laughed. 'No man has ever died merely from drinking Grandfather's whiskey. Though there's many men who drank too much and wished it had killed them.'

'There was Father Connell who rode his horse off the side of a mountain,' a man's voice cut in.

'Oh yes,' Mhairgead recalled, 'but he had been drinking for three days without a respite. And he was a bit strange anyway. His monkey died after drinking a cupful, as I recall.'

'That was whiskey you gave me?' Edward coughed, inter-rupting her recollections. 'Are you certain? It didn't taste like whiskey to me.'

'There is an art to the flavour of a good whiskey,' the woman shot back haughtily. 'And I can attest that this is the best in the county. Grandfather made it himself in his very own still. There's folk who'd gladly pay tuppence a pint for that which you just tasted freely and tried to spit out again.'

'Jesus and all the saints,' the young man gasped, holding both hands over his gut. Suddenly his stomach growled and a great noisy gust of air erupted from his backside.

'I have been poisoned,' he groaned.

'Whisht, and be quiet with you,' Mhairgead mocked. 'What sort of a man makes so much fuss over a glass of the purest?'

'He's a Dubliner,' the male voice explained and now Edward recognised the owner of it. It was the red-haired man called Daniel.

'Take no notice of him, Mhairgead,' the tall man advised. 'They only drink English ale in Dublin. That's why they're always farting.'

'And you mean to tell me,' the woman scoffed, 'that this flat-ulent wisp of a boy shot Major D'Arcy down in cold blood?'

'If we are to believe his story,' Daniel answered, raising his eyebrow to indicate that he had his doubts.

'I wouldn't have thought he had it in him,' Mhairgead declared, dismissing the possibility with a wave of her hand.

'Where am I?' Edward asked, his vision clearing by the moment.

'You are in the house of my grandfather who is known as Hugh Connor,' Daniel replied.

The young rebel sat up a little. His head was still thumping away and his stomach was queasy and tight. As he moved, more wind escaped loudly from his bowel. He quickly scanned the room for redcoats then leaned against the wall and looked about him. At the far end of the room there was a fireplace. Great lumps of turf glowed in the hearth. Outlined in front of the flames were the dark shapes of two men seated on simple wooden chairs.

'Are you going to turn me over to the soldiers?' Edward asked, the apprehension evident in his voice.

'You will have to ask Grandfather that question,' Daniel told him.

The figure seated to the left at the fireplace half turned in his seat. 'Is he awake?' came a strained gravelly old voice.

'He is wide awake now, Grandfather,' Daniel replied.

'Then bring him over to the fire and sit him down. I want to know what manner of a lad goes about the place emptying the contents of his pistol into other men's skulls.'

Daniel leaned in close to Edward and the young man smelled liquor on his breath. 'You heard what Grandfather said. Up and go to the fire. It's not every day you'll have the privilege to sit with two such famous and gifted men.'

Then he added in a whisper, 'Why, there are Englishmen, in Dublin town, who would pay good money to hear that pair speak of the old days. Blind and useless as they both are.' The red-haired man laughed under his breath. 'And here I am with a good pair of strong arms, fine sharp eyes in my head and I can't earn a decent living for my family. You'll wish the red-coats had got hold of you before those two are finished, you poor little man.'

Edward stared at the man blankly, unsure whether he detected a touch of sarcasm in his voice.

'Sit him down, Grandson,' the old man on the left said sternly.

'Yes, Grandfather.'

Edward felt a hand under his arm and he was helped to the fire. Only then did he notice that his coat was gone and he was dressed in only his shirt, shoes and breeches.

'My clothes are dry,' Edward muttered, remembering that he had fallen in the stream.

'I dried them by the fire,' Mhairgead told him, 'while you were asleep.'

She saw the look of shock on his face and her smile broadened mischievously. 'Don't worry, Daniel was outside and those two are stony blind. I was the only one to see you without any clothes.'

She smiled at him again and raised an eyebrow and Edward blushed scarlet.

'Thank you ... for taking care of me,' he mumbled.

'It was a pleasure,' she replied, winking. 'If ever you need taking care of again, I'd be happy to oblige.'

Edward coughed with embarrassment as Mhairgead, laughing, brought a three-legged stool for him to sit on. This she placed between the two old men and a little back from the hearth so that the young rebel could not look directly at either of their faces.

'Grandfather,' Daniel said in a formal tone when the young guest had taken his seat, 'this is Edward Sutler of Dublin. By his own admission he is a cold-blooded murderer and a rebel. It was on his account that Philomena was killed.'

Edward turned around in his seat to protest but Daniel slapped a heavy hand on his shoulder and the young man forgot entirely what he was going to say.

'My name is Hugh Connor,' the old man on the left cut in, turning his head slightly so that the young rebel could just make out the shape of his empty eye sockets, 'from whence my son and grandsons have earned the name McHugh. This gentleman on your right is known as Denis Hempson, a harper of the old tradition and a man of exceedingly good taste and wit, even when he is sober, I am told, though I cannot remember when last that was.'

'It was in the year of our Lord, seventeen hundred and forty-five,' Denis informed all present. 'That was the time of the great rebellion in Scotland and all the Irish whiskey was sent off to keep the army of Bonnie Prince Charlie warm and sociable. There wasn't a drop of liquor to be had in the whole of Ireland for nearly a twelvemonth. They were hard times but, as always, our country gave the best it had to offer to the Stewart cause.' The old harper sighed nostalgically and then gulped the contents of his wooden cup and held the empty vessel out expectantly.

'It is a pleasure to make your acquaintance,' Edward replied politely.

Denis grunted, disgusted that Daniel was not going to fill his cup just yet.

Hempson was an exceptionally thin man with a full head of grey hair. His fingers were remarkably bony and topped with long perfect fingernails shaped like almonds. Edward frowned in confusion when he saw these nails. He could not remember ever having seen anything like them before. He had heard of harpers long ago who had worn them in this fashion, but he thought they were an ancient breed who had mostly died out a generation ago.

'You seem to derive pleasure in a very strange manner,' Hugh observed, picking up on Edward's last comment. 'Due to your foolishness Philomena was shot this morning. She has been my constant companion for ten years. I am beside myself with grief for the loss of her. She was a willing contributor to this household and a kind, generous soul.'

'I had nothing to do with your servant's death!' Edward exclaimed, genuinely unable to recall anyone being killed in the incident by the stream.

'What are you blathering about?' Hugh snapped. 'Philomena was the name of my cow. I will not have any milk for my breakfast in the morning and there is not a pinch of butter in the house tonight.'

The rebel breathed a sigh of relief then noticed the old man's bald head and the dry scabby skin on his face. He couldn't help staring at the deep wrinkles and the masses of freckles around Hugh's eyes and he wondered how old this fellow might be.

'I am sorry—' the young man began but Hugh interrupted him before he could finish the sentence.

'Sorry will not get me milk for my breakfast, nor will it bring back Major D'Arcy from the dead.'

'D'Arcy was a cold ruthless tyrant,' Edward stated quietly but firmly, his voice full of righteous conviction.

'He was a husband and the father of two small girls,' the old man huffed in disgust. 'My own son was an innocent man and a good father to his sons. But because one thick-headed soldier took it upon himself to persecute my boy, he is now rotting in some prison on the far side of the earth. I will never see my son again and Major D'Arcy's daughters will not again see their father in this life.'

'D'Arcy was a bloody murderer,' the young man protested.

'You are also a bloody murderer, if your tale is to be believed,' Hugh spat. 'Do you deserve to die?'

Edward took a deep breath before he answered. 'I am ready to die, if need be, to liberate my country from the yoke of the English.'

'A fine speech,' Denis mocked through a toothless smile. 'You and old Hugh here will quickly become fast friends if you keep talking like that. For when he's sat by the fire with a bumper of whiskey in his hand and a few in his belly, he's a powerful liar and a great hero himself.'

'Your father is quite a wealthy man,' Hugh stated, kicking at the old harper to signal him to keep quiet.

'Yes,' Edward replied politely, determined not to show any offence at all these questions and accusations. He was beginning to realise that his liberty depended on the goodwill of old Hugh.

'And is this how you repay him,' the blind distiller cut in harshly, 'by gallivanting about the countryside murdering honest men?'

The rebel was taken aback by this reprimand. He believed that Major D'Arcy was universally despised. In dispatching him, Edward felt he had done what was best for the country and the local populace especially.

'I don't know what you mean,' he stuttered, struggling to retain an air of good humour.

'Your father has paid for those fine new shoes of yours,' Hugh snapped, 'and your lovely warm coat. He indulged you in your love of books and had you well educated. He pays your bills when your income is compromised. And he has done all this to give you a bright future, such as he never had. Yet you have set off on the path to self-destruction. What in God's name has come over you? Are you possessed by the Devil himself?'

Edward took a deep breath and tried to steady his nerves. Was this man a traitor to the cause of freedom? Or was he simply maddened by years of drinking his own whiskey? 'How do you presume to know so much about me?'

'I can see it in your proud air and your foolish talk,' the old man hissed. 'I see it in the way you sit there fuming when an old man with sightless eyes ventures to tell you things no-one else would.'

'You are blind,' Edward reminded him. 'How can you see these things? How could you have possibly come to these conclusions?'

'I may be blind but I am not stupid,' Hugh retorted sharply. 'After all, vision is merely the art of seeing things which are invisible.'

Edward frowned for a second. He had read that remark somewhere before. Suddenly the answer came to him and he shook his head. 'Dean Jonathan Swift wrote that phrase,' he said, a little surprised that an uneducated country distiller like Hugh Connor would have come across it.

'Indeed he did,' the old man replied, 'and wasn't I with him when he first spoke those words?'

'You could not have been,' Edward objected. 'Dean Swift died over forty years ago.'

'What year is it, Daniel?' the old man cried.

'Seventeen hundred and eighty-eight,' the grandson replied.

'Then I am one hundred years blessed myself,' Hugh laughed.

'Preserved in a hundred gallons of pure bloody alcohol he is,' Denis sniped.

'Were you one of the dean's servants?' the young rebel asked, sitting forward, suddenly interested in this old man.

'I was not!' Hugh shot back, offended. 'I was a friend to poor old mad Mister Swift. Bless his kind heart but there was something amiss between his ears.'

'What do you mean?' Edward asked.

Hugh put a finger to his own temple and swirled it around in the air. 'He was mad. Almost as mad as Miss Maderson the mad maidservant of Maidstone, of whom I am sure you have heard tell.'

'Raving bloody loony,' Denis added under his breath. 'Didn't even know how to milk a cow. That's how mad he was.'

Edward wasn't sure why that should be a symptom of mental instability. 'Where did you meet Dean Swift?' he inquired.

'I was humble servant to Master Carolan, the most renowned harper in all Ireland. We oftentimes resided with the poor mad gentleman Mister Swift.'

'Dean Swift,' Edward corrected him. 'He was the Dean of Saint Patrick's. It is not right to refer to him as mister.'

'He was Mister Swift when I first met him. Besides, apart from the small stipend the title later endowed him, he cared nothing for the job of dean and even less for the Church.'

'The dean was a good Christian and a great writer,' the rebel protested. 'He was a true Irish patriot who used his pen to challenge the might of England.'

The two old men burst into uproarious laughter.

'He was a drunken old tosspot!' Denis guffawed. 'And I only knew him in his declining years when he had begun to slow down. In his youth he was a devil for the whiskey, so they say. And a bit of a one for the ladies too.'

'It is true,' Hugh declared. 'None but my master, Turlough O'Carolan himself, could drink more in one sitting than dear old Mister Swift.'

'Were you really a servant to the great Carolan?' Edward asked, not sure if he had understood correctly. 'The famous harper?'

'I was his companion and his guide,' Hugh stated. Then the old man reached down and felt around with his fingers for the pipe which lay at his feet.

'I suppose a man like yourself would probably have some tobacco about you,' Hugh said. 'Will you take a pipe?'

24

'I have plenty of tobacco myself, thank you,' Edward replied, declining the offer.

'Then let us smell the vintage of it,' the old man demanded, holding out his hand expectantly. 'Would you be so uncouth as to keep it to yourself? And you with a rich father in Dublin who pays for everything.'

Edward rolled his eyes and searched for the tobacco pouch he usually kept tied to his belt. But the belt was missing. Daniel stepped forward then and picked up the tobacco pouch from in front of the fire. The red-haired man checked the pouch was dry then placed it firmly in his Grandfather's hand. Soon Hugh was nimbly stuffing the stringy contents into the clay bowl of his pipe. As he finished, the young woman called Mhairgead picked up a glowing twig from the fire and carefully placed it in the old man's hands.

As she leaned forward she glanced at Edward. Her eyes sparkled even more brightly than before and she smiled again. But it was not a smile of amusement. Nor of joy. It was something else. The young rebel felt himself blushing hotly once more and he fidgeted in his seat.

Edward glanced away but after a moment he noticed the woman was still smiling at him. He turned his head and looked about the room so he wouldn't have to meet her gaze. The young rebel was intensely uncomfortable and confused. He could feel the sweat gathering on his brow. These strange folk held his future in their hands, so he would have to act as politely as possible until he knew what they intended to do with him.

To keep his eyes from Mhairgead, Edward began examining his surroundings intently. The cottage was apparently small. The room in which they were seated was typical of the houses of country-folk. Along the wall there were two enclosed wooden beds with calico curtains to give some privacy. The one closest to the fire was the bed he had been lying in when he awoke. There was a door to the right of the fireplace but Edward had no idea how big the house might be. He reasoned that there must be other rooms to accommodate Daniel and his two brothers.

'Thank you, Grand-daughter,' Hugh said softly as he carefully touched the tip of the twig to his tobacco and inhaled the smoke. When he had taken a few breaths and puffed them out again, he coughed a little. Then he half turned in his seat to face Edward.

'A good Virginia,' he declared with satisfaction, smacking his lips at the taste of the tobacco. 'There is nothing as soothing as a pipe full of Virginia at the close of the day. This would have likely cost your father a shiny shilling or two.'

'I bought it with my own funds,' Edward replied gently, concealing the fact that this old man was trying his patience. 'I have friends in the Americas who supply me with this tobacco. All my other needs are provided from my wages as a tutor in Dublin.'

'The Americas?' Hugh coughed, spitting into the fire. 'So you're connected with the rebels in the New World, are you?' He handed the pouch to Denis. 'What am I going to do with you, my lad?' the old man asked, shaking his head.

'Do with me?' Edward repeated.

'You don't imagine I can let you go free, after you shot down such an important man in cold blood, do you? And you a self-confessed rebel?'

'I don't see why you shouldn't let me go,' the young man retorted, keeping his temper under control, 'if you are a true Irishman who wishes your country to be liberated. D'Arcy was an enemy of the common people. I have rid the land of a vicious villainous despot, and I have done absolutely nothing to harm you.'

'That is where you are wrong,' Hugh snapped. 'You have done a great deal of harm to me and mine, and the smallest part of it ended in the death of my last cow. There will be terrible results from your rash actions.'

He puffed on his pipe again.

'Everyone in this parish will suffer. The English will take their revenge on the innocent. Some guileless young man could very well go to prison or even be hanged on suspicion of having done the deed. The redcoats don't care as long as they have someone to punish. Relations with officers of the Crown will certainly be all the more difficult in future because they will believe that the common folk are sheltering you.'

'Then let me go,' the rebel reasoned. 'I'll be in Dublin by tomorrow and once I am there I will write a letter to the Castle admitting to the deed and notifying them that I acted alone.'

'And what about Philomena?' Hugh insisted.

'I am sorry about your cow,' Edward conceded.

'Philomena,' the old man informed him, 'was descended from a fine animal bequeathed to me by Carolan himself and a personal gift to him from Signor Geminiani.'

'The famous violinist Francesco Geminiani gave you a cow?' Edward exclaimed incredulously.

'He gave it to my master,' Hugh corrected him. 'The signor played the fiddle. And a fine fiddler he was too when he put his mind to it and stayed away from the keg.'

'And when he wasn't chasing the coat-tails of some young gentleman,' Denis added.

'That was merely a malicious rumour,' Hugh admonished.

'I know Geminiani's music well,' the young rebel declared with excitement, ignoring the old men's banter. 'I studied the violin and have played all the Italian's concertos.' Edward stopped all of a sudden as he realised the old distiller was probably not telling the truth. It was possible Hugh may once have met Dean Jonathan Swift. He may even have made the acquaintance of Carolan the harper. But it stretched the imagination a little too far to believe he had also known the renowned Geminiani.

The old man coughed, sensing Edward's skepticism. 'Trained at the college of music, were you? I am sorry to hear it. It's a great pity. For in that case you are not likely to be much of a fiddle player. But tell me, how is it that a scholar of music turns his hand to such dangerous acts of wanton rebellion?'

'My brave companions and I are striking out to free Ireland from the hands of the cruel invader.'

'And at the same time you are destroying the honest business I have spent years establishing,' Hugh sighed. 'You may think you are freeing me and my folk from tyranny, but all you have really achieved is to liberate poor folk, such as myself, from the burden of carrying a full stomach about on old legs.'

'What do you mean?'

'Major D'Arcy bought all his hard drink from me. He purchased the official stores for his barracks from me. He supplied all his soldiers with whiskey distilled and bottled by me and my grandsons. Captain Morgan, on the other hand, the man who will surely be promoted to Officer of Stores in D'Arcy's place, does not touch a drop himself. And he expects the same behaviour of his soldiers.'

'Blind bloody optimism, if you ask me,' Denis grunted.

Hugh drew in on his pipe again then puffed the smoke into Edward's face. The young rebel coughed, but surely the old distiller couldn't have known exactly where he was sitting.

'And even if Captain Morgan decided, by some blessed miracle,' Hugh went on, 'to turn over a new leaf and begin purchasing hard liquor for the comfort of his troops, he would be obliged by his conscience to obtain it through official channels.'

'Morgan's father is an infamous vicar in Edinburgh, you know,' Denis said, meaning to explain the captain's attitude to the drink. 'I've never known a Presbyterian who could bear to see a man enjoy a snout of whiskey. Protestants can't hold the liquor themselves, it is said, and so they begrudge any man who finds enjoyment in it.'

'As a result of your glorious strike for the freedom of Ireland,' Hugh declared, 'I have lost an annual income of over two hundred pounds.'

'I am sorry,' Edward said sincerely. 'I did not mean to cause you hardship. I had no idea that you relied on the army for your income. But I am obliged to point out that you should not be dealing with the English soldiers at all. Not while there are Irish people who are suffering under the tyranny of the foreigners.'

'You stupid boy, who else but the English can afford to drink heavily and pay the prices I charge? Certainly not these Irish folk you run about hoping to set free. They are the poorest folk on earth. Not even the gauger men make a decent living from their trade.'

'The who?'

'Don't you know anything about this country you are professing to liberate?' Hugh coughed in surprise. 'The gauger men work for Dublin Castle collecting taxes on all the whiskey made in Ireland. I and my folk have prospered by avoiding that tax for some years now. In my own way I am also a rebel, though I would never pick up a pistol to prove it.'

'Not a loaded one,' Daniel quipped.

'Hush there!' Hugh snapped and Daniel coughed nervously.

The old distiller drew on his pipe and was already speaking again as the smoke flowed out of his nose and mouth. 'In the old days there was no tax on whiskey or tobacco. Since the coming of the gaugers and the opening of the Scottish distilleries, the taxes have become so high that innkeepers are now watering down their liquor and tobacco merchants are adding dry threshed hay to the blend to flesh out their profits. I pay no tax so my prices are affordable and my whiskey is pure.'

'Where will it end?' Denis hummed in disgust as he took a smouldering stick from Mhairgead and lit his pipe. 'Perfectly undrinkable, that Scots whiskey. And hay in the tobacco makes my chest hurt. I am certain it nullifies all the beneficial effects of a pipe full of Virginia.'

'Now my family are facing starvation,' Hugh cut in, 'and you can summon no more than a half-sincere apology for all the dreadful harm you have caused.'

'If there is anything I can do to make amends—' Edward began.

'There very likely may be,' Hugh answered before the rebel

could finish. And there was the tiniest hint of a threat in his words.

'You won't turn me over to the soldiers, will you?' the young man gasped, suspecting that this must be what the old man had in mind.

'If the price were a little higher, I certainly would have no hesitation,' Hugh admitted. 'But ten pounds would not keep my business healthy and fill the bellies of my large family for more than a few weeks. Evidently even the good Colonel Cumberland did not value Major D'Arcy too highly.'

Denis spat into the fire. 'Ten pounds would buy an awful lot of Virginia.'

Hugh considered this suggestion for a moment but shook his head as if to drive away the temptation. 'There's Mhairgead and her two young children to clothe and feed,' the old distiller said, tallying up his dependants. 'Her husband was imprisoned with my son and is probably tilling the soil in New South Wales by now, so it is my duty to take care of her.'

Hugh thought for a moment. 'There's Daniel, his wife and seven young ones. Finbar has a wife and four boys. That's nineteen mouths to feed.'

'And Francis will be married by the end of the month,' Denis reminded him.

Hugh nodded. 'In his eagerness to begin married life he has a little one on the way.'

'Looks to me like twins,' the other old man stated, playing his hands through the air in front of him as if he were outlining the pregnant woman's belly.

Edward raised his eyebrows and smiled, then he asked himself whether they all shared this house.

'This is nothing to be smiling about, Master Edward,' Hugh rebuked him. 'This is a very serious matter.'

The mirth dropped away from Edward's face straightaway. Then he frowned, wondering how the old man could have possibly known he was smiling. He peered at Hugh's eye sockets, just to make certain he really was blind. There were no eyes at all. The eyelids had long ago grown over and healed shut. The skin was smooth where it had sealed out all light forever.

'I had an accident,' Hugh told him, sensing that he was being closely observed, 'that is how I lost my sight. I had a great distilling shed on the mountainside twenty years ago. And through my own foolishness the precious still caught fire and exploded. I was lucky to survive.'

'You nearly drowned in your own poison,' Denis noted dryly. 'The grass has never grown again upon that hillside. Maybe you got a drop of the wicked stuff in each of your foolish eyes.'

'My whiskey is the best in all Ireland,' Hugh protested indignantly. 'And if there were any poison in it, you would have drunk enough by now to kill a mighty host of griping old harpers.'

'Don't insult me, Hugh Connor. Or I won't give you a tune.'

'If you don't give me a tune,' the old man replied, 'I won't give you another drink to help you on your road.'

'You would drive the Devil to distraction with your heartless bargains,' Denis grimaced. 'But if that's the price of a drop of your whiskey in your house, I'll give you half a dozen tunes and then I'll be on my way.'

'I'll have Daniel open a new barrel in celebration of your bloody good sense and your insatiable desire for liquor,' Hugh declared.

'What would you hear?' Denis asked.

'The Concerto.'

'Not again, Hugh. I have played it three times this month. I have no wish to touch the wires with it any more. My fingers are old and stiff and that is a devil of a tune to trip over.'

'Do you know,' the old distiller said, 'they reckon a man can die a pitiful death of thirst after only a few days of deprivation?'

'I'll die of the love you hold for your old master's music,' the harper hissed.

'You are jealous of Carolan's gifts, Denis, or you would never say such a thing.'

'Rubbish. His tunes were far too fancy for my liking. He never played any of the grand ancient airs. He might as well have been a bloody Italian.'

'The Concerto, Denis. If you please.'

The old harper grumbled under his breath but after a few moments he relented and held out an open palm toward Edward. The young rebel looked at it blankly; he had no idea what Denis expected him to hand over.

The answer came as Mhairgead lifted a battered old harp from where it had been resting by the door. She brushed uncomfortably close to Edward as she handed the instrument to the harper, and he moved back apprehensively in his seat. In a few moments the harp sat in front of Denis on the stone floor. Mhairgead smiled at Edward again but he ignored her.

'Wouldn't you rather hear An Cúileann, Hugh?' the old harper asked.

'No, Denis. I want to hear the Concerto.'

'It is the Lamentation of Limerick I'd gladly play for you,' came the reply. 'A fine air and a fitting sober subject for such illustrious company as our young troublemaker here for it tells of the heroic resistance of King James's army against the Dutchman and his band of cutthroat mercenaries.'

'The Concerto,' Hugh insisted. 'I want to hear the Concerto.'

'I cannot play that without more than a drink or two under my belt,' Denis countered in a frustrated tone. 'So you'll have to wait till I've taken a generous sup of the whiskey.'

'Play me the Receipt then.'

'I do not like to play Carolan's music,' the harper insisted as he ran his fingers over the strings to check the tuning. 'His airs remind me of a sadness suffered in my youth. They bring to memory hard days when I had no bread. Anyway, Carolan did not play true Irish tunes at all.'

'He played his own airs as well as the old melodies,' Hugh reminded his friend. 'And he was the Chief Musician of all Ireland.'

Denis spat into the fire. 'Chief Musician of Ireland!' he

exclaimed skeptically. 'Chief braggart and charlatan is what he was. He was a friend of the English and not much of a harper either. He started his learning too late.'

'He was quick-witted enough to realise where he would likely get his next meal and his next glass,' Hugh said with a cold reprimand in his voice. 'If he did not scruple to play for the English, it was because he had a family to feed.'

'He had a craving for the drink to satisfy.'

'And you would know all about that particular affliction.'

'I'll play SheeBeg SheeMor then,' Denis capitulated, 'for it is the only melody of Carolan's which truly gives me pleasure. Though I have heard many folk say that it is surely not one of old Turlough's tunes.'

'It was his first,' Hugh sputtered, finally losing his temper, 'everyone knows that. Any man who says anything to the contrary is a liar. Only a small man would try to belittle a great one.'

The harper shrugged and took out a tuning tool which fitted neatly into the palm of his right hand. Then he started gently plucking and adjusting the brass wires, starting from the thick lower strings through to the shortest and finest ones near the top of the harp.

Hugh leaned closer to Edward and whispered so as not to distract the musician at his task. 'What am I going to do with you? It would be a terrible pity if you had no chance to redeem yourself to your father and to myself for all that you have done. I would hate to think of you suffering an eternity in Hell merely because I did not give you an opportunity to make amends.'

Edward frowned but said nothing.

'And it would hardly be worth handing you over to Colonel Cumberland,' Hugh went on, 'he will only hang you. A senseless waste of a young life that would be. Even though you have been educated at the college I still have a feeling you might have some intelligence, perhaps even some redeeming quality about you which I could put to use. You will stay here the night while I decide your fate.'

'I have to get myself back to Dublin in case the soldiers come looking for me,' Edward protested.

'They will not come here looking for you,' Hugh assured him, 'unless I send for them.' He turned and called over his shoulder, 'Mhairgead! Fetch the lad some broth. He'll be our guest tonight.'

'Thank you, Grandfather,' the young woman cried enthusiastically. 'But don't you think you should make some further inquiries of him?'

Old Hugh raised his eyebrows and thought for a moment. 'Edward, my young man,' he began, 'are you wedded?'

'No, sir. I am not.'

'Are you agreed to be wedded?'

'I am married to the cause of Ireland's freedom,' the young rebel stated.

'Ireland was very nearly a widow this day,' Denis quipped.

'And if you were to be married,' Hugh went on, 'would your father object if the choice of a bride were your own?'

'My father would not expect me to marry for anything less than the highest ideals of love.'

Mhairgead put both hands to her mouth and sighed with admiration at this comment.

'But I have no thoughts of such matters,' the young rebel added hastily. 'My life is devoted to the great cause of liberty.'

'And you can kiss that goodbye once you're married,' Denis sniggered.

'A handsome young fellow like yourself must be followed about by women like the hounds chasing the fox,' Hugh chuckled.

Edward blushed. 'There have been one or two young ladies who have expressed an interest,' he admitted. 'But I have not had the time to devote to such pursuits. I have been helping to plan the rising.'

Everyone in the room gasped. Daniel slammed the door to the cottage, threw the bolt across and stood by on guard, staring at Edward with suspicion.

'What do you know of the rising?' Hugh demanded.

'I cannot speak of it,' Edward replied, 'if you are going to turn me over to the redcoats. I would rather die than reveal my knowledge of the coming insurrection.'

'Be quiet, you stupid boy,' Hugh hissed. 'What if some redcoat were to hear you talking like that? They hang rebels, you know, and everyone in this house would come under suspicion. Would you like some company on the gallows? Is that it?'

'I am sorry.'

'Govern your wayward tongue, lad.' The old distiller sighed and then turned to where he sensed Mhairgead was standing. 'Will he do?'

'He's fine!' the young woman declared happily and then she bit her bottom lip and hummed to herself.

'Very well then,' Hugh told her, 'we'll keep him.'

'Thank you, Grandfather,' she replied and rushed across the room to kiss the old man on the forehead.

'Think nothing of it, my dear,' Hugh told her. 'It's the least I can do for you and the children after all you've been through. But don't let this one get away.'

'I won't,' she promised and then she rushed off to the kitchen to fetch a bowl.

Edward looked from Hugh to Denis and then across to Daniel. The red-haired man stood by the door stuffing his pipe. When he caught the rebel staring questioningly at him, he shrugged, as if to say he had no idea what was going on either.

'If you have no intention of delivering me to the English, then I must depart immediately and return to Dublin,' Edward declared, his concern mixed with confusion now.

'I never said I had no intention of delivering you to the red-coats,' Hugh told him. 'I said I haven't decided what I will do with you yet. And I also said it would be a pity to see you hang. There is plenty of time for me to come to a decision. We'll sleep on it tonight and in the morning I may have made up my mind.'

'I must return to Dublin,' Edward insisted. 'I have work to do.'

'You have earned yourself a little respite from your work,' the old distiller answered. 'There's not many men who have such a commitment to the cause that they would endanger their lives for it. Sit back tonight and relax. Listen to the music of our beloved Ireland. The music the English would outlaw. This is what you are fighting for. Is it not?'

The young rebel nodded, thinking that perhaps the old man was right. He had risked life and limb for the cause and he did deserve some rest, even some good company and music.

'Very well,' Edward conceded. 'But I must leave first thing in the morning.'

'First thing,' Hugh agreed. 'We'll talk about it first thing tomorrow.'

Before the young rebel could protest the finer points of this arrangement, Denis began playing a lively little tune. Edward did not recognise the melody. He soon realised it must be a tuning air used by harpers to ascertain that the harp wires were well adjusted.

'I have heard Carolan's compositions played on the pianoforte,' the young rebel offered, knowing that it was not considered impolite to speak over the top of the tuning. 'They are quite delightful pieces really, considering he was blind.'

Both old men sighed heavily and shook their heads.

'I don't want to imply that he was not a great musician,' Edward added hastily. 'Just because he was lacking in the faculty of eyesight doesn't mean he was also lacking in talent.'

'The pianoforte is an instrument of the fat-arsed ladies of the aristocracy,' Denis stated with contempt. Then he turned back to his tuning.

'And that instrument does no justice to my master's music at all,' Hugh added. 'For he was gifted by the Gentry with his talent.'

'What do you mean?' Edward asked, confused.

'He was taken away during his illness by the Good People and taught how to play.'

'The Good People?'

'The Faerie folk,' Hugh explained, speaking loud and slow as if his guest was deaf.

'Do you mean to say that Carolan was taken by the Faeries?' the young man scoffed, unable to stop himself smiling at the idea. The old man was obviously joking.

'You can say what you like about King George the Third, or the entire English nation. You can repeat any rumour you have heard about the private and personal habits of the French. You may even rebuke the Irish for their bad luck in battle and their consistent choice of poor leaders. But do not mock the Gentry in this house,' Hugh warned, his voice full of solemnity. 'For they bestowed gifts upon my master which made him the envy of all who met him, and they are to be respected.'

'The Faeries are just an ancient myth,' Edward replied dismissively. 'No-one really believes in them.'

'No-one in Dublin, obviously,' Denis grunted, shaking his head.

'The Gentry are as real as you or I!' Hugh retorted. 'Any man who says otherwise under this roof is not fit to be a guest of this family.'

The old man turned in his seat. 'Daniel?' he called.

His grandson stood up straight and put down his pipe.

'Yes, Grandfather.'

'Go and fetch the colonel. I have a young man here who is no longer desirous of my hospitality. I would like to commend this young fool into the care of the Crown.'

'As you wish, Grandfather.'

'Perhaps you'll feel more comfortable chained inside a prison hulk awaiting transportation,' the old distiller huffed.

'Just a moment,' Edward cut in nervously. 'I did not say that the Faeries were not real. I merely stated that they were an old myth. I wouldn't dream of contradicting my host.'

Hugh did not move.

'Obviously you are very knowledgeable in these matters,' the rebel added quickly. 'I do not profess to have a knowledge as great as your own. Naturally they did not teach us such subjects at the college in Dublin.'

'You concede that you are mistaken?'

'I admit that I have no experience with the Faeries,' Edward compromised. 'And that I should keep an open mind until such time as I do.'

'Then you are a wise and welcome visitor, Master Edward,' Hugh declared.

'I'll saddle my horse in any case,' Daniel informed the old man.

'I don't think there'll be a need for that, Grandson. I have a feeling young Edward is beginning to warm to our simple country ways. Now where's that whiskey?'

Daniel smiled wryly at the old man's talent for manipulation and then stepped out of the house to fetch the jug.

'What makes you believe that Carolan was taken by the Good People?' Edward asked, venturing to pursue the subject and show some interest.

'I had the tale from the master's own lips, I did,' Hugh confided. 'I heard him tell the story again and again over the years. His life was a sad one but he had a fine time of it as it turned out. No man deserves prosperity who is shy of adversity, as the saying goes.'

'Oh Holy Mary in Heaven,' Denis whispered, 'not again. I couldn't bear to hear this bloody tale another time.' The old harper put his hands together in front of his instrument as if to pray. 'Lord above, who calms the suffering of the meek, I'll give up the whiskey forever if you'll just strike this old bugger dumb before he starts that story.'

'Never ask for something which your heart desires with a passion,' Hugh advised, 'for you may well receive what you request. My master made a wish once. And all that befell the great Turlough O'Carolan afterwards happened because he desired something that he was not meant to have. It took him many years to realise the nature of his mistake and by then his life had changed forever.'

The old distiller half turned in his seat again to emphasise his point. The redundant muscles behind his empty eye sockets

38

twitched as he spoke and his eyebrows moved expressively.

'You could learn a thing or two yourself from my master's tale,' he told Edward in his gravelly voice. 'Then, perhaps, instead of running around the village, pistols blazing, you might have the sense to take what troubles life presents to you and turn them to the good of your fellow man. Have you any other talents besides murdering majors and giving the redcoats a chance to practise their skills at musketry?'

'I play the violin and the pianoforte—' Edward began.

'Fat-arsed ladies of the aristocracy,' Denis muttered under his breath as he shook his head. 'Jesus and all the saints, why do I suffer to sit here night after night?'

'I have edited an Irish edition of *The Rights of Man*,' the rebel cut in, speaking over the top of the old harper.

'And what of the rights of woman?' Mhairgead demanded, entering the room with an empty bowl. She went to the fire, lifted the lid on the cauldron and began to spoon out some of the soup.

Edward smiled, thinking the woman was making a joke. She stared blankly back, waiting for his answer, and the young rebel realised she probably had no idea what he was referring to.

'*The Rights of Man* is a treatise on the dignity of all people,' he explained. 'It expounds the belief that all men are created equal.'

'Equally subservient to women,' Denis observed and Mhairgead laughed.

'I am very familiar with the works of Carolan,' Edward went on, deciding it was best not to dwell too much on his rebel activities. 'I have heard many fine musicians perform his work. But as Mister Hempson stated earlier, Carolan was not considered a very good musician in his own time, by all accounts.'

'Not a good musician!' Hugh repeated in outrage, his voice cracking. 'He was the finest harper who ever drew breath. What would you know anyway? Carolan passed on fifty years ago. Long before you were even born.'

'I have heard—' Edward began.

'There are countless silly stories about Carolan,' Hugh stated, 'so many anecdotes that it is difficult to tell truth from invention. It is only fitting that legends arise in the wake of a great man. But I had the whole tale from his own lips. And I was his trusted servant for the last twenty years of his life. I carried his harp and led his horse until the day he died.'

'And that was a talent years in the learning,' Denis mumbled. 'No man in the whole of Ireland was so skilled at leading old nags by the nose. Renowned for it, you was.' The harper chuckled to himself but Hugh ignored the insult.

'The Good Folk were Carolan's patrons,' the old man continued stubbornly, determined to tell his story. 'I know it to be true for my master never lied, unless his honour was at stake.'

Edward frowned but did not point out the obvious contradiction in this last statement.

Just then Daniel returned with an earthenware jug. He brushed the damp soil from around the shoulders of the bottle, removed a fat cork from the neck with a dramatic pop, and filled three wooden cups which had been placed on the kitchen table in readiness. Then he handed a cup to each of the men seated around the fire.

'Is this the one that was buried under the dung heap?' Hugh asked.

'It is indeed, Grandfather,' Daniel replied.

'Slainté,' Hugh offered and Denis repeated the phrase before downing the liquor in one gulp. Daniel refilled their cups again immediately.

'Cheers,' Edward replied awkwardly for he did not have any knowledge of the Irish tongue.

'How long has that whiskey been underground?' Denis asked, passing the newly filled cup under his nose.

'Four months,' Hugh told him.

'Four months!' the old harper exclaimed. 'Jesus and all the saints! Don't you think that is prolonging the aging process?'

'Daniel forgot we had a jug buried in that spot,' the old distiller explained to his guest.

'It's a fine drop, if a little old for my taste,' Denis declared finally. 'With a young woman and young whiskey, a man may live forever, as they say.'

'Who says?' Hugh asked skeptically.

'A great many scholars agree on that point.'

'Rubbish,' Hugh huffed. 'If you would listen to the tale,' he went on, turning his head toward Edward, 'I will tell you of my master's early life long before I met him. Then I will relate all that happened to the great Carolan after I took up the responsibility of bearing his harp.'

"Tis a good story,' Denis pretended to agree. Then he downed his whiskey quickly and reached for his travelling coat which hung across the back of the chair. 'But I've bloody well heard enough for one night,' he whispered to himself.

'Where are you going?' Hugh demanded, turning an ear toward the old harper. 'Why are you making to put on your coat?'

'I was just going down to Finnegan's to taste some fine French claret he has in. I have heard this story a hundred times. Not meaning to be rude at all but I'll come back when you've finished and then I'll play a few tunes before bed.'

'Sit down where you are, you sly old bugger,' Hugh snapped. 'I have dealt you the finest drink in the house and you'll play for me as I tell the story.'

Denis sat back and grumbled as he felt Daniel's large hand on his shoulder. 'Very well,' he conceded, 'but make the telling of it short. I am journeying to Belfast in a few days to meet with a man who'll pay me well for my tunes. A shilling a time, he tells me. And I have no mind to be late because of you.'

'Don't get yourself into a state, Master Hempson,' Hugh advised. 'This tale will not be days in the telling. And anyhow, what manner of a man would pay such a fortune just to hear you play upon your battered old harp? Calm yourself or you'll snap the wires when you pluck at them.'

'I wish the Lord above would snap your bloody wires,' Denis retorted, the mumbled words only half-heartedly concealing his resentment.

Edward raised his eyebrows in amusement at the two old men as he sipped his whiskey politely. The liquor made him gag and numbed his tongue so he was taking it very slowly and carefully. His head still ached and he was feeling very weak. And he was a little concerned that the blow Daniel had struck him might have done some permanent damage.

'Now, what was I saying?' Hugh asked himself with a frown that creased his empty eye sockets and wrinkled the skin around his nose. 'That's right. Now I recall,' the distiller hummed with excitement and he settled back into his chair. 'I was just beginning at the beginning where Carolan's career began.'

Denis sighed deeply and held out his wooden cup for Daniel to refill. Not until the old harper's sharp ears heard the red-haired man replace the stopper in the jug did Denis bring the cup back under his nose once more. The old musician tentatively sniffed the wooden vessel and then swallowed the entire contents in one gulp. He immediately held the cup out again, smacking his lips enthusiastically, but Daniel did not move.

'You'll need your wits for playing, Master Hempson,' the tall red-haired man advised. But then he filled the cup anyway and Denis sat back to sip the liquor slowly and listen to the tale.

'The greatest harper in all of Ireland,' Hugh began, 'present company included . . .' Denis made a snuffling sound to show his disagreement. '. . . was born in the town of Nobber which, as you should well know if you have travelled this land at all, is in the fair green county of Meath. My master's father was a poor farm labourer who, due to hardship, turned to the trade of blacksmith and moved to County Roscommon to work for the MacDermot family. It was there my master met his one and only true love, the woman who captured his heart and for whom he held a lighted candle forever after in his soul. And there in that place at the tender age of eighteen summers he met his dreadful fate at the hands of an invader more ruthless than even the worst of all the English.'

'If you can believe there ever was such a thing created under Heaven,' Denis added.

Hugh coughed indignantly at the interruption.

Denis sipped his whiskey and acknowledged the gentle rebuke by agreeing with his host. 'A curse it was that came upon us all in those cruel years.'

'In the same month that I was born,' Hugh declared, 'Turlough O'Carolan passed his eighteenth year. That is one hundred years ago now. Within a year of my own birth the usurper, King William, who was once the Duke of Orange and an enemy of good King James the Stewart, was proclaimed monarch. That was after the bloody disaster of the Battle of the Boyne. Then began the flight of the earls to France and the dispersion of the old nobility of Ireland.'

'May they all return one day to save us from English tyranny, shoddy Scots whiskey and dried hay in our tobacco,' Denis hummed.

'In the year of my nativity,' Hugh went on, ignoring the interjection, 'sixteen hundred and eighty-eight, a terrible plague of the pox visited these shores, brought on the same winds that filled the sails of the foreigners' ships.'

'That bitter plague took its evil pleasure upon the people of Ireland for fifty years,' Denis noted with genuine deep sorrow. 'Those who did not die a lingering death were blinded, like myself. The less fortunate were crippled and disfigured. I was a child of ten when the sickness struck me.'

'Smallpox?' Edward asked.

'I have often heard it called by that name,' the old harper confirmed. 'But in those days we knew it as the Galar-breac, which means the spotted affliction.'

'The Devil himself would have been more welcome,' Hugh sighed. 'High- and low-born alike were struck down. And so it is said that Satan does not discriminate against a man for the contents of his pockets or the quality of his coat cloth.'

'Many of my family were spared,' Denis continued, 'but most of my neighbours were taken away in the prime of their lives.'

'And for many it would have been better if they had died of the fever,' Hugh said. 'For to live a life without sight or without the use of limbs is hard indeed.'

'Is that how it happened with Carolan?' Edward asked.

'Now if you'll be patient a while,' the old distiller cut in, 'there's much more to the tale and I would have you hear it all.'

'I must be going in the morning,' Edward reminded his host.

'You'll be off to Dublin when and if I decide so. Are you sure you wouldn't rather be resting at His Majesty's pleasure? It can easily be arranged.'

'I am most eager to hear your story,' Edward reassured the old man quickly. 'Please forgive my impatience. It has been a harrowing day for me.'

'It wasn't a very profitable day for Major D'Arcy either,' Denis noted.

Hugh took another sip of whiskey. Then he carefully placed the wooden vessel down on the floor beside him, confident that he had the attention of all in the room.

'Sixteen hundred and eighty-eight was a terrible year. The English were on our doorstep and Lord Mayo, loyal to King James, travelled the country enlisting every able-bodied man to the cause of Ireland's liberty. And in that year Master Carolan discovered his vocation.'

THREE

At the rear of the stone manor house there was a wide court-yard bordered by a large rough-looking timber barn and a blacksmith's workshop. Two broad doors led to the dark depths of the building where a dozen plough mares and a few good hunting mounts were stabled.

In earlier times this building had been a stately hall where magnificent feasts were held. Now the only banquets consisted of sweet hay and well-water. The only songs were the neighing cries of the four-legged beasts lodged within, and the courtly dances of the nobility were replaced by the stamping hooves of restless horses.

Just inside the doors of the stable a young man in his late teens waited, kicking his heels on the grass which grew through the cracks in the stone doorstop. The sun was just going down and his work was finished for the day. Most of the other farm labourers were already sitting down to their evening meal.

But this lad was not going home to eat with his father. Not this night. For tonight he was going to attend an evening of music in the company of his betters. Mrs MacDermot-Rua, the wife of the owner of the estate, was kind-hearted and she had a soft spot for this boy. Since her husband had left to join King James in France, she had sponsored the lad's education.

The boy was sharp-witted and handsome, a hard worker and

honest. He was the son Mrs MacDermot had never borne. His features were smooth and his eyes sparkled like two blue jewels. And he was a quick learner. Under Mrs MacDermot's patronage he had been studying the English language and the complementary skills of reading and writing.

But this lad had one weakness which caused him endless longing, deep pain and hours of unrivalled joy.

She was the daughter of a squire and her name was Bridget Cruise.

Every once in a while the young man looked up toward the house in anticipation. He stared at the kitchen door on the other side of the courtyard, willing it to open. When there was no movement he sullenly looked to the ground and kicked his new shoes at the grass.

'Where is she?' he asked himself aloud as he searched in his pockets for a pipe and tobacco. When he had found the pipe he carefully began to fill it, mindful not to drop a single shred of the precious herb. He did not feel comfortable dressed in his best clothes in the middle of the week and so he loosened the scarf around his neck a little and unbuttoned his waistcoat.

The lad looked up toward the kitchen door again and then he realised he would have to go inside to the hearth to light his pipe. He had only gone a few paces when the kitchen door swung inwards and a girl with golden hair appeared, wearing an embroidered dress of rich burgundy.

Without a moment's hesitation the boy stuffed his pipe back into his pocket and made quickly for the stables. He slipped inside without looking back and pushed the door shut after him. And there he waited, leaning against the wall, his heart beating wildly in his chest.

A long while passed and the lad was tempted to open the door a little to take a look outside. But he held himself back, commanding his impatient heart to wait just a little longer. He forced himself to look at the ceiling, and take his mind off his beloved Bridget by counting the heavy wooden beams that arched above him. And when he had exhausted the possibilities of that diversion he closed his eyes so he could concentrate all his efforts into listening for the slightest sound, the merest hint of her arrival.

Finally, as he was about to relent and go out into the court-yard again, the door opened slightly until it was ajar. A small white hand, delicate and smooth, appeared around the edge of the rough-hewn frame. The lad stood frozen in anticipation, watching the dainty fingers intently.

As he stared the door suddenly swung open and in an instant it closed again. The girl peered back through a small crack in the timberwork, carefully checking once more to make sure no-one had seen her. Satisfied that she had not been followed, she turned around to search the stables.

'Turlough?' she whispered as her eyes adjusted to the darkness. 'Where are you?'

The lad could not move. He was utterly transfixed by the gorgeous creature standing before him. She was a princess. A jewel. A warm, tender loving respite from the harsh work of the forge and the farm.

'Turlough!' she repeated, insistently. 'Don't play games with me. You know I hate it when you tease me.'

With that the young man moved one step closer to her. She jumped a little in surprise and leaned back against the door. But when she recognised the scent of the blacksmith's forge, she smiled mischievously. She raised one finger and beckoned to Turlough.

'Bridget,' the lad murmured, falling into her embrace, 'where have you been? I've been waiting out here for ages.'

'I could not get away,' she told him, stroking his jawline. 'Father is watching me like a cat stalking a mouse. I had to ask the new butler's assistant, William O'Flynn, to distract him.'

'Can we trust him?' Turlough asked with concern.

'I think so,' Bridget replied. 'I caught him sneaking out of the chambermaid's room this morning. I don't think he'd dare say anything for fear I'd tell Mrs MacDermot.'

'Did anyone else see you?'

Bridget put her hand gently to his mouth to stop him talking.

'We don't have much time.' She ran her finger slowly around his top lip. Turlough sighed and threw his head back, savouring every touch. The girl leaned closer, teasing him with the promise of a kiss.

The lad tentatively brushed her shoulder with his fingertips and then gently caressed his way to her neck. His other hand fell to her waist, pulling her close so that he could feel her body hard against his.

Bridget hummed low and contentedly, bringing both her hands up to his face and lightly brushing the skin around his cheeks and across his forehead. She was almost the same height as him so when he focused again he found himself staring directly into her deep blue ocean eyes.

She touched his lip again with her fingernail and then she pulled his face closer to hers. When their lips met the young man felt his knees shake and his whole body tingle with excitement.

Turlough knew she was playing with him. She was teasing him, taunting him. But he did not care. The lad had never known a feeling of such utter joy. He had never been kissed by a young woman the way this girl kissed him. He shut his eyes again and let himself become lost in her.

Bridget nipped at her lover's lips and ran her tongue gently over the edge of his teeth so that he stopped breathing and opened his eyes wide to look at her.

'I missed you,' she whispered.

'I missed you too,' he repeated in a trance.

Her hands ran down over his chest, pushing his unbuttoned waistcoat open, caressing his stomach, moving then to his hips and around behind him to grip his buttocks.

Turlough's hands fell to her shoulders. He was powerless to resist her embrace. Whenever she touched him he melted like golden butter in the pan. It was as if she had placed a magic spell upon him; he had become her unresisting servant. She could have asked anything of him at all. When she had him in this state his will was not his own.

One of her hands strayed to his thigh and his breathing suddenly became deep and rhythmic. He moved a hand to her neck again and then slowly, carefully let the fingers drag lightly across her collarbone. His hand skimmed delicately over the exposed skin and he stared into her eyes all the while.

Then Turlough's fingers pushed the folds of fine burgundy cloth from her shoulders as she kissed him with renewed passion, sighing deeply. At last his hand moved to cup her breast and the young woman groaned. Her hand found his face. She held his chin and breathed lightly, groaning with pleasure.

And then, just as Turlough felt he was losing his senses completely, just as he thought he would drown in the scent of her, in the very presence of her, Bridget pushed herself away from him.

'The music is about to begin,' she hummed with excitement. 'And Lord Mayo is among the gathering. Can you believe it? Lord Mayo himself, deputy to the King's viceroy, the Tyrconnel. And he has with him in his company a harper by the name of David Murphy. What a fine handsome lad he is. He's the same age as you, I'm told, but he's a great musician, despite his youth. The best harper in all the land, folk tell.'

'What folk?' Turlough asked, his voice hoarse with jealousy and frustration. He could have guessed she would play this little game on him. Usually he did not really mind when she pushed herself away because he knew she would relent eventually.

Turlough expected they would have many other opportunities to continue their sport. And in the last six months he had come to enjoy Bridget's teasing games. Indeed he looked forward to the heightened excitement that came from hours of flirting. But tonight he sensed something unusual in her voice, something he had not heard before.

'Mrs MacDermot says that David Murphy is a great musician, and she should know,' the girl retorted. 'Now are you coming in to the music room or are you just going to stand there sulking with your lip dragging in the hay?'

'I'll come in,' the lad replied, struggling to regain his composure and slow his breathing.

'Then tie your scarf up, tidy your waistcoat and fix your hair. Somehow,' she pouted in mock innocence, 'the ribbon has come untied.'

Bridget took a step closer, turned him around and started to arrange his long brown locks so they were neat and presentable. She did not want anyone in the big house to guess what they had been up to in the stables.

'I am just a blacksmith's son,' Turlough reminded her. 'There's no need for me to act grand or dress finely.'

'Mrs MacDermot is providing for your education,' Bridget scolded him as she ran her fingers through his hair. 'If she didn't think you were meant for higher things than the forge, she would not have paid for your English lessons. Nor would she have asked you to attend this recital tonight. Now tie up your scarf and straighten your jacket before we go in. I will not have you embarrass our patroness in front of all the nobility of Ireland.'

The lad grumbled but he did as he was told. 'I thought we would have had a little more time together,' he protested as she pulled his hair too hard, jerking his head back.

'What on earth would I be doing wasting my time with the likes of you when Lord Mayo himself is taking supper in the manor house? You are a strange fellow, Turlough O'Carolan, to think I would want to squander my hours in the stables with a country lad when the man who may one day rule Ireland in the King's name is supping under this very roof.'

'You didn't think it was a waste of time when we had the hayloft to ourselves last week,' the lad winked.

'Shut up!' she gasped in mock reprimand, tugging his brown locks gently. 'If my father even suspected I was spending time with you instead of attending to my lessons, I would be in terrible trouble. And you'd get a fearful beating for your insolence. The only reason we have any excuse to speak to one another at all is that we share a tutor.'

'Bridget Cruise,' he smiled, 'I do believe you are frightened your father will find out what we've been up to.'

'Of course I am,' she shot back.

'Am I not grand enough for you?'

'You'll suffice,' she conceded in her teasing voice. 'In some respects, you are almost the equal of David Murphy.'

She spun him around by the shoulders and began tying up his scarf in a neat knot at the front.

'Would you rather be off with your gallant harper, travelling round the world at the side of Lord Mayo?' Turlough asked.

'The lord is off to France soon to seek the French king's aid in the war against the English,' Bridget declared, mimicking her father's patriotic turn of phrase. 'He is going to bring back a great army of true-hearted Catholics to drive the invaders from these shores forever. And when they've dealt with the Duke of Orange, the valiant army of King James will march back into England to teach the parliament a lesson in humility and loyalty to the Crown.'

'And I expect that harper will go along with them,' Turlough added.

'He will.'

'It is a dangerous voyage,' the young man said, shaking his head gravely. 'Many ships are lost in the high seas. And many more are captured by the English.'

'Lord Mayo and his man will return one day,' Bridget declared.

'If only I was a harper,' the lad muttered.

'What are you talking about?'

'If I was a harper, you would do more than just look sideways at me when we pass in the street. You would not have to sneak to the stables to meet me whenever you wanted my company. You would come to my door and knock without fear of what folk might say. You would be proud of me.'

Turlough put a hand to her cheek. Bridget stopped fumbling with the scarf and looked back into the boy's eyes as his hands dropped to her waist. Then he leaned forward to place a kiss on her lips. But just as they were about to touch, Bridget smiled her wicked smile and pulled back a little.

'If I had fine clothes and played beautiful music,' Turlough said, returning her smile, 'you would want me for your very own. You would not speak to me as if I were nothing more than a servant after we'd spent an hour in the hayloft.'

'Be quiet!' she hissed, the smile disappearing from her face. 'You are forgetting your place. You are the son of a blacksmith. You are nothing more than a servant.'

She caught the flash of anger in his eyes and softened her tone a little. 'You might learn to count one day and to write in the books of the estate. Perhaps you may even perfect your reading skills and increase your knowledge of the world. But you will never be a musician. You are too old to take up the harp and, in any case, your strong hands are needed on the estate. You will always be the son of a blacksmith, Turlough. You can never change that.'

'And you will always be the daughter of a squire who has got himself into debt and relies on the charity of folk such as the MacDermots,' Turlough replied bitterly. 'Your people may have owned half the county once, but you are as poor as I am now. Without Mrs MacDermot's charity you would not even have food in your belly.'

'You don't know what you are talking about,' Bridget snapped, grabbing him by the shoulders and turning him round to face the door.

She tugged on his hair ribbon to make sure the knot was tight. 'When Lord Mayo returns at the head of a French army, the English will flee like rats before the flood. Then King James will go back to London and take his rightful place upon the throne. On that day my father will be restored to his lands and title as a reward for his loyalty. And everyone who has suffered because of the war with the Dutch Prince William will live at peace again.'

'That's a fine old speech but it will take a great army to restore King James to his throne. I have been speaking with old

Teeg the cooper who was at Drogheda when Cromwell came to Ireland. He said the English soldiers are the most brutal stubborn men in all the world. And Prince William of Orange has taken many Dutch and German regiments with him to England to ensure he keeps the throne.'

'With men like Lord Mayo and the Tyrconnel leading his army, King James will be restored soon enough to his rightful place,' she countered. 'The English lords may have no justice in them but the ordinary folk of that country do have a sense of honour. They will not let a usurper rule in place of the rightful monarch.'

'I heard tell that the English are ready to crown William king in place of the Stewarts for he is married to King James's sister.'

'Lord Mayo and the Tyrconnel would never allow them to do that!'

'Well then,' Turlough nodded with a smile, 'I had better go and have a look at him, this great lord with his handsome harper.'

Bridget finished arranging the black silk ribbon in his hair and then straightened his jacket for him and brushed her hands over the shoulders. 'You will have to do,' she sighed, patting the front of the coat.

'Will you give me another kiss, Bridget Cruise?' he asked, smiling broadly and placing a hand at her waist.

'I will not!' she laughed, moving to the stable door. She carefully looked out through the gap to make sure no-one was watching, then she turned to face him again. 'Mind your tongue, or I'll pluck it out.'

'You wouldn't do that, my dearest,' Turlough answered, still smiling. He came up close to her and she leaned back against the door. 'You'd never get the use of it again.'

Bridget grinned and touched her lips gently to his cheek. 'I must go now and you must come with me,' she whispered, but he could tell it would not take much persuading to keep her a while longer.

'I'll meet you after the music has finished,' the girl promised, 'but I will only be able to stay a few minutes. My father wants us to return home early tonight.'

Turlough was about to say that he would rather spend the evening with her than listening to the music of some travelling harper, but before he had a chance to speak they both heard the kitchen door swing open. Bridget looked out through the gap, suddenly frightened.

When she saw a familiar form step out into the courtyard she let out a deep sigh of relief. The man at the kitchen had a black servant's suit and a short grey wig, the mark of a butler's assistant. He was looking across to the stables and wringing his hands.

'Mistress Bridget! Are you coming in? The music is going to start,' William called.

Before young Turlough could entice a parting kiss from her, Bridget opened the stable door and strode out across the courtyard.

'I'm just coming, William,' the girl replied. 'Turlough needed some tidying up and I consented to help him.'

The butler's assistant put a hand to his mouth to feign shock, even though he had a good idea what she was up to in the stables with the blacksmith's son. In a few moments Turlough had caught up with Bridget and was walking calmly beside her.

'Are you two going to stay out there all night?' the butler whispered to hurry them up. 'The best harper in all Ireland is about to begin performing. You'll never hear the likes of him again.'

Then William turned round and went back inside without waiting until they reached the door. Bridget hurried after him, young Turlough close behind. Soon they had passed through the warm kitchen and crossed the broad cold entrance hall. When they came to the music room, which Mrs MacDermot kept especially for entertaining guests, they found the chamber already crowded with people.

Turlough's eyes widened with wonder when he saw all the folk gathered there. He stood on his toes to peer over their heads and gasped at the sight that met his eyes. The chamber was lit by a golden light. Two score candles reflected in the four enormous mirrors which were set into each wall. Their flames flickered gently as the air stirred in the room.

Dressed in their finest, most of the guests stood around the edges of the room, chatting and laughing. The mirrors gave the impression that the chamber went on forever and that there were many more people assembled there than could have possibly fitted into this small space. Red wine flowed freely from a dozen crystal decanters set on silver trays and expertly wielded by bustling servants, some of whom had come from the nearby manor houses to help out, others from as far afield as Dublin specifically for this occasion.

Mrs MacDermot had already taken her seat next to Lord Mayo and was chatting with him as if they were old friends. The lady was arrayed in her finest green dress with long slit black sleeves. While it was a fairly simple design, the colour contrasted starkly with her fiery red hair. Turlough thought she looked like a queen from the old legends.

Turlough leaned close and whispered a question to Bridget. 'How does Mrs MacDermot-Rua come to know Lord Mayo so well?'

'She is a Fitzgerald. The lord's own wife is a Fitzgerald and Mrs MacDermot's cousin. Her ladyship is descended from the ancient nobility of Ireland. That is why she keeps the name of her ancestors, the Rua, the Red Ones.'

'She should be our queen,' Turlough murmured and Bridget laughed at his foolishness.

Just at that moment Bridget's father leaned forward from where he sat behind the lord and whispered something to Mrs MacDermot. Squire Cruise scowled and they both stared over at Turlough and Bridget. The lady nodded, frowned in what seemed reluctant agreement and returned to her conversation with Lord Mayo. Turlough felt his heart sink. He knew they were discussing him.

Mrs MacDermot touched the lord on the shoulder with the

fingers of her black gloved hand and the gentleman spoke a few words to her before standing up from his seat and clearing his throat.

Turlough guessed Lord Mayo was over sixty years of age. The old man's locks were long and grey and tied at the back with a black ribbon. His hair was plaited perfectly so that it hung straight down his back, held in place at the nape of his neck by a silver clasp. His beard was trimmed in the French style to a point on his chin, and he was dressed in the finest black velvet coat that Turlough had ever seen, edged with intricate gold embroidery and lined with linen.

The lord's shirt was black, as was his waistcoat which was also heavily embroidered in sparkling gold thread. His long breeches were tucked into knee-high riding boots. At his belt there was a pistol and by his side a basket-hilted broad-bladed sword like those which the Scots carried into battle.

The old man's clothes were not the fine multicoloured attire of court. They were the garments of a soldier. Despite the fine embroidery, his coat was made to last in the outdoors and provide protection from the weather. Compared to the other men in the room with their fine wigs and their rich stockings, Lord Mayo had an air of strength, experience and wisdom about him.

'Thank you,' the lord began and the room fell silent in awe at his every word. His voice was deep but gentle, like a doting father addressing his children. 'And many thanks to this household for such a satisfying supper. Mrs MacDermot should be praised for her gracious and unstinting hospitality. Her husband serves the King in France and she does her part at home. Mrs MacDermot is a fine example to all. I will be sure to inform His Majesty King James of her heartfelt love and support for even myself, the lowest and most meagre of his subjects.'

Everyone hummed with appreciation at these humble words. They all knew he was far from the lowest or the most meagre in the eyes of the King. Mayo was one of the greatest soldiers of the age and a renowned statesman.

'Raise your glasses, ladies and gentlemen,' the lord went on as he lifted a beautiful crystal chalice in the air. 'To His most Serene and Catholic Majesty, King James the Second by the Grace of God, Defender of the Faith. God save the King!'

'God save the King!' everyone repeated enthusiastically and the room was silent as the assembly solemnly drained their glasses.

The lord glanced at Mrs MacDermot when he had finished his wine. She stood up and Mayo withdrew to his seat.

'And God speed His Majesty's servant, Lord Mayo,' she added.

'God speed,' the guests all wished him as the servants rushed about refilling glasses.

'His Lordship has a special treat in store for us this evening,' the lady announced, her face beaming with excitement. 'His personal harper, David Murphy, who has travelled these last two years with the King in France, will perform a few airs for us tonight. The lad Murphy is well known to all of you by reputation and this evening you will discover how one so youthful could have attained such fame.'

She sat down as soon as she had finished speaking and the room fell into an expectant silence. A thin lad dressed in a dark blue coat which was perfectly tailored to the contours of his body arose from his place behind the lord.

The strands of David Murphy's dark hair were tied back neatly and his scarf was expertly knotted so that it fell across his throat in flawless folds before it disappeared into his waistcoat. The young man coughed, putting a hand to his mouth to cover it with the lace sleeves of his shirt.

Turlough hated the well-dressed harper immediately, from the silk scarf at his throat to the gold buckles on his shoes.

Murphy picked up a small harp from the floor at his feet and moved to a seat in the centre of the room where everyone could hear and see him clearly. Then he took a few private moments to tune his intricately carved instrument. Turlough noticed the boy's fingers were very short and thin. His nails were extremely long and tapered to a fine point.

'That harper's never done a day's work in his life,' he commented under his breath.

'Be quiet,' Bridget hissed, elbowing him hard in the ribs.

When the harp was tuned Murphy looked up from the instrument and smiled warmly to his audience. 'By the Grace of God,' he began, 'and through the incompetence of Duke William's parliament, my lord and I are still free to wander among you. May the day march on when His Majesty King James returns to his loyal subjects and overturns the usurper.'

'Aye,' the guests all agreed.

'I will first play an air that His Majesty has often requested of me,' Murphy went on. 'He tells me that it always puts him in mind of Ireland and the loyal folk who dwell here patiently awaiting his return. It is known to all of you as An Cúileann.'

The young musician took another breath then launched into the opening strains of a gorgeous wistful air. Everyone in the room stared down into their wine in reflective silence as the melody drifted through the room.

The women touched their eyes with their handkerchiefs, pretending to wipe away tears if they had none. The men grasped the folds of their coats with their free hand and hummed approval at the end of each phrase as was the ancient custom. Lord Mayo nodded with pride at the lad's prowess.

The harp was only a tiny travelling instrument which sat on Murphy's lap rather than on the floor. It was more suited to the road than the music room of a great house. But under the nimble fingers of young David Murphy it sang a sweet and plaintive melody. And the enchantment of its song reached out to embrace every heart.

Turlough looked sideways at Bridget and grunted with disgust. He was not surprised that she was so full of admiration for this musician; she always coveted pretty things which had little practical value. But Turlough had to grudgingly admit the harper was exceptionally gifted.

By the time Murphy came to the end of his first measure he already held the room in his power. No-one gave any thought to their mundane lives beyond this room. The bloody conflict over the throne was put out of mind. The troubles of the King became suddenly inconsequential. All that mattered was the magical chiming music of the harp.

The younger women blushed profusely. The elder matrons touched their hands to their cheeks, marvelling at the lad's skill and fair features. David Murphy knew full well the effect he was having on them all. He had no doubt either that he was the most handsome man in the house. And he blessed the day he had decided to follow in his father's footsteps and take up the harp. The instrument worked an irresistible spell on women and he revelled in the power his skill brought him.

At the end of the second measure the young harper took the time to glance around the chamber and nod discreetly at a few ladies. Every woman was staring at him, each with an admiring sparkle in her eye. As usual all the men were gazing at the floor.

The young harper noticed a poorly dressed boy standing by the door in a large coat. The lad's eyes were full of contempt and this surprised the harper until he realised the boy must be jealous. Murphy gave a little bow of his head to acknowledge the stranger's animosity and then he turned his mind back to the music.

Murphy played through the third and fourth measures of the melody with consummate skill and confidence, bringing all his brilliance to bear in the build to the finale. He ended on a delicate trill before repeating the introductory few notes of the first phrase. At that point he stopped for a second, took a deep breath and began to sing the words he had put to this air.

All the men looked up in astonishment and the women blushed even more deeply, now entirely ensnared by this clever youth. It was a rare thing for a skilled harper to have a fine voice as well as such nimble hands.

Murphy had spent many years perfecting his craft. If he knew he was an excellent musician, he was equally certain of the fine quality of his voice. And he had honed his skill before the ladies of the French court. Ladies of incomparable taste and wit who did not stint at complimenting him on his successes or criticising his failures.

'Many hours have I passed,' the young harper began crooning, his voice following the melody his fingers picked out on the harp, 'in the arms of my dear. But I cannot think on her without a sad tear. How often to love me she fondly has sworn. And when parted from me she always does mourn.'

He looked up from his instrument and smiled to his audience before continuing, 'Hardship for me she would cheerfully bear. And at night on my bosom forget all her care.'

Several of the ladies fluttered open their fans and hid their faces, each certain that this handsome young man was directing his song to her and to no-one else in the chamber. A few others held hands to their mouths and giggled as he glanced about the room, again catching an eye here or acknowledging a glimpse of admiration there.

'To some distant climate together we'll roam. And forget all the hardships we met with at home. Fate now be propitious and grant me thine aid. Give me my dear Cúileann and I'm more than repaid.'

Murphy played the opening phrase once more and then he let the brass wires of his harp continue to sound until their humming had faded away completely.

No-one stirred until long after the music room had fallen utterly silent. It was as if everyone were holding their breath in anticipation of another verse. Then Lord Mayo himself began to applaud and the entire gathering was soon clapping enthusiastically in appreciation of this young man's skill at the harp.

Murphy bowed his head politely as the gentlemen called to him and whistled. But across the chamber the strange lad with the dark brown hair was still scowling and the harper wondered for a moment who this fellow was.

Murphy held up his hand to acknowledge the generosity of his audience and when they did not stop clapping he struck a chord on the harp to silence them. The possibility of another tune quietened them quickly.

'I will play for you,' he announced in his clearest voice, and then he waited patiently, for there were still a few folk whispering behind their hands. 'I will play a piece which I recently composed in honour of my generous patron, Lord Mayo.'

The lord smiled broadly. This, after all, was the reason nobles kept harpers by their side, to pay them tribute, to flatter them, to extol their noble virtues. Not for the first time the old lord felt he had been very wise to take on this lad at such a young age. For twelve years Mayo had treated Murphy almost as he might have done his own son. He had showered the lad with gifts and provided him with the best clothes, food and wine. And the best musical education gold could purchase.

Murphy struck a strident chord on the harp and then launched into a stirring march which had the men sitting up proudly as if they had been called to the battlefield that very minute. Most of the ladies also sat up straight and some, those whose husbands or sons were off helping King James raise an army in France, closed their eyes to think on their dear ones.

The harper had got no further than the third phrase of his martial tune when a man dressed in a long blue mud-spattered riding cloak appeared at the door. Turlough and Bridget were gruffly pushed aside as the messenger made his way into the chamber. Once the rider was inside, he scanned the assembly until he found old Lord Mayo. Then, without regard for the wonderful music, the stranger made straight for where Mayo was seated. The old man watched his officer approaching and put a hand to his eyes, thinking the worst. When he looked up again it was only to wave the messenger away as if he had no time for any news just now. But the rider was determined to pass on his dispatch.

He leaned in close to Mayo's ear and whispered a few words. As the man spoke the old man's face changed colour and he put a hand on Mrs MacDermot's lap to grasp her fingers. Then he related to her, under his breath, what the officer had told him. She put a hand to her mouth and stood up straightaway.

Murphy instantly stopped playing. He did not have to guess

what was the matter. The arrival of the commander of the lord's bodyguard could mean only one thing.

Lord Mayo rose calmly and coughed. 'I am sorry to do you this dishonour, David,' he said in a forceful but sincere tone, 'and I must ask you to forgive me this intrusion on your music. But I have just received word that a company of English dragoons, loyal to the Dutch usurper, has been observed on the road less than five miles from this place. It is almost certain they are on their way here in the hope of catching my troopers unawares.'

The room was suddenly buzzing with nervous chatter. One lady fainted and fell forward from her chair onto the floor. Mrs MacDermot rushed to the woman's side and ordered a servant to bring some wine.

'I am terribly sorry,' Lord Mayo went on, addressing the crowd. 'I have not enough horsemen with me to put up a decent fight and so I must hasten away to safety. I regretfully bid you all goodnight. Do not fear. The English will not cause you any harm. They are most certainly searching for me.'

With that the old lord strode over to Mrs MacDermot and kissed her hand, bowing elegantly as he did so. A moment later his officers ushered him from the room, through the kitchen and out into the courtyard where the horses were already being readied.

David Murphy hurriedly wrapped his harp in its leather cover and followed after them, desperate not to be left behind. The throng would not part for him at first and he had to push hard to make his way out. Eventually he made his way to the door and it was there that Bridget reached out and put a hand on his sleeve.

'That was a beautiful song,' she said breathlessly and her cheeks were rosy red as she spoke. 'I hope you will return again soon and grace us with your music.'

The young harper never missed an opportunity to impress a lady, even if it meant he risked being captured by English dragoons. He took Bridget's hand and placed his lips gently on the smooth skin near her knuckles.

'I will come back if you promise me another kiss,' the harper replied as his eyes met hers.

Bridget smiled and leaned toward his ear as if to whisper something, but at the last moment she touched her lips to his cheek. Murphy had a high opinion of himself but he had not expected the girl to be so bold with so many people watching.

'I will certainly return,' he promised, a little startled by her forwardness. Just then the harper noticed the young man who had been glaring at him. The lad was now frowning even more deeply, which made him look a little ridiculous. Clearly this girl was his sweetheart.

'How will I know you when I return?' Murphy asked the girl, purely to antagonise the sullen young man. 'Whom shall I inquire after?'

'My name is Bridget,' she told him, her chest heaving with excitement, 'Bridget Cruise.'

'Until we meet again, Bridget of the golden locks,' he said softly. 'Goodbye and pray for my safe return.'

'Farewell,' she cooed. 'I will pray for you, my gallant harper.' Then she followed the handsome young harper with her eyes until he disappeared through the kitchen door.

'You should not make so free with such a one as him,' Turlough hissed, taking Bridget by the arm. 'He's nothing but a travelling harper.'

'Better that than the son of a blacksmith,' she countered, shaken from her dream. 'He has grace and wit—'

'Pretty clothes and a steady income skimmed from his lordship's coffers,' the lad added before she could finish.

'Be quiet!' Bridget snapped. 'He's a fine young man who is doing his duty to his King.' Then she turned around and pushed past everyone who was milling in the kitchen. She was determined to get one last glimpse of David Murphy as he rode out of the courtyard.

Turlough shrugged and followed her. Once they were outside he tried to put a hand on her shoulder but she brushed him away.

'Leave me alone, you uncouth, unwashed, untutored foolish boy,' she hissed under her breath.

The horses were saddled by this time and the lord had already galloped off with his closest guards. But Murphy was still standing by his mount, having just secured the harp in a large saddlebag. He noticed Bridget as he swung himself into the saddle and he waved to her elegantly and nodded his head. Then the harper spurred his mount and galloped off into the night, leaving the girl and several other ladies standing on the cobbles, staring longingly after him.

'What's so special about Murphy?' Turlough asked in frustration.

'He is a real man,' Bridget replied curtly. 'He is brave and gentle. He is a poet and a musician. He is a guardian of the old traditions which the English would have us abandon.'

'How can I compare with that?' the young lad laughed.

Bridget turned to him slowly, as if she had suddenly woken from a deep sleep. 'You cannot compare with him, Turlough O'Carolan. Perhaps if you were the greatest harper of the age, I might cast an eye at you. If you were as renowned a gentleman as David Murphy and honoured by the great lords of the land, I could possibly consider your attentions as becoming for a lady of my station. But you are a farm labourer. The son of a blacksmith. And you are a petty-minded jealous boy. Now that I have witnessed the heights a man may rise to in this world, I will never waste my time with the likes of you again.'

'What?' the lad stuttered. 'How many times have you told me that you loved me?'

'Be quiet or I will call for my father.' Bridget's voice was full of contempt.

At that moment Turlough felt a hand on his arm. He turned to see William O'Flynn, the butler's assistant. He was a little younger than Turlough but he had an air of authority about him.

'Her ladyship would like to speak with you, Turlough,' William declared, 'before you retire, if you will. She sent me out to fetch you.'

'I'll come along presently,' the lad replied, distracted by the sudden change in Bridget's attitude toward him.

'She wishes to see you now,' the butler insisted. 'Come along. There is much to do before the English soldiers arrive and Mrs MacDermot needs your help.'

'Very well,' Turlough agreed, turning to Bridget once more, 'I'll come.' But the girl walked off before he could reason with her any further. After a few seconds the lad decided to let her be and followed William back into the house.

The butler opened the double doors to the music room and stood waiting for Turlough to enter. As soon as the lad had done so, the doors swung shut behind him. Mrs MacDermot and Squire Cruise were still seated in their places, sipping wine and whispering to each other. They seemed to be quite amicable but there was a tension in the room. The lady looked up as she noticed the boy waiting politely, just out of earshot.

'Turlough,' she began, beckoning him closer, 'good evening to you.'

The young man approached and bowed his head slightly. 'Good evening, my lady.'

'Did you enjoy the music?' Mrs MacDermot asked and the lad thought she looked younger and more fragile than he had ever seen her. It was hard to remember sometimes that she was only twenty-seven years of age, for she had a strong demeanour and ran the household with a stern hand.

'I did enjoy it, your ladyship,' the lad lied.

'Good. Now I have a task for you, if you would not mind. As you probably know, there are reported to be some English dragoons making their way toward our house. They may indeed arrive here at any moment. I would appreciate it if you would go up to the top of Squire Crilly's hill and watch out for them.'

'At the first sign of the enemy,' Bridget's father went on, 'you are to light a torch so that we may see the signal here.'

'That will give us enough warning of their arrival,' Mrs MacDermot added.

'I understand, my lady,' Turlough answered, ignoring Squire Cruise.

'There is one other thing,' she added, 'while you are here.' She glanced nervously at Bridget's father. 'You have heard of the trouble with the Dutch Duke William?'

Turlough nodded.

'The English are rumoured to be preparing to invade Ireland. Lord Mayo is looking for recruits to train in his regiment in case the English attempt to take this country by force and defeat King James. I would like you to consider going off with the lord's regiment and doing your part to protect our land from the invaders.'

'Yes, my lady.'

'Think about it carefully, Turlough. I believe we may be able to spare you about the place, but only if you are willing. A soldier's life is hard and dangerous, but if you go I will pay for your clothing, weaponry and other essential items. And I will provide you with a small income so that you may always have decent food when it is available.'

'Yes, my lady,' the boy repeated.

'Very well, then,' she concluded. 'Off you go to Squire Crilly's hill and make sure you light a beacon at the first sign of danger.'

'I will, my lady.'

Turlough turned to go, knowing full well that Squire Cruise had come up with the plan to send him off to the war to keep him away from Bridget.

'It's for the best,' William offered as he ushered Turlough into the hall. 'I know you are great friends with Bridget, but you must understand it is only because her ladyship provided for both your educations that you ever met. If it had not been for her generosity, you would not have come to know Bridget at all. The likes of you and me are not meant to dally with the nobility.'

Turlough nodded silently. William had obviously overheard Mrs MacDermot speaking with Bridget's father about him.

'You can never make a match with her,' William went on.

'Her family are well-born landholders and despite the trouble they have suffered her father is still a very influential man. We are nothing to folk like them. Our kind can never rise to their station. We must be content with what we have.'

'I know,' the boy cut in. 'I may be no more than a farm labourer but I have eyes to see.' He turned to William and said coldly, 'If you will excuse me, I have a task to complete for her ladyship.' Then he pushed past O'Flynn and made for the courtyard.

Turlough could not see Bridget outside the kitchen where he had left her so he grabbed a torch, a flint, steel and a leather bag. Then he took a small bottle of whiskey from his father's store and set off as fast as he could for the top of the hill which overlooked both the road and the MacDermot estate.

All the way up to the summit he cursed Squire Cruise for his interference. Then he cursed Mrs MacDermot for bending to the old man's will. He cursed his bad luck at being born a poor labourer. But most of all he cursed the sudden appearance of David Murphy, harper to Lord Mayo, who had turned his life upside down in a single evening.

'Bridget would have never thought of forsaking me,' he muttered aloud. 'She would have defied her father if she had not laid eyes on that overdressed, underworked dandy.'

By the time the boy reached the summit the moon had set and the night was utterly dark. A strong breeze rushed up the slopes and whipped his coat about his knees. It sped on to rustle the trees which grew in a round at the very top. Nine old oaks and nine whitethorn bushes stood side by side at the very peak, and the circle they formed provided protection from the wind.

Turlough made for this place and set himself down to lean against one of the oak trees. Far away down below he could just make out the silvery line of the road twisting its way through the fields toward the MacDermot estate.

Even though the trees afforded him a great deal of shelter the air was cold and Turlough considered lighting a fire. Then he realised that even a small blaze on this dark night could be mistaken for a signal by the folk at the house. Besides, he had often been warned about setting fires near ancient places. He did not want to risk upsetting the spirits who dwelt in this desolate spot.

As he huddled beneath the oaks he wondered whether this hill was really a haunt of the Good People, the otherworldly beings folk reckoned dwelt just beyond the fringe of the world. The whitethorn was reputed to be their favourite bough, though he had no idea why.

Certainly, at midnight, alone on this deserted hilltop, the stories of the Faeries, as they were called by those who used the English language, were easy to believe. Turlough found that, rather than dozing off as he feared he might, his senses were wide awake and his mind alert. He took careful note of each sigh of the breeze, every creak of the branches.

The Good People, the Old Ones, were well known for their sport of capturing ordinary folk. They would whisk their captives away to the Otherworld to become slaves or lovers. Or they would steal their poor unfortunate souls and leave the shattered empty bodies of their victims to rot in the forest.

The greatest musicians and storytellers were all reputedly captured by the Faeries, tutored by them and then released once their education was complete. Harpers especially were chosen by the Good People to learn the craft of this ancient music.

'David Murphy is a fine harper,' Turlough conceded bitterly as his thoughts returned to the cause of his sadness. 'I will never have the gifts he has. I am just a poor farm labourer. And now Mrs MacDermot is going to send me off to war just to make sure Bridget and I can never be together.'

The boy wondered whether his beloved would look on him favourably if he became a famous harper. Turlough loved the music. He had always enjoyed a dance and a song.

For a moment he imagined he was standing in David Murphy's shoes. He wondered what it must be like to be able to conjure such gorgeous melodies, to be so superbly dressed, even on a weekday, to have a horse of your own, to be as well fed as any lord, to have the ladies looking at you with fluttering eyes. And even better than all that, to have the luxury of long fingernails which precluded a harper from any menial work. Young Turlough, sitting alone on top of the Faerie hill, closed his eyes and dreamed of what it would be like never to have to till the soil again or drive the cows home from pasture.

'No more cutting turf until my back aches,' he whispered. 'No more horses or sheep to tend. No more harvest work or stacking hay.'

An owl flew out of the trees and Turlough took a sharp breath, startled by the sudden noise.

'If I was a harper I could sleep until breakfast time,' he said aloud to himself when he had recovered from the little shock, 'like all the wealthy folk do. No timber to split for the stove, no milking to be done, no geese to feed or goats to tether. And if I were a harper I would work hard at my craft. I would toil as hard at the music as I have in the fields or at the forge with my father. If it meant I could be closer to my Bridget.'

Turlough looked down at the road. The moon was gone but there was still enough light for him to be sure there were no horsemen riding toward the house. Perhaps, he thought, the English dragoons were not coming at all. The lad did not like the idea of waiting through the whole night without a fire to warm him just in case the enemy appeared.

Turlough thought of the cottage he shared with his father, the warm turf fire in the grate and the little cot covered in blankets. On this hill he could feel the air getting colder by the minute. His skin was tingling; his fingers were numb. There would surely be a frost at dawn.

'I wish Bridget was up here to keep me warm,' the boy said to himself despondently. 'I suppose she will never speak to me again.'

He sighed and lay down among the twisted roots of the oak, leaning his head on one so that he could keep an eye out for the English while he rested. He wrapped his coat close about him and pulled his broad felt hat down over his head to keep warm. Sleep began to grip his weary body. Turlough was used to going to bed long before midnight so that he could rise at dawn and commence his daily chores.

He knew he had a duty to stay alert so he struggled against slumber for a long while, forcing himself to sit up occasionally and take in the cold night air until his lungs ached. Eventually he took out his pipe still stuffed with tobacco, hoping to pass the time with a quiet puff. But then he remembered bitterly that he could not light it. The slightest spark might be interpreted as a signal of the arrival of the dragoons. Deeply disappointed, he put the pipe back in his pocket.

Turlough concentrated his thoughts on Bridget once more and this kept him awake for a long time. But he could not win the battle against weariness and gradually he dozed off. It was one of those little sleeps which he knew he should not be taking but, as we all do on occasion, he made a bargain with himself.

'I will rest for a few minutes,' the lad said softly to himself, 'then I will be better able to stand my watch. The English have not come by yet and they will not likely do so in the next few minutes. I will shut my eyes but only for a short while.'

And so he committed what turned out to be a mistake that would follow him for the rest of his life. Alone on the top of a hill, within the bounds of a Faerie grove, on a night when the enemy was abroad, Turlough O'Carolan fell fast asleep.

Old Hugh stopped speaking and turned to face Edward, his eyebrows pushed down toward his nose in a deep frown.

'What are you sniggering at?' he snarled at his guest.

'This young fellow is an eedjit,' Denis chimed in, 'a bloody eedjit. Don't take any notice of him.'

'Please forgive me, Mister Connor.' Edward tried to control himself. 'It is a very good tale. But surely you can't expect me to believe it. No-one believes in the Good People these days.'

Both old men downed their whiskeys quickly and held their wooden cups out for Daniel to refill.

'You are more English than you are Irish,' Hugh snorted. 'You are from Dublin, I suppose, and that may be the reason for your ignorance. I will forgive you your foolishness. And I pray for your sake that the Old Ones offer you the same goodwill.'

'I hope you do not ever find yourself alone upon the road at night,' Denis added solemnly. 'For if you do, you will wish the redcoats had caught you and filled your body full of lead. Better that than a soul filled full of fear by the Faeries.'

'They are a powerful folk, the Good People,' Hugh agreed. 'They can put a dread upon you that can turn your bones to jelly. Or they may bless you with the measureless bounty of their gifts at their whim.'

'But what manner of folk are they?' Edward asked, amazed that these two old men could hold so strongly to such a strange and archaic belief.

'They are older than the oldest oak tree,' Denis told him in a whisper, 'and wiser than the watching owl. They are of ancient stock. They come from before the times of the Irish people when this land was full of spirits both malicious and kind.'

'I heard a priest say once that the Faeries are angels who fell from grace with God,' Hugh added. 'He claimed they were the servants of the Lord who could not choose which side to take in the wars of Heaven. Because they had not thrown in their lot with Satan, God would not condemn them to the fires of Hell. But because they had not joined the armies of the righteous and helped defeat the Dark One, God decided they had rejected the will of their creator.'

'And so,' the old harper cut in, 'the Lord above had to invent some special penance for them.'

'They were condemned to walk the land of Ireland,' Hugh informed his guest, 'until the return of Christ and the coming of the Reign of Peace. Thus they live separated from our world by a thin veil of enchantment in a beautiful country resembling the fields of Heaven. And because they are undying they are liable to accumulate many more sins than any mortal may in one lifetime.'

'But at the same time their lives are so long they also have a greater opportunity for good works and for redemption,' Denis countered.

'True enough,' Hugh nodded, 'and there are many among them who live only for the happiness they may bring to the world. Though most are of the same sort as we mortals: a curious mixture of good and bad, neither purely evil nor completely saintly.'

'So they are spirits?' Edward asked.

'That is hard to say,' Hugh replied carefully. 'You would have to ask them that question yourself. Though I don't recommend you be so bold. They don't appreciate prying strangers and they relish questions even less. All I know is that some folk who have seen them would swear they were as solid in form as your good self sitting there by the fire with a smirk on your face.'

Edward looked at the old man guiltily but then he remembered his host was blind and couldn't know that he was smiling. 'How is it I have never seen one of these folk if they are so common?'

Both men laughed a little and sipped thoughtfully at their whiskey.

'You have lived your whole life in Dublin, have you not?' Hugh asked.

'I went to London to visit my uncle last year,' Edward answered.

The two old men laughed again.

'You will not find a rabbit living in a foxhole,' Denis told him. 'Nor any of the Good People dwelling in towns or cities. They dwell in the most remote and inaccessible parts of the country, far from our interference. They only come to the towns occasionally on their own business.'

'And if you had come across them,' Hugh said sternly, 'I can assure you, your destiny would have been changed completely. For good or ill, your life would have been turned around. With good reason the Faeries rarely go into the towns where folk are cold, humourless and concerned only with themselves. They do not like the smell of sewers and coal smoke. They prefer the company of country people, if it is mortal company they seek. For country folk have some sense about them. Folk in the villages know which phase of the moon it is and what the weather will bring tomorrow.'

'All townsfolk are like the English,' Denis observed, 'they couldn't find a cow pat if it was floating in a vat of fresh honey.'

'So do not mock what you do not understand,' Hugh admonished. 'Many a man has scoffed at tales of the Faerie folk. Some have been fortunate enough to be allowed to live to regret their mockery. Most are not given that luxury. For the Old Ones do not tolerate foolishness. And as they are under God's penance and have the power to punish, they are dangerous indeed when crossed.'

'And it is your firm conviction,' Edward frowned, 'that Carolan was gifted in some manner by the Faeries?'

'He was and no doubting it,' Hugh replied. 'As sure as this whiskey has been allowed to age too long.' He held up his cup again for a refill.

'We must not let it grow another night older,' Denis agreed, holding his up also. 'Or it won't be fit for drinking.'

Mhairgead came back into the room at that moment and laughed at her grandfather. 'There's some who would say,' she giggled, winking at Edward, 'that drinking too much whiskey attracts the attention of the Good People.'

'If that were so,' Hugh protested, 'then young Denis here would be the King of the Faeries and I would be his chamberlain. For there isn't a man alive can outdrink a harper when he has put his mind to the task. And I have to match him as best I can, of course.'

'Of course,' the young woman laughed. 'So have you seen the Faeries yourself?'

'I have not!' the old distiller snapped. 'And may I never have the misfortune. They are a fickle folk and I would not want to

73

cross them. Though I must admit that since the blindness came upon me I have heard things in the night which no Christian man should hear. I'll swear I have overheard the sound of the Good People making their sport in the front room here. Cavorting and carrying on in wild drunken orgies of unspeakable pleasure.'

Daniel coughed nervously and Mhairgead blushed.

'Go on with you,' the red-haired man said after a few seconds. 'Many's the night you've had so much to drink you wouldn't have heard a regiment of redcoats marching by with a full military band and cannons blazing.'

'I know what I know,' Hugh replied enigmatically.

'Have another drink, Master Edward,' Mhairgead offered.

The young rebel acquiesced and sat back again to sip the liquor. 'How did the Faeries come to play such an important part in your master's life?' he asked, trying not to notice the young woman who stood so close to him.

'That is a good question,' Hugh nodded.

'Well get on with it!' Denis snapped. 'I don't want to be sitting here next week waiting for you to finish your story.'

'Very well,' the old distiller sighed, putting up a hand to still his friend's impatience. But the old harper couldn't see the gesture, of course, so he was not at all calmed by it.

FOUR

The wind had dropped completely when Turlough awoke but his feet were bitterly cold. Almost immediately he stood up and looked toward the road, afraid that more than a few minutes had passed since he fell asleep.

But there was no movement or any sign of English dragoons. All was peaceful. The night was perfectly silent save for the gentle rustling of the branches overhead.

'I would've heard a troop of horses travelling by,' he assured himself, talking aloud for the comfort it brought him.

Then he stretched, yawned and stamped his feet to get the blood moving through his veins. He sat down again after a few moments and for a long while lay back and let his mind wander. His legs were still cold so he pulled his knees up to his chest and locked his arms around them.

'I wish I was a harper,' he sighed, knowing he had almost no chance of attaining such a goal. 'I don't care what hardship I might have to endure. I don't care if it means I never see this wretched estate or Mrs MacDermot ever again. I wish I was the greatest harper that ever lived.'

The wind rose suddenly and as the trees shook the young man turned to look behind him toward the centre of the grove.

'You should be careful what you wish for,' a deep voice cut through the air, 'for you are likely to receive it in abundance.'

Turlough was on his feet in a second, though he stumbled over the roots of the oak tree and fell once more onto his hands. His only thought was that somehow while he had been sleeping a horde of well-armed dragoons had swarmed all over the hill.

In terror the lad raised his eyes to see who the stranger was and if he had companions. A tall figure moved slowly across the cleared space toward him, then suddenly disappeared behind a whitethorn bush.

'Mother of God save me!' the lad cried out. 'I fell asleep on watch and now I'll be murdered by the heathen English.'

His panicked words were answered by a hoarse laugh that chilled him to his bones. It was merry and yet mocking. Turlough looked about him in fear. A thin man was standing a few yards away, obviously much amused at the young lad's predicament.

'Are you an English dragoon?' Turlough asked, trying to mask the terror in his voice.

'You can thank your lucky stars and all the saints that I am not,' the man replied, 'or by now I would have slit your throat and left you for the foxes and the ravens to quibble over.'

'Who are you? What are you doing here?'

'This is my land, Turlough O'Carolan,' the stranger told him. 'Surely I may walk my own ground at whatever hour suits me.'

'Squire Crilly?' the lad asked, squinting to see the man's face in the dark.

'It is,' the squire chuckled, taking a step closer. 'What's all this talk about English dragoons?'

'Were you not over at the big house tonight?'

'I was not.'

'Lord Mayo was there.'

'I heard a rumour that the lord would be about tonight but I had other business to attend to.' The squire looked over his shoulder at the circle of trees.

'I was there,' Turlough whispered, 'when word came that the English were on their way to arrest the lord and all his soldiers.'

'I would be very surprised if the English would be so bold as to try to take Lord Mayo in his own country, Turlough,' Crilly scoffed. 'There are not enough of their soldiers in this land for them to attempt such a daring raid. And surely these dragoons you speak of would have stirred up the whole countryside in their wake. The English rarely ride anywhere peaceably.'

'The lord's bodyguard alerted him to their presence,' Turlough protested.

'The lord's bodyguard are a nervous collection of men. They are paid to be suspicious. The English wouldn't have been able to travel far in this county without facing a fierce resistance. And English soldiers do not travel by night. They are fond of their warm barracks and even fonder of their warm wenches.'

The squire looked up toward the sky in the east. 'It is close to the dawn,' he laughed. Even if there had been a troop of English dragoons on the road, young Turlough would have likely missed them, despite the loud clatter of their armour.

'You're a fine watchman that sleeps through the better part of the night,' he teased.

'God help me if they passed by and I did not see them,' Turlough muttered as he got to his feet. 'Her ladyship will skin me alive if I overlooked them.'

'No Englishmen passed down that road this night, I can assure you,' Crilly smiled. 'I would have smelled their poorly groomed horses and their iron skins. But have you no fear of the Good People that you sleep out here upon their hill in the middle of a moonless night?'

'I was just doing as I was told,' Turlough grumbled.

'So you were,' the squire soothed, 'and I have no objection to you crossing into my lands as long as it was watching for Englishmen that was your only business.'

The man stepped closer and looked hard into the face of the young lad. Turlough was still wearing his best clothes and Crilly frowned quizzically. 'What was it you were saying about being a great harper?'

Turlough looked at the ground and kicked his feet in embarrassment.

'Bridget has an eye for Lord Mayo's musician,' he explained. 'A weedy fellow by the name of Murphy.'

'David Murphy is too big for those tiny boots of his and his size in hats has greatly increased since he took to travelling with his lordship,' Crilly huffed indignantly.

'Do you know him?'

'I have heard him play on occasion.' The squire dismissed the harper with a wave of his hand. 'I am a bit of a musician myself, you know. But Murphy's playing is too bland for me. I have a name for such a poor performer,' he smiled as he stepped even closer.

'What's that?' Turlough asked.

'I call him a tol-lol,' the squire replied, moving his head from side to side in time with the syllables. Then he yawned in an exaggerated manner to press home his point.

'I could not understand why everyone was so excited by his music,' Turlough admitted. 'I didn't think much of him either.'

'What would you know about music? You were blinded by your feelings for Bridget,' Crilly laughed. 'Has she lost her heart to young Murphy then?'

Turlough dropped his head and nodded.

'And you think you can win back her affection by becoming a great harper, do you?'

'At least she might look at me if I was a musician in a fine coat and hat.'

'What would you give to win her back?'

Turlough did not have to think about the answer. 'I would give anything, anything at all, to be a great musician and to have Bridget Cruise look on me as she looked on David Murphy this evening.'

'A harper's life is hard,' Crilly warned. 'I know, for I myself took to the road with harp and horse in days gone by. You might leave your home and not return for years at a time. You might walk the length and breadth of Ireland in twelve months and barely scratch a living in that whole time.'

'I would suffer any discomfort to learn the craft of music. I don't care if I never see the MacDermots or their fat cows and spindly goats again as long as I live.'

Crilly raised his eyebrows and put a hand on the young lad's shoulder. 'You do not know what you are saying,' he said sternly. 'It is the excitement of youth that is guiding your tongue and so I will try to imagine those words never passed your lips.'

'I truly would not be grieved if I never laid eyes on this parish again,' Turlough repeated. 'I want to be as far from this estate and Bridget's father as possible.'

Crilly squeezed the lad's upper arm hard. 'Do not say such a thing. Not here. Not on a hill where the Faerie folk might hear you. Not on a night without a moon to keep them in their homes.'

'Would you teach me?' Turlough asked.

'Would you learn it?' the squire replied, loosening his grip.

'If I had the chance I would spend every spare moment behind that instrument. I would study and practise until I became a master. I would earn the title of Chief Musician of Ireland.'

'And what of the farm work that needs to be done?' Crilly retorted. 'A harper needs good strong fingernails. A farmhand cannot afford such a luxury. And what of Mrs MacDermot's plans for you to join the glorious army of our good King James?'

'How did you know about that?'

'Word travels fast,' the squire answered enigmatically.

'Squire Cruise came to dinner last night and asked my opinion of his plan,' he explained when he saw the look of confusion on Turlough's face. 'Personally I would not like to see you in the army. The harp is a better path than the road of musket and pike. But Mrs MacDermot will have the final say. She has educated you and provided for you. And you owe her a debt of gratitude, so you must go where she sends you.'

'If I became a harper I would do her honour,' Turlough stated, 'just as Murphy does honour to the Lord Mayo. I would compose melodies for her.'

'I will have a word to Mrs MacDermot in the morning,' the

squire promised. 'They may not listen to me at all. But then again they may see the sense of a musical education. After all, they are only sending you away to keep you from Bridget Cruise. You will be as much removed from each other if you are living with me as you would be off risking your life in some senseless bloody battle.'

'I would be most grateful if you would mention it to her ladyship,' Turlough replied, shivering from the gathering frost and wondering if he was dreaming.

'You had best get home to the fire, my lad,' Crilly advised him. 'Not even the most foolish of all English dragoons rides out before the dawn at this time of year. Have no fear, if there is any sign of them I will light the torch. I will be about until long after the sun is up.'

'Thank you, squire,' the lad replied, really feeling the cold now. 'I would be glad of a warm bed and a drop of whiskey.'

'May you always have both,' Squire Crilly murmured, 'and a full belly as well. But remember, be careful what you say on the top of a Faerie hill in the hours before dawn. There may be some folk listening who take your whimsy for wishes and grant you a life that is not all you expected it to be.'

'Goodnight, sir,' the young man said.

'And a goodnight to you, Turlough O'Carolan,' the squire replied and when the lad had gone a few paces he added, 'It sounds fine, doesn't it?'

'What's that?' the boy asked with a frown.

'Turlough O'Carolan, Chief Musician of Ireland.'

The young man laughed then quickly made his way back down the cow path, his thoughts racing ahead of him. One day, he told himself, he would be known as a great musician. He would win back Bridget's heart. And folk would do him the honour they did men like Murphy. And he would play for King James and the royal court in London.

It suddenly occurred to him that it was strange to see Squire Crilly walking the hill in the middle of the night, but he quickly dismissed the idea that Crilly might be an English spy. The squire had always had a bit of a reputation for unusual behaviour.

Elated to think he might have a chance to do what Bridget had told him would never be possible, Turlough began to dance his way to the bottom of the hill, overjoyed that Crilly had promised to speak with Mrs MacDermot. As he reached the path to his father's house he began to sweat. By the time he arrived at the little cottage beside the forge he was dizzy and the world seemed to be moving weirdly before his gaze.

At first he thought he must have caught a chill in the night air. He staggered to the cupboard to look for whiskey and found a half-finished earthenware flagon. He poured himself a cup and drank it down quickly, savouring the warmth of the liquor.

'If that doesn't keep the chill off me,' he told himself under his breath, 'nothing will.'

Turlough lay down in his bed, feeling as if he had drunk too much, though he had only had the one cupful. His head ached. His legs and arms were numb with an aching pain.

'I was foolish to go up there without a blanket,' he muttered to his father when he awoke just after the dawn. 'I was out on the hill all night watching for the English. But they never came.'

John O'Carolan felt the burning on his son's forehead and looked deep into the lad's eyes. This was no chill, the blacksmith feared, but he did not voice his concern to the lad. John had witnessed these symptoms once before and his heart sank to see his son suffering them now. This, he was certain, was the same affliction that had claimed the life of his wife a mere two years ago.

'May God help you, my boy,' he whispered, 'for there is not a living man who can offer you any comfort now.'

Turlough looked up at his father and wondered what he was talking about. He had stayed out without a fire and caught a chill, it was as simple as that.

'May I have a whiskey, Father?'

'You may have one,' John O'Carolan replied. 'And then I am

going to fetch Father Donnelly to say an Ave for you. He survived this curse and so it will not touch him again.'

'I just need to rest a little,' Turlough protested, 'then I'll be up and about my chores.'

'You will stay where you are until a physician has seen to you,' his father ordered. 'Every person you touch, everyone you speak with is at risk. You have seen the last of your friends until this sickness passes. Even I must leave you for somehow this affliction passed over me the last time its curse came to our family. You must prepare yourself for a difficult time.'

'I have to go and split the wood for the breakfast fire.'

'If you go out that door,' John O'Carolan warned, 'you will have the deaths of innocent people on your hands. The pox spreads like rats breeding in a sewer.'

'What are you talking about?'

'I cannot be certain,' his father conceded, 'but until we know for sure whether the Galar-breac has come upon you, it is best that you stay in this bed. I am off to ask her ladyship to fetch the doctor.'

Without another word the blacksmith was gone. Turlough frowned at his father's words, sat up and suddenly felt much better. He went to fetch himself a whiskey from the bottle he kept in the drawer. Then he remembered he had put it in his leather sack to take with him up to the hill the night before.

He found the leather-covered bottle and removed the cork. Then he took a few generous swigs to warm his body. He put the bottle back in the cupboard where it was usually kept.

'I don't feel that bad,' he said aloud, testing his voice. 'I don't really think it could be the Galar-breac.'

But in that very instant the lad felt the floor move beneath him. His head swam as if he had been hit with a heavy club. He was forced to sit down on the edge of his bed and closed his eyes to ease the pain in his head.

When he awoke again, after what seemed no more than a few minutes, his clothes were drenched in sweat. A man with a large red nose and a tattered grey wig balanced precariously on his forehead was leaning over him. The stranger was prodding the flesh of the boy's armpits.

As he poked the man muttered to himself and shook his head in a most peculiar manner. Suddenly Turlough recognised the fellow. He had spoken with the doctor many times. Doctor Lindsay turned his attention to the lad's nose, holding his finger on the end of it while he counted to ten. When he removed his finger he leaned in close to examine the colour of the skin where the pressure had been.

'What are you doing?' Turlough asked.

'I am conducting an examination,' the doctor explained, not taking his eyes from the examined nose for a second. 'Well, your circulation seems good,' he proclaimed after a few moments. 'Bowels open?'

'Yes.'

'And how's your water?'

'Fine.'

'A good steady stream?'

'Yes.'

'And how long have you been feeling ill, Turlough?'

'Since very early this morning. I came down from the hill after standing watch for the English dragoons and—'

'Well,' the doctor interrupted, looking deeply into his patient's eyes, 'it is not the black plague that you have. So that's a good thing. Nor the galloping dropsy. And your teeth seem to be in fine shape, so it isn't that. But I fear the smallpox may certainly have come upon you.'

'I don't understand what you are talking about,' Turlough protested.

'What I mean,' said Lindsay slowly, 'is I think you may have the Galar-breac.'

'Mister Quigley the tailor came back from Dublin with the Galar-breac a month ago,' Turlough gasped. 'He died after a week in terrible agony.'

'Quigley was a man of loose morals,' the doctor spat. 'I have just been to the Widow Keenan's where both her daughters have been struck down with the disease. God save us but Quigley was a fickle man who sowed his crops widely.'

Turlough frowned, not quite understanding what the man meant.

'Squire Farrell's daughter came down with the pox also,' the doctor explained. 'Quigley was a regular visitor to both the Farrell and Keenan households. And he was known to have certain relations with a Spanish woman, down in Dublin, who got him his cloth. That's where the sickness always comes from. Strangers. Foreigners. Spaniards. Travellers. English sailors and the like.'

Turlough tried to sit up, his attention caught by this piece of gossip. 'I had heard a rumour that Mister Quigley was courting Jeannie Farrell.'

'Quigley would have courted every young woman from here to London if he could have got his hands on a boat, a set of oars and a decent set of teeth.' The doctor felt the lad's forehead. 'Have you been to either the Farrells' or the Keenans' in the last week?'

'Squire Farrell's horse threw a shoe on Tuesday,' Turlough began. 'Mister MacDermot loaned the squire a horse and when my father had fixed a new shoe I rode it over to their house.'

'Did you stop to speak with Jeannie Farrell?'

'I did not see her, doctor. I took the horse over and then walked straight back home.'

The doctor muttered to himself in a strange language. Turlough assumed it was Latin. Doctor Lindsay was always making proclamations in Latin which no-one could understand, not even Father Donnelly.

Lindsay looked carefully in each of the lad's ears and put a hand to his own chin in contemplation. 'Well, we should know for certain what is ailing you by this evening,' he decided. 'If it is the smallpox, there will be no mistaking it. You will stay in bed until I return after dark on my way back from the Keenans'. You are to eat nothing whatsoever until I have examined you again. Do you understand?'

'May I have a whiskey?'

'You may not!' the doctor exclaimed. 'I would not doubt it

if that vile substance was at the very root of this terrible illness. If it were not for the foul whiskey dens that line the road from here to Dublin the pox would not have spread as quickly as it has into the countryside.'

The man stood up straight and mopped his brow with a white lace handkerchief that had been tucked into his sleeve. 'A respected and learned physician at the court of King James reckons the vapours brought forth from the distilling of strong drink give off a deadly air which penetrates the lungs and brings on the fever. Once the fever has a hold of you, the pox begins to breed just as the barley ferments when the distiller is preparing the mash.'

The doctor patted at his brow nervously. 'And whiskey is the liquor in which the Galar-breac prefers to propagate. There'll be no strong drink for you until you are fit to walk again. And if you take my advice, you'll never touch a drop again as long as you live.'

'Were you a drinking man once?' Turlough asked, seeing the strange light in the doctor's eyes as he spoke of the evils of liquor. 'Before you were struck down with the Galar-breac?'

'I was not!' Lindsay replied in shock. 'I have never been a whiskey drinker, apart from a brief bout of foolishness when I was a student. I could never understand the allure of that foul liquid. Only the smallpox ever made me sicker than the cursed whiskey.'

'Perhaps you drank it too quickly,' Turlough offered, noticing the doctor's hands were shaking.

'I left it well enough alone!' the doctor exclaimed. 'That is why I survived the dreadful pox when most of my patients died horrible lingering deaths, crying for mercy and beseeching God to take them quickly.'

Lindsay's eyes darted about the room as if he were frightened some demon would jump out and snatch him if he let his guard down.

'There was nothing I could do for those unfortunate souls, poor miserable whiskey-soaked wretches that they were.'

The lad sat back and breathed deeply, less than reassured by the doctor's words. He thought of all the patients the man must have lost to the pox. Then he thought it was probably more to do with his lack of skill than the evils of whiskey. Turlough looked over at the cupboard where his father kept the small flagon of home-distilled liquor. As soon as this old fool was gone, he told himself, he would get himself a drink.

'Well,' the physician said finally, tucking his handkerchief back into his sleeve and regaining his composure, 'all we can do is pray. I'll send for Father Donnelly to administer the last rites this evening.'

'The last rites!' Turlough gasped in horror.

'It's nothing to worry about,' the doctor soothed. 'It's just a precaution. It won't hurt. You wouldn't like to die in your sleep unshriven, would you? And I sometimes find that the extreme unction has the power to cure folk who are otherwise merely looking for an excuse to lie around in bed.'

'I don't know if I want to bother the good father at this time of day,' Turlough replied nervously. 'Surely he has more important folk to attend to.'

'Nonsense, lad. You have nothing to fear. I had a generous dose of the extreme unction myself when I was laid low with the pox. Did me the world of good.' He tapped his chest with the palm of his hand and coughed. 'And look at me now,' he declared proudly, 'apart from mild rheumatism, a lingering cough and six rather loose bowel movements every day, I am as fit as a freshly hatched foal.'

'I think I would like to sleep for a while,' Turlough muttered.

'That is best,' Lindsay nodded and then added, 'if it does prove to be the pox, there must be no light whatsoever in this room while you fight it. The infirmity worsens in sunlight and candlelight and that is the chief cause of the disease spreading, besides the evil vapours of whiskey, of course.'

'Very well, doctor,' Turlough sighed. 'But what will happen to me if I have the disease? Will I perish?'

'Tonight may be very hard on you,' the physician told him,

gritting his teeth as he spoke. 'When I was suffering I had dreams of such a disturbing nature that I cannot in all modesty relate them to any living man. Not even a priest.'

He took his handkerchief out again and mopped his brow with a shaking hand.

'Especially not a priest.'

'What happened?' Turlough asked.

'At one stage,' the doctor admitted sombrely, 'I was convinced that a hundred young maidens came into my room, tore off all their clothing and did unspeakable things to me while I lay back helpless to stop them. I fought them off, you understand, as best I could. But they had their wicked way with me.'

The doctor stopped speaking suddenly, realising he had said too much. Then he coughed a little to cover his embarrassment and stuffed his handkerchief back in his sleeve.

'Of course it was nothing more than a dream brought on by the Galar-breac. My nurse told me that she had been forced to leave my side for the sake of decency halfway through the night. Poor woman. You too may find that you suffer from just such a disturbing experience. Do not believe all that you see. It is merely a delirium made worse by the fever.'

'Thank you, doctor,' Turlough answered weakly. He was feeling very dizzy again and his hands felt as if they were beginning to swell. He tried to turn on his side but found he could not move. In the next second his vision blurred and the shape of the doctor distorted weirdly before him.

'I can see you are feeling much better,' the old man declared cheerfully. 'There's colour in your cheeks now. Have no fear. I am well respected as a physician. I am especially renowned for my skill at guiding folk to their last rest and repose. If it comes to that, you are in the best hands.'

Turlough did not hear this last dubious reassurance. He was already drifting into unconsciousness. When the lad awoke it was just light. He opened his eyes and immediately thought it must be close to dawn. His night on the hill, his fever and the visit from Doctor Lindsay were completely forgotten. It was not until he tried to rise that he began to recall some of what had happened and to fear the worst.

Finally, in a burst of stored energy, he threw back the blanket which covered him and realised he was soaked in sweat. The skin on his arms seemed to be covered in blotches, though he couldn't make out their colour in the poor light. The boy's head ached terribly. Confused, he lay back and stared blankly at the patterns of the thatch in the roof above him.

When Turlough had gathered enough strength to move again, he noticed the room had grown very dark indeed. This frightened him a little so he forced his legs out of bed and sat on the edge of the cot, breathing heavily from the exertion. He was about to stand when a light appeared at the doorway and the door swung open. A man dressed in a black coat entered the cottage carrying a lantern. It was Doctor Lindsay.

'I told you to stay in bed!' the doctor exclaimed, rushing to the bedside to push the lad back down.

'I am sick,' Turlough murmured, not remembering anything of their previous conversation.

'So you are, my lad,' Lindsay soothed, placing the lantern down on the table. He took off his wig, revealing a perfectly bald head. Then he came over to help his patient back into bed.

'Have you been convulsing?' he asked gently, forcing Turlough to lie down.

'What's that?'

'Have you been shaking uncontrollably?'

'No,' the lad replied.

'Well, then there's a chance the Galar-breac will not treat you too badly,' Lindsay lied. He had seen the symptoms many times. In his mind there was no doubt. The only son of John O'Carolan was certainly suffering from the smallpox. The next twenty-four hours would either see the boy succumb to the illness or triumph over it. It was impossible to tell whether he would survive.

'Is that whiskey I smell about you?' the lad asked.

'It most certainly is not!' Lindsay shrieked, quickly putting his hands to his mouth to smell his own breath. 'You must be delirious.'

Then the physician stared intently at his patient's eyes. 'I am going to bleed you a little, Turlough,' he told him as he went to the table and took out a long thin knife and a large earthenware bowl from his saddlebag.

'Once I've rid you of some of the poison, you'll be able to sleep.'

By the time Lindsay returned to the bed the lad was already slipping back into unconsciousness.

'Can you hear me, Turlough?'

The lad shook his head but muttered,'Yes.'

'This will hurt, but it will do you more good than anything I can think of.'

The doctor leaned over the young man and grabbed his arm firmly. Then he placed the earthenware bowl on the floor and quickly ran the fine sharp edge of the blade across Turlough's wrist. Dark blood immediately began to pour out of the wound. The thick red liquid continued to fall into the bowl until the doctor judged he had taken enough.

'The sickness is carried in your blood,' Lindsay explained in his gentlest voice as he wiped the excess away and pressed his hand tightly to the wound. 'So the more blood I can safely expel from your body, the greater the chance that you will live.'

Turlough looked up at the physician blankly and nodded. The doctor began to wrap the wound with a calico strip and when that was done he lifted the bowl of blood to his nose. He took a deep whiff of the contents, winced and decided without a doubt that his diagnosis was correct.

'There is a holy sister coming to nurse you tomorrow,' Lindsay soothed. 'Like myself and Father Donnelly she has suffered the smallpox and survived without any infirmity to her body, which is a blessing. Her recovery has rendered her immune to the disease. So she spends her days caring for those who fall ill with this curse.'

The doctor took the boy's chin and looked into his eyes again.

'The good sister will wash you every few hours. You must not resist her. If you are not kept perfectly clean, the sores that are to come will sour and you will surely die. Remember that your nurse is a holy sister so she means you no harm.'

Turlough's senses were swimming and he was sure he could hear voices other than the doctor's in the room. The headache had passed but it was a difficult thing for him to concentrate on what Lindsay was saying.

'No-one else may visit you until you are well again. Do you hear me, Turlough?'

The lad nodded slowly.

'Your father is sleeping in the big house for the time being. I will tell him how you are. Your mother died of the Galar-breac, is that not so?'

The boy nodded again and then his eyes rolled back and closed. He felt as if his body was spinning in the dark and he gripped the bed to steady himself.

'It was not this way with her,' he managed to say feebly.

'The malady strikes everyone in a different manner,' Lindsay told him. 'Some pass along peacefully and others ...' The doctor coughed. 'I will leave you now. Have a good rest tonight. I will return tomorrow if I do not have too many other cases to attend to.'

With that Lindsay stood up and went to the door where he handed the bowl of blood to William O'Flynn who was waiting outside.

'Pour that into the river,' he ordered. 'And if the lad dies during the night, do not let his father or any of the servants near him. Send me word so I will not waste a journey here in the morning. Only folk who have survived the smallpox may attend to the corpse, unless you want the bloody pestilence to take hold in Ballyfarnon.'

The young butler nodded, wide-eyed and nervous. The doctor returned to the table, placed his knife back in its leather sheath, closed his saddlebag and, after picking up his lantern, silently left the room.

Turlough stirred a little as the door shut. All was dark but he thought he heard someone crossing the floor of the cottage. He opened his eyes wide to look about him but there was no-one in the room and there was no light. He was shivering by now, wondering why no-one else had come to visit him.

Despite the doctor's expertly executed bleeding, Turlough could not sleep for a long while. There was a dull pain in his back which made it impossible for him to lie in one position for very long. This pain gradually became worse and worse until he was groaning in agony and unable to lie still at all.

Finally, after what seemed many hours, Turlough rolled over onto his stomach and spread his arms across the cot. Exhaustion was taking its toll, and despite the stabbing pain in his back he was beginning to drift into a half sleep. Suddenly his back began to feel as though it was on fire. His throat was parched since no water had passed his lips all day and the sweating had continued unabated. And he did not have the strength to sit up, much less to make his way down to the well to draw some water.

Perhaps, he told himself groggily, this was why many folk died of the Galar-breac. No-one dared come near them during the sickness and so, neglected, they died of thirst or hunger.

In his daze Turlough thought he heard Bridget laughing at him, telling him that if he died there would be nothing to stop her running off with David Murphy. And even if he lived she would never love him, for he could not play the harp like Lord Mayo's fine handsome musician.

'I will learn,' Turlough muttered to himself. 'I will be the greatest harper in all Ireland . . .'

No sooner had he made this promise than a light appeared at the door. With immense difficulty the lad lifted his head to see who it might be. Whoever it was did not linger. They merely stood by the door for a while and then departed, taking the light with them. A short while later the light returned and once more the door opened slightly.

Turlough did not have the energy to speak so he groaned to

show he sensed someone's presence. A young woman spoke softly.

'Turlough. Are you awake?'

He recognised the voice immediately. It was his beloved Bridget. She had come to him after all. When no-one else would visit, she had come. His spirits lifted suddenly. Perhaps, he told himself, she loved him after all. Perhaps she had not meant her harsh words. He rallied himself, struggling to get up.

'Turlough,' she said again before he had time to gather the strength to move very far, 'I have come to say goodbye. We are staying here tonight before our journey. Father is taking me to Dublin in the morning. I am to go to school at the convent. He has told me I am not to speak with you but I had to say farewell. We may never meet again.'

Her voice was cracking with emotion. Turlough battled to lift his head from the cot and open his eyes. The girl stood at the door in her nightdress, her golden tresses flowing like a water-fall over her shoulders.

'I am so sorry that I fought with you,' she sobbed. 'I can't help thinking this is all my fault. God is punishing us for break-ing His laws. I am so sorry I brought this on you.'

The lad tried to speak. He forced his mouth to open. But his dry throat would emit no sound and his tongue, swollen and rough, would not move.

'Please forgive me, Turlough,' she begged. 'I knew that we would be caught one day but I did not think that Father would send you out on the hill in the cold night air. If I had even suspected you would fall ill I would have gone on watch in your place.'

Turlough wanted to tell her that the sickness had nothing to do with staying out in the cold night air, that God was not punishing him. But his tongue refused to move.

Then the lad heard another voice and recognised it as that of the MacDermots' new assistant butler.

'Come along, Miss Bridget!' O'Flynn insisted. 'It is dangerous for you to stay here too long. The doctor said anyone who comes here risks falling ill with the pox. And if your father catches us we will both surely regret it. I don't know which would be worse, to catch the pox or to face his wrath, but I would rather not have to choose between the two.'

'I'm coming, William,' Bridget told him sharply. 'I just wanted to have one last look at Turlough and to tell him how much I love him.'

Then she turned back to face the sick lad whose eyes were wide open with surprise and joy.

'Goodnight,' she wished him. 'I will never forget you. I hope we will meet again one day.'

Turlough groaned and dropped his head back down upon the cot, his weakness finally getting the better of him. He longed to tell Bridget that he would never forget her and that he would come looking for her when he was fully recovered. But she was already gone and he was alone in the dark once more.

The lad managed to roll painfully over onto his stomach again. Now he was determined that he would marry Bridget as soon as he was able to walk again. Her father would protest the match but Turlough knew no force on earth could separate two lovers who held each other so dear.

Exhausted, he closed his eyes and resolved that his first task would be to regain his health. In a few days, he told himself, he would be fit again and able to ride. He would follow Bridget down to Dublin and take her away with him. He had almost forgotten his dream of learning the harp.

As he was drifting off he noticed an itching on his left arm like the burning rash left from a stinging nettle. But he did not have the energy to scratch it. As the night wore on, his skin began to sting. However, by then the young man was sleeping fitfully and he only noticed the discomfort once in a while.

After what seemed many hours, another light came to the door and stirred Turlough from slumber. It was still dark, though he had no idea what time of night it was. Then the boy heard the sound of many horses and wondered if the English dragoons had arrived after all.

Once more he tried to get up, but his legs were numb and would not do his bidding. After a long time he found he was so desperate for a drink that his thirst gave him the impetus to rise. When he finally sat himself up he felt very uneasy. The room was deathly quiet. Outside the sound of horsemen had ceased and he wondered if he had imagined it.

He sat on his bed for a few minutes before he managed to stand. Then he slowly staggered to the cupboard where the whiskey was kept. It took Turlough only a few seconds to find the liquor bottle even in the darkness and he was soon swallowing a long draught. The liquor did not quench his thirst though. If anything it made his throat burn even more.

'What are you doing out of bed?' a familiar voice asked him. Turlough turned around to face the door. He had not heard anyone come in. There, standing with a candle in his hand, was Squire Crilly.

'Are you still feeling poorly?'

The young man nodded. 'What are you doing here?' he struggled to say.

'I have come to tend you,' the squire told him. 'You have nothing to fear.'

Turlough put the cork back in the whiskey bottle and placed it on the table.

'You would do better to drink this,' the squire offered and held out a large green glass bottle. Turlough took a few unsteady steps toward him then Crilly strode over and put the bottle to the young man's lips.

Cool clear water filled Turlough's mouth and he suddenly felt quite refreshed.

'Now get back into bed,' the squire ordered, 'or you will not live to be a great harper as you so wish.'

The young man nodded and sat down on the edge of his cot, breathing hard from the exertion of being on his feet.

'Is it still your desire to be the greatest harper in all of Ireland?' Crilly inquired, holding out a hand to touch the lad's forehead.

Turlough nodded again, even though he suspected Bridget would have him anyway. If he could play the harp he would at least be able to feed himself and his wife, that much was clear to him even in this dazed state.

'It is a hard road,' the squire advised, repeating his earlier warning. 'But I sense that your mind is made up. Rest a while longer and I will come to fetch you before the dawn.'

Turlough frowned. What was it Doctor Lindsay had said about not leaving the house or speaking with anyone?

'Do not fear,' Crilly told him as if he had heard his thoughts. 'I will not be touched by the scourge, nor will anyone else be endangered.'

Reassured that Squire Crilly must have once suffered the Galar-breac himself and survived, he lay back and immediately fell into a peaceful sleep. All his pain was suddenly gone, as if it had lifted like a great fog. His throat was cool now and he breathed easy.

When he awoke again it was still dark and the squire was sitting at the table. A candle stuck into the neck of a bottle was burning brightly, giving off a golden glow.

'Are you feeling better, Turlough?' the squire asked without looking up from the book he was reading.

'I am,' the lad answered. His tongue was not swollen any more and he felt much stronger.

'Then we will go for a walk to clear your head,' Crilly told him, closing the little book and placing it in his pocket.

Turlough arose without any effort but his head was still pounding and he felt a little dizzy. By the time he had put on his boots, Crilly was standing at the door waiting.

'The doctor told me I was to stay in bed and not go outside,' Turlough protested.

'What would that old fool Lindsay know?' Crilly scoffed. 'In any case, no-one will know of this little walk but you and I. And I won't be telling anyone, so take care that you don't.'

'I won't tell a soul,' the boy vowed.

'Then come along, lad, we have much to do before the sun

rises. That is if you still have it in your heart to become a great musician.'

Crilly offered the green glass bottle again and Turlough took a deep draught of the liquid. It was sweet like pure mountain water after the snow has melted, too sweet to be merely well-water. Turlough felt immediately refreshed and full of energy as if the veil of sickness had been lifted from him.

'Are there some herbs infused into that concoction?' the sick lad asked.

'Indeed there are,' Crilly replied. 'That water cost me dearly. I had it from a wise woman who lives on the west coast. So mind that you make the most of it. The effects will begin to wear off in a few hours and then there will be no stopping the sickness coming upon you in its full fury.'

'Thank you, squire,' Turlough sighed, full of wonder at how well he felt. 'Perhaps all I needed was a drink of your healing potion. It is as if I was never ill at all.'

'We cannot stand here exchanging pleasantries,' Crilly smiled. 'We do not have much time and there is much to do. Come along.'

Turlough nodded, though he had no idea what the squire had in mind. Crilly opened the door a fraction and peered out through the gap to make sure no-one was about. Only when he was certain they would not be seen did Crilly snuff out the candle and usher young Turlough out into the darkness.

They silently crossed the courtyard and made their way to the path which climbed the hill where Turlough had spent the previous evening.

'You will witness some strange things tonight, my lad,' Crilly told him under his breath as they walked swiftly up the path. 'But no matter what you see, you must not be alarmed. Do not ask any questions. Do not run away.'

The squire stopped to catch his breath and put a hand on Turlough's shoulder. 'Remember, if you do as I say, you will be safe and you may even be granted your dearest wish. With the help of some very influential friends of mine I am going to give you a chance that is not offered to many. Do you understand?'

'I think I do,' the young man replied, completely baffled. A thousand questions filled his head but he dared not ask any of them lest he offend the squire.

After a short rest they set off again and in minutes they were close to the summit. Turlough looked up in alarm when he noticed a large fire blazing amid the trees.

'Who is up on the hill burning so much timber at this time of night?' he asked, shocked at the waste of precious firewood.

'Now there you go,' Crilly gently rebuked him. 'Didn't I warn you not to question anything you see? All will be revealed in a little while. Be patient, and for pity's sake govern your tongue. The folk you are about to meet are kind-hearted but they are quick to anger if their customs are breached. That is the signal fire that brings their folk in for the game.'

'The game?'

'Be patient.'

As the two of them came to the circle of oaks and whitethorns Turlough began to feel inexplicably frightened.

There was no-one standing around the blaze, which was strange because a fire that large ought to be tended. And despite the great flames there was a cold bite in the air which was more chilling than any icy breeze. An unusual scent reached Turlough's nostrils. The fragrance was sweet but disturbingly unfamiliar and it gave the lad a deep sense of unease.

They reached the edge of the trees and Crilly put a hand on Turlough's chest to stop him going any further.

'We will not go inside the sacred circle tonight,' the squire told the boy in a hoarse whisper. 'You must never enter the sacred grove when the fire is burning unless you are invited.'

The wind rose and it seemed to Turlough that the breeze was full of a thousand disembodied whispers. Some beckoned to him to enter the circle, tempting him in seductive tones. Others hissed harshly, warning him to keep away.

'What are those voices?' Turlough muttered. 'Who are these folk you are taking me to meet?'

'You will know soon enough. There is nothing to fear. You are safe as long as you follow my instructions. Are you ready to go on?'

Turlough nodded without a moment's hesitation. He was relieved not to be entering the circle of trees. It was an unearthly place. There was something dwelling there which he had never encountered before in his life. It was obvious to him now that the Faerie folk were gathering here tonight. This strange fire was their beacon. A call to all their kind to come in from the countryside.

'Come along, my boy,' the squire said lowly, taking Turlough's arm urgently. 'We must hurry if we are to make it to our meeting in time.'

'Are you one of them?' Turlough asked, plucking up the courage to speak.

The squire turned to look the lad in the eyes. 'I am not,' he replied. 'I am a mortal like yourself. But my family has always lived in this place and our bloodline has a tradition of service and friendship with their kind. I have been visiting the field since I was a little child. My mother took me to visit the king and queen when I was no more than six years old. I am not afraid of them and neither should you be.'

'What are they?'

'I cannot answer you that,' the squire replied. 'I do not know for certain. I myself have never dared to ask and no-one ever explained the matter fully to me. All I can tell you is that they are folk similar to us in many respects except that they dwell in another place, a land of mists which swallows them up completely. A few of them live among us and pass for mortals. The rest rarely enter our world.'

Crilly looked about him nervously before he went on. 'And I know they are as ageless as the hills. I have been acquainted with some of them all my life and in that time they have not aged any more than you or I might age in one week. Time does not touch them.'

The squire put a hand on Turlough's shoulder. 'I am in a

position to ask a favour of their king, and I have made a request on your behalf. If all goes well, my request may be granted. But these folk are quick to anger. Do not offer any offence. Act with humility and honesty and you will have nothing to fear. Now we really must go!'

Crilly took Turlough's arm and led the way around the edge of the trees. They soon came to the path which led down the other side of the hill toward his family's ancient house. About halfway down the slope there was a great level field which had never in living memory been tilled for any crop. It was known to all in the district as the Hurling Field.

Turlough recalled a legend he had heard as a small child which told that this was the spot where the Faeries came to play their great games in ancient times. The field was also rumoured to be where they held their councils and fought their battles. The lad had heard these stories many times and now, for the first time, there was an air of truth about them.

Turlough had never played much at the hurling. He did not get any enjoyment from running madly up and down a field armed with a crooked stick. To him there was no point in spending an afternoon trying to knock a small wooden ball over a line in the grass. That was why he had never had any skill for the sport. He had no inclination, as his mother used to say.

Nevertheless the other lads on the estate had often pushed him to join their teams in matches against the boys of neighbouring villages. Turlough did not even like to watch the hurling. He had seen too many of his friends fall with broken bones and bruised shins. He considered the game futile and brutish.

Turlough began to wonder what was going on. He hoped they weren't going to have to sit through a game. He didn't care that the players might be the Faerie folk. In his opinion there was only one thing more intensely boring than playing at hurling. And that was having to watch it.

As Turlough looked down on the field he could just make out the dark forms of many folk milling about in large groups. They seemed to be waiting for something.

'We'll be there in a minute,' Crilly whispered.

'What's going on?' the young man whispered. 'Is there to be a match? Who are all those people?'

'I am tired of all these questions,' the squire snapped. 'Didn't I warn you to control your curiosity? Now do as I tell you and guard your tongue!'

As they reached the edge of the field all the folk who were gathered there approached in a seething mumbling crowd. Before long it seemed as if everyone was standing around them in a circle, whispering to their neighbours, pointing at the lad and shaking their heads. Turlough could only stare back in awe at this great group of strange folk.

'Don't say a bloody word,' Crilly reminded the boy.

He need not have worried. Turlough was dumbstruck.

To his surprise the lad found that he was not frightened of these strange beings at all. He had a sense he should be careful not to offend them, but there was no hint of threat from any of them. Some were dressed as if they were going to their own funeral—in shrouds or barefoot Sunday best. A few of the males wore outlandish short pantaloons that puffed out around their backsides and long stockings that reached up to the tops of their thighs. Many of the men and women wore iron breastplates like those the English dragoons sported. One or two had rusty helms upon their heads.

And all of them were exceptionally ugly. Turlough searched through the crowd for any sign of beauty. But all he could see were large noses, red like overripe apples or short and squat with huge nostrils. Some folk were incredibly hairy. Others had not a single hair adorning them at all.

The squire bowed to several of the folk and addressed them by name. Without exception he received courteous replies. One large fellow patted Crilly on the head affectionately and inquired about his cat.

By this time Turlough had completely forgotten his illness. And Crilly's order to remain silent was beginning to seem absurd. The lad was burning with curiosity. He was about to open his mouth to ask a question when the gathering suddenly became agitated. In a few seconds Turlough noticed the crowd parting. Most of the strange folk were removing their hats and headgear and falling to their knees.

Then the boy glimpsed two tall figures dressed in dark clothes making their way through the throng. As the stately looking couple passed by, some folk reached out to kiss their garments. But the strange pair did not slow their pace or look to either side as they progressed regally through the crowd.

At last they approached the spot where Turlough and Crilly were waiting to be received and the lad got a good look at the two strangers.

The woman had black hair which shimmered with traces of silver in the moonlight. She was dressed in a gorgeous burgundy velvet dress which hugged her body tightly, accentuating her curves, and then swept out behind her in a long train. Two short attendants followed behind her to make sure the train did not drag in the dirt.

This beautiful lady flashed her dark eyes at Turlough through a veil of delicate black lace as ephemeral as dew on a spider's web. As she did so she squeezed the arm of the pale-skinned gentleman at her side. The lady was shorter than her companion but Turlough sensed she was a woman not to be trifled with. All the folk in the crowd stared at her with such admiration that it could have been mistaken for worship.

The gentleman wore a long black coat much the same as the one Lord Mayo wore, except that this was made of velvet and embroidered in black. The man's headwear was a small simple three-cornered hat unadorned except for a single red ruby set into a fold of black silk above his left eye.

He had a bunch of black lace around his neck for a scarf and black lace at his cuffs, and his shoe buckles were of shimmering silver. As the pair came closer the man handed his silver-topped cane to one of his attendants and caught his partner's eye with a mischievous wink.

A beautiful melody suddenly struck up from somewhere out

of Turlough's sight and the lad thought it the most haunting piece he had ever heard. The tune complemented the lady perfectly.

Turlough did not recognise the instrument at first but in the end he decided it must be some type of flute. Then he had the inexplicable notion this melody was not only dedicated to the lady but that somehow the music and the lady were inseparable.

'Don't look directly at her,' Crilly whispered urgently and the lad forced himself to stare at her companion.

'Why not?'

'Don't ask questions,' Crilly hissed. 'And bow your head low.'

Turlough glanced up at the strange gentleman as he bowed his head. The stranger's skin was incredibly pale and smooth. His eyes were unbelievably dark. His hair was as white as freshly fallen snow and yet there was not a wrinkle on his face. The man seemed to be no more than thirty years of age. Turlough had never seen anyone like him in his life.

'Is this the boy?' the gentleman asked in a deep clear soothing voice which was filled with a bright mirth and a soulful weariness all at once.

'This is young Turlough,' Crilly replied respectfully, prodding the lad to lift his head.

The stranger left his lady's side and walked around behind the boy, looking him up and down. The gentleman stopped, poked at Turlough's shoulders with his index finger and then sighed.

'He is well enough built,' the stranger conceded. 'He might well suit our purpose.'

'He is a hard worker,' the squire enthused. 'Intelligent. Well educated. A credit to his patron. And he has the passion.'

The gentleman raised an eyebrow but it was the lady who spoke.

'He has the passion? Are you certain?'

'He was set upon this path over the love of a young woman,' Crilly answered.

The lady hummed with admiration. Then she stepped forward and grasped Turlough's chin so that he had no option but to look deep into her eyes.

They were the blackest black he had ever seen. Blacker than coal. Blacker than midnight in a deep dark cavern. But in the blackest part of them the boy thought he glimpsed the tiny flicker of a flame. When he blinked, the light disappeared, leaving him wondering whether or not he had imagined it.

'He is very handsome,' she said, not taking her eyes from Turlough's for a second. Her voice was deep and gravelly and the lad found himself breathing hard. He coughed nervously and the woman smiled, but she did not let him go.

'Yes,' the white-haired man snapped impatiently, 'all of that means very little to me. Can he dance?'

Crilly looked blankly back at the gentleman for a moment. 'I am not sure,' the squire stuttered, casting a nervous glance at the young lad. 'Can you dance, Turlough?'

'I can,' the lad replied confidently. 'I can dance a storm up.'

'There won't be any need for that,' the gentleman retorted. 'If I feel like a storm, I'll have one of my own people arrange it.'

The lady raised an eyebrow. 'I am sure you are a very able dancer,' she cut in and a sweet smile played across her lips. Turlough thought her lips were exactly the same shade of red as the ruby in the gentleman's hat.

'I believe he is almost perfect,' the lady declared.

She released Turlough's chin and he bowed his head slightly to her as she withdrew to take the gentleman's arm again. At that moment the lad realised this lady had the same teasing tone in her voice as Bridget.

'Can you hold a hurling stick?' the gentleman pressed impatiently, frowning deeply as he tried to assess the lad's worth.

'I can.'

'Are you skilled at the game?'

It crossed Turlough's mind that he should tell the truth here no matter what, that any false statement would incur unspeakable wrath. But the lady was still smiling at him with obvious admiration and his pride was beginning to get the better of him.

The lad glanced at Squire Crilly, who raised his eyebrows and nodded his head, silently encouraging the lad to speak.

'I am a fine player,' the young man lied.

'Very well then, Crilly,' the white-haired gentleman replied in his cultured voice, not taking his eyes off Turlough for a second, 'you have your bargain. If my people win the match and my wager is secure, I will arrange the terms just as we discussed.'

The gentleman held out a hand to retrieve his long walking stick.

'And if your party should lose?' Crilly asked in a strained voice.

'Squire Crilly,' the white-haired gentleman smiled, tapping his walking stick lightly onto Turlough's shoulder, 'I hardly need tell you what will transpire if you have led me astray. And as for your friend here ...' The man lifted his stick and waved it dismissively. 'He would not have lived anyway in all likelihood.'

Crilly nodded and then turned to face Turlough. The gentleman led his lady through the crowd, raising his walking stick in the air as he went. The lady glanced back at Turlough and smiled as her companion commanded, 'Let the game begin.'

A great chorus of hoots and jubilant cries filled the air as everyone in the crowd began to cheer.

'There is to be a hurling match here tonight before the coming of the dawn,' Crilly explained, dragging the boy aside. 'His Majesty's team was short one man and you have been chosen to make up the numbers. Do you understand?'

'I do,' the young man answered. 'His Majesty? Is he the king? And who was that lady?'

'Do not ask me any questions,' Crilly cut in tersely before Turlough had a chance to open his mouth again. 'Play your best and if His Majesty's team is victorious, your wishes will certainly be granted.'

Turlough frowned. He did not understand at all.

'Just get yourself ready for the hardest game of hurling you have ever played in your life. Thank God you are a good player or the odds would certainly be against you.'

'Actually,' the young man admitted, 'the truth is, I'm not a very good player. I hate the game. I haven't played in years.'

Squire Crilly's mouth dropped open in shock. 'You lied?' he muttered in horror, taking the boy by the shoulders. 'You lied to Their Majesties? You spoke a falsehood to the King and Queen of the Faeries?'

'Is she the Queen of the Faeries?' Turlough gasped.

'Of course she is, you stupid boy,' the squire hissed. 'Who in Heaven's holy name did you think she was?'

'And that gentleman was the King of the Faeries?'

'Indeed,' the squire informed him. 'Did you lie to him?'

'I did.' The lad lowered his gaze in remorse.

'Then may he have mercy on your immortal soul,' Crilly whispered, 'for you are about to receive the soundest whipping of all your life.' Then the squire thought for a second. 'And my own fate won't be all that pleasant either. At least I was not aware of the falsehood, so there is a chance I may be treated mercifully.'

The squire handed the young man a stick which resembled a narrow old-fashioned shovel except that it was curved at the blade.

'Take this,' Crilly told him. 'And do your best, for it is too late to extricate ourselves from this mess now. We have to hope that you can stay away from the action for the most part and not get your foolish head knocked off.'

'Are we ready?' the king bellowed impatiently.

'Ready,' Crilly replied with false bravado as someone handed him an iron helm. The squire placed it on the lad's head and it immediately slipped down and covered Turlough's eyes.

'There's nothing to worry about,' Crilly assured him. 'If you can survive the first ten minutes, you will probably escape with only minor injuries.'

'What?' Turlough protested, unsure that he had heard correctly. He pushed the helm to the back of his head so he could see properly. 'You didn't mention anything about injuries.'

'You didn't mention that you hadn't played at hurling for years,' Crilly countered. 'Do your best.' And he pushed the young lad out onto the field.

Just then another tune began to play. It was a lively piece and full of joy. Turlough's feet began to tap instinctively as the melody built up a pace and he would have happily launched into a dance if the circumstances had been different. As it was, his heart was beginning to race with apprehension.

The white-haired king raised his walking stick high in the air. 'Let the match between the ancient folk of the Big Hill and the venerable people of the Small Hill commence.'

There was another raucous cheer as Crilly pushed Turlough further out onto the playing ground until he was surrounded by hundreds of folk. Then the squire retreated to the safety of the sideline.

The players faced each other in two enormous, haphazardly arranged teams. There was a clear space of about forty paces between the opposing sides but this was the only spare room anywhere on the field. Most of the players carried hurling sticks, some also wore strange armour, and several of them were amongst the ugliest folk Turlough could ever remember having laid eyes on in his life.

The lad saw that a good number of his team-mates also carried long shields shaped like teardrops. And a few were brandishing swords. When he noticed this, he realised there were also knives, clubs and maces hanging from players' belts. Turlough looked around, desperately seeking out Crilly. But his vision was blocked by the mass of Faerie players.

'I think I may be in trouble,' he mumbled to himself. 'If these folk are truly the Good People, I might have been safer marching in the army of King James than playing in one of their hurling matches.'

On the other side of the flat grassy pitch he could just make out the opposing team. They were all dressed in very much the same way as the folk on his own side. Their clothes were many different colours, some wore helms or breastplates, a few carried great axes. But there was really nothing in anyone's dress or manner to distinguish one team from the other. Turlough had no idea how he would tell his team-mates from the opposition once the game had started.

'A hundred men on each side and murder in all their eyes,' the boy muttered under his breath. 'Holy Mary, I am in the middle of a bloody battlefield.'

Suddenly all the players around him erupted into a chorus of deep-throated cries. They brandished their sticks, swords, axes and shields and stomped on the ground in a menacing rhythm. Turlough felt his guts begin to turn to water as the shouts rose in intensity. He had never witnessed a battle before. Now he desperately wished he had not told the King of the Faeries that he was an experienced player.

The lad was still cursing his foolish tongue when the chanting abruptly stopped and the field fell silent. It was not a calming silence. It was a tense quiet punctuated by the heavy breathing of the folk who pressed close to him. Their sweaty bodies made the boy gag and he was beginning to feel dizzy again.

When the earth beneath his feet began to rumble, Turlough thought his heart would burst with terror.

He looked about him for a way to escape and glimpsed an awful sight: the opposite team were raising their various sticks, shields and weapons in the air and commencing their own unnerving war cry. Turlough felt his blood turn to ice. Sweat began to roll down his forehead.

'I am going to die,' the boy told himself with certainty as he searched frantically about him for a break in the crowd through which to run.

Then for some unexplained reason he recalled Doctor Lindsay's warning that the Galar-breac often had an unwelcome effect on the mind. Perhaps all this was no more than a bizarre delusion brought on by the fever.

'This is a dream,' Turlough reassured himself and this calmed him immensely. 'I am very ill. None of this is real. This whole illusion has been brought on by the smallpox. This is a fantasy created by my troubled mind. I have nothing to fear.'

For a moment he started to relax. Then, close beside him, one of his team-mates, an ugly fat creature with a huge bottom lip, began to laugh. The stranger rolled his eyes in merriment and great gobs of spittle rolled onto his chin as he guffawed and gasped. His breath reeked of wild onions.

When the fat man had regained control of himself, he leaned in close to Turlough. 'You'll bloody well wish this was all a dream,' he cried, tears of laughter running down his cheeks. 'Before this night is out you'll see more blood spilled on this field than you could expect to witness in Oliver Cromwell's poultry pen on Christmas Eve. If I were you, I'd be quaking in my breeches and checking my armour for gaps.'

Turlough recoiled from the stench of the stranger's breath, then realised this foul odour could not possibly be the product of a dream. The stink was unimaginably disgusting. Suddenly the boy's heart was racing again.

'We've been waiting all night for you to turn up so we could put our army on the field,' the fat man explained. 'There's not much time left before the sun rises. And the side with the most goals when the first rays spill over the horizon will be named the victors. So play hard, strike low and pray that you still have a head on your shoulders at breakfast time.'

The sky was already beginning to pale as the sun made its journey back to the world. Turlough realised that this would have been a dangerous match at the best of times. But with no more than ten or fifteen minutes until sunrise, it was going to prove particularly brutal as each team fought to score the first goal.

Abruptly all the players around him erupted in a chorus of cries again and the young man noticed Squire Crilly standing in the space between the two opposing teams. In his hands he nursed a heavy red wooden object about half the size of a cannon shot.

The squire held up the ball and everyone on the field stopped their chants and fixed their eyes upon it.

'That is the holy red hurling block,' Turlough's fat team-mate informed him with a deep-throated giggle that sounded like the growl of a wolfhound.

With infinite care Squire Crilly placed the sacred ball on top of a tiny mound of earth in the centre of the field. Then he faced each team in turn before he raised his hand high.

'Let the battle begin!' he shouted and the words were no sooner out of his mouth than he was running as fast as his legs could carry him toward the sidelines. As he approached the king and queen they nodded politely to acknowledge him.

'That was well placed, Crilly,' the king complimented him.

'You have an uncommon grace,' the queen added.

'Thank you, Your Majesties,' the squire puffed as he took his place beside them.

'There's no need to be so formal with us,' the king rebuked him gently. 'We wouldn't want you to forget yourself in other circumstances and embarrass us, would we?'

'Of course not,' Crilly replied. 'Thank you,' he said and then his attention turned to the game.

In the next instant the air around Turlough erupted with wild, violent shouts. No sooner had the cacophony begun than his whole team moved forward as one, charging as fast as they could toward the ball on its little mound. The young man was too frightened to move with them and let his team push past, hoping to be left behind.

'I thought you said he was a good player,' the King of the Faeries snapped coldly at Crilly without taking his gaze from the match.

'I never said that!' Crilly gasped, then realised how suspicious that sounded. 'My lord, he is among the best players in all Ireland.' Crilly's voice wavered slightly and he coughed to hide his lack of conviction.

'He is simply biding his time,' the squire assured his patron. 'He is a tactician.'

'A tactician,' the king repeated with some skepticism. 'This is a hurling match. What use are tactics in the game?'

'That is the secret to his success,' Crilly countered and the king took his eyes from the game for a moment to regard the squire carefully.

'I have a feeling he will do very well,' the queen declared confidently. Then she smiled at Crilly and he gulped loudly.

'Yes, my lady. I certainly hope so.'

'So you should,' the king added, returning his attention to the game.

The opposing teams were running headlong at each other, screaming and waving their sticks. Turlough decided that he had to try to escape this battle fury if he did not want to get himself seriously hurt.

'This is madness,' he told himself as he dodged the horde of wild combatants charging recklessly at each other.

A few seconds later, as Turlough was still trying to find his way through the seething mass of players, the front ranks of the opposing armies met with a great clash of sticks, swords, fists and curses. There was a sickening crunch as the melee ground to a halt and degenerated into a shoving and slogging match. Screams, cries and agonised grunts filled the air, punctuated by thudding metallic crashes and the loud cracks of breaking bones.

The holy red hurling block was hopelessly lost amongst this senseless throng. Indeed it seemed to Turlough that the little red ball was not really that important to the players at all. Most of them were putting all their energy into beating each other's heads and torsos with various blunt and not so blunt implements. In the confusion it was impossible to tell who belonged to which side.

'The doctor was right,' Turlough told himself in shock, 'this is the strangest dream I have ever had in all my life. It is very disturbing. I think I want to go home now.'

Eyes wide with horror, the young man surveyed the wild battle, too stunned by the spectacle to run. All around him there were folk lying on the ground, groaning, clutching at damaged limbs, mopping blood from their faces or simply motionless.

Others wandered around aimlessly, stunned by the blows they had received. In the midst of the carnage the able-bodied survivors battled on desperately with any weapon that came to hand.

'Your lad is not doing very well,' the king observed dourly.

'He needs to warm up,' Crilly explained quickly. 'He is waiting for the right moment to strike.'

Turlough flinched as his fat team-mate with the foul breath fell lifeless in front of him, a great broadsword embedded in his chest. A second later the lad saw a break in the crowd and he needed no further prompting. Without a moment's hesitation Turlough ran through the gap and out onto the open field away from the heaviest fighting.

When he had cleared the melee, he turned around to look back at the battle from a safer distance. He still could not believe his eyes. He had never seen anything like this savage fight. There did not seem to be any sense in it at all.

He would be safe here, Turlough thought. But at that very instant he noticed an object flying through the air, sailing gracefully toward him. Instinctively he dodged to get out of its way. At first he thought it was merely a poorly aimed projectile tossed from somewhere deep within the groaning mass of combatants. But when the bright red ball bounced on the grass no more than a few feet away, the boy recognised it immediately.

It was the holy red hurling block and it rolled along the ground until it came to rest right at Turlough's feet.

The young man looked down at the object dispassionately for several seconds before a terrible realisation hit him.

'Mother of God!' he whispered, throat dry with terror.

He looked up and saw that all those players who were still capable of standing, as well as many who weren't, had their eyes firmly fixed on him. There was an awful tension in the air as the fury of the battle subsided and the word passed around that the mortal had found the ball.

Turlough could feel his whole body shaking and thought he was probably going to faint long before he died from the blows of the enemy's axes. This idea didn't make him feel any better at all.

Before Turlough had a chance to pass into unconsciousness, however, both opposing armies raised their fiercest cries anew. And in the next second every able-bodied player on the field was charging headlong toward him. Turlough's mouth dropped open in fright and he felt his heart skip a beat. And then another.

There was nowhere to run.

'It is only a dream,' he stuttered, not believing it for a second.

None of the players was even looking at the holy red hurling block. All their rage was focused at the mortal lad they had waited all night for. Turlough felt their fury reach out before them like a great wave of wrath. His heart hammered so hard in his chest he thought it would surely burst his ribcage and he was frozen to the spot with fear.

The rabid mob was no more than thirty paces from him and picking up speed with every step. Turlough held his hurling stick in front of his face to protect himself and as it touched his nose he had a flash of inspiration.

Surprised at himself, Turlough let out a mighty scream, more from terror than any attempt to disturb the other players. He had very little time if he was to save himself from the frenzy of the screaming crowd.

With shaking hands he hooked the holy red hurling block up into the crook of his stick. But it immediately rolled out onto the grass. Turlough's whole body was quivering violently with fear as he hooked the ball up again. Desperately he flipped the stick around in his hands and hefted the holy red hurling block with all his might back in the direction of the charging players. Then he let his knees buckle under him and slumped onto the grass to await the impact of the charging mob.

But it never came.

Turlough had not played at the hurling for years. Any skill he might have acquired in his boyhood had deserted him long ago. He had intended to throw the ball directly into the mob of oncoming attackers to distract them and stave off their advance, but he had missed his aim entirely.

The holy red hurling block had spun upwards out from his stick in a long elegant arc high over the heads of all the other players. Turlough watched the ball soar, following the curve of its flight with his disbelieving eyes, mouth still hanging open in fright.

The charging players were also following the ball's heavenly journey. Eyes full of wonder, they halted their headlong sprint and stretched up to impotently wave their sticks at the bright red object as it passed them by. Out of reach it flew, clearing the entire crowd, until it disappeared completely from Turlough's view.

At the sidelines Crilly stood with mouth agape. He could see what Turlough could not. And the squire quickly realised where the object was going to land.

The holy red hurling block bounced at the far end of the field and rolled a long way across the grass, beyond the reach of the enemy players. Before it came to a halt the bright wooden object tumbled over the line which marked the goal of Turlough's team.

At that very instant the first rays of the sun appeared above the horizon and the writhing frenzied mob erupted into cheers and spitting insults, depending of course on their point of view.

The young man, saved from certain death, or maiming at the very least, fell forward on the grass, his jaw still locked open. All he could think to do was to recite the Ave nine times.

As Turlough lay there the sun bathed the whole countryside in liquid gold. The players turned their faces away from the light to shield their eyes. The dead returned to life, the injured to health. All the spilled blood was soaked up by the soil. And even the ugliest among the players seemed suddenly to attain some gracefulness.

Turlough finished his last round of the Ave then got up on his knees to look around him. As he watched, the Good People of the Big Hill and the Small Hill melted into the air as if they had never existed.

Turlough O'Carolan was left all alone in the middle of the grassy field, clutching an archaic curled stick. He stared blankly in front of him, trying to make sense of what he had just witnessed. He was so shocked he did not notice the three figures walking briskly toward him.

'Well done, lad,' Crilly yelled triumphantly at the top of his voice from across the field. 'I have never seen such a magnificent hurl in all my life. You're a bloody champion!'

The white-haired king and his dark queen were smiling, and when the three of them reached Turlough, the Queen of the Faeries leaned down and offered the hero her hand.

'A champion indeed,' she said with admiration in her voice. 'I predict great things for you, young man. It was worth the loss of a wager to see such a masterful stroke. I dare say you'd give even my consort a run for his money on the field.'

The king coughed loudly as Turlough got to his feet and for a second time looked into the queen's deep eyes. Try as he might, he could not look away. Then all of a sudden the lad started to feel very ill again.

'Well, Crilly,' the king declared dryly, dark eyes flashing full of suspicion toward his queen, 'he turned out to be a tactician after all. It seems I must now keep my end of the bargain. You will receive word from me in a few days' time. The old woman I have in mind for the job will be passing by Ballyfarnon shortly. Now take the lad home to rest. We will do what we can for him, and if he survives the spotted curse, we will be his patrons.'

The squire opened his mouth to thank the king but did not get the chance. Before he could speak, Turlough's knees began to buckle beneath him. The squire moved quickly to keep the lad on his feet, catching him around the waist.

By the time Crilly had Turlough standing up again, the king and queen were gone, disappeared into mist like their people.

'Who were those two?' the lad asked through a haze of pain and confusion.

'I told you earlier. The King and Queen of the Faeries,' Crilly whispered softly. 'He is the King of the Big Hill and she is the Queen of the Small Hill but she is the senior of the two of them.'

Turlough, however, did not hear the squire's explanation. He was already insensible to the world around him.

FIVE

Edward put the whiskey cup to his lips and drained the contents as he eyed old Hugh suspiciously. The firelight cast a deep red glow over the old man's nose and the young rebel reckoned that many gallons of illicit liquor had passed under those nostrils during Hugh the distiller's first hundred years.

'I hope you don't expect me to believe that your master played a hurling match with the Faeries?'

'Whether you believe it or no,' the old man protested, 'that is the story he told me, word for word and phrase for phrase.'

'With only minor embellishments,' Denis added under his breath, 'to help the tale flow better.'

Hugh coughed to show his displeasure at this interruption.

Edward's eyes narrowed, then he looked up at Hugh's grandson and held out his cup to be filled. Daniel obliged with a shrug of the shoulders, as if to confirm that he too held some doubts about the truth of the story.

'I don't know what to think of you, old man,' Edward said as he took the cup back. His speech was a little slurred and a broad smile had crept over his face. 'I really don't know what to think of you,' he repeated, taking another swig of the homemade spirit.

'When all this happened I was little more than a babe at my mother's breast,' Hugh informed his guest, 'so I was not a witness to these events. But the good Master Turlough told nothing but the truth in all his years upon this earth.'

'Unless he was certain he would not be discovered lying,' Denis mumbled mischievously.

Mhairgead giggled as she pulled up a seat behind Edward and began darning a pair of woollen stockings.

'Are you going to lean on that harp all night,' Hugh snapped at Denis, 'or are you going to play something for us?'

'There's no call for impatience,' Denis admonished, putting up a hand as if old Hugh wasn't blind. 'Are you in a hurry? Do you have some other fireside you're rushing away to? Or a hurling match perhaps?'

'Whisht, you old drunkard, and play me the Concerto.'

'I'll play it when I'm good and ready,' came the harper's sharp reply. 'For the time being you'll have to endure SheeBeg SheeMor. Is that not a fitting air to play?'

'It is indeed right and proper after hearing that part of the tale,' Hugh agreed and sat back to listen. Edward looked carefully at his host and thought from the old man's expression that he would have shed a tear, if he could, at the prospect of listening to one of his master's tunes.

Satisfied that the harp was in good tune, Denis launched into a sprightly rendition of the popular melody. Edward shut his eyes and listened with all his heart to the gorgeous golden notes dropping like honey from the instrument's wires. Denis's seasoned hands skipped along, effortlessly drawing life from the hard timber and brittle brass of the harp.

Suddenly Edward noticed his mind was spinning along with the familiar music in a wild dance. His eyelids were heavy now that they were closed and he felt his head loll forward onto his chest. It was as if some magic spell were contained in the sparkling notes and it had wrapped itself around him tight like a spider's web.

In his imagination Edward saw the high hill where the hurling match had been played. He could make out the two armies arrayed at opposite ends of the playing field ready to contest their honour. In the harp's droning bass notes he discerned the dark chanting of the armies. In the tinkling upper notes he saw their brightly coloured clothes and glimpsed the figure of a mortal man in amongst the great host of Faeries.

Too soon the tune ended and the humming wires stilled until the room was perfectly silent again.

'My master learned that from the Faerie folk, you know,' Hugh said in a low voice so as not to break the mood. 'It's the merriest melody I have ever heard and it was his first. It was to commemorate the battle in which he took part and its title pays honour to the Faeries of the Big Hill and the Faeries of the Small Hill.'

'It is one of the few of Carolan's pieces that I know nearly off by heart,' Edward told his host, 'though I have played many of his tunes.'

'If you can't recite the airs note by note,' Denis quizzed, 'how do you play them?'

'I have taught myself to read musical notation.'

'What's that?'

'The notes are all written down on paper so the musician can read them while he's playing,' Edward explained. 'In that manner I don't have to even hear a piece of music to be able to play it.'

'Sounds very clever,' Denis replied scowling and it was obvious the word clever was no compliment in the harper's vocabulary.

'I would be happy to show you tomorrow,' Edward offered. 'It's really quite simple.'

Denis turned to the young man and frowned and Edward could have kicked himself. It had never occurred to him before that the old blind harpers had to learn every tune they played by listening over and over to someone else's performance.

'I have as much hope of teaching you common sense as you do of teaching me to read,' Denis sighed and then he leaned the harp against his seat and held out his hand in Daniel's direction looking for his cup.

'That tune was learned from the Faerie people by my master,' Hugh began, steering the conversation back to his tale. 'It was the tune he heard when the hosts were preparing for battle. He remembered another tune as well and that was the melody which accompanied the Faerie Queen wherever she went. And he named that air after her. The Faeries gave him good melodies all right. They even provided him with the finest harp teacher in the whole of Ireland. But I am jumping ahead of myself again.'

The old man put a hand to his chin and thought for a few moments.

'Now, where were we?'

'Weren't you going to tell us what happened to Bridget Cruise?' Mhairgead asked.

'Not at all,' Hugh replied. 'I was going to tell you how Carolan met the true love of his life.'

'But you have already told us how he met Bridget,' Edward protested.

'Not her!' Hugh exclaimed. 'She wasn't his true love. Carolan just *thought* Bridget was his true love. No, the real woman of Turlough Carolan's dreams was a simple girl with no family name and she loved him like no woman has ever loved a man before or since.'

'I love this part of the story,' Mhairgead said dreamily as she leaned forward to touch Edward on the shoulder.

The rebel felt her hand caress him and he turned to look at her fingers. He suddenly felt confused and his head was beginning to ache.

'What time is it?' he asked.

'It's time for the next part of the story,' Mhairgead replied quickly.

'It's time for another whiskey,' Denis declared.

'It's time you all shut up and let me get on with it,' Hugh grumbled.

Daniel poured another drink for Edward, who swallowed it down without any hesitation. When the cup was empty the young rebel realised that he had hardly tasted the brew.

'Is my tongue numbed by this stuff?' he asked Daniel. 'Or did you put water in that drink?'

'Never water another man's whiskey,' Hugh advised, 'or sleep with another man's wife if you aspire to an untroubled existence free from strife.'

'Is that how the saying goes?' the harper sputtered, shaking his head.

'Of course it is,' the old distiller answered sharply.

'Well I have discovered too late that I misunderstood the meaning of that phrase entirely,' Denis sighed.

'What are you talking about?' Hugh snapped.

The harper breathed deeply and touched his forehead as if thinking about something. He mouthed a few words and shook his head again.

'Well, at least I can say in all honesty,' Denis conceded, his speech slurred slightly, 'that I never watered another man's woman or slept with another man's whiskey.'

'You old fool.' Hugh shook his head. 'Where on earth did you lose the wits that God gave you when you were brought into the world?'

'There is no water in your whiskey,' Daniel told Edward with a grin. 'It's just that after a while the mouth mellows to this liquor and it seems to be less potent.'

'I see,' the young man replied, even though he did not.

'I will come to the next part of the tale,' Hugh announced, 'if you three gentlemen and the young lady will allow me.'

'As you wish,' Denis said. 'But spare a thought for me. I always suspected that my youth was misguided and misspent. And now, when I am too old to make amends, I have the firm evidence for it.'

'Be quiet,' Hugh hissed, his temper simmering.

At that moment Denis put a hand in the air and gasped. 'Did you hear that?' he said through clenched teeth.

'Horses,' Hugh decided after a few seconds.

'They're a fair way off,' the old harper added.

'I don't hear anything,' Daniel said.

'You must learn to trust our blind ears,' his grandfather scolded him. 'Denis and I can hear things that you never could.'

'Is it the English?' Edward asked apprehensively.

'It may well be,' Hugh said solemnly. 'They must be determined to find you if they are venturing out of barracks after sunset.'

'You must hide me!' the rebel cried in shock. 'What if they come here searching for me?'

'I will not let them find you,' the distiller promised. 'Not until I am ready.'

'What do you mean?' Edward was not at all reassured by this promise.

'Do not trouble yourself,' Mhairgead advised. 'He's just pulling your leg. He has a habit of playing jokes on well-meaning folk.'

She stroked Edward's hair and put a hand on his arm. 'Don't fret,' she soothed. 'The redcoats won't take you. Will they, Grandfather?'

Hugh thought about that for a second as Edward frowned and slumped forward. Not even the prospect of English soldiers nearby could stave off the effects of the whiskey. In a few seconds the young rebel was breathing deeply.

'Is he asleep?' Hugh asked.

'He's having a little rest,' Mhairgead said as she checked that Edward's eyes were shut. 'I'm not surprised. You've been filling him full of your liquor all night.'

'Are you sure you've made up your mind, Grand-daughter?' the old distiller whispered.

'I knew as soon as I saw him. He's handsome and wealthy and he won't be running off with some redhead from Dublin at the drop of a hat.'

'If the redheads don't get him, the redcoats will,' Hugh pointed out.

'Then you had better make sure the redcoats don't get him,' the young woman replied.

'What has it got to do with me?' Hugh protested.

'If anything happens to this lad,' Mhairgead warned, 'I'll be down at Dublin Castle so fast not even the mail coach will be able to catch me. And I'm sure the lords in that fair city will be very interested to hear about your stills, your illicit whiskey trade with three garrisons, and your treacherous dealings with Major D'Arcy.'

'You wouldn't dare,' Hugh spluttered.

'I would. And I'm sure I'd get a decent reward for my information too. More than enough to set myself up in a fine house for the rest of my life.'

'Who would have thought my own flesh and blood would have turned traitor on me?' Hugh gasped in shock.

'I'll wager the magistrate in Dublin will see it differently.'

'How do you mean?'

'They might not think me the traitor at all. They might well judge a man who buys good English muskets from a roguish redcoat officer and then sells those guns on to the rebels as the true villain,' she whispered. 'They would surely hang such a man for supplying arms and corrupting servants of the Crown. But the young rebel who bravely dispatched the greedy and disloyal Major D'Arcy would surely be accounted some kind of a hero. Edward might even get a reward on his own account.'

'I can't believe I am hearing this,' Hugh hissed. 'I am your grandfather. I nurtured you as a child. You ate the food I provided for the table. Your father is my own son.'

'My father is rotting in Botany Bay because you and Major D'Arcy were not careful enough in your dealings.'

'I have fed and clothed you, how can you threaten me so?'

'I am not getting any younger mending your stockings, cooking your meals and cleaning up after your drunken friends. I want a good man who'll take care of me and my children. And maybe take me to Dublin on occasion.'

'And what was wrong with the husband I arranged for you?' Hugh demanded.

'That bloody fool!' Mhairgead laughed with venom and Edward opened his eyes. 'He was a worse drunk than even you were! The only good thing he ever did was get himself transported!'

'What's that?' the young rebel asked. 'What was that about transportation?'

'It was nothing,' Hugh soothed. 'Daniel!' he called. 'Go out and see what all the noise is about. If it's a troop of redcoats, lay them off the scent.'

'Yes, Grandfather,' Daniel replied with resignation. He grabbed his coat and in a minute was gone to do as he was told.

'Have the redcoats come upon us?' Edward asked, his head beginning to spin.

'All will be well,' Hugh reassured him. 'Daniel has gone out to deal with them. You have nothing to fear. Fetch the young gentleman another drink, Mhairgead,' the distiller insisted. 'We can't have an honoured guest going dry, can we?'

The young woman smiled. For the moment at least, she had the upper hand.

'Were you going to tell us the next part of the tale, Grandfather,' Mhairgead asked as she brought the earthenware jug to Edward and filled his cup.

'I was only waiting for our young hero, Master Edward, to recover his senses,' Hugh said with just a hint of sarcasm in his voice.

'I'm wide awake,' the rebel assured his host. 'If the English are abroad tonight, it would be well for me to stay on my guard.'

'Then you'll need another drink to fortify you against sleep,' Denis cut in. 'God only knows, the storyteller won't likely keep your attention.'

'I was going to tell you about my master's recovery from the smallpox,' Hugh snarled.

'We are all waiting on the edge of our seats,' Denis replied.

Turlough's eyes opened to bright sunlight. The door to his father's house was open and the yellow light was tinted with gorgeous shades of honey and gold.

The scene was so beautiful that Turlough drew a deep breath and held the cool sweetness of it in his lungs for a few moments. 'Am I dead?' he asked aloud.

'You are not,' a young woman's gentle voice replied. 'You are still with us yet.'

Startled, Turlough turned his head and saw a fresh-faced young woman with pale skin and black hair. She was smiling down at him as she folded a wet cloth. Her dark eyes shone in the light and Turlough had to blink several times to make sure she was real.

The girl's serene face reminded him of paintings he had seen in church of the Blessed Virgin.

'Are you sure I am not dead, for you are like an angel from Heaven.'

'You are talking to me,' the woman laughed. 'So it would be quite remarkable if you had passed over. Anyway, where would you have seen an angel?'

'Who are you, if you're not the Mother of God herself?'

'My name *is* Mary,' the young woman admitted as she dipped a piece of cloth in a bowl of water and wiped his face. Then she thought for a second before she added, 'But I'm not that Mary.'

'My name is Turlough.'

'I know that.'

Then the boy remembered the doctor's warning. 'You must go,' he urged her. 'You are in danger of losing yourself to the Galar-breac.'

'Be quiet now,' she answered softly. 'I had it when I was very young and it left me whole. It cannot touch me. I am safe. I have come to nurse you. As long as you are kept well washed, you will survive the sickness also.'

'Are you a blessed sister of the hospital order?'

The girl laughed out loud and her eyes sparkled with merriment.

'Whatever made you think I was a nun?' she giggled. 'You seem to have a fascination with holy women. Were you hoping to become a priest one day? Or a bishop perhaps?'

'No!' the lad exclaimed. 'God help me, that's the last thing I want. The doctor told me there would be a nun coming to take care of me.'

'I didn't hear about any nun,' the young woman told him. 'My grandmother and I stayed with the MacDermots last night and when the good lady heard that I had overcome the plague, she asked me to nurse you.'

'Are you friends with the MacDermot family?'

'No,' she said simply, 'we are travellers.'

'Travellers?'

'My grandmother and I have always travelled from place to place getting what work we may.'

'How do you manage?' Turlough gasped. 'Times are so hard!'

'That's enough questions from you now. Still your tongue or you'll have no strength for your recovery.'

'I had a strange dream,' Turlough muttered as the details of the hurling match came back to him. 'It was so real that I am sure it must have really happened.'

'I had strange dreams also.' The girl mopped his brow. 'Almost everyone who suffers the Galar-breac experiences vivid visions. You must put them out of your mind.'

'I want to learn the harp,' he said under his breath as he closed his eyes. 'I will be the greatest harper in all Ireland one day.'

'Will you?' the girl smiled. 'Well, we shall see, won't we? What did you dream?'

'There was a field up at the top of the hill,' Turlough began dreamily, 'and it was full of strange folk playing at the hurling in the middle of the night.'

'Was it indeed?'

'It was a great gathering of the Good People, and I played at the hurling in front of the King and Queen of the Faeries.'

'Sleep now,' Mary soothed as she touched his face with the wet cloth. 'Sleep peacefully and do not trouble yourself. The visions will pass away.'

Her voice was so calming that Turlough sighed and breathed

easy. Before long his head rolled back into the centre of the straw pillow and he drifted off.

Mary mopped her patient's brow again and then pulled the sheets up to his neck. As she did so she realised there was something odd under the bedclothes. She rolled down the sheets and as her hands touched the object she frowned.

Mary shook her head with a smile as she prised an old battered hurling stick from Turlough's grip, wondering how on earth it could have come to be in his bed. Then she tucked her patient under the covers again, placed the stick in the corner of the room and returned to bathing his brow.

Turlough slept quietly for a while then he began to toss fitfully until some hours later he passed into a deep sleep. When the boy opened his eyes again it seemed at first that only a few minutes had passed. But he soon noticed that the room was once again dark. The door was shut and there was no candle in the room at all.

'Who was that woman who was here bathing my brow?' he whispered.

'What woman?' a man's voice said with a hint of urgency.

'The girl with the black hair and the shining eyes.'

'I do not know her,' the voice replied and suddenly Squire Crilly was leaning over Turlough, grasping at the boy's chin and staring into his eyes.

'Are you fit enough to rise?' the squire asked.

'I am very tired. I want to go back to sleep.'

'We must go visiting tonight, for it is very likely you will be unable to move after tomorrow. The sores are close to maturing and once they have unleashed their poison, you must lie perfectly still or endanger your life.'

'Where are we going?'

'To see the king and queen.'

Turlough looked at Crilly's eyes and noticed they were sparkling in the same way as his nurse's eyes had done earlier.

'I don't want to play in any more hurling matches,' the boy stated firmly.

'The king and queen wish to congratulate you on your skill. They were very impressed with that winning shot. They're holding a party for you.'

'I am too tired,' Turlough protested.

'Whatever happens to you,' Crilly admonished in a stern voice, 'no matter where you are or how tired you may be, if they summon you, then you must go. That is if you know what's good for you.'

'What do you mean?'

'The king and queen have agreed to become your patrons,' the squire explained. 'With their help all your dearest wishes will come true.'

'Why would they do that for me? I'm just the son of a blacksmith.'

'It suits their sense of irony, perhaps,' Crilly smiled.

'I don't understand what you mean.'

'That's enough interrogation, my lad. And remember, you must never ask a question of the king or queen directly. Do you understand?'

'Yes.'

'Good. Now drink some of this liquor. It is not whiskey but it will give you the strength to attend the court and pay your respects.'

'Please let me sleep,' Turlough begged as the squire put the bottle to his lips.

'It is too late for that, my boy. You made your wish and you were foolish enough to be overheard by one who is a friend of the Good People. If you agree to the bargain, you must live it through to the end of your days.'

With that Crilly poured a few drops of the liquor into the lad's mouth and then carefully replaced the stopper in his precious bottle.

'How are you feeling now?' the squire asked.

To his surprise Turlough suddenly felt like he had slept a long and peaceful sleep and was ready for a good day's work.

'What is in that bottle?' the boy asked.

'Don't ask too many questions, lad, and you'll find life treats you much easier.'

The squire helped the young man to rise and dress in breeches and a shirt. Then he threw a fine dark blue cloak around Turlough's shoulders. 'This will keep you warm and make you look a little more respectable.'

'Where are we going?'

'You really are going to have to learn to curb your curiosity,' Crilly berated him. He sighed and said, 'The king is holding court in the stables tonight in honour of your astounding victory at the hurling. There will be some very interesting folk gathered there. A few of them may prove to be great friends in the future should you stand in need.'

Turlough nodded, though he didn't really understand, and then quickly pulled his boots on. In a few minutes the two of them were standing in the courtyard. All was quiet and dark in the middle of the night. There were no lights in the big house. Even the kitchen fire had dulled to a glow which barely showed beneath the door.

The young man looked across toward the stables. All was perfectly silent. Nothing stirred, not horses, dogs nor any other animal.

'Are you sure we are supposed to be meeting the king and queen in the stables?'

'I am.' Crilly led Turlough by the arm to the stables door then held a finger to his lips and whispered, 'No matter what you see when this door opens, you must not make a sound. Do you understand? Not a sound.'

'I understand,' Turlough replied and then Crilly pushed the door ajar.

Suddenly the air was swimming in a glorious golden light and as the creaking wooden door swung wider the light changed from orange to red and then to a rich purple. Turlough's jaw dropped open. He took a deep breath to cry out in dismay but the squire had his hand over the boy's mouth before he could make a sound.

'Be still,' Crilly hissed. 'All will be well.'

In the next instant he had pushed Turlough into the stables and shut the door fast behind them. In the courtyard all returned to silence as if nothing untoward had happened.

The very moment the stable door was closed behind them, the beautiful light grew less intense, fading back through all the colours of the rainbow to a pale yellow glow. Turlough rubbed his aching eyes. He blinked several times and when he could focus again he saw that the stables were bedecked from top to bottom with hundreds of candles.

All around the stalls there were fresh garlands of whitethorn sprigs, oak leaves and holly. The ceiling of the ancient hall was covered by a huge hanging square of white lace of the finest workmanship. The double doors to the building were framed by an arch woven of living ivy branches arranged in the most intricate and beautiful patterns.

A great round black cauldron sat over the blacksmith's fire, bubbling merrily, and from it rose a sweet aroma. Nearby there was a low table covered with every type of food imaginable, as well as some delicacies Turlough did not recognise at all. Laid out at one end of the table were many cups of silver with long stems and deep bowls, each etched with a different pattern.

Despite the strange rearrangement of their stables, the horses stood in their stalls contentedly as if nothing were amiss. One of the hunting dogs slept soundly in a corner amongst the straw and the animal was so quiet that Turlough thought for a moment that it must surely be dead. But on closer inspection he found the animal to be breathing deeply, wrapped in the secure embrace of untroubled slumber.

The young man turned to Squire Crilly, eager to learn what was going on. But then he realised that all this must be one of the strange delusions the Galar-breac brought with it.

'This is not a dream, Turlough,' a woman's voice soothed. 'But then who is to say whether dreams are less real than anything else in the world?'

The young man turned around but there was no-one else in the stables apart from Squire Crilly.

In that instant the candles abruptly ceased their glow, leaving only a small circle of light around the bubbling cauldron. Turlough gasped with wonder as two figures stepped out from the edge of the darkness.

A tall man dressed in a long black coat led a younger-looking woman also dressed in black. As the two strangers approached Turlough, the white-haired man raised one hand in the air and the candles burned brightly again.

Turlough then recognised the couple, though he could not remember their names.

'Bow your head,' Crilly hissed and Turlough did as he was told.

'You are the young man who has the desire to become a harper?' the lady asked.

Turlough raised his gaze without lifting his head and looked into the woman's eyes. They were two dark jewels set in a perfectly shaped face. Her lips were of the purest ruby red and they were glistening with moisture in the candlelight. Her jet black hair fell about her forehead in long straight locks which framed her glowing face.

The strange lady smiled at him then laughed a little, putting a milk-white hand to her mouth as she did so. Turlough thought she was, for an instant, like a young woman, coy and sweet, though her eyes held the wisdom of great age.

'Answer the queen,' the squire whispered.

Turlough tore his gaze from the woman and stared at the floor, resisting the urge to look up again at the lady. 'I would dearly love to learn to play the harp,' he said finally. 'It is my wish to one day become a master of that ancient instrument.'

'Is it true that you would do this for the love of a woman?' the queen asked.

'Yes.'

'Then we will grant you your wish,' the man with the snow-white hair answered. 'Under the terms we will set later.'

Crilly's eyes widened and he stepped forward slightly. 'What terms?' the squire asked nervously.

'It is none of your concern, good man,' came the stern reply.

'Forgive me, Your Majesty,' Crilly began cautiously, 'but I was not aware there were going to be any terms to this arrangement. Turlough is not fit to negotiate at the moment.'

The King of the Faeries smiled and there was a glint in his eye as he leaned in closer to whisper, 'I was not aware you had a stake in this bargain.'

'I am only thinking of the lad's wellbeing,' Crilly protested.

'Indeed,' hummed the king. 'Do you think I will look to anything less than his wellbeing? It is my wife here who has the reputation for changing her mind in such matters, not I.'

The queen coughed and touched the king on the shoulder. 'I do beg your pardon,' she said addressing Crilly, 'but my consort seems to be a little confused about the circumstances surrounding this arrangement. To begin with it has obviously slipped his mind that I am the senior partner in this marriage. I can assure you, Squire Crilly, that once I have made up my mind about a course of action I will stay with it to the end. I am as dependable as the sunrise.'

'The clouds do occasionally compromise the rising sun,' the king noted with a smirk on his face and a wink in Crilly's direction.

The squire did not reply. He did not dare make a single move. It was plain to him that there was trouble brewing between this pair and he knew he would be well advised to stay out of it. Their disputes were the stuff of legend.

'Husband, you have frightened the man,' the queen stated with a giggle in her voice when she saw Crilly's worried expression. However, her eyes were flashing with fury as she spoke.

The king thrust his face close to Crilly's and peered at him. 'He does seem to be concerned,' the king noted as Crilly began to sweat across the brow. 'But I don't think it is I who has upset him, my dear wife.'

'I am not your wife!' the queen hissed. 'You are my consort! The chieftainship follows the female line.'

'Not in the world of mortals,' the king replied confidently. 'Is that not true, Crilly?'

'I beg your pardon, my lord?' the squire stuttered, certain that no matter what he said he would be in trouble.

'Is it not true,' the king repeated, rolling his eyes at the tediousness of having to explain himself, 'that in the mortal world the husband rules the wife by long custom?'

'That could be said to be true,' Crilly replied, but when he saw the queen's face turn from smile to frown he added, 'and so it may seem to be. But I believe that nature would not allow such a state of affairs.'

'What do you mean?' the queen barked.

'A bull may rule the herd,' the squire offered, 'but it is the cow that gives the milk.'

For a moment both the king and queen fell completely silent, their faces stern and unamused. Crilly squirmed in his shoes, sure that he had gone too far, and cursed his flapping tongue and dull wits.

Then suddenly the queen laughed. The king took a pace back and stood beside her. Then he nodded slowly and appreciatively with a broad grin on his face.

'You are a wise man, Crilly,' the king congratulated him. 'You will live to be a great age if you always use your head as well as that.'

'Thank you, my lord,' the squire stammered.

'If you listen to Squire Crilly,' the queen told Turlough, 'you will learn much. He has a sweet tongue and a polite manner.'

'I will take your advice, my lady,' the young man managed. A few minutes earlier he had been convinced that everything he was seeing and hearing was a strange figment of his dreaming mind. But now he was not so sure. Turlough touched the velvet fabric of the cloak Crilly had loaned him and the texture tickled the tips of his fingers. The cloak at least seemed real enough.

Abruptly the king raised his hand in the air and instantly the stables were full of hundreds of folk arrayed in the finest clothes. Turlough gasped in surprise. The gathering had appeared out of nowhere. The lad felt faint.

The multitude of strange folk were chatting away as if they had been there all evening. The room echoed with the sound of laughter, the clinking of fine crystal glasses and the spirited conversation of people enjoying themselves. In one corner a harper sat playing a merry tune on an instrument that was made of pure gold.

'Mother of God!' Turlough mumbled to himself as he felt his knees go weak beneath him.

He shook his head, closed his eyes and waited a few seconds, hoping to clear his mind of the disturbing visions. But the sounds did not cease. And when he opened his eyes again the guests were still enjoying the party with great enthusiasm.

'If these are Faerie folk,' the lad said in bewilderment under his breath, 'why do they seem to be no different from anyone I have ever met?'

'Why should we be any different?' the queen asked him. 'We can take any form we wish. So why would we not cloak ourselves in radiance and beauty? There are those of our kind who prefer to present themselves as frightening or cruel, but most of us find this pretty form suits our tastes much better. In this guise we can walk in the world of mortals and not attract too much attention. Unless it suits our purpose.'

'Why would you want to walk amongst our kind if you can take any form you like?' Turlough asked.

'That is a good question,' the king interrupted. 'I will condescend to answer it, though I am sure you should have been warned about our attitude to prying.' The king glanced coldly at Crilly to show his displeasure.

'I suppose we like to think we are doing some good in the world,' the king went on. 'Lending a helping hand where it's needed, giving advice, delivering windfalls, rewarding generosity, that sort of thing. It gives us a sense of purpose and helps keep us amused down the centuries.

'Everything, even the most beautiful things, can become a

little tiresome after a while,' the king continued. 'Keeping oneself gainfully occupied is not as simple a matter as it may at first seem. It is very tempting to spend hundreds of years doing nothing other than dancing, singing, drinking and indulging the senses.'

'It may be tempting for you,' the queen observed, 'but that merely confirms your base nature. I have no trouble whiling away my time, helping folk who are in need.'

'You do indulge yourself,' the king smiled. 'Remember that young poet?'

'What young poet?' the queen snapped.

'That fellow a hundred years ago or more. The one you spent all your time alone with. You remember surely. He was completely enchanted with you.'

'He was not such a great poet after all,' the queen grunted. 'His verses were trivial and tiresome. I don't know why they are still popular amongst mortals.'

'You grew weary of him and in time you discarded him like all the others,' the king said, holding up a finger of reprimand.

The queen's eyes flashed and Turlough thought he saw tiny flames leaping about deep within the blackness of her pupils.

'Will you have a drink with us?' the queen offered sweetly, changing the subject and holding out a tall silver cup to Turlough. 'This is the finest whiskey you'll ever taste. Distilled in the palaces of the southern Faerie folk.'

The lad suddenly found himself to be extraordinarily thirsty. His mouth was dry and his tongue swollen.

'I would be honoured,' Turlough replied, taking the cup from the queen. He was about to take a long draught when he noticed the squire shaking his head furiously at him.

'Is there something the matter, Crilly?' the queen asked sternly, not taking her eyes from Turlough or dropping her smile.

'No, my lady,' the squire replied, coughing to cover his nervousness.

'Then perhaps you should take a breath of fresh air. You are looking rather pale. Come back when you are feeling better.'

'I'll take Turlough with me,' Crilly said, gripping the lad by the arm. 'He isn't feeling that well himself as you may recall.'

'Let me drink a toast first,' Turlough offered, 'and I'll be right with you.'

'Don't drink the whiskey!' Crilly hissed under his breath.

'What did you say, Crilly?' the queen snapped.

'I was just reminding Turlough that whiskey doesn't agree with his stomach.'

'What are you talking about?' the lad began but he felt an elbow jab him hard in the ribs and he spilled the liquor on the floor of the stables.

He looked down in wonder at the spot where the whiskey was soaking into the floorboards. Almost immediately a small bush erupted from the floor and in moments it had sprouted the most beautiful and diverse fruits.

The king waited patiently for the tree to mature then picked himself a juicy red apple and bit deeply into it. He offered Turlough a taste but the lad was too awe-struck to move.

'Perhaps you would like to try one of these fine sugar cakes,' the queen suggested, taking the empty cup away.

'He really shouldn't be eating such rich food in his state,' Crilly advised her. 'It will only compromise his chances of recovery.'

The queen smiled tightly and put the tray of cakes back down upon the table. 'You are probably right,' she conceded. 'Let us see what manner of musician he turns out to be before we feast him finely. There will be plenty of time for food and drink later.'

Then she turned to whisper something to the king and in a second the two of them were laughing uproariously.

'You mustn't eat or drink anything, Turlough,' Crilly whispered urgently. 'Don't you know anything?'

'What are you talking about?' the lad replied, confused.

'If you eat their food or swallow their drink, you will not be able to leave. You will become like them. Immortal. Beyond the redemption of Heaven.'

Suddenly there was a hush and the king stood up on a stool to speak. 'There were harps and harpers long before the Irish people came to these shores,' he began.

'In the days of the Tuatha-De-Danaan,' Turlough murmured, unprompted.

'You speak well,' the king told him. 'It is a great pleasure to meet a young man who values the old tales.'

'My mother told all the stories to me when I was a wee lad.'

'Then she was a good teacher,' the queen noted. 'Are you ready and willing to submit to another teacher?'

'A harp teacher?' Turlough asked.

'One who will be able to help you nurture any talent you may have for music,' the king's voice boomed.

'I am ready,' the boy answered.

'You are very lucky,' the king told him. 'My queen has petitioned me to favour you with this gift. You have certainly impressed her. Make sure you always give a good impression of yourself.'

'I will,' the young man nodded without hesitation.

'My male *consort* and I,' the queen went on sternly, her eyes flashing at the king, 'are to be your patrons from this day forward. I have consented to benefit you with my generosity. Do you know what that means?'

The king breathed out heavily in exasperation as he rolled his eyes toward the ceiling.

'I have an idea that you will dress me in fine clothes and ensure I am well fed.'

'If you prove to have any talent, that may well be the case,' the king informed him. 'But I think my good wife is referring to your obligations to us.'

'I see,' Turlough stammered, but he didn't really.

'What my consort is trying to say,' the queen continued, making it quite clear that she considered herself the senior of the two, 'is that it will be your duty to attend to us at our command. It will be your pleasure to compose airs which flatter us and speak of our many fine attributes. And you must never allow any man to slight our names. If we should but ask, you will return your life and livelihood willingly to us. If you serve us well we may grant that when you pass away your spirit comes to dwell with us in our kingdom.'

'Oh,' the lad said with a frown of confusion. Then he made a move to speak.

Crilly had a hand over the boy's mouth in a second and mumbled a brief apology to the king and queen. Then he took Turlough by the shoulders and stared into his eyes.

'I thought I told you not to ask any questions,' he whispered.

'But I don't like the sound of all that obligation business,' Turlough protested.

'What are you worried about? I have known these two all my life. They have always kept their word. They are a kind and gentle lord and lady who will always take care of your wellbeing as long as you keep your faith with them. But ask them too many questions and you will surely see their wrathful side. For it is just as easy for them to remove their gifts as it is to bestow them.'

'I am not so sure that this is what I want after all,' Turlough shrugged.

'Believe me, my boy,' Crilly said solemnly, 'this affair has progressed far beyond the point where you are able to change your mind. A sickness has come upon you. And the only chance you have of recovery is with the help of these two folk who stand before you.'

'The lad seems very distressed,' the queen cut in. 'Is the pestilence far advanced?'

'Tomorrow he will begin to suffer the worst of it,' the squire replied.

'Then take him back to bed,' she said in her sweetest tone. 'It is senseless to have him out and about when he should be conserving his energy for the fight ahead.'

'We will leave him in your hands, Crilly,' the king added. 'You will let us know if he needs anything. The old woman will be staying for a while yet. Her grand-daughter has a duty to young Turlough. She will bring him through the darkness and into the light again, and when the girl's duty is finished, the old woman will begin the work of teaching him. We will grant you sufficient funds to pay for his education.'

'Thank you, Your Majesty,' Crilly said, bowing low.

Then the king stepped off the stool and approached the squire. 'Of course you understand,' he whispered, 'that he has seen us?'

'Yes, Your Majesty,' Crilly sighed. 'I understand. But I would ask your mercy in this matter. I have seen you many times and I am allowed to retain my eyesight.'

'You come from an old established family with ancient links to my own. You are almost kin.' The king put an arm around the squire. 'I trust you as I would a brother. But we cannot take a risk with this young fellow. He may not be able to cope with all that happens to him. And besides that, he expressed a heart-felt wish. He said he didn't care whether he ever saw this estate again.'

'I beg you not to take that rash statement too literally,' Crilly cut in.

'He should not have asked for it if he didn't want it,' the king said petulantly and the squire wondered how these two could justify everything they did as good works. There was a good deal of mischief about them, for all their kind acts.

'Please reconsider,' Crilly pleaded. 'He is only young. The young make hasty decisions and foolish judgments.'

'I do not remember being young, it was so long ago. But young or old there is a price to be paid for everything. Turlough named his price very early in the negotiations. It would be dishonest of me to change the terms of our agreement after the bargain has been struck. Fear not. He will have a good life.'

Crilly looked at the king and queen and sighed. Further argument would achieve nothing.

'Thank you, my lord and lady,' the squire said humbly, taking Turlough by the arm. And then he backed away toward the door, dragging the lad along with him. By this time Turlough was sweating profusely and his face was flushed as the effect of the liquor began to wear off.

The boy could no longer focus and he was feeling very dizzy. Crilly held the lad up as they stepped out of the stables and into the cold dark night once again. The warm radiance of the king and queen was replaced by the indigo of the clear night sky. The lad found himself wishing he was back in the Faerie hall, bathed in the glorious amber glow of the many candles and listening to the grand merry music.

'Is this the boy?' a strange voice demanded, and Turlough heard Crilly answer, 'It is.'

'Let me see him.'

Through his haze Turlough made out a short stooped figure stepping out of the shadows. An old woman reached out a hand to the lad and he felt her fingers brush against his face.

She pulled back the headscarf from around her face to reveal two empty eye sockets. Then she cackled loudly, 'You are a handsome young fellow. I can tell you will be a fine musician one day.'

'You can tell whether he will be a good musician simply by touching his face?' the squire cut in.

'Have you ever met an ugly harper?' the old woman retorted sharply.

Crilly stopped to think carefully about his reply. He resisted the urge to say the first words that came to his mind. 'No, of course not,' he replied diplomatically.

'He will suit the purpose,' the old woman declared. 'I will do what I can with him if he lives.'

'He is strong.'

'But that alone is not enough to ensure that he will survive the Galar-breac. I know of many good strong folk who have succumbed simply because they have been unable to wash themselves or fetch themselves a drink.'

'He has a good nurse,' the squire reminded her.

'She is a very able nurse,' the woman agreed. 'But it will take more than good nursing to bring this boy back from the edge of death. It will take deep caring. If he lives, I will do my best to teach him.'

'Then I pray that he does live.'

'Pray all you like, it won't make any difference,' the old woman snorted.

'Thank you for your help,' the squire stuttered, feeling decidedly uncomfortable.

'Don't thank me. Thank Their Majesties. If I hadn't given them a solemn oath to serve at their bidding, I would not be here now myself. I would be sitting at home dozing by the fire. Goodnight, Squire Crilly. Goodnight, young Turlough. One day you will be known as a fine harper if you take heed of my teaching.'

Turlough grunted a goodnight, already slipping back into the sickness.

'Take him to bed, Squire Crilly,' the old woman muttered as she melted back into the shadows. 'I can't teach a corpse anything of any value.'

SIX

After that night the sickness took a terrible course with the young Turlough O'Carolan. For five days he lay in his bed, senseless to his surroundings and to the nurse who bathed his sores and watched over his ordeal.

The boy's whole body was gradually covered in large blisters which stretched his skin mercilessly. When the sores burst, the pus escaped from the wounds to burn his flesh, spreading the inflammation.

Turlough's mouth was always dry; the sweat poured out of him and when he woke, which was seldom, he cried out for water. His body shrank miserably as he lost weight. His hair became lank, his breath foul.

Mary was powerless to halt the disease. All she could do was sit beside him in companionship, bathe his wounds as often as possible and hope for the best.

No-one could tell whether Turlough would survive. Doctor Lindsay gave up hope very early and afterwards only visited rarely. He convinced Mrs MacDermot that the only thing to do was purchase a coffin so that the body could be disposed of quickly when death finally took the lad.

Mary knew that smallpox was indiscriminate in its choice of victims. It could strike the strong and kill them easily, yet a weaker person might be left almost untouched. No matter how well she cared for him, young Turlough would have to win this battle alone.

After the first week the lad's fevers began to abate a little and his sweating ceased almost completely. But the sores covered the whole of his face and the inside of his mouth and tongue. The red pustules stank of sweet decay when they poured out their poison. This vile liquid, sometimes clear, sometimes yellow and brackish, soaked into the bed sheets and the straw mattress.

Each day Mary removed the linen and washed it. If Turlough was to have any chance of recovery, she would have to keep his skin as clean as possible and free of the tainted pus. By the sixth day of his senselessness the boy's eyes and nose were also covered in open weeping sores.

Mary considered it a blessing that Turlough woke seldom, for he only did so when the pain was at its worst. Though Doctor Lindsay had forbidden it, she gave the lad whiskey to calm his breathing and still the agony of consciousness. This, sadly, was one of the worst cases of the disease Mary had ever seen, and when the sores spread to the lad's eyes she came to the reluctant conclusion that there was very little hope for his survival.

Early in the evening of the tenth day of the fever there was a knock on the door. Mary went to see who it was and was relieved to find Doctor Lindsay standing outside, his bag under his arm.

'How is he faring?' the doctor whispered.

'You need not keep your voice low,' Mary answered, 'he will not hear you. He is in the deepest sleep I have ever witnessed.'

'That is a pity,' Lindsay replied as he pushed past her into the room.

'There was nothing I could do to prevent the poison seeping under his eyelids,' Mary shrugged wearily and the doctor grunted acknowledgement as he sat on the bed.

'You have done a remarkable job in keeping him alive this long,' Lindsay noted as he opened the lad's jaws with the end of a metal spoon. The doctor peered inside Turlough's mouth.

'The sores seem to be healing on his tongue but I fear they have done their damage to his eyes.'

'Will he be blinded?'

'It would be too much to hope that he will come through this ordeal unscathed,' the doctor replied, careful not to commit himself. 'That is, if he survives at all.'

'Surely you can do something?' Mary sighed.

'I could bleed him,' Lindsay conceded, seeing the distress in her eyes, 'but in his weakened state that might also be the death of him. His mouth is dry so I suppose he should be given as much water as his body can take. Otherwise I have done all I can. I am merely a physician. Turlough's recovery is in the hands of God.'

The doctor prodded one of the sores on the lad's face and it obligingly split, splashing pus onto the pillow. Lindsay quickly covered his nose with a lace handkerchief to stifle the foul odour.

'I have seen this stage many times,' he coughed. 'When the pustules break around the eyes and are full of dark yellow poison, there is little hope the patient will live. His body is worn out from the fight. He has no strength left. Perhaps he would be better off if he succumbed now. It would save him a lot of pain.'

The doctor touched the young man's ear at a point where there was no infection. 'He is cold to the core. He will be gone by morning. And we should look on that as a blessing.'

The doctor looked down at the boy and at that moment Turlough opened his eyes a little. The lids were almost completely stuck together with a thickened mucus, but this small movement was enough to convince the doctor that the young lad was still fighting.

'Keep the eyes clean,' Lindsay advised. 'What good if he recovers from the illness and ends up blinded by the sores?'

He picked up his bag and made for the door. 'One last thing. If he dies, you must make sure his body is only handled by those who have survived the pox. Even after death his corpse will be a danger to anyone who has never been touched by the disease.'

Lindsay put his broad-brimmed hat on his head. 'I will be in the big house. Call me when it is over.' Then he left, closing the door quietly behind him.

Mary turned away. She was determined now that this young man would live. No foolish old doctor was going to pronounce a death sentence on Turlough O'Carolan.

'You will live,' she whispered to the sick young lad. 'I do not care what that stupid old drunkard says. I will not let you succumb. Do you hear me?'

Turlough struggled to open his eyes again and Mary placed a clean wet cloth across them.

'Bridget?' he murmured.

'You must not move,' Mary told him. 'Save your strength. The fight is not over. If you keep opening your eyes, the poison will get under the eyelids and you will risk losing your sight.'

The young man opened his mouth slightly and Mary went to the table to pick up a jug of cool water. When she returned she lifted his head and placed the jug to his dry, cracked lips. Turlough drank deeply and then lay back down again. The effort had exhausted him almost completely.

'Have you been dreaming?' Mary asked and the young man sighed as to indicate he had. 'Do not take much notice of your dreams. I remember how confused I was when the sickness hit me. I suffered nightmares all the time and could find no peace in my rest. Though I slept heavily, I was sure I was awake and wandering through the world.'

Once again the lad heaved a sigh but he could make no other sound. The inside of his mouth had become a mass of infected sores. To move his tongue was extremely painful.

'You have asked for Bridget many times in the last week,' Mary said softly. 'She must be very dear to you.'

Turlough coughed and tried to nod.

'Sleep now as best you can,' she soothed. 'I will sit by you through the night and wash your face. If you need anything, I will be here.'

Turlough made one last effort to open his eyes. Through a blur of pain he could just focus on the face of the young woman who sat at his side. She smiled back at him, though her features were etched with worry. The suffering boy tried to smile back but could not, so he closed his eyes and slept.

Turlough survived that night, though Mary despaired for him more than once before dawn. The next day he seemed a little better and slept soundly without any moans or sighs.

Within a few days it was obvious the lad was regaining his strength. The sores were beginning to heal and there were no fresh infections breaking out. But it took three weeks before the last of the ugly wounds began to disappear.

Some days the boy slept solidly without waking at all. At other times he lay in bed awake, absolutely silent, his eyes bandaged tight against the light. As he began to gain strength Mary tried to coax him into speaking. At first she would make passing comments about the weather or the gossip around Ballyfarnon. She understood that the lad was probably in great fear of losing his eyesight.

It took her many attempts to get any manner of reply out of him. But when he had begun to relax in her company they would regularly sit together through the middle of the night. They would speak of all manner of things until Turlough fell asleep completely exhausted.

Mary took to sleeping during the day or catching a few hours' rest by the bedside in the early hours of the morning. Her patient's skin still needed to be washed and his eyes were slow to show any sign of improvement. Following the doctor's advice she bathed and bandaged them each day.

Mrs MacDermot made sure the nurse was fed and that she had a bed in the big house. But Mary never slept in it. She stayed constantly by Turlough's side, only leaving the cottage to talk with her grandmother or to relieve herself. She even took her meals at the table in the blacksmith's home.

In time the sores around Turlough's eyes began to dry out. The doctor ordered that under no circumstances was the lad to be allowed to open the lids. Lindsay expressed the hope that the eyes would not be damaged and would, with rest, heal themselves.

One morning, eight weeks after young Turlough O'Carolan had sat on the hill watching for English dragoons, Doctor Lindsay visited the lad for the last time.

'It is a miracle,' the doctor gushed as he sat down at the end of the bed. His breath stank of liquor. 'A bloody miracle,' he repeated in awe. 'Praise God for His infinite mercy. And bless the learned gentleman who taught me my skill. I told you that you would be better off without the whiskey, lad. You were wise to heed my words. The Lord has rewarded you for your determination to eschew the Devil's potion.'

Mary coughed to cover a giggle. She had been giving her patient a small cupful of liquor every day for weeks. And it was obvious the good doctor had tasted the spirit more than once already that morning. Turlough smiled but Lindsay did not guess why.

'Now we will see whether my knowledge of the healing craft has saved your sight,' Doctor Lindsay told him as he leaned over the bed to unwrap the bandages. 'Keep your eyes shut for the moment. The light may be too much for you at first.'

When all the cloth was removed from around the lad's head, the doctor tossed it on the floor. 'Make sure you burn that,' he told Mary.

Lindsay brushed away a little dried mucus from the lashes and then touched the corners of each eye. He hummed to himself in satisfaction at what he observed.

'You may open them up now,' Lindsay advised. 'But slowly.'

Tentatively the lad lifted his eyelids. The doctor peered closer, a smile on his face. In a few seconds Turlough's eyes were moving and he was blinking.

'What did I tell you? A bloody miracle!' the doctor cried triumphantly, turning to Mary. He did not stop congratulating himself until he felt a hand on his sleeve, tugging hard.

'I cannot see anything,' Turlough murmured anxiously. 'Everything is dark.'

Lindsay leaned in close to get a better look. First he gingerly lifted the right eyelid and then the left. Next he retrieved a magnifying glass from his bag and held it close to each eye so that he could observe them both in detail.

'The eyes have healed,' Lindsay stated solemnly, 'but new skin has covered the pupils entirely and blocked out all light.' He put a hand on Turlough's shoulder. 'I am sorry, lad,' he said sincerely. 'There is nothing I can do. There is no cure for this. Your eyes are useless.'

Mary took Turlough's hand and squeezed it hard.

The doctor, his face flushed with embarrassment at having raised the boy's hopes so, packed his glass away. 'At least your face and body are not badly scarred. You can thank the diligence of your nurse for that mercy. It's not that bad.' But he was not convinced by his own words. He put on his coat in silence, reaching into his pocket to fondle the little bottle, reassured that he could take a swig as soon as he was outside.

After the doctor had gone, Mary and Turlough sat for a long time together clutching hands. They neither moved nor spoke until much later when the room was dark. Then Mary got up and lit a candle. She went to the cupboard and poured out two generous cups of whiskey.

'Will you have a drink with me, Turlough?'

'I will,' he replied in a hoarse, defeated voice.

She brought the cups over to the bed and placed one in his hand. Then they poured the whiskey down their throats as if they had not had a drink in years.

'I was looking forward to seeing you,' the lad whispered. 'I imagine you to be wearing a grey servant's dress.' The boy reached out to touch her sleeve. 'The material is coarse like linen. And to me it has the colour grey about it.'

'It is grey,' she told him gently. 'How did you guess?'

'I have only ever seen this dress in my imagination. Yet I

know what colour it is,' he laughed. But the humour dropped away from him quickly.

'Tomorrow I will be getting you up out of bed,' Mary told him. 'It is time to start building up the strength in your legs again.'

'I'll need another whiskey then if I am to be back at work so soon,' Turlough replied. Mary got up and brought the bottle back with her to the bedside and together they finished it.

It was another two weeks before the lad had regained the strength to walk more than a few steps at a time. Even then he could not do so without an arm to lean on. Each day Mary led him to the edge of the fields and then back to sit by the fire in the cottage.

Turlough spoke seldom and even when he did he said only a few words. The shock of losing his sight had been so great that nothing seemed to cheer him at all. Mary tried to coax conversation out of him but to no avail. At the end of the day he was often sullen and angry, prone to flares of temper and never more content than when he was left alone. At night he begged his nurse to leave him by himself and she took to sleeping in the bed Mrs MacDermot had set aside for her in the big house.

But Mary missed their late-night conversations and sometimes crossed the courtyard after dark or in the early hours of the morning to check on the lad who had become her friend. One night as she passed by the cottage she heard Turlough sobbing and so she knocked gently on the door.

'Turlough, are you feeling ill?'

There was no answer.

'Turlough, may I come in?'

There was not a sound.

'Turlough, let me sit with you for a while.'

Still there was no acknowledgement from the lad. Finally Mary pushed the door open and peered into the darkness. She could not see anything inside the cottage and it struck her that this was how Turlough would always view the world.

'Turlough?'

'You may come in,' the lad said grudgingly.

Mary made her way to the bedside without lighting a candle. She sat down, found his hand and held it for a long time in silence.

'I understand how you must feel,' she said eventually.

'No, you don't!' the lad snapped, his voice full of bitterness. 'Don't try to soothe me. It will not work.'

'I am sorry,' Mary whispered, taken aback. 'I'll go back to bed and leave you.'

Turlough coughed.

'It's all right,' the lad murmured, squeezing her hand in remorse. 'You can stay if you want. I shouldn't be angry at you. I am truly grateful for all that you have done. You have looked after me so well. I am sorry for treating you so harshly.'

'Don't fret,' the young woman replied softly as she took his head and cradled it in her arms.

'I have a great sadness in me,' Turlough said lowly.

'Tell me about it,' Mary whispered.

'There is a girl,' he began. 'I care so much for her. I am sure I love her with all my heart.'

Mary hugged the boy's head and brushed the hair from his face. Then she noticed her heart was beating fast and she moved away from him, embarrassed.

'I had the thought that this girl cared the same way for me.'

'How do you know that she doesn't love you as much as you love her?' Mary blushed.

'Perhaps there was a chance for us to be together once,' the lad said solemnly. 'A slim chance, granted, with me nothing but the son of a blacksmith.'

'Perhaps there is still a chance.'

'If I was a whole man. If I had my sight. But I am blinded. I am useless. I will never be able to live without the help of others.'

'Which of us can?' Mary pointed out. 'We all rely on the goodwill of our neighbours.'

'But I will never have any of the things I dreamed of,' he protested.

'What things?'

'I had it in my mind to become a harper and make great music for the pleasure of this woman.'

'Blindness does not preclude you from becoming a harper, though you are a little old to be starting at the music.'

'I had no sense of music before I was ill. What chance do I have of getting any skill if I cannot see the strings?'

'I have met many blind harpers, Turlough O'Carolan, and most of them never had the benefit of eyesight. At least you have some memory of the world. You will be able to compose melodies with those memories in your mind.'

'What sort of a woman could love a man who cannot find his way around without an arm to lean on?'

'I know a few women who would not flinch at such a man,' she replied with a smile. 'I also know many husbands who have the full use of their eyes yet are blind to the thoughts, desires and feelings of their wives. And at least if you are blind you cannot be accused of having a roving eye. That quality alone is a rare thing in a man.'

Turlough laughed a little at the joke but his mirth soon melted away. There was a dark cloud gathered over his mind which no laughter would dispel.

'You are a very handsome young lad,' Mary told him. 'And you have a good heart. You may be surprised to find that this woman perhaps feels very deeply for you. And that she will not think any differently of you even though you are blinded.'

'It was my idea to learn the harp to impress her,' the boy admitted. 'I thought it was the only way to win her affection.'

'When it is won in such a manner, affection cannot live long,' Mary sighed. 'Much better that the woman love you for your good nature and your kind heart, not the tricks you can perform. Clever tricks soon become tedious.'

'I'll never see her again,' the boy sobbed gently.

Mary stroked his troubled forehead and frowned. She had nursed a secret hope that Turlough was speaking about her. Now she suddenly recalled that during the worst of his sickness he had asked for someone named Bridget.

'You will always see her in your heart,' Mary offered, voice faltering.

'I am a fool to love her so much,' Turlough cursed. 'Bridget Cruise has a haughty manner. She is selfish and cruel. But she has a way with her teasing that is so enthralling that I have been enchanted by her. I will never see her again and she will never look on me either. She would not have married me when I was but the son of a blacksmith. Now I am the blind son of a blacksmith my heart will be broken forever.'

Mary could not say anything. She bit her tongue, held her thoughts close and thanked Heaven that Turlough could not see the tears gathering to roll down her cheeks.

'What will I do, Mary?' the lad asked her. 'I am so sad and angry that this terrible fate has befallen me. Have you ever had your heart broken?'

'I have, my friend,' she whispered. 'I have.' Mary wiped the tears away with her sleeve and the two of them sat for a long while in silence.

'Mrs MacDermot wants you to move into the big house in the morning,' Mary told the lad before she left to go back to bed. 'You will have the room next to mine. Mrs MacDermot has been very generous. Now that the sickness is past, people will be able to visit you.'

Turlough nodded, half asleep, and Mary left as quietly as she could.

The next day the lad was moved into a room in the servants' quarters of the big house. All the serving folk gathered in the kitchen to share hot oatcakes and sip real Indian tea from the Far East, supplied for the occasion from Mrs MacDermot's private stores.

The lady sat in the kitchen with her servants, relieved to see that Turlough's face was not badly scarred and genuinely overjoyed that he had returned to them at last, though he was withdrawn and unresponsive.

When the tea had all been finished and the oatcakes were gone there was a strained silence in the room. Turlough wondered what was going on. He could hear whispers and the shuffling of chairs.

'Where is my father?' he asked when he could stand the quiet no longer.

Mrs McDermot coughed loudly. 'That's enough excitement for one day,' she declared. 'Off to bed with you now and take your rest. Most of these folk have got work to be going on with and you are keeping them from it.'

The lady turned to the butler's assistant. 'William, take Turlough up to the room we have prepared for him.'

The servant nodded and silently helped the lad to his feet. When they were gone the lady and the rest of the servants sat in absolute silence for a long while.

'You must tell him,' Mary said finally as she rose from her seat.

'Yes, I must,' Mrs MacDermot replied. But it was not until after dinner that evening that she knocked on the door to Turlough's room and let herself in.

The boy was lying across the bed in the dark.

'Turlough,' Mrs MacDermot began, 'are you feeling well this evening?'

He did not stir.

'Turlough, I know you are awake. Mary was in here five minutes ago. I heard the two of you speaking some foolishness at the top of your voices.'

The young man breathed deeply but said nothing.

'Turlough, you cannot stay here indefinitely,' the lady went on. 'This room belongs to William O'Flynn. He has graciously consented to give it up to you until some other arrangements can be made. I am sorry to say that the estate cannot support an idle pair of hands. And it would not do for you to while your life away here without any purpose.'

This caught Turlough's attention and he sat up to listen. He had expected he would be allowed to live close by his father as long as he wished.

'Where will you send me?' the boy asked.

'For a while I thought to give you into the care of my eldest brother in Dublin,' she explained. 'He manages a house for folk who have been blinded by the pox.'

'I have never been to Dublin,' Turlough told the lady. 'I would have liked to have seen the city.' Then he laughed harshly to himself. 'When I had my eyesight, I probably never would have had the chance to travel anywhere. Now that I cannot appreciate the wondrous sights of the city I will be sent to live in Dublin against my will. It is a strange fate I have.'

'If you really don't want to go to my brother's house I will try to make other arrangements,' Mrs MacDermot offered. 'But the times are hard and we are pressed to feed everyone on the estate as it is. Ballyfarnon is not a wealthy town and there are many folk who need our assistance.'

'I understand, my lady.'

'I have given the matter much thought over the last week,' she continued. 'I don't want to send you away. I really don't think it would be beneficial for you at this time to be shifted too far from those who care about you. And I have listened to the views of my friends and neighbours.'

'And what does my father say?' the lad asked.

'Turlough,' Mrs MacDermot breathed, taking his hand, 'I decided to keep something from you while you were ill. I thought that the news would distress you and hamper your recovery.'

'What are you talking about?'

'It is my sad duty to inform you,' she went on with a deep breath, 'that your father was struck down with the pox a few days after you were. He was a strong man and he put up a brave fight. But in the end he succumbed. We buried him alongside your mother in the churchyard at Ballyfarnon.'

Turlough swallowed hard as the shock hit him. 'You had no right to keep this from me,' he stated after a few moments.

'I thought it was for the best. I am sorry if it was the wrong thing to do. Please forgive me.'

'Now I am alone as well as blind.'

'Your father is at peace now,' Mrs MacDermot soothed, placing a hand on his shoulder. 'No-one can tell who will be taken by the plague and who will be spared.'

'I would have been better off if it had taken me,' Turlough replied with bitterness. 'What use am I to anyone like this?'

'Others have suffered from this pestilence and they are not cursing their luck at being spared.'

'How many others have found themselves in my position?'

'Too many,' the lady sighed. 'The Galar-breac struck this parish with a terrible vengeance. There are many orphans in Ballyfarnon now and you are not the only one to have been blinded.'

Turlough fell silent and pulled away from Mrs MacDermot's reach.

'Shall I leave you alone for a while?'

The lad did not answer.

'Turlough?'

'I do not want to speak with you any more,' he replied in a whisper. 'I have heard enough for one day. I do not want to speak with anyone ever again.'

'I understand how you must feel,' Mrs MacDermot consoled him. 'You must be very confused by all that has happened to you.'

'How would you know?' the lad snapped. He instantly regretted the harshness of his tone but it was too late to take the words back.

'I will allow you your grief,' the lady told him. 'You are entitled to it. But I will not let you wallow in your misery. I will not allow you to withdraw yourself from the cheering company of all those in this household who care for you.'

'They do not care. They hardly spoke a word to me today.'

'It is you who have not been speaking to anyone, Turlough,' the lady rebuked him. 'Apart from Mary. But she has a way with you, that is certain. You sat in the corner of the kitchen today feeling sorry for yourself, refusing to pass even the simplest pleasantries with those who love you and wish you only the best.'

The lady moved to sit on the end of the bed.

'My lad,' she went on, 'I'll wager that you have not even had the decency to properly thank the young woman who saved your life.'

'What do you mean?'

'If it had not been for Mary taking the time to sit with you through your illness, to bathe your sores and mop your brow, to ensure you were fed and clean, you would not have lived at all. I know of folk who lost the use of their hands, arms or legs after the pox struck them down. You have still got your limbs, your handsome features and the full use of your wits. It is only your eyesight that is damaged.'

The lad dropped his head in remorse, beginning to understand that he had been thinking only of himself for some time. But then Bridget came into his thoughts again.

'What use am I to anyone like this?' Turlough whispered.

'Squire Crilly visited me the other day,' Mrs MacDermot said, seemingly changing the subject. 'He has had a guest staying with him these past two months. She is an old woman known as Mhaire Dhall. She is a very famous and talented harper. In her time she was renowned throughout the kingdom. She once played before His Majesty the late King Charles who was a great patron of the arts. And as you may have guessed from her name, she too is blind and has been since birth. Young Mary, your nurse, is her grand-daughter.'

'Mary's grandmother is a harper?'

'Yes, Turlough. Squire Crilly tells me you once expressed to him an interest in learning the harp. Is that true?'

'It is.'

'And the squire tells me that he believes you would be a good student.'

'How can I play without eyes to see the strings?'

'Old Mhaire manages quite well, as do many harpers of the old tradition. I am told it is actually much easier to play the instrument without the distraction of eyesight. And I am afraid there are not many other opportunities open to you for making a living,' the lady sighed.

'It is an honourable profession. There are still a number of travelling harpers who call in at the big houses and perform for their meals and a place to sleep. Some of them live quite well. You may not always be able to rely on the goodwill of the MacDermots. Times are changing and the English are talking about seizing Catholic lands in Ireland. You will need a profession to carry you through life.'

'And I might as well be a harper,' Turlough shrugged, 'as anything else.'

'As it happens, you are very fortunate indeed,' Mrs Mac-Dermot went on. 'Mhaire is too old to travel now and her grand-daughter is at the age when she should be thinking of finding herself a husband or securing herself a good position in a wealthy household. So it is that the best teacher in all Ireland will be staying at the Crilly residence.'

Turlough said nothing, only turned his face away.

'Turlough, I cannot keep you here,' Mrs MacDermot told him gently. 'Rumours abound of imminent war. Some folk say that the new king, William, is making ready to bring his army to Ireland. King James is mustering his forces in France. Ireland will be the battlefield, just as it was less than a generation ago in the time of Cromwell. And the result will likely be the same as it was then—famine and destruction.'

'I would not wish to be a burden to you,' Turlough cut in, 'especially in such difficult times.'

'Squire Crilly has made a suggestion,' Mrs MacDermot said, 'and a very generous suggestion it is too. He has offered to feed and clothe you and to give you a place to stay in his household if I will contribute something to your education at the harp.'

Turlough lifted his head.

'Indeed, there are folk who say that you are too old to learn. Even old Mhaire does not hold much hope that you will be a great musician. But I believe it is a fine solution to the situation.'

'I will live with Squire Crilly?'

'You will,' Mrs MacDermot replied. 'And Mary will continue

to take care of you until you are able to fend for yourself. Her grandmother, who is very old and nearing the end of her days, will have a warm place to sleep in Squire Crilly's house and some money in her pocket besides. She tells me it will take three years or more for you to become proficient at the instrument. I have forwarded the squire a sum which will guarantee you have at least that much time with your teacher.'

'It is all settled then?'

'It is,' the lady confirmed. 'If you are agreeable. Remember, I only want what is best for you, Turlough. But there are thirty folk living on the estate and I must consider the needs and well-being of each of them. At least you will have a greater degree of independence than you would have in a house in Dublin. You will be able to decide your own destiny. That is more than can be said for most folk in these troubled times.'

She sighed wearily. 'You must look on this change in your life not as a misfortune but as a gift. Squire Crilly, Mhaire Dhall and myself are willing to help you get started, but in the end it is up to you to view your affliction either as an opportunity or as a disaster. I understand that at the moment your life seems bleak and cruel, but in time you may feel differently.'

'Perhaps you are right,' the lad offered and he felt his face blushing. 'I am grateful for all your help. I know you have only my interests at heart. I will try my best to learn the harp and make a life for myself.'

'You are still a handsome young man, Turlough. You are lucky that the pox did not scar your features as it did your eyes. One day you will find yourself a fine woman and you will have children of your own. If you work hard at the harp, you will not have any trouble feeding your family. I asked Tómas Burcá the harp maker to find you a small lap harp for your first instrument. He has heard of your plight and has kindly offered to give you an old instrument which needs some repairs. It should be ready in a month or so.'

'A harp of my own?'

'It will not be a grand instrument such as the one David

Murphy carries. It is quite battered and Tómas would not have offered the instrument if he could have found a buyer for it. But it will be a beginning. When the harp is ready you will move into a room in Squire Crilly's household.'

'I will never forget your kindness.' Turlough raised a smile, suddenly understanding the extent of the lady's generosity.

Mrs MacDermot stood up and walked briskly to the door. She opened it and for a second looked back at the young man.

'In time I hope you will come to understand that everything that happens in life is for the best,' she told him. 'It may seem at first that the obstacles put in front of us are too great to overcome. But life has a way of steering us onto the path we thought it impossible to take, and we must all learn to look for opportunities where they are least expected. One day you may even come to bless this blindness which now seems such a burden.'

'Perhaps in time, my lady,' the lad replied doubtfully. 'Perhaps in time.'

'But you were going to tell the tale of SheeBeg SheeMor,' Edward protested and he felt his head spinning slightly as he spoke.

'Yes, I was,' old Hugh agreed. 'You are not a patient man. You have to know the whole story. There's no point in me telling you just little pieces of it here and there.'

'You should never have let him start,' Denis complained, turning his head toward Edward. 'We could be trapped here for days while he spins this yarn.'

'I have to be getting back to Dublin in the morning,' the young rebel insisted and he was suddenly conscious that his speech was very slurred and his tongue rather numb. 'But for now I must get to bed so that I may rise early and be on my way.'

'Every redcoat in the country will be out looking for you,' Hugh laughed. 'You've no chance of making it back to Dublin tomorrow. You're going to have to lie low for a few days.'

'I must be in Dublin on Thursday at the latest,' Edward said, frowning as he tried to remember why. 'There is something very important I have to do there.'

'What could be so important that you would forsake a cup or two of whiskey from the stills of old Hugh?' Denis asked in shock.

Edward's frown deepened. The young rebel was feeling quite strange now. The light from the fire seemed much brighter and warmer than it had earlier. His ears seemed still to be ringing from the sound of the harp. And his mouth was unusually dry.

Suddenly he remembered what he had to do in Dublin on Thursday.

'I have to attend a tea party my father is giving for the anniversary of the rising of the American rebels.'

'You'll be attending your own hanging if you leave the safety of my cottage in the morning,' the distiller reminded him sternly. 'What sort of a fool would waltz right into the preparations for his own execution? There are hundreds of soldiers out looking for you. You foolish boy. You wouldn't get two miles before the air was filled with lead and curses.'

'Where did I leave my pistols?' Edward asked, remembering that he had been carrying one when the soldiers began firing at him.

'One of them is lying safe in the middle of the stream,' Daniel laughed as he closed the door behind him.

'The other one is well hidden,' Hugh reassured him. 'A fine piece of workmanship, Daniel tells me. Worth ten pounds at least. Do not fear. It is safe and will be returned to you in due course.'

Then the distiller addressed his grandson. 'Was it redcoats I heard?'

'It was, Grandfather,' Daniel replied. 'Thirty grenadiers marching toward the garrison after scouring the hills all day. And a dozen Scottish dragoons on huge dapple greys who complained bitterly that they should be out looking for the killer of an English officer. I think they would like to congratulate you, Edward.'

'All that for Major D'Arcy?' Hugh asked. 'I did not realise he was so well liked.'

'The dragoons told me,' Daniel went on, 'that D'Arcy was

involved in some plot which was uncovered on account of his untimely death.'

'What sort of a plot?' the distiller snapped.

'The Scotsmen did not know,' the red-haired man said. 'They reckoned it was the nature of English officers to be engaged in plots and could not understand all the fuss. But they will be abroad tomorrow and there will be many more redcoats besides searching for our young hero.'

'Indeed he is a hero,' the old distiller sighed with mock admiration. 'It is almost as if fate led him into our hands.'

'How do you mean?' Daniel asked.

'That his rash act in murdering Major D'Arcy should uncover a plot.'

'We do not know what sort of plot,' Daniel noted.

'Indeed,' Hugh conceded. 'But how many plots can one English officer be involved in?'

'I see your point, Grandfather.'

'There's nothing for it,' the distiller decided. 'Young Edward must not be found here. We are risking drawing attention to ourselves if the soldiers come searching.'

'I am going to saddle a horse,' Mhairgead announced.

'Bide your time, Grand-daughter,' Hugh protested. 'We must come up with a good story to explain his presence here at the house in case the English should make inquiries.'

'He might pass for a cousin from Dublin,' Daniel suggested.

'But that does not give him an excuse to be visiting us, does it?' the distiller pointed out. 'If we had rich cousins in Dublin, would they visit us?'

'I suppose not,' the red-haired man shrugged.

'We could tell them that he is my betrothed,' Mhairgead offered.

'You are a wily one, like your mother,' Hugh laughed. 'You could have been an English officer yourself if you had been born a man.'

'I probably would have ended up as a whiskey distiller,' she quipped.

'That's the answer then,' Hugh decided. 'Edward Sutler of Dublin has come to ask for Mhairgead's hand in marriage and is staying a few days to celebrate. If he is recognised as Major D'Arcy's murderer, there can be no suspicion laid on this household. We know nothing of such matters.'

'A fine solution,' Daniel nodded. 'But wouldn't it be easier to toss him out and let him fend for himself?'

'I'll be ready to ride in half an hour,' Mhairgead informed her grandfather.

'No, no,' the distiller soothed hastily. 'There's no need for that. If Edward were arrested he might mention his sojourn in this house. That could prove uncomfortable for us. We don't want any suspicion laid on us for helping rebels.'

'What a bloody mess,' Denis said, shaking his head. 'Why don't you just blow his brains out and dump him in the stream? That would be an end to your worries.'

'That would be the beginning of your worries,' Mhairgead reminded Hugh. 'Add murder to the list of crimes, along with rebellion, trading arms, profiteering on government goods, illicit whiskey and communicating with the French. That is known as high treason, I believe.'

Hugh put both his hands up to his forehead and sighed deeply.

'She's right,' he conceded. 'Daniel should have knocked him on the head and put an end to it then and there. It is too late for that now.'

'Why?' the red-haired man asked.

'Don't you listen?' Hugh snapped. 'Mhairgead has an eye for the fellow.'

'Mother of God!' Daniel spat. 'And you would betray your own family for that pale-skinned piece of town flesh?'

'I would,' Mhairgead assured her brother. 'For he's better than anything I'll find around these parts. He has money. He has no taste for the drink.'

'That I will concede,' Daniel said as he looked at Edward slumped in his chair.

'And he has a passion about him,' she went on. 'It may be a misguided passion at the moment, but I am sure I can redirect it, given time.'

'I wouldn't doubt you could redirect the moon and stars given time,' Hugh grumbled.

The old distiller turned his head to the young rebel. 'Did you hear that, young Edward?'

'What?' The young man shook his head and sat up when he heard his name.

'Welcome into the Connor family, my lad,' the distiller enthused. 'Now, will you join us in a drink?'

'I have to go to sleep,' Edward stammered, tripping over his tongue. He shook his head again for a few moments but had to stop when the floor began to heave under him. He held his face in his hands until the sensation ceased. Then for the first time he noticed his mouth was tingling and raw. He touched his tongue with the tips of his fingers.

'I must bid you all goodnight,' Edward protested, holding out a hand to Hugh. It was a little while before he realised the old man had no idea he wanted to shake hands, so he turned to Daniel and said slowly, trying to master his thick tongue, 'Thank you for saving my life.' He reached out to touch the tall man on the arm in a friendly manner. 'One day I hope you will be able to do it again.'

'Given your propensity for landing yourself in difficult situations,' Daniel smiled, 'I think that is very likely.'

Edward noticed Mhairgead leaning against the door and giggling.

'And thank you to the lovely lady of the house,' the young rebel went on, 'the grand-daughter of this most excellent host,' he swept his arms out in a wide arc to encompass everyone in the room, 'Mhairgead of the shining eyes.'

'A toast to Mhairgead,' Denis declared.

'To Mhairgead!' Edward answered immediately and took another drink.

Everyone in the room sat perfectly still. Those who had their eyesight watched the young man take a great mouthful of drink. Those who did not listened intently. But the rebel did not notice. He was too far gone to care.

As soon as Edward had swallowed the contents of the cup, Daniel filled it yet again.

'Now I really must go to bed,' the young man reasoned. He could feel the veil of drunkenness descending upon him like a thick black cloud.

'Nonsense!' Hugh cried. 'The evening is young. It's still light outside.'

Edward frowned again and moved to peer out through the window for confirmation, but the wooden shutters were closed tight. He was so drunk by this time that it never crossed his mind to ask how an old blind man would know whether it was day or night outside.

'Nevertheless, I must retire,' the rebel mumbled, waving his hand in the air again. 'I have had quite a day.'

'And so you should be celebrating,' Denis told him. 'It's not every day one gets an opportunity to strike for Ireland's freedom.'

'To Ireland's freedom!' Edward declared. Then raised his cup and solemnly drank from it in honour of the cause.

When the rebel had downed this toast, Daniel tried to fill his cup again but Edward held his fingers over the top to stop him.

'That is enough for me, I think,' the young man stated. 'I don't feel right about taking so much drink from you after all the trouble I've caused.'

'It was only a little trouble,' Hugh admonished. 'And tomorrow you will surely make amends for the harm you've done.'

The old man spoke so sweetly that Edward frowned in confusion. He was not quite sure whether he was being threatened.

'Your stories are grand, if a little exaggerated,' the young man told his host magnanimously. 'Though I am sure there is an element of truth buried deep within them. It has been very entertaining sitting here with you rustic folk. It is simple country peasants like yourselves who make the cause of liberty worth fighting for.'

'That is very gracious of you, Master Edward,' the distiller replied in a monotone.

'Indeed,' the rebel went on, oblivious, 'I think if I had any more of your fine whiskey to drink I would no longer question that the Faerie folk do indeed exist.'

'The beginning of wisdom is when a man realises the extent of his ignorance,' Denis hummed.

'How true,' Edward said, feeling the full force of the profundity of that statement. He sat back and swayed on his chair, a blank look on his face.

'Would one more drink hurt you?' Hugh asked gently. 'I would be honoured if you would take a drop with me and listen to the part of the tale about SheeBeg SheeMor. I promise you that my grand-daughter will have you up bright and early if you still wish to be on the road to Dublin in the morning.'

'I must go home early tomorrow,' Edward nodded. 'No offence to your hospitality at all.'

'None taken,' Hugh replied. 'One more drink to prove beyond a doubt that you have enjoyed our company.'

Edward tried to think, but he found it very difficult to form any sort of coherent thoughts at all. In a few moments he was staring at the floor trying to remember how he had come to be here in the first place.

'Will you stay for one more drink, Master Edward?' Hugh pressed.

'I will,' the young rebel said without another moment's hesitation, for he could not remember the reason why he should stay sober.

Before he had the opportunity to change his mind, Daniel handed him a cup full to the brim with golden whiskey. The young rebel stared at the cup for a few seconds, unable to focus.

'Slainté!' Hugh declared.

'Slainté!' Denis repeated.

'Slant yer!' Edward muttered and took a mouthful of the liquor. He had always had great difficulty with the Irish language but now he reckoned he was having no trouble at all getting his mouth around the strange words. It must be the good influence of these two old men, he decided. Daniel filled Edward's cup surreptitiously while the young rebel was lost among his own thoughts.

'This is a fine jug,' the harper declared after taking a sip.

'I've been saving it for a special occasion,' Hugh whispered, leaning toward his old friend.

'And you think this might be a one, do you?' Denis asked, cocking his head in Edward's direction.

'Mhairgead seems to think so,' the distiller answered. 'She has had a hard time of things and deserves better. Perhaps he'll suit her nicely.'

'Very nicely,' Edward repeated, senseless to what the two old men were saying to each other.

'In any case, for the time being no other answer seems to be presenting itself,' Hugh shrugged.

'This whole affair has become unnecessarily complicated,' Denis agreed.

'It could be worse,' Daniel cut in. 'The redcoats might have turned up at the door.'

'I'm not so concerned about redcoats,' Hugh whispered to his grandson. 'It is Seamus Kelly and his compatriots I am worried about. What will I tell them?'

'I'm sure you'll think of something,' Daniel smiled as he shook his head. 'You always manage somehow.'

'May you always manage somehow,' Edward wished him.

'A toast, gentlemen,' Hugh offered, changing the subject. 'To the three sacred pastimes of old Ireland. Music, storytelling and whiskey.'

'Whiskey!' Edward cried as he downed another mouthful of the stuff.

Hugh and Denis took the tiniest sips from their cups, listening carefully to the young rebel.

Edward threw his head back as he drank down his liquor, reclining in his seat as he did so. When the cup had been drained of its last few drops, the young rebel found himself staring at the ceiling of the little cottage. It took several seconds for his eyes to focus but when they did he had to blink repeatedly. He simply did not believe what he saw.

High up in the rafters there were literally hundreds of gleaming brand-new muskets stretched from one beam to another. Alongside them there were pikes and long swords and the unmistakable shape of a small cannon with its carriage and wheels lying alongside.

When Edward realised he was staring at a huge arsenal of weapons, enough to arm a small force of soldiers, he put his hands to his eyes and rubbed hard. The young rebel teetered for a second on two legs of the stool, just long enough to whisper a blasphemous utterance. And then he fell backwards.

When he landed on the wooden floor of the cottage he bumped his head and had the wind knocked out of him. He struggled for a few moments but then the whiskey got the better of him and he rolled over and lay face down by the fire.

Mhairgead was at his side in a second, cradling his head in her arms.

'Well,' Hugh said cheerfully, 'I suppose it's time for bed then.'

'You are right,' Denis agreed. 'It's been a long day and I am not as young as I used to be.'

'Thank God!' the old distiller laughed and the harper giggled along with him.

'I'll play some more for you tomorrow if it pleases you,' Denis assured his host.

'I am sure that would be grand,' Hugh nodded. Then he turned to his grandson. 'You will take care of the lad, won't you?'

'Don't worry, Grandfather,' Daniel smiled. 'I'm sure he's safe in my sister's hands.'

'I wouldn't place any sort of wager on that!' Hugh retorted. 'I'd rather deal with the Devil himself than my grand-daughter.'

'Goodnight, Grandfather,' Mhairgead replied sweetly. 'Now get to bed.'

SEVEN

E dward opened his eyes for no more than a split second but it was enough for him to sense that there was something very strange happening to him. The world was utterly dark. Not just the sort of dark there is on a moonless night. This was the sort of darkness only experienced in the deepest parts of the earth.

And the air was stifling as well, tinged with a strange musty odour that reminded him of truffles, mould and moss.

And there was another aroma as well. Edward inhaled a deep breath trying to ascertain exactly what it was.

'It reminds me of freshly tilled soil,' he murmured and his voice sounded dull and lifeless to him within this confined place.

In that instant a fear gripped him that was more urgent and more real than the fear he had suffered when the redcoats were firing their musket balls at him. His heart beat loud and hard, thudding against his ribcage as if it were trying to escape the obviously doomed confines of his body.

Edward put his hand out and his fingers immediately rapped hard against a flat timber board only a few inches from his face. Panic really began to take hold of him now. In a flash he moved his hands out to either side of him. To his horror he found there were boards there also.

He was a prisoner. He was trapped in this box. A terrible

thought crossed his mind as the damp rawness of fresh earth enclosed him in a pungent cloak, wrapping tightly round him like a funeral shroud.

'They have buried me alive!' the young rebel gasped under his breath.

In horror he began punching the board above him.

'Let me out of this bloody coffin, you murdering bastards!' he screamed at the top of his lungs. 'You can't bury me and expect to get away with it!'

The box filled with dust from his violent outburst and Edward had to stop yelling to cough some of it out of his lungs. He wiped the grit out of his eyes and then fell silent again, waiting to hear if there was any reply. A few minutes passed but he heard no sound whatsoever.

He was done for, he told himself. All his money and his pistols were gone. He should have known better than to trust the old bastard.

His heart sank and he thought carefully, trying to remember what had happened the night before. But the last thing he could recall was old Hugh telling some tale about Turlough O'Carolan and the Faeries.

'Jesus,' he muttered. 'I was a fool to be so taken in by that rogue. They got me drunk, put me in this box and buried me. I'll never be found. I'm finished.'

He knew he should concentrate on finding a way out of this mess. But no obvious solution presented itself. So he began screaming again and he kept it up until he thought he heard a noise.

Somewhere above him he could just make out a few muffled words in Irish which of course meant nothing to him. Edward realised he was under the floorboards of the house. At least he wasn't buried in a field somewhere.

'I know you're up there, you bloody villains!' he cried at the top of his voice. 'Let me out!'

The boards immediately above his face suddenly moved and bright light poured into the long box in which he was laid.

Edward squinted and put his hands over his face to stop the dirt falling in his eyes and mouth.

It only took a few moments for him to focus. But the light was behind his rescuer and he could not make out the features of the face looking down at him.

'Who are you?' Edward cried. 'Where am I?'

'It's Daniel,' a familiar voice said calmly. 'What's all the bloody row about then?'

Edward furrowed his brows in confusion. 'What am I doing in this box?'

'You must have been well away last night when you and the old boys finished drinking. Don't you remember?'

'Of course I don't remember!' Edward shouted. 'Your bloody grandfather got me drunk!'

'Sure he forced the whiskey down your throat he did,' Daniel sniggered. 'Calm down or you'll have every redcoat from here to Derry town dropping by to see what the fuss is about.'

Edward shook his head, feeling a little silly all of a sudden. He did not recall very much about the previous evening at all. In fact his head ached so badly he was having trouble putting words together.

'After you fell off your chair,' Daniel explained, 'Grandfather decided it was time for everyone to go to bed. Just as Mhairgead was pulling the warm blankets around your head, we heard the sound of men coming up the path. It was a dozen redcoats searching the country round for one Edward Sutler, late of Dublin, accused of murder and suspected of being a rebel leader.'

Edward sat up quickly. The sudden move made his head ache sharply and he had to put a hand to his forehead to still the pain.

'Jesus!' he hissed. 'Redcoats?'

The young man's stomach growled deeply and he was very dizzy. In a few seconds he had stopped worrying about the soldiers and was thoroughly engaged in feeling extremely ill.

'I think Grandfather would have turned you over but for the fact that you have not heard all of his stories,' Daniel smiled.

'If I were you,' he whispered, leaning in close, 'I would continue to be an appreciative listener. Do you take my meaning?'

Edward nodded, instantly regretted moving his head at all, and then mumbled as best he could, 'I think I understand.'

'Then you had best get up and have yourself some broth,' Daniel told him as he grasped the young rebel by the wrists and pulled him up out of the box.

In the next instant Edward found himself standing in the middle of the room. Pretty stars danced before his eyes and he felt his face go cold as it drained of blood. He had to put a hand to his mouth as he felt his stomach turn again. Then a great belch of air escaped his guts and he groaned.

Daniel sat Edward down on the same stool he had occupied the previous evening, then carefully replaced the boards over the hole in the floor and spread the rushes about to cover any evidence of the secret place.

'We thought this was the best spot to hide you,' Daniel explained. 'It's where we usually keep an emergency supply of whiskey in case the gauger men have the scent for it. I hope it wasn't too uncomfortable.'

Edward groaned and felt his stomach turn again. Then a gust of air escaped from his bowels with such force that he sat up straight and gasped.

'Christ, man!' Daniel exclaimed, holding a hand over his nose. 'That's not Mhairgead's broth did that to you,' he added, grimacing.

'I think I am going to be sick.' Edward swallowed hard.

'You'll find the dung heap out through that door,' Daniel advised, seeing the paleness of Edward's face.

The young rebel bowed his head in thanks, not daring to speak in case his bowels erupted in midsentence. In a few moments he was out the door and leaning over the dung pile, retching up the entire contents of his stomach.

A long while later he staggered back to the house and sat down by the fire, totally drained. He clutched his head in one hand and his aching belly in the other.

'I'll never drink again as long as I live,' he vowed, breathing deeply and wiping the sweat from his brow.

'Surely you'll have a drop of this,' Mhairgead said with a smile, her eyes flashing with mischief. 'It's pure water from the stream and it'll do you the world of good.'

She handed the young man a wooden cup. He sniffed the contents warily and only when he was satisfied that there was no whiskey in the vessel did he gulp the contents down.

'Don't feel too bad about those two old buggers getting the better of you,' the woman said softly, putting an arm about his shoulders. 'I know plenty of grown men who would have hit the floor long before you did. Few folk can keep up with Grand-father once he sets his mind to drinking. You should be proud of yourself for coming so close to outlasting him.'

'Exactly how close did I come?'

'Very close indeed. A matter of only a few drinks, I would say.'

'Mother of God!' the young rebel groaned and put his head in his hands.

'Will you take some broth, Edward?' Mhairgead said, turning to pick up a bowl of the steaming liquid from the table. The young man looked up as soon as he smelled the thick soup. He placed his nose over it, testing his stomach against the aroma for a few seconds. Finally he reached out to take the bowl but just then his guts began to churn again. The next thing he knew he was making rapidly for the door.

Throughout the rest of the morning Edward struggled back and forth to the dung heap, finally succumbing to the exhaustion of the battle shortly after midday. He saw no sign of Hugh and assumed the old man was off attending to his still. Mhairgead put the young rebel to bed close by the fire and tucked the covers up around his head. Then he slept soundly all afternoon.

The room was almost completely dark when Edward woke and he lay on his side for a while, looking at the glowing embers. Then he heard the sound of several voices speaking loudly outside the house. His first thought was that the soldiers had come for him. His second thought was that it might be better for him to surrender rather than risk another night with old Hugh. In the end he lay absolutely still because he couldn't bring himself to move.

Edward pulled the covers up over his face as if that could keep him safe from danger. He listened carefully but the men were speaking Irish and he could only understand a few phrases in that tongue, though he knew many folk who spoke it in their daily lives.

Then Edward thought he caught Major D'Arcy's name mentioned a few times followed by his own, and his heart raced a little faster. The conversation outside went on and on and D'Arcy's name was mentioned again and again. Eventually it dawned on Edward that English soldiers would be unlikely to be able to speak Irish. Then his curiosity got the better of his common sense and he decided to find out what was going on. If old Hugh was going to turn him over to the soldiers, it would be better to face it like a man.

Edward took three deep breaths to still his nerve. Then he threw the covers off and strode across the room. He swung open the wooden door and stepped out into the dusk. Conversation immediately ceased and all eyes turned to him.

Three strangers sat on barrels in a courtyard bounded by the cluster of four houses. They faced old Hugh and Daniel who were seated on low three-legged stools. Each of the three strangers immediately scowled maliciously. Daniel whispered a few words to his grandfather.

'Edward Sutler,' Hugh began, 'I would like you to meet Seamus Kelly, Connor O'Grady and Teeg Malley.'

The three men nodded but their expressions remained full of animosity.

'These gentlemen have come to look for you, Edward,' Hugh explained. 'It seems your reputation has preceded you. They claim you owe them money.'

Edward shook his head carefully to clear it and thanked God the pain was bearable after his sleep.

'I have never seen these men before in my life,' the young man protested. 'I know of no debt I might have incurred to them.'

'You were responsible for the death of Major D'Arcy?' the man called Seamus asked in a thick country accent.

'I am the man who killed D'Arcy,' Edward admitted, confused.

Seamus laughed as if he didn't believe it. 'What do you know of the major?' he asked, his voice full of menace.

'He was a bloody tyrant and the country is better off without him.'

'Are you an English agent?' Seamus pressed.

'Now, Seamus,' Hugh cut in, 'we agreed there'd be none of that talk.'

Seamus scowled. 'You're right, Hugh. He hasn't the guts for it.'

Then he turned to look Edward squarely in the eye. 'D'Arcy owed me twenty pounds for tobacco he bought for his officers.'

'I am owed forty pounds for cloth with which he outfitted his soldiers,' Connor O'Grady piped up.

'And I claim ten pounds for lead shot which the major purchased a month ago,' Teeg Malley added. 'I was promised payment in thirty days.'

'How are you going to settle with us?' Seamus demanded.

'I sympathise with you all,' Edward began, 'but surely Major D'Arcy's debts are none of my concern, gentlemen.'

'They most certainly are,' Seamus insisted. 'I have a family to feed and a business to run, as do my friends here. The army will not return the goods we supplied to the late major nor will it honour any receipt signed by him. They say he did not keep the books very well and that he is suspected of dealing with rebels. You have robbed us of our income as surely as if you had held a pistol to our heads and demanded the gold from us.'

'D'Arcy was no rebel,' Edward scoffed, then he noticed the dour expressions of all the men in front of him. 'Was he?'

'That's what the army is saying,' Hugh replied. 'It may be

just an excuse for not settling the accounts, but I suspect they have good grounds for the accusation.'

'Where's our money?' Seamus pressed.

'This is a matter between yourselves and the garrison commander,' the young rebel protested. 'With all due respect for your injured feelings, I must insist this has nothing to do with me.'

'You murdered D'Arcy,' Connor O'Grady growled, 'so you should settle his debts.'

'I don't understand where you get the impression that I am responsible for the major's financial problems.'

'He didn't have any financial problems till you shot him dead,' Seamus stated, raising his voice slightly.

'Now his family are his only beneficiaries,' Hugh explained calmly. 'It would not be decent for honest merchants such as these gentlemen to claim payment from a woman so recently widowed.'

'Of course not,' Edward conceded. 'But shouldn't the army sort this out?'

'It seems the regiment has no record of the transactions in question,' Hugh explained. 'The major was not known for his clerical efficiency. Indeed, that may be the basis of Colonel Cumberland's suspicion as to D'Arcy's loyalty.'

'If there are no records,' Edward began, 'how do we know these men are telling the truth?'

'Do you doubt my word?' Seamus shouted and Edward stepped back behind Daniel.

'No, not at all,' the rebel stammered nervously.

'Bloody Dubliners, coming up here and interfering in matters which are no concern of theirs!' Seamus bellowed at the top of his voice. 'You'd be wise to mind your own bloody business, you stupid boy! Months of planning went into our enterprise and you come along and knock it all over, thinking you are doing us some sort of favour.'

'Now, Seamus,' Hugh intervened, 'we wouldn't want young Edward to think any of us were involved in anything untoward, would we?'

'Shut up, you foolish old drunkard,' Seamus snapped.

'I'm very sorry for the injury that's been done to you,' Edward began.

'Then when can we expect to see our money?' Seamus demanded.

'Where am I going to get seventy pounds?'

'You should have thought of that before you shot that poor man down in cold blood,' the tall man advised.

'He wasn't a poor man, he was a bloody tyrant!' Edward protested. 'He was but one of a legion of cruel Saxons who seek only to trample our native land and restrain our people in the iron bonds of slavery.'

The other men looked from one to another with raised eyebrows.

'He's talking Dublin rebel rubbish again, Daniel,' old Hugh said sadly. 'Take him back inside and make sure he lies down near the fire till the fit passes.'

His red-haired grandson grunted and took hold of Edward's elbow, but the young rebel pulled away from his grasp.

'I am perfectly well,' Edward insisted indignantly, struggling to steady himself. 'And I am sure we can sort this minor disagreement out with a little patience and understanding.'

'The major kept my family alive,' Seamus stated. 'If it weren't for the business he brought to me, my children would have starved long ago. Now it looks as though they will go without any food this winter. And it's all your fault, you foolish boy.'

'But he was an officer of the enemy! He was responsible for the deaths of many men and the imprisonment of countless others.'

'He was no enemy to those whose livelihoods depended on him,' Hugh commented. 'To most of those folk he was a saviour. He bought their goods when no-one else had the money to do so. And I have to say he may have held some rebel sympathies.'

'What?' Edward asked, horrified.

The old man smiled and shrugged his shoulders. 'I heard tell that he stole arms from the garrison and sold them to the rebels.'

'D'Arcy?' the rebel gasped. 'No! He was a bloody tyrant.'

'He might have seemed that way to some,' the distiller conceded. 'But it was all part of an elaborate ruse to put his superiors off the scent.'

'He wasn't a tyrant?' Edward stuttered.

Hugh shook his head.

'Nor a bloody murderer?'

'I fear that you were ill informed,' Hugh shrugged. 'If anything D'Arcy was a saint who was willing to risk his life, his career and his reputation for the cause of liberty which is so dear to your heart.'

'I don't believe it!'

'The sad thing is that he was so adept at covering his own tracks that he attracted your attention.'

'What have I done?' Edward put his hands to his face and covered his eyes in shame.

'Now the saviour of our parish has perished,' the distiller went on, 'and it is all your doing, young Master Edward.'

'Then he wasn't a murderer?'

'No,' Hugh replied bluntly. 'But you are.'

'This is a war,' the rebel pointed out defensively. 'A war for our liberty. There are bound to be casualties. And even if D'Arcy was sympathetic to the cause, he had been a soldier all his life. Are you trying to tell me that he never did wrong?'

'Murder is murder,' Hugh shrugged. 'I am sure many an English soldier has gone into battle and killed the enemy joyously because he thought his country had called him to the task. And so in those soldiers' minds it was the right and proper thing to do. Does that make it acceptable to kill another human being?'

Edward hung his head. He rubbed his eyes with the heels of his hands, thankful his host could not see how upset he was.

'Every man commits sin at some time in his life,' Hugh said gently. 'But given the opportunity, every man will probably also do some things that benefit his fellow human beings. Would you condemn a man for all his evil acts and not bring into balance the good he may have done? Besides, you must also ask yourself if you have a right to deal out the punishment.'

The young rebel sighed, seeing the point.

'D'Arcy was not compelled to trade with us for his supplies. He may have done so because of his alleged sympathies with the cause of Ireland's liberty. Whatever the reason, we all came to rely on one another over time.'

'If one of us had been murdered by the soldiers, D'Arcy would have seen to it that all debts were paid and our families compensated in some way,' Seamus added.

'But now there is no-one to make sure his debts are paid,' Hugh went on. 'The quartermaster of the barracks is a greedy man with no morals whatsoever. I have no doubt that he has destroyed the official invoices for the goods and pocketed the money that should have been paid to these gentlemen. He may have discovered some incriminating evidence which pointed to D'Arcy's treachery. All we can be certain of is that we have no recourse through the army.'

The young rebel swallowed hard and looked down at the ground. 'I think I understand how you must all feel,' he admitted.

'Very well then,' Hugh said cheerfully, 'that's settled. I am so glad you've decided to see some sense.'

'I beg your pardon?' Edward looked up sharply.

'Since you understand the plight of these poor men and their families, it will not be burdensome for you to settle all the debts in D'Arcy's name.'

'I don't have seventy pounds!' Edward cried.

'Ninety pounds,' Hugh corrected him. 'D'Arcy owed me ten and Philomena the cow was worth another ten.'

'I didn't shoot Philomena!'

'Indeed,' Hugh agreed, 'but there would have been no lead in the air that morning at all if you had not attracted the attention of the redcoats. If you had not shot the good major down in cold blood, or if you had chosen another valley in which to hide, my cow would still be alive. And she would still be giving me milk for my breakfast.'

Edward suddenly wished sincerely that he *had* chosen another valley in which to hide from the soldiers.

'How will you pay us if you don't have the money to hand?' Seamus grunted threateningly.

'I am sure we can come to some amicable solution to this vexing problem,' Hugh cut in, raising a hand in a gesture of peace. 'Give me a few days to consider all the circumstances and I will let you know my decision. You three have lost no less than I as a result of this boy's foolishness. But leave the young man here under my care for the time being until we can work something out.'

'I want my money,' Seamus growled.

'And so you shall have it,' Hugh told him. 'But you will not have it today. You can only get as much whiskey out of a jug as you can put in it. The young man obviously has no money on him. Perhaps we should consider writing a letter to his father in Dublin.'

'No!' Edward protested, knowing what his stern father's reaction would be. 'Not that. I'll find a way to repay you all. I promise.'

'There you have it, gentlemen,' Hugh sighed, satisfied. 'The young fellow has given his solemn word on the matter and we have my grandson here to bear witness to the bond of his promise. Come back in two days and I am sure we'll be able to settle all question of debts once and for all.'

Seamus nodded grudgingly and the other two men followed suit.

'Goodnight to you, gentlemen,' Hugh added, standing up to lean on his grandson's arm. He did not have to be able to see their faces to know that their silence meant they were satisfied for the time being.

The three men said their goodbyes and departed, leaving the old man, Daniel and young Edward to return to the fireside.

'That was very wise of you, young man,' Hugh smiled as he

slid down into his chair and pulled the blankets over his knees. 'They came here looking for your blood. I persuaded them of the folly of murdering you and the good sense in claiming some compensation instead.'

'How will I repay you all?' Edward shook his head. 'I have no money.'

'Quiet now, lad,' the old distiller said. 'There's no need to worry yourself. Some solution will present itself, I am sure. We have two days to think about it.' He turned and addressed Daniel. 'Is that old harper coming in tonight?'

'I am not sure, Grandfather,' came the reply. 'I haven't seen him all day.'

'Then go to the village and find him,' Hugh demanded. 'He still owes me a tune or two from last night. I'll bet he's down at Finnegan's treating himself to their watery Spanish claret. The sly old bugger.'

'I'll go straightaway, Grandfather,' Daniel replied obediently and in a moment he was out the door striding off to the village.

'Good lad!' the old man called after him.

Edward sat down on the same stool he had occupied the previous evening. His head was not pounding as badly now but he felt faint and weak at the knees.

'Will you join me in a drink, young Edward?' the old distiller asked.

The young rebel rolled his eyes. 'Not for me, thanks. It's still too early.'

It suddenly occurred to Edward that with Daniel gone, he could easily run out of the door and never come back. He could be in Dublin the next morning and from there, with his father's help, he could take ship to America. The redcoats would not be able to track him down, and neither would Seamus and his friends. No-one would be able to find him.

He licked his lips nervously as he eyed the door.

'Edward?' Hugh said. 'Are you there?'

'Yes, I'm here,' the young man said, standing up quietly, breathing heavily. To stay here would be foolish. The soldiers were sure to find him eventually. Or someone would turn him over to the authorities in return for the reward. It was obvious now that D'Arcy had many friends in the parish. Any of the villagers could claim the reward and have revenge on the major's murderer at the same time. Edward realised it was more than foolish, it was downright dangerous for him to remain in this place a moment longer.

In the next second the young rebel strode across the room and pulled the door open. He stopped for a moment, considering thanking old Hugh for his hospitality, but then he thought better of it and walked out through the doorway straight into the waiting arms of Daniel.

'Where are you off to then?' the red-haired man asked.

'Just out for some air,' Edward stuttered.

'You had best stay in by the fire,' Daniel advised him in a deep menacing tone. 'There's all sorts of folk about tonight. You'd better be careful or you might find yourself at the bottom of a ditch with your throat cut.'

'Yes,' Edward replied quickly, seeing the other man's point immediately. 'I should probably go back inside. I'm sure I've had enough fresh air for one evening. There's a lot of consumption about. I don't want to strain my lungs.'

'You're a wise man, Edward,' Daniel told him sternly, eyes narrowing as he spoke. 'You may yet stay alive long enough to live a long life.'

Edward smiled nervously and went straight back to the fire.

'You're back then?' Hugh said in a cheery tone.

'I'm back,' Edward replied, stretching his hands out to the fire.

After a while Mhairgead came in from the kitchen, lifted the lid from the pot nearest the fire, sniffed the contents and then went to get some bowls. She doled out the boiled bacon in its thin soup and handed it to the two men.

'She's a fine cook, my grand-daughter,' Hugh snorted as he drank the soup straight from the bowl. 'A pity her husband will never return. Off to Botany Bay. As good as dead he is.'

'He was as good as dead drunk before he left,' the young woman reminded her grandfather.

'It was a weakness he had,' Hugh admonished her. 'I was working with him to improve his attitude to the drink.'

'I'll say you were,' Mhairgead groaned. 'You improved his attitude so much he could hardly stand up most of the time.'

'There you go again,' the distiller grumbled, 'making light of the effort I've made for you.'

'Be quiet or I'll make light with your dinner.'

'You wouldn't threaten your old grandfather, would you?'

'Will you marry again, Miss Mhairgead?' Edward interrupted, trying to defuse the situation. 'Or will you wait in hope of your husband's return?'

'Mother of God!' she exclaimed. 'I bless the day the soldiers took him. Drunken sod. Never did a day's work in his life unless there was a chain about his ankles and a cat-o'-nine-tails at his back.'

'Now be fair,' Hugh intervened, 'he helped your father on many an occasion.'

'He helped my father get transported,' Mhairgead shot back. 'My husband was supposed to be the lookout. He was so drunk he fell asleep at his post and the soldiers arrested the lot of them without a fight. My father got away but my husband was so sozzled he told Colonel Cumberland the whole story, named all his accomplices and every single one of them was in gaol the next morning.'

'He wasn't a bad man,' Hugh protested. 'He was just a bit foolish with the bottle.'

'And a bit of a one for the ladies,' Mhairgead added. 'Married and all, we were, mind you. But that didn't stop him. I don't know what those poor women saw in him. He was usually too drunk to be of any use. But he was afflicted with a rambling eye. Now his eye can go a-roving to the far side of the earth and see if he bloody well likes it. Botany Bay was too good for that bastard.'

'I see,' Edward replied, wishing he had never broached the

subject. 'So have you found yourself a man to take his place?'

Mhairgead strode the few paces between them and leaned in close. She touched a finger to his cheek and smiled, showing her remarkably white teeth. For what seemed an age the young rebel was transfixed by her sudden move and her penetrating stare. He simply could not tear his eyes away from hers.

'I don't know what the fashions are in Dublin, Master Edward,' she began, 'but here in the country we don't discuss such matters in front of our elders.'

Edward touched his hand to his throat and swallowed loudly. He was about to ask her what she meant when she whispered, her breath in his ear, 'If you're not too drunk at the end of the evening, I'll be outside looking up to the moon and stars. The night sky is so pretty at this time of year.'

Edward panicked. She had mistaken his meaning entirely. 'I was just asking,' he stammered. 'I mean to say ... you're very pretty of course, Miss Mhairgead, but I wouldn't want you to think that ...'

'Be quiet, you two!' Hugh grumbled. 'Can't a man eat his bacon in peace? Off with you, Mhairgead, and out of here unless you can keep silent while I have my dinner.'

'Yes, Grandfather,' she replied meekly, taking the old man's empty bowl and refilling it. When she grabbed Edward's bowl she winked at him and he let go of the vessel in shock. It immediately fell to the floor and shattered loudly.

'Be careful, child!' Hugh snapped. 'And enough of your foolishness. You can have the lad to yourself when we older folk have all gone to bed.'

'No,' Edward began, 'I don't think you understand.'

But the old distiller did not let him finish. 'No need to be ashamed, lad. She's a fine young woman who would make you a good wife.'

'I'm not looking for a wife.'

'Nonsense,' Hugh laughed. 'I never knew a man who wasn't looking for a wife at some time in his life.'

The old man thought for a second and then shook his head.

'Apart from that unusual friend of Mister Swift's who told everyone he was looking for a husband. But that fellow was another story entirely.'

'I am not looking for a wife,' Edward repeated.

'Most men like to do a lot more than look before they decide to make a woman their wife,' Hugh noted with disgust. 'And there'll be none of that in this house, do you understand, Edward?'

'I do,' the rebel shrugged. It was useless arguing with the old man.

At that moment the door swung open loudly and Denis the harper made his way in, led by Daniel.

'Was it quiet down at Finnegan's tonight then?' Hugh asked.

'It was,' Denis replied bitterly. 'Especially after your grandson arrived.'

'Sit down here and stop your moaning,' the old distiller admonished.

Before he was properly settled, Denis had a bowl of boiled bacon in his lap and a cup of whiskey by his foot at the fire.

Edward and Hugh soon held wooden cups of their own. This was despite the fact that the young rebel had made a solemn vow to himself he would not drink at all tonight. The young rebel looked at his cup and decided a sip or two of whiskey probably wouldn't do any harm. He did not lift his eyes from it as Hugh began to speak.

'Now, I believe that last night when young Edward fell off his seat and the redcoats arrived I was about to tell how Carolan got his education at the harp. But that is a very long story for it took three years of practice before the master could play even the simplest of tunes.'

'He was not known for his skill with the fingers,' Denis concurred, chewing his bacon fat as he spoke. 'In fact I have it on very good authority that he was a clumsy harper.'

'Whose authority?' Hugh gasped.

'David Murphy. The famous harper to Lord Mayo.'

'Bloody Murphy,' the old distiller shuddered. 'What would he know?'

'Carolan was a poor harper,' Denis insisted. 'By all accounts.'

'But his melodies are fine indeed,' Edward cut in.

'I'll get to that part of the tale presently,' Hugh snapped. 'Be patient. And do not criticise your betters, Denis Hempson. It is a rude habit you must have acquired in Dublin town.'

'He took up the music too late,' the harper pressed.

'But which of your melodies will be played fifty years after your death?' Hugh countered crossly.

'I'll be remembered for my skill,' Denis told him flatly. 'I took the harp on my knee when I was a lad of six and the music has been with me ever since. Carolan was eighteen years of age when he first leaned an instrument into his chest. His fingers were hardened by the tilling of the soil and never attained the suppleness required for a good performer. And his ear was never keen enough to keep the tuning.'

'And old Mhaire Dhall recognised all of those handicaps,' the distiller shrugged. 'But she had promised her patron she would do what she could with the lad. Her life was ebbing away from her and she was grateful for a warm place to sleep and dependable mealtimes. She worked her student hard. And Carolan often related as much whenever some student of his complained of the tediousness of practice.'

'She was said to be a fine player,' Denis agreed.

'She made him strike the wires until his fingers bled,' Hugh cut in and Edward thought that hearing these two men pick up on each other's thoughts was like listening to one storyteller with two voices.

'The wires of the old harps were set close together,' Denis informed the young rebel. 'Not like this one I have now.' He turned his head and waved his hand with disdain in the general direction of the instrument. 'This cupboard is just a poorly constructed copy of the ancient instruments made bigger by some fool craftsman who thought the sound would be improved if the harp was made larger. Bigger does not always mean better.'

'A good philosophy for life,' Hugh interrupted.

'Harps were built differently in those days,' the musician went on. 'They were sturdy and small. And there was none of that Italian nonsense in the music.'

'He means,' Hugh explained, 'that before the departure of good King James, foreign musicians were rare in Ireland. When they came later to entertain the new aristocracy, they brought with them all sorts of pretty ideas that did not sit well with the old music.'

'I was taught to play the harp as if it were an extension of myself,' Denis said proudly, waxing lyrical. 'Under an old harper's fingers the sea breeze was invoked and the seagull upon that breeze. The stirring sounds of battle roared upon the wires and the voices of the Faerie folk melted the heart of the sternest warrior.'

'I have heard a modern harper play,' Hugh said, screwing up his nose in disgust. 'They do not use the brass wire any more for fear of damaging their dainty fingers. They do not wear the long nails on their hands. They do not strike the chords but play little tinkling melodies underneath the tune to confuse the listener and draw attention away from their lack of skill.'

He stopped to search for his pipe but Daniel had already filled it in anticipation. He handed it to his grandfather and the old man put the pipe straight to his mouth.

Mhairgead picked up a glowing twig and touched it to the pipe as Hugh drew in the smoke, then she took the empty broth bowl from Denis. When she had stacked it with the others in a half barrel of water she went outside, glancing back over her shoulder as she left the room to catch Edward's eye. But the young man looked firmly away.

'There are many differences in the style of the old harpers,' Denis continued. 'The chief one being that the brass wires ring much longer than the gut strings. So the harper must learn when to stop the wires from sounding, as much as when to strike them. This is the most difficult of all the skills. And because the learning of it takes such dedication, no-one bothers any more.'

'Everyone is in a rush these days,' Hugh nodded.

'No time to do things properly,' Denis moaned.

'So young Master Carolan was taught the instrument of ancient Ireland under the tutelage of one of the last great harpers to walk the road,' Hugh said. 'Mhaire Dhall herself came from a long tradition. She could trace her lineage back to Ruarí Dhall O'Cahan who lived in the time of Queen Elizabeth of England. But Mhaire had no idea that Carolan would be amongst the last of that glorious line. Nor did she realise that within two generations there would be but a handful of harpers left in the land.'

'For even in the three years that Carolan was learning his craft,' Denis added, 'changes were to come upon Ireland which could not have been guessed at.'

'A year after the young master suffered his sickness and was blinded,' the distiller went on, 'the English deposed King James the Second from the throne and elevated the Dutchman, William, Prince of Orange, to the monarchy.'

The old man drew on his pipe and then continued, 'You surely know the story. King James landed with Patrick Sarsfield, his commander, at Kinsale and the whole country rejoiced. Catholics rushed to his banner and very likely Carolan would have joined them had he not been blinded. Perhaps, if he had been sighted, he would have died in some senseless battle for he often lamented that all his childhood friends passed away in the next few years.'

'A hard time,' Denis noted with bitterness. 'A hundred Galarbreacs would have been easier to bear.'

'For a long while it seemed that Ireland would remain free with her own king and parliament,' Hugh explained. 'But in the summer of the second year of Carolan's tuition King William's army made landfall at Carrickfergus. The Dutchman had cannons and mercenaries and, as you know, he won the day. Eventually the whole land fell under the rule of the new aristocracy.'

'I was two years old,' Denis said, 'when the Dutch, Danes and German troops came to our village. But they were decent folk, my mother said, compared to the English soldiers who were paid in plunder for their services.'

Daniel handed the old musician a lighted pipe and the blind man nodded his thanks.

'My mother's younger sister,' the harper began, 'had a baby boy at her breast when the English came to the town and then indulged themselves in the bloody slaughter of innocents. My aunt told me that when she heard the sound of screaming and shouting she fled to hide under a small bridge, her babe in her arms. But as night came down, the cold air made the baby cry and this attracted the attention of a group of soldiers.'

Denis sucked on the pipe and blew a billow of blue smoke toward the fireplace.

'An English officer ordered one of his troopers to find the crying baby and to kill it. The man soon located mother and son cowering in fear beneath the bridge. But the soldier had not the heart to do the deed. For though he was a Protestant, he was Irish and he understood the whispered pleas of the mother. So he waited a short while with her and then returned to report to his officer.'

Once again the harper drew in on the pipe and the bowl glowed brightly orange.

'Well, the officer asked the soldier how he had dispatched the child and the trooper told him it was by the bayonet. But there was no blood on the weapon so the officer ordered the gentle soldier to return and do the job properly or it would be his own blood upon that cold steel.'

Denis shook his head. 'Cruel times they were,' he sighed.

'The soldier returned, but still he could not bring himself to murder this young mother and her child, even though his own life might be forfeit if he did not follow orders. So the soldier came up with a daring plan. He took the babe, though the mother shrieked at him to give her son back, and cut off his little finger. That done, he smeared the blood all over his bayonet and gave the boy back into her arms. She silenced the child and the soldier disappeared. She slipped away a few hours later and knew not what became of the man.'

'A lucky escape,' Edward cried, engrossed in this tale of English barbarity.

'Lucky indeed,' the harper agreed. 'And that was but the start of all the trouble. For the soldiers did not abate in their blood lust for many years. And their officers made things worse by mistreating the men and withholding their pay. Though there were some good men amongst the cruel.'

Denis sucked on the pipe and was silent for a moment.

'But that is not the end of the story,' he cut in, just as Hugh was about to speak. 'For twenty years later a stranger came to our door. I remember his voice well. As was the custom, since he spoke our language, he was invited to stay the night and share a meal. Over a jug of whiskey he told us he was a Protestant who had served in King William's army at the Battle of the Boyne. He had just been paid off and was a wealthy man.'

Denis smiled. 'My young cousin decided then and there he would follow the stranger after he left the house in the morning and murder him for his gold, for this man was a Protestant and had served the enemy. But at breakfast the old soldier told the story of a young woman and her baby whose lives he had saved twenty years before. My cousin held up his hand, the one with the missing finger, and you could have heard a feather fall upon the floor we were all so astounded,' Denis chuckled.

'The old soldier ended up staying another week. My aunt had lost her husband in the war, you see, so it was no surprise to anyone when the soldier and she were married the next Thursday. He became a good Catholic to make amends for his wicked life.'

'If he had not spoken up, your cousin would have killed him,' Edward said in shock.

'Surely he would. But things usually turn out for the best in my experience.'

'So this was the state of Ireland when Master Carolan finished his apprenticeship,' Hugh interrupted, trying to wrestle control of the conversation again.

'And no sooner had Carolan finished his three years' training,'

Denis added, 'than most of his potential patrons sailed off for France, never to return.'

'That is true.' Hugh nodded his head. 'In the summer of sixteen hundred and ninety-one the Irish garrison at Limerick surrendered. They made a treaty with the English. Those who stayed in Ireland took the Protestant faith. The rest went into exile forever. Most of the old aristocracy went with them to France to serve in the armies of King Louis.'

'All the old lords went off,' the harper recalled, 'including Mayo. But years later his son returned and took to the Protestant ways in order to alleviate the pain of his suffering people.'

'Yes, and thank God he did,' Hugh replied. 'There were some who called young Mayo a traitor when he forsook the Catholic Church, but the ordinary folk would have had no voice if he had not had the courage to return.'

'The Flight of the Wild Geese,' Edward whispered, a tear welling in his eye.

'That's a very poetical turn of phrase you have, young man,' Denis commented.

'Wild bloody fools they were,' Hugh scoffed. 'Three days after Limerick town surrendered, a French army of ten thousand men arrived to relieve them. But Patrick Sarsfield, King Jamie's general in the field, would not go back on his word and he stuck to the surrender terms.'

'He was an honourable man,' the harper hummed.

'Pity the English didn't have any among them with the same standards,' Hugh hissed, 'for in later years they broke every article of the treaty Sarsfield had signed. And they brought a famine on the country that was only outdone by the ferocity of the Galar-breac.'

Denis drew in another lungful of smoke and sighed loudly. 'It was a terrible time to be alive. But I am glad I lived through it all.'

'It was that same summer after the siege of Limerick that Master Carolan was summoned to the MacDermot household,' the old distiller continued, 'three years after he had begun his studies at the ancient music. It was Mrs MacDermot's idea to have him play for her and some of her honoured guests on the occasion of her daughter's birthday. Squire Crilly even provided the master with a fine suit of clothes.'

'But fine clothes don't make a good harper,' Denis snapped.

'In your case it could be said that even fine harpers have very little idea of how to dress well,' Hugh quipped.

Denis grunted and sucked in the sweet blue smoke of his pipe. Edward sipped at his whiskey. These tales of the old days stirred in him feelings of patriotism and righteous outrage, and he listened with renewed interest as blind Hugh Connor once again took up the story of Turlough O'Carolan.

EIGHT

The summer was a particularly dry one. It had not rained for three days. So Turlough's journey to the MacDermot estate was uncomfortable and slow. He was dressed in a fine dark green coat which was a gift from Squire Crilly, a red waistcoat and a tall black English-style hat. He was sweating profusely.

His horse plodded away beneath him and the servant assigned to lead the animal grumbled incessantly from the moment they set out. It was a journey of no more than two miles but it felt like twenty.

Turlough sat in the saddle and reflected on the last three years. During that time he had barely left the confines of Squire Crilly's house, only emerging to go to mass at Holy Week or to touch the first snow of the season for luck.

His fingernails were long and shaped like elegant teardrops for catching the wires of the harp. His fingers were toughened by long hours of practice and they were forever fidgeting, unable to keep still, as if eager to play even when the harp was put down.

Mhaire Dhall was a hard teacher. She had pushed her student at a gruelling pace to learn techniques which might have taken another apprentice many years to master. But the old woman was determined Turlough would be able to support himself as a musician before she was too old to teach him anything more.

She did not tell him how happy she was with his progress lest the praise go to his head.

Turlough had endlessly practised the tuning, the trills, the grace notes and the melodies she set him. Turlough often sat behind the instrument day and night until his thighs were numb from being in one place for too long. He played till his fingers cramped with pain. In time he no longer felt the agony in his hands or limbs. Turlough was too enraptured by the harp and the sounds he could coax from it to be bothered with his own discomfort. The three years had passed quickly, he realised. Now he was on his way to perform publicly for the first time.

His harp, a small instrument which stood no higher than a man's thigh, was slung in its case across the unfortunate servant's shoulder. Turlough sat in the saddle, occasionally rehearsing the few pieces he felt confident enough to perform by running his fingers down the buttons of his waistcoat.

By the time they arrived at the house and Mrs MacDermot had greeted him, Turlough was already exhausted. In the last three years the only part of him that had got any real exercise was his fingers. His legs ached from the saddle and his back was twisted. And he could feel his face was a little sunburnt.

The young harper was led into the house by the assistant butler, William O'Flynn, who took him by the arm into the music room. Once the young man was comfortably seated, his harp was placed on his lap and the tuning key in his hand. Then he was left alone.

Turlough tried to picture the room as it had been on that night a little over three years ago when he had heard David Murphy play. But all he could remember was the way Bridget had eyed his rival. Then Turlough suddenly remembered that this room was lined with mirrors. He thought about that for a moment and, for some reason which he could not explain, the idea made him very nervous. He tried to drive the thought of the mirrors from his mind. It was a ridiculous thing for a blind man to be worried about, he told himself.

'That was the night Bridget was lost to me forever,' Turlough said under his breath. 'And the night I first wished I would become a harper.'

'And now you are,' a familiar voice hummed.

'Mary?' Turlough blurted, embarrassed that she had caught him talking aloud. 'Three years! I haven't heard your voice in all that time.'

'It is three long years,' she replied. 'I am sorry for creeping up on you.'

'How are you?' he asked her. 'Is the life of a serving maid suited to you then?'

'It is,' the young woman sighed. 'Though I am yearning for a good husband to steal me away.'

'Your grandmother sends her kind regards,' Turlough said.

'She can be so stuffy,' Mary laughed.

She walked up to where he was seated and hugged him close to her. Turlough resisted her at first, shocked that she would be so open with her affections where anyone might walk in on them.

'We'll be caught,' he warned her. 'And then what will you do for a living?'

'The door is shut to give you some privacy,' she whispered. 'What's the matter with you? You seem very out of sorts.'

'It's the mirrors,' Turlough explained. 'I can't stand the thought of all the mirrors in this room.'

'What do you mean?'

'I know I can't see them, but I remember well what this room looks like. There are mirrors all around the walls and they make me nervous.'

Mary looked at him and giggled. 'You are a strange one, Turlough O'Carolan.'

'Please, Mary,' he said, pushing her away. 'I am afraid of what will happen to you if Mrs MacDermot were to walk in on us.'

'Oh don't worry about her,' the girl told him. 'In any case, I am finished here. Grandmother cannot teach you any more and so that is the end of her stipend from Mrs MacDermot. So I am going to work for the squire.'

'Mhaire cannot teach me any more?' the young man cried in dismay. 'But she has only just begun to pass on her knowledge. I haven't learned nearly enough to prepare me for the wandering life.'

'It was wise of her not to tell you,' Mary noted dryly, realising her grandmother had left it to others to break the news. 'She must have known you would be upset.'

'Upset!' Turlough coughed. 'I'm outraged. Only this morning she was telling me that I would never be a decent musician and that she could spend three and thirty years teaching me and still it would do no good.'

'That's her way, Turlough,' Mary laughed. 'You know she means well beneath that hard exterior.'

'A bit like her grand-daughter,' the young lad replied mischievously.

'I don't have a hard exterior!' she protested. 'I am as gentle as a lamb.'

'You are as soft as the dew on the cobwebs first thing in the morning,' Turlough told her. 'I was just teasing you.'

'You haven't forgotten the girl of your dreams, have you?'

'Bridget?'

'That's her,' Mary grimaced.

'I have not forgotten her. And I still hope one day to win her back.'

'Would you not try to win another hand if it was offered to you?'

'What do you mean?' Turlough asked, genuinely confused. But Mary did not have a chance to answer. The door to the chamber swung open and William O'Flynn strode in.

'What are you doing here, Mary?' he snapped.

'She is a dear friend of mine,' Turlough retorted. 'She nursed me through my infirmity. So I'll ask you to speak well to her.'

'I am sorry, Master Carolan,' the butler apologised, 'but she is meant to be packing her things ready for your journey tomorrow.'

'What journey?'

'Didn't I tell you?' Mary waved at the butler to keep his mouth shut. 'I am to join Squire Crilly's household as a serving maid. But first I am going to accompany you to the house of Squire Reynolds tomorrow. He is himself a well-renowned harper. He has agreed to listen to your playing, give his opinion and teach you what he knows. And he may prove of great service to you for he is acquainted with many folk in Dublin.'

'Squire Reynolds?' the young man asked. 'Mhaire doesn't think much of him.'

'Nor does he think much of her,' Mary admitted. 'It is an old quarrel and neither side can remember how it began. But they are both stubborn enough to keep it going.'

'Would you like a drink before the performance?' O'Flynn asked, remembering what he'd come in for.

'You could get him a whiskey,' Mary said straightaway.

'Bless you, my girl,' Turlough laughed. 'You'll make some lad a very happy fellow one day.'

'I pray that it will be the one of my choosing.'

'Indeed so do I.'

'Careful, Turlough. You don't know what you are saying.'

'What are you all doing in here?' Mrs MacDermot cried from the door. 'You can catch up with him later, young woman. Let him be to tune his harp. I will be bringing the guests in in ten minutes. Is that enough time for you, Turlough?'

'It is, my lady.'

'I hope your hands are steady,' Mrs MacDermot said.

'They will be when I have had a glass or two of your best hand-steadying water,' he answered, and Mrs MacDermot laughed.

'But now,' the lady declared, clapping her hands, 'everyone out and leave the lad alone to prepare his harp for his first performance. There'll be time enough for all this chatter later this evening.'

With that she ushered Mary out of the room and waited until O'Flynn had delivered a glass of whiskey.

'My lady,' Turlough piped up as Mrs MacDermot was

leaving to return to her guests, 'have you any word of Bridget and her father?'

'Squire Cruise passed away two months ago,' she told him. 'His heart was weak they say and he caught a chill one night. Within a few days he was gone. And as for Bridget, she is to be married in a few months to a young officer.'

'An Englishman?' Turlough gasped in horror.

'A Protestant,' Mrs MacDermot told him. 'But I believe he is from Belfast. Now that is enough news for the moment. I'll tell you everything there is to know after supper.'

With that she shut the doors behind her and Turlough was left alone.

The young man sat back in the low chair and breathed deeply. Bridget was to be married. He was too late!

Turlough was hungry for more information but he decided it was best that he concentrate on his performance for the moment so he began to check the tuning of his small harp. Gently he ran his fingers over the wires in the manner that Mhaire had taught him. Immediately he knew something was very wrong. All the wires seemed to have shifted tune dramatically. Whether it was the journey or the hot weather or simply that this harp was not the finest instrument to begin with, he could not tell.

All Turlough could think of was that he had less than ten minutes to completely retune the instrument. He set about his task as quickly as he could, but he was flustered and his mind kept returning to Bridget. He had not expected the harp to need so much attention. Why did this have to happen now? He had never had this trouble before.

But he had never taken his little harp out of Squire Crilly's house before and he had certainly never travelled with it. The wires had stretched in the heat, flattening most of the upper notes until they were all at strange pitches.

Fortunately the lower notes were not much out of tune because the wires were so much longer and so could move a little more without damaging the tuning as much.

Turlough was still adjusting the wires when Mrs MacDermot came back into the room to check on him.

'Are you ready?' she called out.

'In a few minutes,' he replied without taking his attention from the harp.

She frowned and shrugged her shoulders, closing the door behind her.

One or two wires refused to keep their pitch no matter what Turlough did. So he quickly decided to avoid striking them if possible. This left him with only a few tunes in his repertoire to choose from.

'Mother of God!' he hissed to himself.

No sooner had he spoken those words than he heard the doors open again and the sound of people chatting as they entered the room.

How many people had Mrs MacDermot invited, Turlough wondered in shock. He began to shake with fear, asking himself why on earth he had agreed to this. He wasn't ready for a public performance.

The room quickly filled and Mrs MacDermot came to stand beside Turlough, placing a hand on his shoulder.

'Welcome one and all,' she began. 'This is young Turlough O'Carolan, the son of our late blacksmith who has spent the last three years studying the harp. I am very proud of him. He has struggled hard against his affliction and I am told that he has completely overcome the disadvantage of his blindness.'

There was restrained applause.

'He is going to play a few tunes for us before dinner. I would beg you to encourage him.'

She stepped down and took her place in the front row. Turlough nodded and put his hand to the wires. He felt his fingers trembling, then he concentrated all his attention on the instrument in front of him.

Though he could not see the harp, old Mhaire had taught him how to feel its presence. He quickly and gently brushed each of the wires in turn with the very tips of his fingers as he breathed in the gorgeous ringing that rose from the sound board.

As Turlough launched into his first tune he felt the audience breathe a collective sigh of relief. They had obviously been expecting his playing to be awful.

The tiny instrument hummed but it was not as well made a harp as the one Murphy had carried. That was said to be over three hundred years old. The wires on Turlough's harp rattled in the lower range and thudded in the upper registers, but he managed to disguise most of these problems. No matter how hard he tried, however, he could not conceal the fact that this harp had been damaged once and not very well repaired. Secretly he was glad of its shortcomings for it meant that the listeners might be more forgiving of any of his mistakes.

He performed three tunes and then put the harp by his knee, hoping that would be enough. There was enthusiastic applause and Mrs MacDermot arose from her seat to speak again.

'Thank you, Turlough,' she said proudly. 'That was truly wonderful. You have learned in three years what it takes other men a whole lifetime to master.'

Turlough blushed and bowed his head. 'Thank you, my lady.'

'My lady,' the butler announced, 'dinner is served.'

'Thank you,' she replied, turning to the servant. 'Ladies and gentlemen, please make your way into the dining room.

'Well done, Turlough,' she whispered taking his hand. 'I am so proud of you.'

'You are very generous, my lady,' he answered.

'Are you coming to dinner?'

'To sit with you and your fine friends?'

'You will have to get used to it. You are a harper now and you will command great respect for your skill. You will sit at the high table in many houses if your career goes well.'

'I'll be along presently,' Turlough replied, still uncomfortable with the notion.

'Very well. You pack up your harp and I'll have William wait for you.'

'Thank you.'

'Congratulations, young man,' a man's voice interrupted and Turlough pricked up his ears, thinking he had met the owner of it somewhere.

'You have done well to learn so much of the craft in such a short time.'

Turlough felt a cold shiver run through his body as he recalled exactly where he had heard this voice.

'Turlough,' Mrs MacDermot began, 'this is Squire Sheehan and his wife Elizabeth who have come from Donegal. They are amongst the most fashionable folk in the kingdom. I wish you could see the fine clothes they are wearing. It is such an honour to have them visiting us. They are going to be staying with Squire Crilly for a while.'

'It is a pleasure to meet you, young man,' a woman's voice spoke up and Turlough felt his jaw drop in shock. He knew her voice too. He could even picture her face perfectly.

'Have you visited us before?' the harper asked.

'Once,' she replied with a smile in her voice. 'About three years ago. But I would have remembered you, surely,' she purred. 'Have you the notion that we have met somewhere else?'

'I have.'

'I don't recall making the acquaintance of any handsome harpers when last we passed this way,' she teased.

'I have it in my mind that you are a woman of exceptional beauty,' Turlough recalled, 'with long black hair and eyes like deep pools of fresh water at midnight. You might in other circumstances be mistaken for a queen. And your husband is a youthful-looking man whose very presence commands respect.'

'Turlough,' Mrs MacDermot gasped, 'either you have an astounding memory or there are some other gifts lurking inside you alongside your talent for music. You have described the Sheehans exactly.'

'How could I forget so gracious a couple? I will hold your images in my mind for many years to come.'

'You are very kind,' Mrs Sheehan smiled.

'I am sure we will meet again, young man,' the squire cut in. 'We have a house in Dublin. And we would be honoured if you would grace us with your presence if ever you are passing through that town.'

'I would be the one to be honoured.' Turlough bowed his head.

'You are very polite,' the lady told him. 'I think you have had a very good teacher.'

'I am very grateful for her wisdom,' the lad replied. 'As I am for my gracious patrons.'

'I foresee great things for you, young man,' Squire Sheehan told him.

'Thank you,' the lad bowed.

'We'll leave you now to pack your harp away,' said Mrs MacDermot. 'Come in when you are ready.' And then she led her two guests out of the room, whispering under her breath to them all the way.

The young harper came in to dinner shortly afterwards but he did not get a chance to ask Mrs MacDermot anything more about Bridget. The lady was busy introducing him to all her friends and acquaintances.

When he finally went to bed in William O'Flynn's room in the servants' quarters, Turlough knew nothing further about Bridget and he almost felt his heart would break if he didn't find out who this officer was that she intended to marry.

The thought came to him that he should go straight to Dublin, find her and play for her. He was sure she would fall into his arms and leave this captain forever once she heard him. Just as he had convinced himself this would be the best course of action, there was a knock at the door.

'Turlough,' Mary whispered, 'I just came to say goodnight to you.'

'Mary!' he called. 'Thank goodness you have come. Did you hear that Bridget is to be married?'

'I did,' she replied. 'Next week in Dublin.'

'Next week!'

'Indeed. That is what I heard.'

'Then I haven't a moment to lose,' he told her. 'Will you help me pack?' And with that he stood up from his bed and made his way slowly across the room. He started patting around the chest of drawers for his clothes to stuff into his travelling bag.

'It's no good, Turlough,' Mary soothed, putting a hand on his shoulder. 'I am told she is very much in love with the man. He's a fine handsome soldier who'll be a colonel one day, so they say.'

'But she told me she would always love me!'

'But three years have passed. She has not heard from you in all that time. She has probably forgotten you by now.'

'She would never forget me,' he denied. 'We were lovers!' Then he blushed, realising he had said too much.

'Don't be embarrassed,' the girl reassured him. 'I was in love with a young man once. He only had room for another woman in his heart. But he did not know that this other woman cared nothing for him. So he pursued this other woman in his thoughts without guessing how I felt.'

'What did you do?'

'I let him have his dreams, even though I knew they would come to nothing. One day he would realise how I felt about him. It would have been foolish for me to chase after him. He probably would have laughed at me for wanting him so much.'

'Nonsense!' Turlough scoffed. 'I have only seen you once but I know you are very beautiful. I am sure any man with sense would want you for his own.'

Then the penny dropped. Turlough breathed deeply and blushed bright red again.

'Me?' he asked tentatively.

'Yes, Turlough.'

'Oh Mary,' he began, wishing he had been blessed with a bit more good sense. 'I am so sorry. I had no idea.'

'I know that,' she murmured. 'And that is why I can forgive you.'

'It was not my intention to hurt you. I have only ever had

one woman in my heart. Truly I have been blinded in more ways than one.'

'Bridget is not meant for you,' Mary asserted. 'If you'll forgive me saying so. Mrs MacDermot tells me the girl is a spoiled child who is not happy unless she has the best of everything. The finest clothes, the most expensive shoes, the most exotic dishes at her table and the most handsome men in her bed.'

'Mary!'

'It is true!' the girl insisted. 'And she'll do anything to get what she wants. Bridget has had every man in Dublin chasing after her and I've heard that she does not always run very swiftly, if you take my meaning.'

'Mary, don't speak so about her.' Turlough was horrified.

'Her father died of shock when he found out about her ways.' Mary was not about to stop now. She had held her tongue too long. 'He had converted to the Protestant faith and you know how staid that lot can be. But then he was too ashamed to attend church, they say, for fear of what his new-found friends would say. Eventually the gossip became so loud he could not ignore it. He fell ill with worry and in the end he passed away with her name on his lips.'

'I don't believe you.'

'And he was not the first man to lose his life on her account,' Mary continued. 'The officer she is to marry fought a bitter duel for her with his best friend. The captain was so smitten by her beguiling ways that he did not question the act of piercing his comrade's breast with a steel-pointed sword to win the heart of Bridget Cruise. But the truth is, though others lose their hearts to her, she has no heart at all herself, Turlough.'

'No,' the harper protested. 'I won't hear you speak of her that way.'

'She did not even attend the funeral of the rival, even though she had professed her love for the poor man a mere three weeks earlier. If the captain can keep her in check, then good luck to him, for it has been beyond the skill of any other man.'

'You are only saying these things out of jealousy.'

'I wish it were so,' Mary said sincerely. 'Mrs MacDermot did not want to tell you about all this because she knew of your feelings for the girl. But somebody has to let you know what sort of a person she is so that you can forget her and continue your life in happiness without her shadow haunting you.'

'I can't,' Turlough muttered, his throat choking with emotion. 'I love Bridget. She loves me.'

'The only love Bridget Cruise has ever known is the love she has for herself.' Mary bowed her head at that, seeing that Turlough was beginning to shake with emotion.

'I care too much about you to tell you anything that I did not know to be true,' she sighed. 'There are many other things said about her which I would never repeat to you because they cannot be proved.'

Mary reached out a hand to take his and in a moment he had thrown his arms about her and was sobbing uncontrollably.

After a long while the lad calmed down a little and Mary left him to sleep, but he lay awake all night. There was no sense in him being a harper any more and he suddenly didn't care whether he ever picked up the instrument again. These past three years he had only been driven by his infatuation. Now he saw how foolish he had been and his passion was burned out. It was gone, only to be replaced by bitterness.

The next morning was overcast and dark. Rain clouds had blown in during the night and the temperature had dropped so the air was chilly. Shortly after dawn, before there was any light, Turlough and Mary set out for Squire Reynolds's house. It was a journey of almost four miles from Ballyfarnon.

The day warmed as the morning wore on but it rained lightly most of the time so they both wore their coats. Turlough dozed under his tall broad-brimmed felt hat, the rhythm of the raindrops gently lulling him as his mare plodded along.

Finally, just before eleven, they came to the boundary of the Reynolds estate. Mary had never been to this house before. She gasped in awe and excitement as they approached the great iron front gate.

'Mother of God,' she hummed with obvious delight, looking down the long lane toward the mansion, 'it's the grandest house in all Ireland.'

Turlough said nothing. He had lost interest in the whole idea of being a travelling harper. His heart was broken and his dreams had been shattered like a fine porcelain cup under the forge hammer. He did not even lift his head to acknowledge her enthusiastic cries.

As they rode up to the house servants came scurrying out to attend to them. The harp was removed from its saddlebag and taken indoors. Mary leapt from her mount eagerly, then remembered Mrs MacDermot had told her she should curb her excitement and remain restrained and ladylike during the visit. Mary bowed her head, placed her hands in front of her and walked sedately to the front door.

When she turned around she noticed Turlough was still seated on his mare, the rain pelting down on him. Her heart went out to him and she would have gone back to help him down but Squire Reynolds's servants were already at his side.

In a few moments the harper was standing on the gravel. He offered no resistance as a butler led him to the front door to stand beside Mary. Then the two of them entered the main hall to await the squire.

'Are you tired after the journey?' Mary asked.

Turlough did not move or acknowledge the question in any way. He just stood with his arms limp by his side as if he were deaf as well as blind. Mary decided to take no notice of his moodiness.

'This is such a beautiful house, Turlough,' she told him. 'Full of paintings and hunting trophies and the finest furniture. I wish you could see it.'

The young harper sighed and put his hands in the deep pockets of his coat. No sooner had he done that than a butler came to help him remove his travelling clothes. Turlough sighed again and let the man take the coat and his hat.

'You can't go on moping about like this,' Mary whispered

when she was sure the servants were out of earshot. 'You have to play for the squire this afternoon.'

There was no response.

'Turlough!'

The young harper turned his head away.

'I'll be fine, Mary,' he told her. 'Sit me in the garden for a while and you go off and have a look around the house.'

'It's raining, Turlough!' she laughed. 'You'll catch your death of cold in the garden.'

'Oh yes,' he replied. 'Well sit me by the hearth then.'

Mary shook her head and asked a serving man to see the harper to the fire. But she did not leave his side. The servant brought Turlough to a long seat covered in finely worked leather which had been placed in front of a small fireplace. Mary sat quietly at the other end of the room, keeping an eye on her friend.

They were not there very long when the door opened. A large well-dressed gentleman with a balding head appeared, followed by another stranger, a young man of about the same age as Turlough.

Mary rose from her seat and made a gentle feminine curtsy, just as Mrs MacDermot had taught her. She was careful to keep her back straight and tilt her head forward only a fraction.

'Well!' the balding man exclaimed. 'I see it has not taken long for the fashions of the French court to come to Roscommon. My name is Reynolds,' he told Mary. Then he made an attempt at an elegant bow himself, bending his left knee, thrusting his right calf forward and doubling his body as he flourished a hand in the air.

'I am not as dainty as you, my dear,' he laughed, 'but I hope you can see through my clumsiness and appreciate the sentiment. May I present Mister McCabe. He is himself a student of the harp.'

'My name is Mary,' she replied, handing a bundle of papers to the squire. 'These are letters from Mrs MacDermot. The first one is our letter of introduction.'

Reynolds took the papers and laid all save one on a small table. Then he tore open the seals on the remaining letter and went to the window to read it by the faint sunlight.

'"My dear squire,"' he began, reading it aloud. '"It is my honour to present to you Turlough O'Carolan who has been studying the harp under the expertise of Mhaire Dhall Maguire."'

Reynolds blew the air loudly through his lips to show how much he thought of the old woman.

'"He has done remarkably well at his studies. This evening he performed in front of a gathering of many of my friends and was generally acclaimed for his progress. Thank you for your kind offer to help him further his education at the harp. I believe that with the right tuition he will one day be regarded highly."'

Reynolds grunted. 'If we can undo the harm Blind Mhaire has done to him.'

Mary frowned but he did not notice.

'"My maidservant Mary accompanies him,"' the squire continued. '"She was his nurse during the illness and will be able to see to his needs. She will be returning to service at the home of Squire Crilly when you have found a suitable guide for Turlough. Once again, thank you. I hold you in the kindest regards. Mrs MacDermot-Rua."'

Reynolds walked back over to the table and put the letter down.

'Well, where is he?' he asked Mary, throwing his arms in the air.

She pointed to the leather sofa and the squire strode across the room. Turlough was lying down across the seat, hidden from Reynolds's view. When the squire approached he was surprised to find that the lad seemed sound asleep.

'Is he ill?' Reynolds inquired.

'The journey was long and he is not used to travelling,' Mary replied tactfully.

'He'll have to get accustomed to it mighty quickly,' Reynolds laughed. 'He leaves on his first tour in a few weeks. That is if I consider him to be worthy of the travelling life.'

The squire looked closely at the lad, who drew a slow breath in his slumber. And then the old man smiled.

'I will not wake him now. I can see he needs some rest. Have you eaten, Mary?'

'No, sir,' she told him. 'We have barely dismounted and taken off our cloaks.'

'Where is that butler?' Reynolds said to himself. 'I told him to have things prepared.'

'Will you teach Turlough the harp?' the girl asked.

'It will be more a case of him learning to forget everything Mhaire Dhall has taught him,' the squire explained. 'That silly old woman was never very skilled and her technique is extremely limited. I don't know what possessed good Mrs MacDermot when she arranged for that old crone to be Turlough's tutor.'

'I have heard you have engaged in a long dispute with Mhaire Dhall,' Mary said coldly.

'She is a foolish old hag with no sense of rhythm and as tone deaf as she is blind,' Reynolds laughed. 'And her temper is legendary. Do you know her?'

'She is my grandmother,' Mary answered in as polite a voice as she could muster.

The young man called McCabe coughed in surprise and then held a hand over his mouth to stifle a laugh. Squire Reynolds blushed deeply.

'Forgive me, my child,' he offered. 'It is an old dispute and I sometimes forget myself when I speak of it. Indeed I have forgotten how it all began. But such is the way of petty disagreements if they are allowed to fester. They can easily become a nagging wound that refuses to heal. I probably should have approached Mhaire years ago and apologised for my part in the whole thing, but my pride would not allow it. Once again I would ask you to forgive me.'

'If you'll pardon me saying so, it sounds to me as if you

should be saying those words to my grandmother,' Mary told him, 'not to me.'

The squire looked sternly at the girl for a few seconds and she thought he was going to berate her for her forthright comment. But the cloud passed from his face and he smiled. 'Perhaps you are right,' he agreed. 'Now, shall I have the servants bring some refreshment?'

'Thank you, sir,' Mary answered, bowing elegantly again.

'McCabe and I are off to take the air,' the squire said. 'We should be back in an hour or so. Then I will wake our young prodigy and see what all the fuss has been about.' With that the squire turned on his heel, grabbing the other letters from the table as he did so, and, followed by McCabe, left the room.

An hour later when the two returned, Turlough was still lying on the couch with his eyes shut.

'That boy could sleep through an English siege!' the squire declared. 'What's the matter with him? Is he still suffering from the aftereffects of the pox?'

'His present malady did originate with the Galar-breac,' Mary answered tactfully.

'I'll have my physician look at him,' the squire decided. Then he marched across the room and prodded the lad in the leg with his walking stick. Turlough did not move, though he breathed loudly and snorted once as if he was snoring.

The squire leaned in close and slapped the young man in the face. Turlough's eyes opened with a start and he rolled off the seat onto the floor. In a second he was on his hands and knees, trying to work out what had happened to him.

'Are you awake now?' Reynolds asked in a loud voice. 'Have you got your wits about you?'

'I am awake,' Turlough coughed. 'And I am blind not deaf, so please refrain from yelling. I also have my wits, which is more than can be said for you, whoever you are.'

'I am your host,' Reynolds declared sharply.

'You are the squire?' the young harper asked, putting a hand on the seat to steady himself as he rose. 'But I was told that

Squire Reynolds was a man of exceptional good taste and learning. I heard that he was intelligent and compassionate. You are an ignorant oaf who assaults a blind man while he is sleeping. You cannot possibly be the squire.'

'How dare you speak to me in that manner, young fellow?' the squire bellowed.

'You have no conscience about deriding my teacher in front of me,' Turlough went on. 'Or did you think I couldn't hear you? And then to throw me off my seat in your impatience to hear me play! If this is the way a harper is treated in the Reynolds's house, I will go out to the stables and sleep with the horses.'

'You have spent too long in the company of Mhaire Dhall,' Reynolds berated him, forgetting any kinder feelings he might have been harbouring for the old lady. 'You have acquired her inflated sense of self-worth. You are not a harper until another harper has approved of your playing. You may have performed for the gentlefolk who make Mrs MacDermot's acquaintance, but none of them have the slightest idea about music. Most of them believe a bassoon is a large hairy creature which lives deep in the forests of India. They are ignorant of the finer points of harping and would excuse even a badly tuned instrument simply because they know no better.'

'My teacher warned me about your bad temper,' Turlough replied. 'She told me that it blinds you to the world about you.'

'You are impudent and ill-informed,' Reynolds screeched. 'I am as sedate a gentleman as ever lived in this land.' The squire's voice was gradually rising in pitch and his face had turned red with rage. 'How dare you accuse me of having a wild temper?'

'I did not say it was wild,' the harper pointed out, 'I said it was bad.'

'Be quiet!' Reynolds shouted. 'I'll tell you what you said, you young puppy!'

By this time the servants were running in to see what the matter was.

'If you want to sleep with the horses,' the squire bellowed, 'then you shall do so!' Reynolds surveyed the gathered servants quickly and when he spotted his chief butler he snapped his fingers at the man. 'O'Shea, fix this man a bed in the stables.'

'My lord,' the man replied, hurrying over to his master. 'My lord, the stables are full of horses this night. There is simply no room for the young gentleman.'

Reynolds's face changed from red to bright purple. He turned suddenly on the butler and with a mighty punch knocked the man to the floor. For a few brief seconds the other servants stood with mouths wide open in astonishment. Then they all scurried back to their work, none of them wanting to be the next object of the squire's attention.

As soon as he realised what he had done Reynolds calmed down. His face paled. He shook his head and slapped himself on the cheek. Then he bent over to take the butler's hand and help him to his feet.

'I am terribly sorry, O'Shea.' The squire was genuinely remorseful. 'I don't know what came over me.'

'That is quite all right, my lord,' the man stuttered nervously, rubbing his jaw. 'I'll go and see to the accommodation then, shall I?'

'Put this young fellow with the stinging tongue in one of the guest rooms,' Reynolds said in a subdued tone. 'And see that young Mary has a good bed in the servants' quarters.'

'Yes, my lord,' the butler replied, straightening his long waist-coat and brushing his sleeves.

When the butler was gone the squire rounded on the harper. 'You have embarrassed me in front of my servants, young man,' he hissed, his rage seething. 'I will forgive you if you turn out to be as talented as everyone says you are. But if you have been wasting my time, you will be sorry for it.'

With that the squire stormed from the room, slamming the oak-panelled door behind him.

A few seconds after he was gone, the man called McCabe broke out into fits of laughter. 'I haven't seen him that stirred up since the last time old Mhaire came to visit,' he chortled.

'Congratulations. But I am afraid it pretty much ruins your chances of gaining his patronage.'

'What do I care about his opinion,' Turlough dismissed.

'He knows everyone who is anyone in Ireland,' said McCabe. 'On his recommendation you could walk into any of the finest houses and be treated like a king.'

'I am not a king,' the harper scoffed. 'Why should I wish to be treated like one?'

'But men of your profession are a rare breed these days. Since the time of Cromwell there have been fewer and fewer folk taking up the harp. How Mhaire Dhall survived the reign of the Puritans I'll never know. I suppose she hid herself well. But a great many harpers were burned at the stake by Cromwell and his men. And almost all the harps in Ireland were destroyed along with them.'

'I know that,' Turlough replied tersely.

'Did you also know,' McCabe asked, 'that the few harpers who have survived are not necessarily the best of their breed? The finest harpers are dead or have had their hands mutilated. Even today if a harper is arrested in Dublin on any charge, the soldiers will remove the musician's top finger joints so the nails cannot grow back.'

'What are you trying to say to me?'

'That you will be regarded as highly as any of the greatest harpers who once roamed this land, simply because you are one of the very few who still exist. Before the English came, harpers were the equal of any chieftain or king. They were treated with honour. Their visits were an occasion of great feasting. Folk still yearn after those days and you will be accorded high honours if you are talented and skilled. You have embarked on a life which will take you to places and allow you to meet people no son of a blacksmith could hope to encounter.'

'I understand,' the harper answered humbly, beginning to see McCabe's point.

'I have been studying the harp with Squire Reynolds for five years,' the young man told him. 'I am the son of a squire myself.

My father turned Protestant so that his land would not be confiscated by the Crown. But though he and many like him have adopted the religion of the English, we are still Irish at heart. The traditions, language and music of our people are important to us.'

'So I will be well patronised?'

'If you have any real gift for the instrument,' McCabe affirmed, 'you will have a grand life ahead of you. You will be welcomed with open arms amongst the old Irish aristocracy as well as many of the folk who represent the new order. I advise you to try and get on Reynolds's good side. He has a kind heart really and his approval would be invaluable.'

'Thank you for your advice, Mister McCabe,' Turlough nodded.

'My first name is Cathair,' the man smiled, 'but the squire will not let anyone call me that since it sounds too much like the Irish word for chair. Reynolds reckons that would be undignified for one of the harping profession.'

'Then what name do you go by?'

'I am afraid the squire decided that a rather uncouth foreign name would suit me best,' McCabe winced. 'You must call me Charles.'

'You poor unfortunate bastard,' Turlough sighed, shaking his head. 'Stuck with a name that would curdle milk. I shall call you Cathair, if you don't mind. I prefer a restful name to one that sticks in your teeth like lumpy cheese.'

The harper reached out and found the sleeve of his new friend. 'Sometimes I may call you by the name of Chair,' Turlough whispered. 'You must not think I do this in anything but fun.'

'I don't mind,' McCabe smiled.

'And you, sir,' the harper went on, 'may address me as Turlough.'

McCabe took the harper's hand and shook it firmly.

'I'll be off and see to the squire,' McCabe said. 'Hopefully he will have calmed down by now. Get your harp out and start tuning. I'll bring him back as soon as I can. The best way to win his support is to play well.'

'Thank you, Cathair,' the harper answered politely, though he really had no heart for playing.

Mary brought the harp to him, laid it down at his feet and began untying the straps which held the seal-skin flaps shut.

'What has come over you?' she whispered. 'Why were you so insulting to the squire? He only wishes to help you.'

'No-one can help me,' Turlough sighed.

'I have heard enough of that talk,' she snapped. 'You have worked hard for the last three years learning to play. Mrs MacDermot and Squire Crilly spent good money on a tutor for you. You have been given a harp and a horse and the opportunity to play for the wealthy and the powerful of this land. Everyone is doing whatever they can to help you on your way and yet you are so ungrateful. What more could you ask for?'

'The one thing I can never have.'

'Will you shut up about bloody Bridget Cruise!' Mary spat. 'She's gone. And you'll have to get used to that. In the meantime you have a life to live and obligations to your patrons to fulfil.'

Turlough nodded hastily. It was not often that Mary lost her temper and he did not want to upset her any more. He took the small harp from her, sitting it on the floor in front of him. Then he ran his fingers over the strings, shaking his head when he discovered that it was once again terribly out of tune.

'This harp does not like to travel,' he cursed. 'I had this same problem after the journey back to Ballyfarnon. The timbers are not secure enough to stretch the wires.'

'It was the best Mrs MacDermot could do,' Mary said, trying to buck him up. 'In time you will be able to buy a better harp of your own. You are about to embark on a wonderful adventure, enjoy yourself.'

Just then the door opened and Squire Reynolds marched in, closely followed by McCabe. They stopped in front of the fireplace.

'Are you ready to show me your skill?' Reynolds barked.

'I must adjust the tuning,' Turlough replied. 'I hope you can give me a few minutes.'

'I can.'

The harper ran his fingers over the wires again and the squire raised his eyebrows in dismay. 'That is a badly tuned harp,' he declared. 'Indeed I have never encountered one so poorly tuned.'

'She does not like to travel,' Turlough explained.

'Nonsense, lad. I have never known a harp that did not like to travel. It is in their blood. The road is a part of their spirit.'

'Well this one does not like it,' the harper insisted. 'She was in tune when I left this morning, but the journey has put her out.'

Reynolds grunted as if to say he did not believe Turlough. The squire warmed his hands in front of the fire while he listened to the harper's tuning. Occasionally he would wince and groan to show that he thought a wire was still in need of adjustment, but apart from that he was silent until the young man had finished.

'What will you play for us?' the squire asked when Turlough had completed the task.

'Ríon in Uaigneas,' Turlough replied in Irish. 'The Forlorn Queen.'

'A grand tune,' McCabe pronounced it, 'and one of my favourites.'

Reynolds was not so impressed. 'It is too slow and mournful a piece for this time of day. But if you need to warm up with an easy melody, then so be it.'

Turlough ignored this sly insult. Carefully placing his fingers against the wires, he commenced the air the very moment Reynolds stopped speaking.

The piece was very mournful, evoking the sorrowful mood that had come over Turlough himself since last night. He played it slower than was usual, imbuing the music with all the power of his emotions. Occasionally the young harper would pause in the middle of a phrase when he felt it appropriate. His teacher had instructed him in this technique. It was an old trick harpers used to keep their performances fresh. In this way no tune was ever played the same way twice.

When Turlough had finished, the wires lingered on into silence. Only Mary knew that her friend had put all of his own anguish into the tune. The tears welled up in her eyes at the thought of the pain he must be suffering.

'Play Brian Boru's,' Reynolds asked before McCabe had a chance to compliment the young harper's playing. 'I want to hear you play one of the truly ancient pieces. There is nothing like a stirring march to fill the heart with joy.'

Turlough nodded and placed his hands on the wires again, struggling to conjure the mood of this piece in his mind. The melody was said to come from the time of the great King Brian who drove the Vikings out of Ireland many centuries before. It was a tune of war. But the harper was not in the frame of mind for fast-moving tunes. He could not concentrate on the particular flavour of this melody. He paused.

'Come along then,' Reynolds urged. 'Every harper knows this piece.'

'It was the first one I learned,' McCabe agreed.

Turlough took a deep breath and struck the first few notes lightly. It was his intention to build the piece to a crescendo but the notes rang out so softly at first that the harp was barely audible. The squire leaned forward to hear the melody, frowning and grunting with displeasure as he did so.

Distracted by this, Turlough began to build the intensity of the piece before he was ready and he inadvertently struck one wire too hard. It rang over the top of the other notes, spoiling the effect of the chords underneath.

Reynolds coughed. Turlough played on, becoming more and more frustrated and knowing full well this was not his best performance. As he raised the volume of the harp by striking the wires more stridently, he struck a string which slipped its tuning and went terribly out of key. He flinched and tried to avoid that wire as he played but in a few seconds another wire slipped and then another. The harp was not responding well to being set so close to the fireplace.

But it was too late for Turlough to do anything about that. He played on regardless until he finished the march on a note that was so out of tune everyone in the room, including the harper, gritted their teeth.

Before the discordant note had rung out Reynolds spoke up. 'You have some skill,' he conceded. 'But you are impatient and you do not know how to care for your instrument.'

'It is not a very good harp,' McCabe pointed out in defence.

'A good musician can make the worst of instruments sing under his fingers,' the squire retorted, raising his voice over any further objections. 'You clearly do not practise enough. You should be playing eight hours a day.'

'If I play eight hours a day,' the harper asked, 'how will I have the time to travel between one great house and another?'

'You will stay here for a week and we will see what improvements diligent practice can achieve,' Reynolds told Turlough, ignoring his cheeky remark. 'But my advice to you is that you are not a gifted player. You have no feeling for the old music at all. That may come with time but I suggest that you try your hand at composing instead. You have one week to present to me a piece of your own. The piece must be completely original. On that performance I will judge whether you are worthy of beginning a career on the road.'

'One week!' Turlough gasped. 'Mhaire Dhall would not allow me to compose. She told me that was only for the most accomplished harpers. I have never played anything but the melodies she taught me. I don't know how to compose.'

'If you don't learn to compose melodies this week,' Reynolds smiled, 'you will stay here until you have learned. Even if that takes another three years. For I will not allow you to go out that door if you have not got something worthy to offer your patrons. If you can compose tunes in tribute of your betters, you will have an easy life. I am doing you a great favour.'

'Are you asking me to produce a melody in honour of yourself?' the harper asked resentfully.

'No, that would be too easy. I am readily flattered. I think a tribute to this house and this land would be a far more fitting subject.'

'I have no eyes to see your house or your land,' Turlough hissed, suspecting that there must be some trick in the setting of this task.

'Then Charles will take you out around the boundaries,' Reynolds countered, 'and he will describe the countryside to you and the house and anything else that might be worthy of a melody. He will be your eyes.'

'Thank you, sir,' the harper replied rather sarcastically.

'I will see you this evening at dinner,' the squire informed him. 'You have a few hours of light left. Since you have only a week to complete this task, I suggest you set about it immediately.'

'I would be happy to go with you,' Cathair told Turlough. 'Give me time to change into my walking clothes and I'll be with you.'

'That's settled then,' Reynolds proclaimed, clapping his hands with glee. 'I am off to see to the stables.' He bowed slightly to the young men. 'Good day to you, gentlemen.' Then he bowed to Mary. 'And to you, my dear.'

'Good day,' they answered as one and the squire left the room.

'He didn't think much of me,' Turlough said sullenly when he heard the door shut.

'You are quite wrong,' Cathair commented. 'George Reynolds is a hard man. He rarely has a good word to say for anyone. I believe you have impressed him. I was here twelve months before he ordered me to try my hand at composition. He is just being harsh because he wants to see if you can take criticism. I'll meet you out the front of the house in a short while and we'll go for our first walk together. There is so much to see on this land.'

Turlough nodded and McCabe went off to get changed.

'You played beautifully,' Mary said.

'Thank you,' Turlough replied and he was truly grateful for her kind words.

'I must go to make our rooms ready,' she told him. 'I will see you this evening.'

Then she came close and brushed her lips against his cheek. 'Enjoy yourself this afternoon,' she said and then left him to ponder the difficulty of creating something from nothing.

With the butler's help Turlough wrapped the harp in its seal skin. Then he made his way outside just as Cathair was walking down the stairs.

'I'll take that,' McCabe offered, slipping his arm through the strap on the harp case. 'It wouldn't do any harm to bring the instrument out. The rain has eased off quite a bit. We might even get some blue sky.'

'I have lain my harp across the shoulder of a steady chair,' the harper quipped as he put out his arm to be led. McCabe laughed at the joke and headed down to the gardens.

'Where would you like to go first?' Cathair asked Turlough.

'Into the fields,' the harper replied immediately. 'I haven't laid down in a green field for three years. I've been stuck inside at my lessons without respite all that time.'

'The ground will be wet,' Cathair advised.

'I don't care.'

'Very well. We shall go to the fields. And I can tell you some of the local legends. Every hill hereabouts, every rocky outcrop, every oak tree or ash or yew has a story attached to it. And Squire Reynolds knows all the tales.'

Turlough grunted a reply. He would have preferred to forget Squire Reynolds for the moment.

They had walked for about half an hour when McCabe came to a halt and announced, 'Here we are.'

'Where are we?' asked Turlough.

'The palace of the King of the Faeries.'

'What?' the harper cried, thinking he must have heard incorrectly. He felt a shiver run down his backbone.

'That is the other name this hill is known by,' McCabe informed him. 'But most folk call it simply Shee Beg.'

Turlough frowned, certain he had heard that name before,

though he could not remember where.

'It is a famous hill, for under a cairn at the top lies the last mortal remains of Fionn MacCumhal,' Cathair explained, 'the greatest hero Ireland has ever known.'

'I've heard tell of him,' Turlough acknowledged with sarcasm in his voice. Everyone knew the tales of Fionn.

The harper reached into a deep coat pocket and pulled out a leather bottle. He removed the cork and took a generous mouthful of whiskey. 'Would you like some, Cathair?' he offered.

'It is a little nippy,' McCabe answered, not sure whether Squire Reynolds would approve. 'I'll have a drop since you're offering it.'

McCabe took the bottle and placed it gently on his lips, taking the smallest of sips. Then he handed it back.

The harper weighed the bottle in his hand for a moment then passed it back to his companion.

'Oh go on, man, take a good swig. It'll do you good.'

Cathair smiled and nodded. Then he took a mouthful of the liquor. In seconds the poor fellow was coughing and gagging at the strength of the whiskey. He struggled for a few minutes to control his breathing. Finally he stood up straight and cleared his lungs with one great phlegm-filled hack.

'Where did you get that?' McCabe gasped when he had caught his breath again. 'I've never tasted anything like it.'

'Squire Crilly and his family make it,' Turlough replied, politely ignoring the fact that McCabe obviously had very little experience of whiskey. 'Tell me, Cathair,' the harper said after he had retrieved the bottle and taken another gulp of whiskey, 'what part of the country are you from?'

'Lough Erne.'

'What sort of harpers do they have up there on Lough Erne's shore?'

'I don't know what you mean.' McCabe smiled. 'Fat ones. Thin ones. Short ones. Tall ones. The same as everywhere else.'

'I don't think you understand me,' Turlough said. 'I mean to say, what sort of a harper does not occasionally touch the drink?'

'My father won't allow strong liquor in the house,' McCabe explained a little sheepishly. 'He has strict rules about it. And Squire Reynolds made a solemn vow to him that I should have none while I am staying in his home. I've never been a one for the whiskey anyway.'

'I guessed that.'

The harper handed the bottle back to McCabe. 'And so does it worry you that we might be caught breaking the rules?'

Cathair took another swig, coughed a lot less this time, and placed the bottle back in Turlough's hand. 'I don't care much for rules, as a matter of fact,' he sputtered.

'Neither do I,' the harper laughed as he lifted the bottle to his lips. Before long the two of them had sat down on the side of the hill called Shee Beg to finish Turlough's small supply of whiskey. And in a short while they were laughing together like two long-lost friends.

'I have learned many things from Squire Reynolds,' Cathair said, holding up a finger to Turlough. His eyes focused on the extended digit rather than the harper. 'And I will not hear him derided. Not even by you.' McCabe's finger wandered off and his bleary eyes followed.

'I am sure you have learned a lot from the squire,' Turlough smiled. 'But why have you not been sent out on the road like myself after your five years of learning? If harpers are so scarce, why keep a fellow like yourself indoors?'

'I am not that skilled really,' Cathair muttered bashfully. 'You are a much better player than I am. I can't seem to relax when I am performing. My fingers tumble over one another uncontrollably. I can't keep a good tempo.'

'What's a tempo?'

'A steady beat.'

'I don't understand you exactly.' The harper cocked his head to one side in interest.

Cathair beat his hand on his leg and hummed the march called Brian Boru's.

'That is a steady beat.'

'Mhaire taught me to think of music as a series of breaths,' Turlough replied. 'And breaths may vary in length from one to the next.'

'How would two musicians playing a piece together know how long each breath was intended to be?'

'I have never played with another musician,' the harper admitted. 'Mhaire would play melodies to teach them to me and I would copy them note for note. I know how to vary each performance to give freshness to the music and that means varying the breaths. But I have never heard the harp played along with another instrument.'

'You must have heard a chamber orchestra play at Mrs MacDermot's,' McCabe frowned.

'Yes,' Turlough conceded.

'Didn't you wonder how the violins, the cellos and the violas played together in perfect unison?'

'That was before I was blinded,' the harper explained. 'And before I had any interest in music. I didn't take much notice.'

'I will take you to hear a recital of the works of an Italian composer whose music I admire,' Cathair offered. 'His name is Corelli. Archangelo Corelli. His melodies are sublime.'

'That would be fine,' Turlough laughed. 'I have heard his tunes and Vivaldi's too. It's fine music.'

'But you'll have to give me some more of that whiskey in exchange,' McCabe told his companion.

'I have several fine bottles at home and the promise of a further supply whenever I should need it.'

'It certainly has made me feel different since I had that drink. It is as if I have become instantly brave and invincible.'

'That's what happens,' Turlough nodded. 'The trick is to enjoy the feeling without believing in it at all. Once you start to think you're invincible, you'll get yourself in terrible trouble.'

'I am sure I could play the harp now like I never have before,' Cathair announced. 'I suddenly don't care what anyone thinks of me or my skills.'

'Why don't you pick it up then?'

'Your harp?'

'Why not?'

'Thank you, Turlough,' McCabe smiled. 'I would be honoured.'

'I would be honoured with a tune, Cathair,' the harper replied.

'But let's go up the hill a bit further,' McCabe suggested. 'From up higher I can get a clear view of the sister hill to this one. And I will describe it to you.'

'What's that hill called?' the harper asked.

'It is known as Shee Mor.'

'Shee Beg and Shee Mor,' Turlough repeated under his breath. 'Where have I heard those two names before?'

But Cathair had already put the harp on his shoulder and was reaching out a hand to his friend. 'I am a bit unsteady on my feet,' he stammered. 'I am not used to drinking that much.'

'That wasn't much,' Turlough laughed as they headed off. 'I'll wager Squire Crilly's cat drinks more than that for breakfast.'

'I've heard tell it is quite a cat!' McCabe hummed in agreement.

'I've seen it. It is not an animal to be trifled with.'

Halfway up the hill Cathair stopped in his tracks, breathing heavily, obviously exhausted.

'This will do,' he stated and put the harp down on the ground.

'Now that I wish to sit down,' Turlough grinned, 'I regret not bringing a chair with me.'

'You did bring a chair,' McCabe replied in a flash. 'But it won't do you any good to imagine you'll be sitting on it. You find your own seat and envy me. For I have a chair wherever I go.'

The harper laughed and found himself a place to sit while McCabe unpacked the instrument from its case and sat down to touch the wires. 'She has held her tuning well,' he said, raising his eyebrows in surprise. 'I cannot believe you had so much trouble with her.'

'She always keeps her tuning for other folk,' the young harper replied bitterly. 'I don't think she cares for me.'

'Perhaps she does not like having novices like ourselves touching her all the time,' Cathair suggested. 'Perhaps she prefers an experienced hand.'

'Just like a woman,' Turlough muttered. 'But a fellow has to learn the art of handling them some time. And if they won't let us study diligently, how are we to improve ourselves and satisfy them?'

'Are you talking about harps or women?'

'The two are very similar in my opinion.'

McCabe laughed and then launched into a lively tune which Turlough recognised as a piece by a famous harper who had lived in the time of the first King James. The melody reminded him that he, Turlough O'Carolan, was merely one in a long line of musicians. Harpers had played for their supper in the great houses of Ireland ever since the ancestors of the Irish had landed on this isolated island at the western edge of the world.

As he dwelled on the lineage from which his knowledge had descended, Turlough lay back with the clear understanding that he had a responsibility to carry on the ancient tradition even in these dangerous times when men and women of musical skill were looked on with suspicion by the authorities.

The gift of learning he had been given was precious, beyond value, and it was his duty to share his music with as many folk as possible. His unhappiness over Bridget Cruise should not be allowed to get in the way of that duty. Even the blindness that had come to him might be considered a gift, he thought, for it had led him to the life of harping.

As Turlough drifted off to the sweet melody, the drink taking effect, the young harper tried to remember where he had heard the names of these hills before. Was it in some old tale? Or a song? Or had Squire Crilly mentioned them?

The music ceased after a while and the blind harper lay on the hillside, letting his mind drift off. He had not been dozing long when he sensed the presence of someone standing nearby.

Since the onset of his blindness, all his other faculties had sharpened.

'Cathair?' he whispered, a little afraid. 'Is that you?'

'He is asleep,' a familiar voice said softly.

'Who's that?' the harper gasped, sitting up. When there was no reply, he rolled over onto his side and stood up.

'Stay where you are, Turlough,' the stranger said gently. 'I mean you no harm.'

'Who are you?'

'We have met before,' the man told him. 'Don't you recognise me?'

'I am sorry, sir,' Turlough admitted. 'You have the advantage of me. Perhaps we met before I was blinded.'

'Indeed we did meet once or twice before you were blinded, though you perhaps do not recall the circumstances,' the stranger teased. 'You also met my wife. And we saw you again at Mrs MacDermot's house last night. We heard you play there and complimented you.'

'Squire Sheehan,' the harper suddenly realised and he bowed low. 'Your Majesty.'

'Indeed it is,' the squire replied with delight in his voice. 'I am touched that you remembered me. But it is unwise to be so formal with me. I am Squire Sheehan to the world of mortals. My wife and I do not like to attract too much attention. In the past it has caused us some degree of discomfort.'

'I understand,' Turlough replied. 'What are you doing here? I thought you were intending to stay with Squire Crilly for a while.'

'Still asking questions,' the squire commented with a smile in his voice. 'I forgive you your inquisitive nature. It is the mark of a fine musician. My wife and I came over to spend the evening with Reynolds. He is an old friend. We were told you would be playing tonight. My wife has taken quite a liking to you, young man.'

Turlough was suddenly flooded with memories of the strange vision he had suffered in his sickness. 'Whilst I was ill I dreamed that the King of the Faeries and his queen presided over a hurling match,' Turlough began. 'Until this moment I was certain that it was only a delusion, a symptom of the Galar-breac. Now I am beginning to believe that it was something more.'

'If it eases your mind,' the squire told him, 'then I have no objection to you recalling the experience in whatever terms you feel most comfortable with. As long as you remain true to my wife and I and do not betray us.'

'I made my oath.'

'So you did,' Sheehan said. 'And we have kept our part of the bargain. How are you enjoying your new life as a harper?'

'I am warming to the idea.'

'I am sure you will have a grand time,' the squire laughed. 'So will you perform something for us before dinner?'

'I may do,' the harper replied cautiously.

'Will you grace us with a composition of your own?'

'I have never composed music before,' Turlough admitted. 'And I have been given one week to come up with a piece for Squire Reynolds.'

'Plenty of time,' the gentleman scoffed. 'Have you found a suitable subject?'

'I have not.'

'Perhaps I might suggest something?'

'Please do.'

'I have a favourite tale which comes from these parts,' the squire began. 'It concerns a battle which took place between the people of these two hills, Shee Beg and Shee Mor.'

'A battle?'

'A battle it ended,' Sheehan smiled. 'But it began as a friendly hurling match between the Faeries of that hill and the Faeries who dwell under this one.'

'Faeries?' the young harper coughed.

'Yes,' the squire nodded. 'The Old Ones. The Gentry. The Good People. What you will.'

Turlough crossed himself. 'Mother of God,' he mumbled, 'what have I got myself into?' He'd had his suspicions but was shocked to have them confirmed.

'Don't tell me you're one of those religious fanatics!' Sheehan exclaimed.

'No,' the harper admitted. 'I never much think about religion till there's trouble.'

'Very wise,' Sheehan replied sternly. 'Do not fear. My wife and myself and our kind are not agents of the Devil as some foolish priests would have you believe. We are no less created by God than anything else in this world. We are just different. If you would hold that up as reason to consider us evil, then perhaps you are not the lad we thought you were.'

'No, no, I do not get the impression that you are evil at all,' Turlough cut in hastily. There was a frightening edge to the squire's voice.

'Because we are not. Believe me, if ever you meet true evil, you will know it instantly.'

'Tell me the story of the battle,' Turlough gulped, keen to distract the squire from this train of thought. He knew he would recognise the tale, but the conversation was taking a rather dangerous direction.

'I am surprised you do not remember it,' Sheehan said archly. 'I was under the impression your mother was quite a good storyteller.'

'She was.'

'Then how is it she never told you this one?'

The harper frowned deeply as half-remembered images came into his mind, remnants of dreams, nightmares and old songs all mixed together.

'A great game was arranged between the folk of this hill, Shee Beg, which is a fine hill. The finest for many miles about, though it is the smaller of the two. A game was arranged with the Faeries who make their home under the hill of Shee Mor, which if you were granted your sight again right now you would be able to perceive directly in front of you.'

'How did the game turn into a battle?'

'That is the interesting part,' Sheehan went on, choosing not to take offence at the lad's curiosity. 'The Faeries of Shee Beg were one player short so the game was held up until a suitable subject could be found to fill the position. The King of the Faeries sent his minions out in search of a mortal since all the Good People had been drafted in from the countryside and there were none left.'

'Did they find a mortal?'

'They did. They found a lad seated upon a hill alone on a moonless night and asked him to join their team. The next evening the hosts gathered and, according to the rules, the game began. But the Faeries of Shee Mor were angered that their opponents had a mortal on their side. They protested to the King and Queen of the Faeries but to no avail.'

'So the game went on?'

'It did. Though the folk from Shee Mor decided to bend the rules slightly.'

'In what way?'

'They armed themselves with weapons, shields and all the gear of war,' Sheehan explained. 'The folk of Shee Beg decided, for their own safety, that they should do the same. And a great battle began from what should have been a friendly match.'

'Who won?' Turlough gasped. He'd never quite known which side was which.

'There was blood all over the field and bodies strewn from one end of the valley to the other before the winning goal, the only goal of the match, was struck.'

'And it was the mortal who struck it!' the harper exclaimed. 'He claimed a goal for the folk of Shee Beg.'

'And I won the wager,' Sheehan declared happily. 'I am very grateful to you for that. It is not often I get the upper hand with the queen on anything.'

He leaned closer.

'You are lucky the queen took a fancy to you. The last time she lost a wager her wrath was unstoppable. But your presence at the game seemed to quiet her immensely.'

The squire clapped his hands enthusiastically. 'And in gratitude for securing them the victory, the King of the Faeries of

Shee Beg promised to grant the mortal his dearest wish and to watch over him for the rest of his life. And the Queen of the Faeries of Shee Mor promised to be his patroness forever after.'

'Are you truly the King of the Faeries?' Turlough blurted, mindless of the offence this question might give.

'I am,' Sheehan laughed. 'But that must be our secret for you will meet many mortals who would not understand. There are a large number of your folk who live in fear of my people.'

'I have heard that the Faeries steal mortals for their sport,' Turlough ventured.

'Rubbish!' Sheehan dismissed crossly. 'That is just a bit of mischief. And it is usually visited upon those who rightly deserve it. Didn't Crilly warn you about asking too many questions?'

'He did,' the lad replied.

'Since you won me the wager,' Sheehan stated, 'I will allow you a few, to satisfy your curiosity.'

'What manner of folk are you?'

'Just the same as you, Turlough. Except for the fact that we live for a long time.'

'How long?'

'A very, very long time,' Sheehan replied with a sigh. 'But there are compensations to the tedium of immortality. Our private world is very beautiful. There is music, poetry and dancing. Everyone is filled with joy and there is no sickness.'

'Why do you choose to live in our world if yours is so wonderful?' Turlough asked with suspicion in his voice.

'A few of us like to think we can influence mortals to some degree,' Sheehan explained. 'That can be quite an amusing pastime. You folk are such timid creatures. Mortals rarely change their fashions or their ideas. They would like the world to stay as it always was.'

The squire laughed heartily. 'If left to your own devices, you lot would all still be dressing as you did in the time of the Romans. But the curious thing is that when your folk observe some brave soul wearing an outrageous style of wig, or a coat with long tails and wide cuffs, they often jump around with excitement and desire the new thing themselves. Mortals just need to be led on a little by folk who have a developed taste.'

'Mrs MacDermot did say that you and your wife were leaders of fashion,' Turlough remembered.

'Indeed we are. In clothing, in music, in cuisine. Even in the jewellery we wear and the friends we keep. My wife and I are looked up to by most of polite society. We represent an ideal which few mortals can achieve. We are young, eternally so I might add; witty, that comes from experience; wealthy, another result of having lived a long while; and, above all, easily bored, which is why we like to influence change in the world as much as possible.'

Sheehan sat down beside Turlough and put a hand on his shoulder. 'Once in a while of course, we do strike some opposition.'

'What do you mean?'

'That nasty business with Oliver Cromwell a few years ago. He and his Puritan followers set out to destroy all the joy, music, mirth, merriment and fashionable dress in the land. Of course they didn't realise it was my people who had had a hand in all that frivolity. Cromwell just hated having a good time.'

Sheehan thought for a second and then went on. 'You know,' he said incredulously, 'the thought often crossed my mind in those days that the Puritans did not even believe in the existence of my people.'

'English folk are said to scoff at the belief in Faeries. Squire Crilly told me that there are no Good People in England at all.'

'A great many of my kindred left Britain in the time of Cromwell, I heard tell,' Sheehan agreed, 'because they couldn't continue to live in a land where music was outlawed.'

'I have heard that Cromwell burned many harpers on great bonfires built from their own harps.'

'That is no crime at all compared to the cut of his clothes,' Sheehan spat. 'Those Puritans had absolutely no dress sense whatsoever. Dour old men they were for the most part. And Cromwell! He was the worst of them all. Face like a stewed fig, completely uncorrupted by any trace of a smile. All he really needed was a damn good woman and a bit of illicit fornication to lift his spirits. That would have set him to rights. Things would have been different, I can tell you, if he and his wife had enjoyed a bit of fun in the straw now and then.'

Sheehan laughed at a memory, but the joy dropped from his voice as he went on. 'The poor fellow couldn't even enjoy a fine glass of port without imagining the Devil looking over his shoulder. I mean to say, what sort of a man spends eight months of his life drafting a law against the wearing of lace? Weren't there any hospitals to build? Or roads to mend? Weren't there more important problems for the Lord Protector to be concentrating on?'

Turlough shrugged. To him Cromwell was just a disturbing story which old folk told to frighten the children.

'Now it is all happening again. Another flock of frightened mortals are coming to reform Ireland. A Dutchman this time! The Dutch have no sense of humour in my experience. You'd easier get witty comment from a priest than a smile from a Dutchman.'

Sheehan tightened his grip on the lad's shoulder and Turlough squirmed uncomfortably.

'They have to be stopped,' the squire hissed urgently. 'These people who would have us living in a drab grey world where obligation and duty are more important than friendship and generosity. A world where trust is something you keep to yourself and all that gets shared is opinions.'

Turlough was starting to sense just how outraged the squire was.

'They would create a world where mere money is the common currency of everyday life. A world where music and dancing are valued by their weight in wealth not the depth of their delights. If these dismal folk have their way, the mortal lands will become a barren landscape where people are housed like caged animals in long featureless halls built of stone.'

'Like Dublin Castle is said to be,' Turlough cut in.

'They'll have everyone dressed in uniforms,' Sheehan ignored the interruption, 'not just soldiers, everyone. They'll tell folk what to eat and what not to eat. They'll persecute anyone who does not agree with their religion. They'll decree that fun is something for children and that grown men and women must leave their joy behind when they enter through the gates of adulthood.'

'Will they outlaw whiskey?'

'I wouldn't be surprised if they tried,' Sheehan shook his head in dismay. 'These poor scared souls will be the death of a good time if we let them.'

'I won't let them!' Turlough promised.

'Good lad!' Sheehan bellowed. 'That's what I like to hear. There's not many mortals who'd dare take up the challenge of facing the pompous, formal, stodgy folk of this world. You are one of a rare breed.'

'What else have I got to do with my life?' the young harper sighed. 'I will devote it to bringing joy and merriment to mortals. And I will show the Puritans up for what they really are!'

'Bravo!' the squire exclaimed. 'I knew we could depend on you, my lad. I could tell by the way you struck that glorious goal that you were a fellow who would not be frightened of a challenge. You're a true tactician.'

'What's that?'

'Never mind,' Sheehan frowned. 'I'm overjoyed that you've joined with us. Harassing dour mortals can be so much fun. Old Squire Reynolds used to be like you, a long time ago. But he forgot us when the concerns of the mortal world began to burden him. Now he's as sour as the dried-up fruit from a Puritan's lemon tree.'

'A light heart lives long,' Turlough said, repeating an old saying he had heard as a child. 'That's your secret, isn't it?'

'That's a large part of it,' Sheehan smiled. 'So let's have a bit of fun with Reynolds, shall we? What do you think about the Battle of Shee Beg and Shee Mor as a fitting theme for your first composition?'

'Indeed it is a fine idea,' the harper agreed. 'A worthy subject for a lively melody.'

'Then take the idea away with you and perhaps you will have a tune by this evening.'

'By this evening!' Turlough laughed. 'That would certainly irritate the old man.'

'Reynolds will be impressed if you present that story to him,' Sheehan confided. 'It is a tale very dear to his heart.'

Then Turlough heard Sheehan yawn.

'I have spent too long out in the fields today,' the squire stretched.

'I know what you mean,' the young harper replied. 'I have just had a little sleep myself.'

'Did it improve your mood?' Sheehan asked.

'I don't know what you mean,' the harper replied cagily.

'Reynolds told me that you had words with him this afternoon.'

'That is true,' Turlough admitted.

'Are you feeling better about the world then?'

'I am. I was clinging to a dream that will never come true.'

'You strike me as a young man whose wishes come true with alarming regularity,' Sheehan laughed. 'If I didn't know better, I'd say that you had been touched with a special gift. But it is a wise man who knows when to abandon one foolish dream and pursue another. Indeed often the original wish takes us off on another journey altogether and we forget what it was we first desired.'

'I will never forget what I first wished for, but I have learned that some things are not meant to be and that everything happens for the best in the long run.'

'You have an old head on those young shoulders,' the squire complimented him. 'If I had learned that lesson when I was younger, my life would have been much easier. It may have been much shorter and certainly less adventurous, but it would have surely been far easier.'

The squire laughed again before he went on. 'Once I understood that there is nothing on this earth worth getting upset about, I truly began to enjoy my life a lot more. And believe me, if you're going to live as long as I have, you might as well enjoy it.'

'As for one such as myself,' Turlough continued, taking up the squire's theme, 'well I am only here for an allotted time and I suppose I should make the best of it. Those who do not grasp the sweet opportunities life presents to them are wasting their time here.'

'So is our pact sealed?' Sheehan wanted to know. 'You will work with my folk to bring some joy into the world and to educate the begrudgers. And in return we will ensure your belly is full and your bed is always a warm one. And you may learn any tune you hear our folk playing and claim it as your own Agreed?'

'Agreed.'

'I must ask you one last question,' Sheehan ventured. 'Are you not bitter about your blindness?'

'I was for a long time,' Turlough admitted. 'But I think I am coming to realise that it has changed my life and it is beyond my power to do anything about it. So I may as well enjoy the other gifts which I have been awarded in compensation.'

'You are right. Every gift can be considered an affliction if it is misused or undervalued. It is just a matter of perspective.'

'And every setback should be cherished for the lessons it brings,' Turlough hummed. 'Even if we were allowed to live for a thousand years, one day we would be called to leave this world and seek the next.' Then the harper stopped to think. 'Do the Faerie folk live that long?'

'Longer,' Sheehan acknowledged with deep sadness in his voice. 'A great deal longer.' He paused for a moment then stood up. 'It is time I was getting back. I will see you this evening.'

'And I will hear you,' Turlough quipped. 'Because I cannot see anything. But before you go on your way could you pass me my harp without disturbing my friend Cathair?'

'Of course,' came the reply and in a few moments Turlough felt the instrument lowered down into position at his left side.

'I wish you an enjoyable afternoon,' Sheehan said merrily. 'The sun has come out and the birds are singing. Sunset is not far off. It will be a pleasant walk back to the Reynolds manor house. Goodbye.'

'Good day, sir,' Turlough replied respectfully and he listened to Sheehan's footsteps disappear down the hill.

The harper knew now that he had been allowing himself to wallow in self-pity and disappointment. The news of Bridget's impending wedding had been a bitter blow to him because he had been working all this while with one thought in mind: to win her back. His desire for her had led him off on an unexpected path, but even though she was out of reach, he had still gained a valuable and rare skill.

Mary was right. It was time to forget Bridget, if he could, and think seriously about his own future. He was blinded and trained in the ancient ways of the harp. There were few options open to him other than the life of a travelling musician. If he practised his skill and proved to have a talent for composition, he would at least have a fairly comfortable life. If he did not work at his profession, he would starve. It was as simple as that.

Turlough's mind wandered and he thought again of the hurling match. Strange that he had put the whole experience out of mind for so long, but he had thought of it as a dream and hadn't paid it much heed. He vowed to listen to his dreams from now on and to draw on them for his music.

Then a vague recollection arose from the depths of his memory. In a flash he heard the echoes of the barest bones of a tune. It was a melody that had featured prominently at the hurling match. In the next instant he was sure he could still hear the sweet tune which had been playing before the game.

At first Turlough could only vaguely recall the opening phrase. But once he had hummed that to himself a couple of times he heard the second and third parts of the air in his head as well.

His heart racing, the blind harper ran over the whole melody in his mind. Then he sat still for a few minutes and tried to calm himself. Was this a gift from the King of the Faeries? He had not invented it but had picked it up at the hurling match. It would be a source of great embarrassment to him if someone else recognised it.

Try as he might, the only place he could ever recall hearing the melody was at the start of the hurling match.

Shaking slightly with excitement, Turlough placed his fingers on the harp strings, finding the starting note and gently touching the wires in order until he thought he had the tune worked out. It was a simple melody, but an elegant and enticing one.

He decided he would practise the tune then play it for McCabe when he awoke and ask him if he recognised it. If he knew it then Turlough could not claim to have heard it at the match. He could have heard it anywhere. At the hiring fair or in the music room at Ballyfarnon. He must not claim it as his own until he could be absolutely certain it was the Faeries that taught it to him.

And so he sat there while his comrade slept soundly and in less than an hour he was performing the melody with confidence and conviction. In his vivid imagination he conjured the visions of that strange game. He recalled to mind the host of Faeries that had gathered on the playing field above Squire Crilly's house and he played the tune as if he were there again.

The very moment he heard McCabe stirring, Turlough put the harp down. 'Are you awake at last?' he asked.

'I am,' Cathair yawned. 'I haven't slept so well in years.'

'That will be the whiskey,' Turlough told him.

'Mother of God,' McCabe exclaimed, 'it is almost dark! We had better be making our way back to the house. I wouldn't like to be out after sunset tonight. It is a new moon and it will be so dark we will risk getting ourselves lost.'

'Now you know how I see the world,' the harper smiled. 'Before we go I want you to hear a piece I have been practising.'

'As long as you play quickly,' Cathair agreed.

Turlough lifted the harp and launched straight into his new piece. Cathair sat with his mouth open wide in astonishment as the blind harper played.

As the last chords were dying, Turlough turned to McCabe and asked him what he thought.

'It is quite beautiful!' Cathair exclaimed. 'Where did it come from?'

'You don't know the piece?'

'I have never heard anything quite like it,' McCabe said in admiration.

'I believe that the Faerie folk taught it to me,' Turlough admitted.

'The Faerie folk?'

'The Good People.'

'You have the gift of composition,' Cathair said. 'And either you are too modest to admit it or you are simply a man with an untamed sense of humour. I am not yet sure which.'

'We must get back to the house,' the harper urged. 'I want to play this piece for Mary. She has heard her grandmother play a thousand different tunes since she was a little child. I want to be sure she has not heard it. If Mary does not recognise the piece then I will claim it as my own.'

In a second Cathair was on his feet and had taken the harp from his blind friend. McCabe wrapped the instrument in its seal-skin cover as quickly as he could and soon both men were making their way back to the Reynolds house.

Along the way Turlough began putting together a few words in his head to make a song about the Faerie battle. It was surprisingly easy to find the right phrases to fit the music. By the time the two of them came to the front door, the harper had a poem to complement his melody.

'Take me to my room,' he asked McCabe when they were inside the house and had removed their coats. 'And then bring Mary to me as quick as you can.'

Within ten minutes Mary was sitting at the end of Turlough's bed as he played the tune to her.

'I have never heard it before,' she told him when he had finished. 'It is one of the most gorgeous melodies I have ever heard.'

'Are you sure you don't recognise it?' the harper pressed.

'I am certain,' she confirmed. 'I would have remembered such a charming air. It has an ancient echo to it, yet there is another quality which I have never heard before. I would not be surprised if you told me that you had heard the music of the Faerie folk and then simply copied one of their tunes.'

'Faerie music,' Cathair agreed. 'It does have a flavour of the Otherworld about it. Perhaps you did learn it from the Good People.'

Turlough smiled broadly, extremely pleased. 'Perhaps I did,' he replied enigmatically. 'I intend to present the melody to Squire Reynolds this evening as my first composition.'

'If you are going to play before dinner,' Mary told him, 'you had better get changed into a clean shirt and breeches. And your stockings have grass stains on them too so I'll find you a clean pair.'

'I'll go and tell Reynolds that you will play for him,' McCabe volunteered. 'He probably won't believe me.'

'Probably not!' Turlough laughed. 'But Squire Sheehan and his wife will not be surprised, I think.'

'Why is that?'

'He gave me the idea for this piece,' Turlough explained. 'In some ways you could say he inspired me to compose it.'

McCabe stood up and made for the door. 'You only have half an hour at the most,' he warned. 'Are you sure you'll be ready?'

'I'll be ready,' the blind harper smiled. 'I'll be ready.'

He recited the words of his song to Mary after McCabe had gone and she was surprised. 'That is a good story. Where did you learn it?'

'Squire Sheehan taught it to me this afternoon,' he admitted. 'Though the phrases are my own.'

'What has changed your mood, Turlough?'

236

'The squire pointed out to me,' he began, 'though it was you who first told me, that I am a very lucky man indeed. I have decided to drive Bridget from my mind. I will forget my sadness and look to a life of joy. What other purpose can God have intended for all of us? Certainly He would not be happy if we squandered His gifts. I must earn a living like anyone else, but I have been given an opportunity to do something which I once thought impossible. To play music for my bread and to bring a little happiness into a drab, cruel world.'

Turlough took Mary's hand in his and squeezed it tightly. 'I have much to thank you for, my dear friend. First of all you nursed me through the sickness of my body and now you have nursed me through the sickness of my soul. How can I ever repay you?'

'You can start by showing Squire Reynolds that you are worthy of his patronage,' she replied. 'And then,' she paused, 'we will have to have a little chat, you and I.'

'Very well, then,' the harper chirped. 'If you will help me get dressed, I'll get the Squire Reynolds business over as quickly as possible.'

He paused for a second and took the sleeve of her dress. 'This is fine blue wool.'

'Indeed it is,' Mary smiled. 'It was a gift from Mrs Mac-Dermot. That is quite an unusual talent you have for discerning colours. How do you know?'

'I have no idea really,' Turlough admitted. 'The colour just comes to my mind as I touch the fabric. But it only works with you. With anyone else I have not a hope of guessing the colour.'

Mary brought out a fresh shirt for the harper and he dressed in his dark green coat with the wide folded back sleeves which Crilly had given him. At his throat he wore a white neckerchief with a small amount of lace sewn into the end.

By the time Turlough entered the drawing room the guests were already seated in a semicircle around the fire. Mary led the harper in, describing the chamber in a whisper so he would know where each individual was seated.

She led him to an empty chair with its back to the fire with his harp lying at its feet. Turlough sat down and adjusted the skirts of his coat so that he was comfortable. Then Mary lifted the small instrument up and placed it carefully on his lap. At last she leaned in close as if to whisper words of encouragement but instead she managed to kiss him on the ear without anyone in the audience suspecting a thing.

Turlough smiled, relieved that his face had not turned bright red as it usually did when he was embarrassed.

'Squire Reynolds,' he began as Mary retreated to her seat, 'I listened carefully to all your words this afternoon. And I have taken some of what you had to say very seriously.'

The squire grunted. He was not sure whether he was being insulted.

'I went for a walk into the hills,' Turlough went on. 'With a good guide who shared with me the joyous spirit of ...' The harper paused. Cathair turned pale. '... the joyous spirit of the harp,' Turlough concluded with a smile. McCabe breathed a sigh of relief.

'I was told a story,' the harper continued, 'of a great battle which took place here in times gone past between the tribe of folk who lived under the hill of Shee Beg and the Faerie clan from the hill of Shee Mor. And I thought that would be a fitting tale for a composition.'

'You came up with a new composition in only a few short hours?' Reynolds scoffed. 'You are wasting my time. You have neither the skill nor the good sense to perform such a feat.'

'You have not heard the piece,' McCabe cut in. 'Perhaps you would be advised to listen to it before you pass judgment. I have heard it and I think it is remarkable.'

Reynolds turned his head slowly to look at McCabe. He could hardly believe his ears. 'What did you say?' he hissed, barely containing his outrage. 'Has everyone in this house lost their senses? How dare you speak to me in that manner? I am your teacher.'

'You are,' McCabe conceded. 'And I respect you greatly. But I think you should listen to the melody before you make any judgment.'

'That lad could not even keep his harp in tune this afternoon!' the squire laughed maliciously. 'I find it hard to believe that by this evening he could have composed a melody of any substance.'

'There is only one way to find out,' Turlough heard Squire Sheehan say. 'Let him play.'

The room fell silent for a few moments before Reynolds spoke again.

'Very well, Turlough,' the old man said in a measured, controlled voice. 'So as not to offer offence to my guests I insist on you performing your piece. I hope you realise that you run the risk of embarrassing me and making a complete fool of yourself. But I can see that my opinions will not be heeded until everyone has shared the experience of this fine composition of yours. Play on.'

'Thank you, sir,' Turlough replied politely. And then he checked the wires were in tune. They were perfectly set. The harper silently thanked Cathair with all his heart. He played a little chord, running his fingers over the wires while he spoke the first verse of his poem.

'A great quarrel came between the two kingdoms,' Turlough began, 'because they could not restrain their anger on the Faerie hill. It began with a little taunt and before long harsher words were added. Tempers frayed and the battle commenced.'

And then the harper launched into the melody. As he liked to do, he started touching the wires lightly, running his fingers gently over the bass notes to build the intensity slowly. But this time he was careful not to strike any of the strings too hard.

Squire Reynolds's mouth dropped open at the end of the first phrase and by the middle of the second he had shut his eyes to listen more carefully. Cathair and Mary smiled at each other. The Sheehans sat back in their chairs and touched hands, their eyes sparkling with delight.

Turlough sang the song he had composed, strumming the

chords of the harp to accompany his voice and occasionally plucking the upper strings to reinforce the melody. Mhaire Dhall had taught him this form of accompaniment. She had told him the style was as ancient as the harp itself.

When the song was done and Turlough began to restate the melody on the harp, even Squire Reynolds had a broad smile on his face.

The harper finished his piece with a delicate run down the strings, which he deftly repeated before striking a chord in the bass which rang on after the melody ended.

There was total silence as the vibrations of the resonating wires died out. No-one moved. No-one dared speak. Turlough lifted his head a little to hear if anyone would say anything. Suddenly he was concerned that he was about to get the same response from Squire Reynolds as he had received that afternoon.

The pause dragged on until the harper could not bear it any longer. 'Well?' he whispered. 'What do you think?'

'That is a fine tune,' Reynolds spoke up finally with a cough of discomfort. 'And a good story. Worthy of a great musician and an accomplished poet.'

'Thank you,' Turlough replied with relief, hardly able to believe his ears.

'But I do not think it is your own composition,' the squire accused.

'What do you mean?' McCabe gasped. 'Have you heard it before?'

Reynolds cast a glance at Sheehan who stared back blankly, giving nothing away.

'It was charming,' Mrs Sheehan cut in. 'I think he has done a splendid job for his first composition.'

'Where have you heard it?' McCabe pressed Reynolds.

'I cannot be certain,' Reynolds admitted. 'But I will lay money on the fact that it is not an original composition created in one afternoon by young Turlough O'Carolan.'

'Until you can recall the time and place where you heard it,'

Squire Sheehan interjected, 'and the name of the melody, it is rather unfair to condemn Turlough for claiming the piece as his own. Even if he did take an ancient tune and embellish it slightly, I cannot see what all the fuss is about. Clearly he plays beautifully with a real feel for the music. And the song was most entertaining.'

'I am sure I have heard those words before,' Reynolds objected in a sterner voice, shaking his head. 'They are not his own doing.'

'They are his own,' Sheehan announced. 'I told him the story this afternoon as he was resting on the hill of Shee Beg.'

Cathair frowned. He could not recall Squire Sheehan's presence on the hill.

'He may have heard the tale before,' Sheehan went on, 'but he did not know all of it. I had to tell him how the story began. So he must have come up with the words in the few hours since we spoke together.'

Reynolds looked at the squire and his wife and a troubled expression came over his face. 'I don't recall where I have heard the song before. Perhaps it is only a half-remembered dream.' He was scowling deeply now.

'Would it be too much to ask,' Sheehan suggested, 'for you to consider praising the lad's efforts?'

'I concede,' Reynolds snorted, realising there was nothing else to do until he could come up with proof that the melody was stolen, 'that the tune was quite pleasant and the song a well-rendered version of the tale. But that does not make Turlough O'Carolan a good harper. I noticed many instances during the performance where his fingers slipped or tumbled unnecessarily.'

Everyone in the room let out a sigh of exasperation.

'Nevertheless,' Reynolds went on, 'I can imagine that the young man may one day make a fine musician if he practises daily and nurtures his apparent talent for composition.'

'Will you send him out on the road?' McCabe asked.

'Certainly not!' the squire scoffed. 'He's not ready for that.

A few weeks here won't do him any harm. He still has a thing or two to learn.'

Before anyone could protest at the seeming injustice of this last remark Turlough spoke up. 'Thank you, Squire Reynolds. I would be honoured to attend lessons. And I would be happy to spend time practising with yourself and Cathair if that is what you have in mind.'

'It is ... And by the way, his name is Charles. We do not call him the Chair in this house.'

'I will endeavour to remember that,' Turlough sighed. 'And I look forward to beginning our work tomorrow morning.'

'I have a gift,' McCabe spoke up, 'which I would like to give to Turlough in praise of his performance.'

'What gift?' Reynolds demanded. Only the most renowned harpers received any sort of a token after a performance. 'He is still an apprentice. He is not entitled to gifts.'

'Nevertheless, I have one for him,' McCabe declared. 'Since he has so much trouble with the tuning of his harp, I have decided to give him mine.'

'That instrument cost your father fifty pounds!' Reynolds cried. 'You can't give it away to this fellow.'

'I shall have his harp,' McCabe decided. 'For I will never have the talent Turlough has been blessed with. And I only need an instrument to practise on. I do not intend to make my living from music. He needs a good harp much more than I do.'

'Thank you, Cathair,' Turlough whispered, shocked at the extravagant gift but very grateful.

'His name is Charles!' Reynolds bellowed and everyone looked at the floor to hide their smiles.

NINE

Old Hugh the distiller drew in the smoke of his pipe and blew out a grey-blue cloud.

'That is the origin of the first tune my master ever composed,' Hugh told the young rebel. 'SheeBeg SheeMor was Carolan's most famous and most popular piece. And he was fast friends with McCabe ever after.'

'And you still insist that the Faerie folk were Carolan's patrons?' Edward smiled.

'I have told you,' Hugh asserted, tapping the ash from the bowl of his pipe, 'that is the way my master told the story, and who am I to doubt the truth of it?'

'So this Squire Sheehan,' the young rebel asked, 'was really the King of the Faeries? And his wife was the queen?'

'She is not his wife!' Hugh hissed. 'He is her consort. Do try to remember that and you may save yourself a great deal of future embarrassment.'

'But you said yourself Carolan sometimes told folk that he had heard the tune in a dream,' Edward pointed out.

'And that is what he probably preferred to think for a long time,' the old distiller admitted. 'Perhaps he did not like to imagine himself as anything special. Perhaps he found he was ridiculed for claiming the patronage of the Good People. I have already told you that even Mister Swift mocked my master cruelly when Carolan mentioned his encounters with the Faeries.'

'It must have been a dream,' the young rebel argued. 'That makes much more sense.'

'Believe what you will,' Hugh snapped. 'It makes no difference to me. But if you ask anyone who heard the master play, they will tell you he had a gift that did not come from this world.'

'I heard him play,' Denis declared. 'I didn't think much of his performance.'

'That was in the last years of his life,' the old distiller retorted. 'He was slowing down just as you are.'

'I have not slowed down in my old age,' the old harper chortled. 'I have only just started to warm up.'

Hugh laughed along with his friend. 'You have left it a bit late, haven't you?'

'Call me a slow bloomer,' Denis shrugged.

Edward looked at the two old men laughing at each other's wit and he couldn't help but smile himself. 'You are both nearly one hundred years old,' he commented, 'and yet you are both so full of life. What is the secret to living so long?'

'Plenty of relaxation,' Hugh replied. 'Avoid worry.'

'As well as landlords, soldiering, press gangs, priests and politics,' Denis added.

'A moderate amount of work taken daily,' the old distiller said, raising a finger, 'preserves the body from any malady. Too much work brings on fatigue of the bones and that leads to an early death.'

He stopped to throw another cupful of liquor down his throat.

'A good woman,' the old harper continued.

'Who is also a good friend,' Hugh pointed out. 'And not too young either.'

'The young ones lead a fellow to premature mortality,' Denis confirmed, shaking his head.

'How many of our dear comrades have had their lives extinguished,' Hugh asked, 'by the wistful—'

'Fickle,' Denis interrupted.

'Wistful, fickle,' Hugh agreed, 'enticing smiles of a pretty girl? I'd gladly face cannon fire any day than the wilful attentions of a young woman with one thing on her mind.'

'What would that one thing be that's on her mind then?' the harper asked innocently.

'How would I know?' Hugh retorted. 'It would be on her mind not on mine. I'm a hundred years old. I haven't thought about such things for months.'

'The other qualities essential to long life are equal portions of laughter, love, liquor, mirth, mischief and music,' Denis giggled.

'And if you mix them all in the right proportion, you will live to be as old and handsome as we two,' the old distiller confirmed, showing his toothless grin. Then he turned to his friend. 'Play us a tune,' he demanded. 'I'm not filling you full of the best whiskey so you can sit there and waste away the hours in philosophical conjecture.'

'I will not play if you insist on insulting me,' Denis stated emphatically. 'I have never engaged in philosophy. I find it distracts me from the important things in life. Like the eternal question of where my next cupful is coming from.'

'You are a lazy old whiskey sop,' Hugh snapped.

'There you go again,' the harper sighed. 'You can't help belittling me, can you?'

'Play us a tune.'

'What would you like to hear?'

'The Concerto.'

'Jesus and all the saints! Not that again! I will play it when I am good and ready. You ought to be grateful to have a harper under your roof. Not even the grand houses are fortunate enough to have my kind visiting them any more.'

'Most of the grand houses refuse to have your kind visit them,' Hugh informed him. 'Because they dole out their finest food and drink and then have to wait three days for a melody.'

'Something else then?' the harper offered. 'Is there some other tune you would like to hear?'

'What would you play, if not the Concerto?'

'What was the second tune Carolan composed?' Denis inquired.

Hugh sat back and thought for a moment. 'I have a notion it was the Hewlett,' the old distiller said finally, 'though I cannot be certain.'

'That is a fine melody, though I have heard it was a tune McCabe composed himself and then Carolan learned it from him.'

'That is not true!' Hugh spat. 'You have been ill informed, Denis Hempson. McCabe and my master remained the best of friends for the rest of their lives. Indeed they were always playing tricks on one another. I do not think Master Carolan would have claimed a tune belonging to his best friend.'

'The Hewlett is a lovely piece,' Denis told Edward. 'Full of mirth and good humour. I have a notion that it may have been composed as a celebration of friendship.'

'Indeed it may,' Hugh conceded. 'My master and Cathair McCabe travelled all over Ireland for many years and they were very close.'

The old distiller searched in his pockets for some tobacco. Edward reached across and placed his pouch in Hugh's hand.

'Thank you,' the old man said. 'Now, what was I saying? Oh yes.' He paused. 'I remember the master telling me of an instance when they were in Dublin together.'

'Do you want a tune or not?' the old harper interjected.

'In a minute! Keep your wig on,' the distiller groaned. 'Where was I?'

'In Dublin,' Edward reminded him as he sipped his whiskey.

'That's right,' Hugh said, snapping his fingers. 'Carolan had been on the road for several years when one bright summer day he arrived in Dublin to meet his old friend McCabe who was staying with a certain Doctor Delany while he attended the college. And who should Cathair McCabe introduce my master to?'

'I have no idea,' the young rebel replied, shaking his head.

'Bridget Cruise. She was a married woman by that time of course. McCabe had met her at a recital and she had latched onto him like a black barnacle on the backside of a barge.'

'Is that true?' Denis gasped.

'It is,' the old distiller confirmed. 'McCabe had thought to surprise her by introducing her to the already renowned Carolan. But it was McCabe who got the surprise when the master inquired after her husband before the introduction was even complete. Carolan told me he had recognised Bridget the moment she entered the room, before she had even spoken a word, even though he was blind.'

'I was like that with my wife,' Denis admitted. 'I could tell when she had entered the house or when she had something on her mind that was causing her to fret. But it was purely for reasons of avoiding a bitter bruising in my case.'

'After that meeting,' Hugh went on, ignoring the old harper, 'Carolan composed a beautiful haunting melody in commemoration of Bridget Cruise. It was the most touching air I have ever heard played. I could not listen to it without tears coming to my eyes.'

'I feel the same way about your stories,' Denis mumbled.

'I myself first met the master a short while afterwards,' Hugh continued. 'My father, Old Hugh Connor was his name, had been working for Mister McCabe as an artificer-coachman. He was in his fifties at the time. When Mister McCabe used to go off travelling with Master Carolan my father would go to lend a hand to the two gentlemen.'

'But how did you come to be Carolan's serving man?' Denis asked, though he must have heard the tale before.

'I was working for the good Doctor Delany in Dublin town,' the distiller explained, 'in the same trade as my father, a coachman. One afternoon news came that my father had suffered a terrible seizure. I went straight round to Mister McCabe's little house to look to the old man and there I met the renowned Turlough O'Carolan for the first time. He was playing a soothing air for my old man who lay on a large bed looking like he was gasping his last. I was so touched by the scene that I offered my services to Master Carolan.'

'Did your father pass over?' Edward asked solicitiously.

'No,' Hugh giggled. 'It turned out that my father had swallowed a bit of apple the wrong way. It got stuck in his windpipe. Then the old boy had a touch of indigestion afterwards of course. He lived into his nineties and would still be here today if he hadn't gone for a walk along the coast on that bitterly cold autumn day in seventeen fifty. It was a wet and miserable morning. I tried to tell the old boy how foolish it was to be going out in that weather all on his own. But he was a stubborn man, my old father.'

'Such foolishness in one so elderly.' Denis shook his head. 'Did your father die of the chill?'

'No,' Hugh replied shaking his head. 'He choked on an apple he had taken with him for his lunch.'

Hugh sighed deeply and then swallowed his cup of whiskey in one swig.

'But that chance meeting with Master Carolan,' the distiller went on, 'was the beginning of a long association between us. I was paid a penny a day, which in those times was considered a bloody fortune.'

'That's more than a shilling a fortnight!' Denis cried. 'How did you not come to save any of that vast amount of money?'

'Master Carolan was not always punctual with the distribution of my wages,' Hugh explained.

'I always suspected you of being a spendthrift,' the old harper sniped, working out the sum with his fingers. 'In four months you would have earned close to a pound sterling!'

'I told you,' the distiller retorted through clenched teeth, 'I was not always paid on time. I often had to make do.'

'Then why did you stay with Carolan?' Denis wanted to know.

'We became friends,' Hugh explained. 'He needed me. And after Mister McCabe took up his studies at the college there was no-one else to guide the master on his journeys. So it was left to me. And anyway, it wasn't such a hard life. I always had a full belly and a warm place to sleep. And often there was more strong drink available than I could have possibly consumed.'

'So there were compensations,' Edward laughed.

'Indeed there were,' Hugh smiled.

'And a few adventures, I'll warrant,' Denis added.

'More adventures than I have time to tell,' the distiller nodded.

'Thank God,' the harper mumbled.

'And you met many of the folk the master composed his music for?' Edward asked.

'I met them and oftentimes became good friends with them.'

'But Ireland was a different place in those days,' Denis cut in. 'It was safe to travel the roads.'

'Whenever Cathair McCabe was taking a rest from his studies,' Hugh continued, 'he and my master travelled together to all the big houses. In that time no grand estate was more than a day's journey from the next. Of course it is quite a different story today. I doubt that many folk in the country would open their doors to a stranger since the advent of all the wars and deprivations.'

'The land is full of brigands,' Denis agreed. 'It takes me all the courage I have to walk out the door sometimes.'

'And often you are compelled to consume quite a bit of my courage before you will consent to leave,' Hugh quipped.

Daniel entered the room, saw that the cups were empty and did the rounds, filling them up again. 'I'll go for a walk and keep watch in case the redcoats come calling,' he declared. Then he took his pipe and went to sit outside, for the night was clear and not too cold.

'Carolan composed an air for Elizabeth Nugent at her father's house which was still being requested from him in the last year of his life,' Hugh recalled. 'He was present at the death of Sir Ulick Burke and composed a lament for that gentleman, as well as one for Finbar MacDonough; both men were of the old aristocracy, you understand.'

Hugh threw the whiskey down his throat and went on, 'Captain John Irwin became friends with McCabe and so Carolan created a lovely piece as a tribute to him. I can still remember how it goes.'

'Did he compose music for all his patrons?' Edward asked.

'No,' Hugh shook his head. 'Only those who offered him the best hospitality and the finest liquor. Only the ones who could afford to reward him handsomely were honoured with a melody.'

'If he had no income, how could he afford to travel?'

'The master took students and was paid for his tuition. And he often stopped at inns and would play in return for a meal and a room. He once composed a piece for Squire Jones who was one such innkeeper. That man had a taste for claret and he drank it from great bumpers which could hold as much as four of my cups. I can remember many an evening spent singing Squire Jones's song and inventing new verses to suit the present company.'

The old man put his hand to his chin in thought. 'Pick up that harp, Denis Hempson,' he called and as soon as the harper struck a chord Hugh burst into song.

'You good fellows all,' he began, and Edward was surprised at the strength of Hugh's voice, considering his claim to be a hundred years old. 'Who love to be where good claret's in store, attend to my call, there's one who's never frightened but often delighted with six bottles more!'

After the exertion of the first verse Hugh rested while Denis played on. The old distiller was content to hum along until Denis came to the end of the tune. Then, without announcing it, the old harper launched into a slow melancholy piece full of longing.

'This is the first air Master Carolan composed for Bridget Cruise,' Hugh whispered, 'the day after he met her in Dublin. I only ever heard him play the piece a few times for it made his heart sick to recall the occasion. I have no idea where Denis might have learned it.'

'I got it from McCabe,' the old harper said without breaking the flow of the melody.

Mhairgead came in and leaned against the door when she heard this piece. Edward looked up at her and saw that her eyes were welling with tears. She wiped the drops away when she noticed the young rebel staring at her and then came over to the fire to see to the whiskey cups.

As soon as Denis finished playing he put the harp down by his side and Mhairgead placed a full cup in his hand.

'That was the saddest tune I have ever heard you play,' she told him.

'I don't play it often,' Denis conceded. 'It makes me think of folk long passed over who I am grieved to be parted from.'

'It makes me feel so lonely,' Mhairgead sighed. 'As if I were the only person left in the world.' She glanced up at Edward, a half smile playing across her lips.

'But the tune Carolan composed for his teacher was an even more sorrowful piece,' Hugh informed her. 'The tribute to Mhaire Dhall is sweet, merry and mournful all at once.'

'It is a lovely lament,' Denis agreed. 'But I heard that she taught it to him before she passed over.'

'Will you not let the man's soul rest in peace?' the old distiller raged. 'Are you incapable of giving him any credit for his achievements?'

'Those melodies that are his own I will grant him,' the harper retorted. 'Some of them are very fine, though they are the devil to perform. Those that he borrowed from other folk I will not pass judgment upon for I have only the word of men like McCabe to go by.'

'McCabe never said an ill word against Carolan in his life!' Hugh protested. 'I know because I travelled with the two of them over the long roads between the great houses. Cathair McCabe may have been a trickster with a taste for hard liquor, but he was a gentleman who loved my master like a brother.'

'But I remember you telling me the story of McCabe's death,' Denis shot back. 'Was that the act of a friend? To deliberately pass away under such distressing circumstances?'

'I don't understand,' Edward interrupted after taking another sip of whiskey. 'Was McCabe responsible for his own death? Did he commit suicide?'

'Good God no!' both old men responded and then they chuckled.

'It was a much more amusing mortality than any suicide,' old Hugh confided. 'He died at the hands of a highwayman.'

Edward frowned, not seeing the joke.

'It happened in the same year as the master composed his tribute to Lord Inchinquin.'

'What year would that be?' Denis asked.

'Seventeen hundred and nine or ten it must have been,' the old distiller replied, calculating quickly in his head. 'I was twenty-one years of age and I had been in the service of Master Carolan for little more than a year or two.'

Edward shook his head to clear the pall of the whiskey. Then he stretched out his legs, ready to hear another part of the tale. Mhairgead came over as Hugh was stuffing his pipe again and she drew a chair up close beside the young rebel to listen with him.

The great draughthorse stopped in the middle of the road and would go no further. Turlough sat in the saddle and kicked it as best he could. He swore at the animal. He pleaded with it. He called down a curse upon it and all its descendants. Finally, in desperation, he invoked the power of all the saints in Heaven. But the horse would not move.

'Where are you, Hugh?' the harper called out, frustrated. 'Why won't you help me get this animal moving?'

'I'm as exhausted as she is,' the servant replied. 'I am having a lay-down in this dry ditch. The grass is soft and I am content.'

'Have you been struck with the lazy fever?' the harper boomed. 'I want to get on. I have no mind to be out here after dark.'

'It is midday,' Hugh replied. 'We have been going all night and most of yesterday. I need to sleep. The mare needs to eat, drink and rest. Leave us be.'

'I am anxious to get to Jones's house. I have heard there is to be a great party there tonight to celebrate the return from France of some good friend of his.'

'We'll never make it,' Hugh sighed. 'It's five miles. I'm finished. You go on without me.'

'Mary is to be there,' Turlough went on. 'I haven't seen her for a year. And I have something very important to ask her. Cathair is going to perform a composition of his own, I've been told. Come along.'

'Go on without me. If I don't rest I'll die.'

'I can't go on without you. You are carrying my harp. What good am I without the instrument of my profession?'

'I am going to shrivel up like a corpse if I don't get a good sleep,' Hugh grumbled. 'There will be other parties.'

'Shift your fat arse or I will not pay you this month.'

'You didn't pay me last month or the month before,' the servant responded calmly. 'I am beginning to get used to that state of affairs. It is an idle threat.'

'Now, Hugh, you know that times have been hard,' the harper soothed. 'What with the long war, the sickness of King William and the resulting instability in the kingdom. And then there was that business with the Jacobites. There is not that much good fortune going around.'

'I know,' Hugh cut in without opening his eyes. 'I have heard this speech before. Next you are going to tell me that I should be grateful for a full belly and a warm place to sleep at night. And then you'll remind me of the charity afforded to me by my privileged position at your side. "There are plenty of folk starving for the want of a spoonful of boiled cabbage,"' he went on, mimicking the harper's voice, '"and here you are, Hugh Connor, feasting on game and fine baked vegetables every night. And there are highwaymen robbing the poor people of the little they have, so what have you got to complain about?"'

'There's no need to take that tone.'

'I'm tired!' Hugh snapped, rising up on his elbow to make sure he would be heard.

'Very well,' Turlough conceded. 'I suppose it won't do any harm for us to take a short rest. Half an hour or so perhaps.'

'Don't worry, I'll still be here when I'm ready to leave.'

'Very funny.'

Hugh ignored his master and put his head back down on the ground. But no sooner had his cheek touched the grass than he heard a strange thudding sound in the earth.

His eyes darted open.

'Who would be galloping a horse at that pace in the middle of the day?' he whispered to himself and in the next instant the answer came to him. 'Highwaymen! I should not have joked about it.

'Get down off that mare, master!' the servant yelled, springing up to tug at the harper's coat.

'What is wrong with you, Hugh?' Turlough cried. 'I will get down in my own sweet time. Have you gone raving mad?'

But by then they could both hear the hoof beats on the levelled road. Turlough turned in the saddle and frowned.

'I have an awful feeling about this,' Hugh pleaded. 'Please get down and find a hiding place in the ditch. I heard of a harper who was robbed two months ago and the devils shot his servant before they stole everything the poor fellows owned.'

'If highwaymen are after shooting servants, maybe you should be the one to hide,' the harper suggested. 'No robber will get anything from me.'

'You are brave, master. But I beg you to come down.'

'Hugh,' Turlough said emphatically, 'no highwayman is going to steal anything from us. We have no gold. We have no food. No drink. Nothing of any value but the harp. And no brigand would be fool enough to try and steal a harp. What would he do with it? Even if he could get it on the back of his horse?'

'I never thought of that,' Hugh admitted and he felt a little better. Not much, but certainly a little better.

By that time the horseman was much closer and the servant's heart soon began to beat in time with the heavy hooves.

'Please get down, master,' he begged again, 'just in case there is trouble.'

But it was already too late. The rider had seen the two travellers and was upon them.

The stranger was dressed in a long black travelling cloak and a broad-brimmed hat turned up in the French style to make three crisp corners. His face was covered by a thick black lace handkerchief tied behind his neck to keep the dust of the road from his mouth and nose.

The stranger reined in his horse and brought it to a halt only a few paces away from Turlough and Hugh. Then the rider leapt from the saddle and led his sweating animal toward them.

'Good day, gentlemen,' the stranger called out in a hoarse voice.

'Good day, sir,' Hugh stuttered.

'Good day,' the harper replied.

'Are you in some difficulty?' the rider asked, his throat obviously straining with the effort of speech.

'No,' Hugh snapped.

'It is strange that you have stopped here between one village and the next. Has your horse thrown a shoe?'

'No,' the servant said emphatically, looking at the rider with suspicion. 'We might ask a similar question of you.' Hugh felt a little bolder now. 'Why are you galloping along the road at such a pace in the middle of the day when the weather is warm? Do you not care for your horse?'

'I am a messenger,' the stranger explained. 'I have been sent out by Squire Jones to find Turlough O'Carolan, the harper.'

Turlough opened his mouth to speak but Hugh prodded his master in the leg, warning him to be quiet.

'Why would Squire Jones be wanting to get a message to the famous harper?' Hugh demanded.

'The squire heard that Carolan was travelling this road on the way to the great party and asked me to escort him.'

'We don't need an escort,' Hugh snorted. 'So be on your way and tell the squire we'll be in around sunset.'

'Is this Carolan?'

'I am,' the harper spoke up, pushing Hugh away with his hand. 'Please don't take any notice of my serving man. He has not had any sleep since yesterday and he is a little too fond of the bottle.'

'My name is O'Halloran,' the stranger declared, his hoarse voice straining. 'I have a message for you. Sad tidings, I fear.'

'What's that?' Turlough asked apprehensively. 'Has some tragedy befallen the good squire?'

'No,' O'Halloran replied. 'I take it you have not heard the news.'

'What news?'

'Charles McCabe is dead.'

'Cathair? Dead?' Turlough gasped. 'But how?'

'He was stopped by a highwayman three days ago, not far from this very spot. He put up a valiant fight, as I am told was his nature. But the thief was armed with a pair of firelocks. McCabe was shot in the back and died of his wounds before any aid could be brought to him. He was buried in the church-yard half a mile from here yesterday morning.'

'Cathair!' Turlough cried. 'Mother of God! He was a good man and a great friend.' The harper started weeping loudly.

Hugh looked at the stranger with suspicion. He was still con-vinced that there was something about this man which wasn't quite right.

'We should be getting along,' the stranger urged. 'The high-wayman is still at large and could be lurking anywhere along these ditches waiting for a chance to attack.'

'Take me to Cathair's grave,' the harper sobbed. 'I wish to visit my friend and pay my respects.'

'What's that?' the stranger answered with just a hint of panic in his voice. Hugh was quick to notice the rider's eyes darting this way and that.

'I want to sit by his grave and mourn for Cathair McCabe,

the gentlest poet in the whole of Ireland,' Turlough said with genuine sadness.

'Very well,' the stranger replied with a slight quiver in his voice. 'He was laid in the churchyard further down this road. I will lead you there if you wish.'

Hugh felt the hairs tingle at the back of his neck. His instincts told him this rider was lying. But he dared not move against the stranger just yet in case he was mistaken. Then as O'Halloran turned to calm his horse and his long black cloak parted, the servant noticed a slender pistol hanging from the stranger's belt.

It was an expensive-looking firearm with gold inlay over blackened wood. And it was a flintlock. The latest and most reliable model brought over from France. Hugh had been shown one of these weapons at Lord Inchinquin's house just a few days earlier.

'Jesus,' he mumbled, turning quickly to pretend he was adjusting the bridle on his master's horse.

The stranger looked directly at the servant for a second and then turned away again. Hugh began trembling as he tried to work out what he should do. Finally he decided to bide his time and watch the rider carefully. At the first sign of trouble, he told himself, it would be his duty to protect his master.

O'Halloran mounted his horse again and Hugh took note of the fact that the animal was a fine cavalry mount. It still had a fleur-de-lis brand on its rump to mark it as a French military steed which had arrived in Ireland with the recent unlucky Jacobite army. The man was probably a former trooper fallen on hard times since the failed landing of the French a few years earlier. Hugh could not see any sign of a sabre or a sword, nor of a carbine. It seemed the only weapon this stranger carried was his pistol.

'He'll get one shot,' the servant whispered. 'God help me if he turns out to be a marksman.'

'How far is the churchyard?' Turlough asked in a quiet, defeated tone.

'Half a mile,' the stranger replied. 'If we ride at a trot we'll be there in no time.'

'You'll have to wait for me,' Hugh cut in, panicking slightly. 'I am on foot and carrying this harp. There is no way I can keep up with two trotting horses.'

'We'll wait for you at the churchyard,' O'Halloran suggested. 'It is not far.'

'I would rather stay beside my master, if you don't mind.'

'Hugh,' Turlough said softly, 'I will be fine. The news has not really touched me yet. Perhaps I need to be alone with my thoughts for a while. We'll ride on. You catch us up when you can. I know you are exhausted, so take your time.'

'Master,' the servant insisted, really beginning to worry now, 'if the highwayman is still at large, would it not be best for us to remain together? Surely if there are three of us he won't be so bold as to attack?'

'I have an argument that would keep a highwayman at bay,' O'Halloran laughed, and he drew the long pistol from his belt. In a second he had levelled the weapon and tilted it to the left slightly so the powder would not run out of the pan. He pointed the pistol at Hugh's head as he squinted one eye to take aim.

'Don't shoot!' Hugh cried. 'We have nothing worth taking. Only the harp and this old draughthorse. She's a plodding stupid mare, you wouldn't get a shilling for her.'

O'Halloran's eyes sparkled.

'What's going on?' Turlough cried. 'Has he got a gun?'

'I have,' the stranger declared. 'I was just showing it to your man.'

In the next second the stranger had dropped the weapon to his side and slipped it back in his belt.

'So you see, Hugh of the Freckles,' the rider declared in his husky voice, 'your master has nothing to worry about and neither have you. I will take care of Carolan. We'll meet you up on the top of the churchyard hill near to where the old yew tree grows.'

With that the stranger grabbed the reins of Turlough's mare and took off at a pace.

'Don't be too long!' the harper called back to Hugh. 'I still must try to make Squire Jones's house tonight so I may learn the full circumstance of this terrible occurrence.'

'Master,' Hugh called out, 'don't leave me! Stay and walk with me.' But his appeals went unheard. Turlough had already bowed his head, holding on tight to the mare's neck as they trotted off towards the churchyard.

'Oh Saint Brendan,' Hugh prayed aloud, 'protector of all travelling folk, put a veil of safekeeping around my master. He is a trusting soul who never harmed anyone. I do not know what this stranger is up to but I know it cannot be any good.'

In a few minutes the two riders turned a corner in the road and disappeared from view. Hugh picked up his pace, walking as fast as he could with the weight of the harp on his shoulder.

Carrying the load was a fairly easy matter when moving at a moderate stroll. But the faster Hugh strode the more the harp moved around, rolling against his side and nearly knocking him over with its unwieldy weight.

All the while Hugh kept praying to Saints Brendan, Patrick and any others who would listen to watch over his master and not let any harm come to him.

At last, perspiration pouring down his cheeks from his exertions, Hugh reached the bend in the road. From there he looked up and could plainly see the top of the hill with its yew tree and the little cluster of headstones. His master was kneeling in front of one of the stones while the stranger tied up their horses at the old tree. Hugh was relieved to see that the harper had not yet been murdered but he was sure this suspicious O'Halloran was just biding his time.

Hugh hurried on as fast as his legs would carry him. Then a terrible realisation dawned on him and almost stopped him in his tracks.

'How did that man O'Halloran know my nickname was Hugh the Freckled?' he muttered to himself. 'I have never met this fellow before.'

The servant thought for a moment.

'He must have learned that we would be passing by from poor old McCabe just before he shot him.'

With mounting fear Hugh redoubled his efforts and hastened on.

'I would have been up there already,' he cursed, 'if I hadn't been walking all through the night lugging this harp.' He did not dare put it down in case O'Halloran rode off with it.

Hugh was drenched in sweat by now, hot and thirsty too. He remembered that he had not eaten that morning and he felt his stomach growl in protest. His head began to spin from the exertion but he did not falter in his determination to stand by his master and defend him to the death if necessary.

At last he reached the churchyard gate and leaned against the stone wall to catch his breath. The sun broke through the clouds to shine down upon him and he could not remember ever feeling so hot and drained of energy.

'What use will I be to my master when I get there?' he asked himself. 'I'm bloody exhausted.'

Hugh stripped off his coat and unbuttoned his fine red waistcoat. Then he shouldered the harp again and began his climb up the hill. He could still see Carolan kneeling at the gravestone. The stranger was standing a little way back from him with his head bowed.

Halfway up the hill there was a small chapel which offered some shade from the heat. Hugh stopped there to steady his resolve. His eyes fell upon a stone font just inside the tiny building. The bowl was filled to the brim with holy water.

'All merciful God,' he begged, 'forgive me.' And then he dipped his hand in and drank a mouthful of the sweet water to appease his dry throat.

'I am sure that must be a mortal sin,' he sighed. 'I hope the saints don't hold it against me if I should need their help to rescue my master.'

Hugh crossed himself and suddenly wished he had exercised some restraint. He was sure he would need all the help he could get. Then he pressed on, passing through the rows of stones, crosses and unmarked mounds of soil until he came to where the stranger was standing.

Hugh's shirt was hanging out, his stockings had fallen down around his ankles and his long red hair had come out of its ribbon. He stumbled past O'Halloran like a man who has been out on the town and is just staggering home.

The stranger put a hand on Hugh's shoulder to stop him. 'Don't you think you should dress yourself properly? Out of respect for the dead?'

Hugh glared at the man. 'Don't you think you should remove that mask so I can get a good look at you?'

O'Halloran was plainly smiling under the lace, but he made no move to take it off. 'I was wounded in the failed rebellion,' he explained. 'A musket ball struck my jaw and shattered it. You would not want to see what is left of my face.'

'Is that you, Hugh?' Turlough called out from where he knelt.

'It is,' the servant replied, turning away from O'Halloran.

'Then bring me my harp,' he called. 'I have composed a eulogy for my dear departed friend and I wish to play it for him.'

Hugh glared at O'Halloran and then pushed past him to the harper's side. He quickly unwrapped the instrument from its seal skin and placed it beside his master. Then Hugh turned his attention to tidying his own appearance.

Just as he finished buttoning his waistcoat the harper began to play. The tune was mournful but all the more so because the wind lifted the notes from the harp and scattered them in a hundred different directions. Like smoke dispersing on the breeze the melody drifted by Hugh and he closed his eyes and thought of Cathair, the Chair, McCabe.

'Pity me,' Turlough sang in a voice choking with emotion, 'I am tired from my long ride. I sit at the grave of my friend. My shirt is soaked with my tears. I found nothing when I got here but a hard flat stone and a lonely bed beneath the clay.'

Hugh had to wipe his eyes with his white lace cuffs and then his shirt really was soaked with tears.

'My friend Cathair was no common Chair,' Turlough went on. 'He was no Chair of the nobility either. There has never been a Chair like my friend Cathair. A fine Chair as entertaining as he was a harper.'

The stranger stepped forward but Hugh refused to look around at him. At that precise moment he didn't care whether O'Halloran turned out to be a highwayman or not. The servant was lost in his grief.

'There is no pain on earth,' Turlough sang, 'no loss, no torture, no sickness as saddening as the death of a friend or the parting of companions.'

Hugh saw the harper put down his instrument as soon as he had sung those words. Such was his grief that Turlough could not even finish playing the melody. The servant ran to his master's side and put an arm around him in comfort.

Hugh stared at the grave for a long while as he held his master in that embrace. His eyes took in the upturned clay and it was hard for him to think that Cathair McCabe was now part of that soil. The servant looked at the headstone cut from a piece of blue granite, smoothed and engraved with a message.

'Read what it says about him,' Turlough asked.

'What's that?'

'On the headstone.'

Hugh focused on the fresh inscription and spoke the words slowly, for he had never learned the skill of letters too well.

'"In loving memory,"' he began.

'Go on,' the harper urged.

'"... of the dearest soul,"' Hugh continued, '"I ever met."' He focused on the next few words and tried to pronounce the longest one slowly. '"My darling wife, Kathleen Mary Brady."'

'Are you reading the right stone, Hugh?' Turlough whispered tersely.

'I am reading the one that is right in front of us.'

Just at that moment O'Halloran stepped forward and

coughed loudly. 'This is where it ends, gentlemen,' he announced hoarsely and Hugh turned around on his knees, his eyes flashing wildly.

'I had a feeling about you!' he cried, standing up, all his suspicions confirmed. 'Now I suppose it will be "Stand and deliver, your money or your life"?'

The servant glanced over at the horses as he searched for a way past the rider. But Hugh could plainly see that he would have a long run to the cover of the tree and O'Halloran could easily get a clear shot in before he reached it.

'What are you talking about, you foolish man?' Turlough asked Hugh.

'The story of McCabe's death was all a trick to get us up on this hill away from the road,' Hugh said with terror in his voice. 'This stranger, who calls himself O'Halloran, is a highwayman.'

'It was all a trick,' the stranger declared, admitting that Hugh had guessed right. 'Your servant has unmasked me.'

'Then Cathair is not dead?' Turlough cried.

'He is not,' the stranger stated and then he put a hand to his mouth. In one swift tug he removed the lace handkerchief which covered his face.

'My God, master!' Hugh gasped, falling back to his knees in shock. 'Jesus save us!'

'What is it, Hugh?' Turlough cried.

'It is Mister McCabe.'

'What is?'

'There,' the servant mumbled, still in shock. 'O'Halloran is really McCabe.'

'Hello, Turlough,' Cathair offered, the hoarseness gone from his voice. 'I am sorry. I couldn't resist playing a little trick on you. But I thought we would get as far as Squire Jones's before you worked out who I was.'

'Cathair?' Turlough stood up, leaning on Hugh's shoulder. 'Are you safe? Have you been hurt at all?'

'I am fine,' Cathair hummed. 'It was all a harmless joke. I certainly had you fooled, didn't I?'

'So you were never in any danger at all?' the harper asked with relief.

'No,' McCabe smiled, coming closer to take his friend's hand.

'Well you bloody well are now!' Turlough bellowed, lunging forward to grab at McCabe. 'Just wait till I get my hands on you!' the harper yelled. 'I'll bloody well murder you.'

'Now, Turlough,' McCabe protested, dodging out of the way, 'I thought you would be happy to see me.'

'For the first time in my life I can truly say I am happy not to be able to see you, you scoundrel.'

'Calm down, Turlough,' Cathair begged. 'It was only meant to give you a laugh.'

'A laugh?' the harper asked incredulously.

'Yes, a laugh.'

'Laugh at this!' and Turlough kicked hard in McCabe's direction. The harper's boot connected with the other man's shin and in the next second McCabe was on the ground clutching his leg in agony.

'Jesus, Turlough,' he cried, 'leave off. You'll hurt me.'

'I certainly hope so, you vagabond,' came the reply.

'We'll be late for Squire Jones's party,' McCabe warned and that calmed Turlough down immediately.

'Very well,' the harper breathed, 'we will go on to the house of Squire Jones. But I am only relenting in my rebuke of you because I do not see the sense in disputing this all day long. Especially when there is a cellar of the best French claret awaiting our arrival.'

'I am glad you have seen sense,' McCabe replied.

'I thought you were dead, you vagrant!' the harper hissed.

'It was a touching piece,' Cathair told him. 'I can't thank you enough for your glowing tribute. And I am honoured to know that I am the only man in the whole of Ireland who will one day be able to tell his grandchildren about the eulogy composed for him by the famous Turlough O'Carolan.'

'You are still a vagabond,' the harper grumbled. 'And had I

known the truth I would have said so in your tribute. Indeed now that I think of it, I don't know why I omitted to mention your scheming, deceiving nature.'

'Let's get going,' McCabe suggested, wisely changing the subject. 'Jones is putting on a fine supper tonight.'

'Is he?' Hugh drooled, instantly forgiving Cathair. The servant had not eaten since yesterday and his stomach was growling. 'What's the occasion?' he asked as he began wrapping the harp. 'We heard the squire has a guest from France.'

'An acquaintance of his has just returned from the French court,' McCabe explained. 'I don't know the man's name but he is apparently a very famous musician.'

'A harper?' Turlough asked.

'I cannot be certain,' McCabe replied. 'I had the news from a friend in Dublin who had heard it from a fellow in Cork.'

'Then let's get a move along,' the harper bustled. 'Jones's parties are always entertaining and his guests are usually enthralling.'

'He has extremely good taste,' Hugh nodded.

'Take me to my horse,' Turlough demanded. 'Let's be off!'

Hugh led his master to the mare and helped him mount, then waited until McCabe was astride his saddle.

'You can ride up here with me, Hugh,' Cathair offered. 'I can see that you ran your legs off to get up that hill.'

'That is most kind of you,' the servant replied, beginning to forgive McCabe's heartless prank.

They rode on slowly, singing songs and laughing until they reached Squire Jones's house just before nightfall. The squire, a man with a great belly which flowed over his belt, greeted them cheerfully.

McCabe told the tale of the lament Carolan had just composed, and Jones bent double with amusement. Turlough smiled through gritted teeth.

'Who is this friend of yours,' the harper asked, 'who is having a party held in his honour?'

'You may have heard of him,' Squire Jones replied. 'He is

famous both here and on the Continent. And he has played before King Louis of France.'

'Well, what's his name?' Turlough insisted.

'David Murphy.'

Turlough shook his head and smiled that he had rushed all this way to attend a party in honour of his one-time rival.

The three travellers had just enough time to wash and change out of their riding clothes before the guests began arriving.

Turlough dressed in a fine new coat of green which had been a gift from Lord Inchinquin in payment for a tune. Green was his favourite colour and it marked him out in a crowd. Under this coat he wore a black velvet waistcoat and a white shirt with a black cotton neckerchief.

As was his custom he waited in his room until Hugh brought word that all the guests had congregated. Then he made his way downstairs to take advantage of a late entry. He always found this was the best way to attract maximum attention.

McCabe met the harper and his servant at the foot of the stairs and leaned in close to whisper to his friend. 'She's here,' he said under his breath.

'Mary?' Turlough replied.

'Yes, Mary is here,' McCabe answered, 'but that is not who I mean.'

'Who are you talking about?' But the question had barely passed the harper's lips when a name came to mind.

'Bridget Cruise.'

'Bridget,' the harper whispered as if the name alone held some magical power over him. 'I will play an air for her later,' he announced. 'I haven't bumped into her in years.'

'Very well. If that is your wish,' McCabe replied. 'I will tell Jones.'

At that moment a woman dressed in a gorgeous pale cream silk gown approached them. She was closely followed by a man in an outlandish sky-blue coat richly embroidered with gold thread and studded with pearls. The buttons on his coat were pure gold and the whole garment was lined with the same cream-coloured silk as his companion's dress.

The man was surrounded by a small group of young men who were dressed in almost exactly the same fashion. They stayed very close to the fellow in the sky-blue coat, even when he walked at quite a pace.

Hugh leaned close to his master to describe this strange assembly. He was still talking to the harper in a muffled whisper when the group came to a halt immediately in front of them.

'Turlough?' the woman said softly, putting her hand in his so that he could kiss it. 'I would like you to meet a dear friend of mine.'

'Hello, Bridget,' the harper replied politely, holding up the outstretched hand and touching his lips to it. 'How nice it is to meet you again.'

'I have missed you,' she told him.

'How is your husband?' the harper retorted.

'He is off again in Flanders with his regiment fighting against the French,' she replied with disinterest. 'Or is it the Germans this time? I can never remember which. How are you?'

'I am very well. All things considered. Have you any children yet?'

'Good God!' she cried. 'With my husband? That, my dear, would be a miracle.'

She took the harper's hand and squeezed it tightly, then addressed her companion. 'Turlough O'Carolan is a childhood friend of mine.'

Turlough tried to picture what Bridget must look like. Over twenty years had passed since they had been lovers and five since Cathair had reintroduced them. The harper knew she must have aged but the only image he could bring to mind was of the young woman with whom he had been so very much in love.

'I would like you to meet David Murphy, Turlough.'

'Mister Murphy,' the blind harper bowed, not in the least surprised that the two of them were friends. 'We have met before.'

'Have we?' Murphy answered in a high-pitched tone of exaggerated surprise and an affected French accent. 'Where would that have been?'

'At the same place where you first met Bridget.'

'At the theatre in Dublin?' the man laughed. 'I don't think so. What would a man such as yourself be doing at the theatre?'

'What do you mean by a man such as myself?' Turlough demanded.

'You have no eyes,' Murphy said in a low voice, as if he were divulging a well-kept secret. 'You wouldn't really be able to appreciate the theatre, would you?'

'You and I met at Mrs MacDermot's the night Lord Mayo visited us,' Turlough scowled.

'Oh yes, I remember you now,' Murphy grinned. 'You were wearing a coat three sizes too big for you and harbouring a grudge twice those proportions again. I see that things have not changed very much. At least the coat fits you better.'

Murphy turned to laugh with a few of his gathered friends. Bridget put an arm around the man and giggled.

'Don't take any notice of David,' she chuckled. 'He is such a wit. He simply can't help himself. Can you, darling?'

'I have a flair for it,' Murphy admitted.

'And I see that you have not changed much either, Mister Murphy,' Turlough sniped. 'How is Lord Mayo?'

McCabe leaned in close. 'He hasn't seen his lordship in some months,' he explained. 'Murphy is banished from the household.'

'I am not banished,' Murphy snapped. 'We had a little disagreement and I decided to let his lordship calm down somewhat before I return to grace his household with my music. Mayo has had a terrible time in France, you know, and he must be over eighty years of age. The strain is beginning to tell. And now the Prince Regent of France has asked King James to leave the country for Italy. It is all too much. Of course His Lordship's nerves are on edge.'

'Of course!' one of his friends repeated. The others nodded and hummed sympathetically.

'It has been devastating for the old man,' one fellow chimed in.

'David has been such a solid support to his lordship throughout this terrible crisis,' another agreed.

Turlough guessed that Murphy was unaccustomed to allowing truth to interfere with his version of events. There was obviously more to the story of Lord Mayo's displeasure than was being openly discussed.

'I am told that you have played before the King of France,' Turlough remarked.

'That is true,' Murphy replied, raising his voice so that everyone in the room could hear. 'I have performed for King Louis many times. I was his favourite.'

His friends applauded him and he bowed to them, affecting an air of humility.

'Is everything they say about King Louis true?' Turlough asked.

'That and more,' Murphy bragged, turning to catch an eye here or return a smile there.

'I have heard that the Sun King is tone deaf and prefers the sound of lowing cattle to the music of the harp. Indeed I was told he prefers the company of cows and sheep in his bed to that of the Queen of France.'

Murphy scowled and gripped his silver-topped walking cane with whitening knuckles.

'Is it true that Louis keeps a farmyard in one of the rooms of the palace?' Turlough continued. 'And that the great King of the French sneaks out in the middle of the night to visit his favourite lambs?'

'You are mistaken,' Murphy retorted sharply. 'But then I am hardly surprised. You obviously spend a great deal of time with empty-headed gossips who have nothing better to do than deride great men.'

'I heard that tale from a fellow who was deriding sheep actually,' Turlough replied with a shrug. 'But I was wondering if it was true. And I thought you would probably know better than most.'

'I have heard, from reliable sources,' Murphy fumed, 'that you have become very popular with the common people. The more common the more likely you are to be popular with them.'

'Common people. Nobles. Clergy. Royalty,' Turlough smiled. 'I have admirers in all the professions. I have often been thankful that I do not have to play before the high and mighty every day of my life. They can be such tedious creatures.'

'Indeed,' Murphy jeered. 'A flea may consider a dog to be tedious if he does not remember that is where his next meal is coming from.'

'Then I am a flea,' Turlough admitted, 'flitting from one dog to another. And I don't mind entertaining the other fleas along the way. But no dog has ever banished me from his backside. You must have bitten Lord Mayo a little too hard.'

'You should be more careful,' Murphy declared venomously, raising his voice for his friends to hear. 'You are nothing but an ignorant wretch pretending to be a musician.

'You may call yourself a harper,' Murphy hissed, 'when you have been playing for as long as I have. Until then you are nothing but an upstart. I mean to say, you have not even found yourself a decent tailor. What sort of a musician are you?'

'I have been somewhat surprised at meeting you,' Turlough answered and Murphy's eyes narrowed. 'I had been told that you were a self-centred, soft, spoiled and boastful man with a propensity for foolish conversation. I was informed that you lived for the praise heaped on you by your foppish friends. And that your weak-withered wit was one of the more endearing aspects of your personality.'

Turlough paused for breath.

'But now I see that your detractors were only partly justified in their appraisal of you.'

'I am a wealthy man,' Murphy told Turlough, speaking between clenched teeth. 'I have played before the crowned heads of Europe. I am the most successful harper you will ever meet. I could see to it that you never play again in any house in Ireland. I could destroy you.'

'I am sure you could,' Turlough nodded. 'It warms my heart that you consider me such a threat.'

'It would pay you well to take some notice of the way I carry myself,' Murphy hissed, 'if you aspire to a life as rewarding as mine.'

'You will need help carrying yourself out of this house if you threaten me,' Turlough warned him. 'Consider your words carefully or I will box your ears.'

'If you can find them,' Murphy smiled.

'That would not be difficult,' Turlough laughed, 'as they are attached to the sides of a large soft empty head. I am sure I could sound out a few skulls until I found the one which made the greatest noise when knocked.'

'I would challenge you to a duel, blacksmith's son,' Murphy replied scornfully, 'if I thought you would be able to tell one end of a rapier from the other.'

Murphy's friends broke out into great guffaws of laughter at this comment.

Turlough opened his mouth to speak. He was going to tell the other harper that he knew which end of the rapier he would like to stick up his backside. He wanted to say that he thought Murphy was the vainest person he had ever met and that if success resulted in stupidity Turlough O'Carolan would rather lie in a ditch and play dances for the local badgers.

But McCabe stopped his friend before he could speak. 'Come now, Turlough,' he cut in, taking the blind harper by the arm, 'what's all this talk of duels? Didn't you say that you had a tune to play in honour of Bridget Cruise?'

'I did.'

'Then let's hear it!' Squire Jones yelled as he arrived on the scene and passed out jugs of whiskey and bumpers of claret.

'Bridget,' the harper nodded, 'the tune I will play for you was one of the first I ever composed. The song reflects the way I felt for you when we first parted company all those years ago. I will perhaps speak with you later.'

Bridget giggled. 'Do forgive David his wit. He cannot help himself.'

'I never met a fool who could,' Turlough replied.

Then the harper turned and put his face close to McCabe's. 'Where is Mary?' he whispered.

'She is standing in the corner,' Cathair replied.

'As soon as I have finished reciting this piece I want you take me over to her.'

'As you wish,' McCabe nodded and then he led Turlough to a seat.

Hugh placed the harp down at his master's feet and Turlough leaned into the instrument.

In a few seconds the whole hall had hushed to listen to the music of Turlough O'Carolan. The melody was one of his most enchanting. The harp began humming gently with each brush of his fingers.

'Sweet Bridget, this song is for you,' Turlough began to lilt. 'I am without strength and you do not even notice my distress. Yet I follow after you, pearl of the golden tresses.'

The verses went on and the compliments became more personal. Bridget blushed at all the attention she was receiving, but plainly she was enjoying it immensely. After a few minutes she moved away from Murphy and sat down close by Turlough's side so she could better hear the beautiful tune he had composed for her.

Murphy made sly comments under his breath to his friends throughout the performance but Bridget ignored them. She stared up at this man she had known when he was a lad and clearly she was impressed with the harper he had become.

At last the melody concluded and Turlough let the harp ring out. Then he suddenly arose and without acknowledging Bridget's presence at all took McCabe's hand. Cathair led him directly to where Mary was standing at the edge of the room.

'Did you hear the song I composed for Bridget Cruise?' Turlough asked her.

'I did,' Mary replied, looking at the floor, feeling confused and hurt. 'It was beautiful. She is very fortunate to have such a gorgeous melody composed in her honour.'

'Perhaps that is so,' the harper answered. 'But she never cared that much for me, if the truth be told. And I'd rather be among friends I can trust than fickle folk who blow with the wind and change loyalties as it suits them.

'There is an old saying,' he went on before Mary could interrupt. 'It is fine to be infatuated with a pretty woman who preens her feathers and thinks very highly of herself, but marry the kind and beautiful girl who you know will be your friend through hard times as well as good.'

'What is it you mean to say?' Mary asked, taking his hand.

'You have taken care of me since the day we first met. You have never treated me with anything but kindness. You have been my friend and my confidante. And now I am asking you to be my wife.'

Mary passed pale and had to lean against the wall.

'Well?' the harper whispered. 'What do you say? Everyone in the room is waiting for your answer.'

'There is nothing on earth that would please me more,' Mary replied with a gasp and the chamber broke into a spontaneous cheer.

Murphy took Bridget Cruise by the hand and led her to a corner of the room. They and their friends were the only folk who remained silent.

Squire Jones brought out more claret to celebrate the occasion and soon the room was full of spirited conversation. The party that had started out in honour of Murphy's return to Ireland became a celebration of Turlough and Mary's engagement. And the irony was not lost on David Murphy.

Turlough took the sleeve of Mary's dress.

'This is a finely woven cloth,' he said. 'And the colour reminds me of the saffron cloak Mrs MacDermot used to wear when she was younger.'

'It is precisely that colour,' Mary replied with tears in her eyes.

'I can tell,' Turlough smiled. 'I don't know how but I can almost see the very shade of it in my mind.'

As the night wore on, Turlough, Mary and McCabe sang together, danced together and drank the finest French claret in Ireland. Then when the harper felt his legs weakening from too much liquor, he sat down and put the harp against his shoulder.

Turlough played SheeBeg SheeMor. Then he played his lovely tribute to Lord Inchinquin. He played his drinking song composed for Squire Jones. Then he performed some older melodies before finishing the evening with another new composition.

'This piece,' he explained, 'I have dedicated to the Queen of the Faeries who has been my patron now since before I was blinded and without whom I would never have taken up the harp.'

A few folk giggled. Murphy and his friends broke out into wild laughter.

'I am sure she will be enthralled,' a woman spoke up nearby and Turlough turned his head in recognition.

'Is that you, Mrs Sheehan?' he asked.

'It is,' she replied. 'My husband and I have just arrived in time, it seems. Will this really be your last tune of the evening?'

'I will play for you in private when I come to Dublin next,' Turlough promised, feeling uncomfortable all of a sudden.

'I would expect nothing less,' Mrs Sheehan replied.

'But for the time being perhaps,' he went on, 'you can imagine that you yourself are the Queen of the Faeries. I would very much like to know what you would think of this melody if you were she.'

'I will listen as if it were composed for my ears only,' she told him, and Turlough could picture the sparkle in her dark eyes as she spoke.

The harper struck up the slow, stately air and played the composition with grace and reverence. The room was perfectly still as the golden notes dropped from the instrument, filling the air with their bright tinkling.

In his mind the harper pictured the queen wearing a long

trailing black dress with a dark hood over her head. She was, he imagined, passing through the ranks of her people and they were bowing before her as she made her way to her throne made of woven flowers. He conjured such an intricate portrait in his head and brought it to life in his tune so beautifully that the entire audience gasped with delight.

The moment Turlough struck the last note the room erupted in wild applause and rapturous acclaim. The harper felt small fingers grasp at his own and then he sensed a woman's lips against the back of his hand.

'You are a master, Turlough O'Carolan,' Mrs Sheehan declared. 'And if I were the Queen of the Faeries I would be very glad that I had offered you my patronage.'

'And if I were King of the Faeries,' Squire Sheehan interrupted light-heartedly, 'I would be concerned that this harper was going to steal my wife.'

'Your consort, my dear,' Mrs Sheehan corrected him. 'Everyone knows the Queen of the Faeries is the senior partner in the marriage. The king is merely a mate chosen for his ability to father healthy offspring.'

'Nevertheless,' the squire countered overly politely, 'I would be more than a little worried about the undue attention the queen showered on her harper. He is only a mortal after all.'

'The queen is free to do as she pleases,' Mrs Sheehan asserted archly. 'And perhaps she sometimes prefers the company of mortals.'

'And that is perfectly understandable,' the squire replied casually. 'I have no doubt the king has had the odd dalliance with a mortal woman.'

'Indeed?' Mrs Sheehan snapped. 'And how often do you think the consort might stray from his queen's bed on average?'

'Very rarely,' the squire answered in a conciliatory tone, raising a hand to calm her. 'But if the queen is permitted to do so, then surely he has some rights as well.'

'Do you imagine so?' Mrs Sheehan laughed disparagingly. 'You have forgotten your place.'

'Let us be reasonable,' the squire begged. 'I do not want another fight.' Suddenly he paused and realised several folk were listening intently to their every word.

'Will you excuse us, Turlough?' the squire asked.

'Yes, of course,' the stunned harper replied. The Sheehans withdrew, still speaking harshly to one another in subdued tones. He laughed to himself at their ongoing disagreement.

He shook his head and then realised he had taken too much claret.

'Mary!' he called. 'McCabe! Take me outside for some air. I am feeling queasy.'

In a few moments Cathair had one of his arms and Mary had the other and they all staggered out into the night, hoping the cool air would sober them up a little. Hugh stayed in the room to pack away the harp and when he had done that he joined them on the lawn.

'That is a lovely story about the Queen of the Faeries,' Mary remarked. 'Did you really meet her?'

'I did but I would rather not discuss her right now. I am not feeling all that well. I must have taken too much drink.'

'You are always on about the beautiful Queen of the Good People,' Hugh laughed, propping his master up. 'You even had me believing the story for a while.'

Turlough felt for his servant's throat and drunkenly took him by the collar. 'Don't you ever say anything untoward about the Queen of the Faeries,' he warned. 'I swore to defend her name whenever anyone dares to insult her.'

'I wasn't insulting her,' Hugh protested. 'I was insulting you.'

'And you better be sure it stays that way,' the harper mumbled.

Mary laughed loudly, then looked around when she heard more raucous laughter nearby. Other guests had come out into the garden to take the air and the small group now approached them.

'What do you think of Turlough O'Carolan's music?' a voice asked loudly.

'It is not for me to say,' David Murphy answered.

'Do tell us, David,' Bridget pressed him.

Turlough let go of Hugh and turned to listen to what the harper had to say.

'His music is full of good intentions,' Murphy said solemnly. 'His tunes are charming in their simplicity. But the melodies are rather like a leg of beef that has had the flesh boiled off it.'

'How is that?' one of his friends asked.

'They are all bones and no meat.'

The small group fell about screaming with drunken laughter and before Hugh could stop his master, Turlough had launched himself in their direction.

'I'll play you a tune with a bunch of my fingers,' Turlough screamed as he somehow managed to grab hold of Murphy. 'And you can put what beef you like to the bones.'

The harper threw a punch which landed far from its mark but knocked one of Murphy's friends flying. Then he got a hold of his rival's hair and began kicking at him.

'Stop him!' Murphy cried, shrieking with fear in a high-pitched voice. 'He'll surely murder me.'

Two of Murphy's friends managed to restrain Turlough. The man who had been knocked over by the harper got up and landed a punch in the blind man's stomach. The harper took the blow and then immediately stood up straight. His jaw dropped open and he swayed a little, which made Murphy's friends laugh again.

In that instant McCabe and Hugh struck in revenge. In seconds the whole garden had erupted into a wild free-for-all between the supporters of Turlough O'Carolan, who were many, and the friends of David Murphy, who were only a very few.

But Turlough was oblivious to the mayhem around him. He was lost in a drunken stupor. He heard Murphy's voice nearby and he reached out a hand to grab at the man.

The blind harper must have been particularly lucky that night for he managed to catch hold of the other man for a second time. But the exertion exhausted Turlough and he fell over, still clutching at Murphy's coat.

As he felt the ground rise to hit him in the face the harper heard a loud tearing sound followed by what he thought was the bleating cry of a small animal screeching in terror. And then Turlough knew no more.

TEN

Old Hugh breathed deeply and held out his cup. Mhairgead raised the jug and poured some of the golden home-made liquor into it.

'They were married that month,' Old Hugh said. 'Turlough and Mary. And they were the happiest couple I ever knew.'

'He was off travelling half the year, that's why,' Denis explained.

'But even in the six months they spent together each year,' Hugh added, 'they were always good natured and loving to one another.'

'They had six children,' the old harper chortled. 'They must have enjoyed a few mutually entertaining pursuits.'

'Five daughters came to them,' Hugh reminisced. 'And one son. One lad who was the laziest, stupidest boy I have ever met in my life. And when he grew up he became a stupid lazy handsome man.'

'A dangerous combination,' Denis sighed.

'Young Terence inherited his father's good looks. The bright eyes. The noble chin. The flowing hair. This lad had them all, but not a brain in his skull nor a purpose in his walk. And for that reason he never had a penny in his pocket.'

'What happened to young Terence in the end?' Edward asked.

'Not long after my master's death,' the old distiller said in a mysterious tone, 'young Terence went out one night for a stroll in the cool air. He told his sister not to wait up for him and she thought it mighty strange that he was going for a walk at that time of night. But she never asked him where he was going. He kissed her once on the cheek and then he walked out the door. He was never seen again. He disappeared forever.'

'Disappeared?' Denis gasped.

'Off to England with one of his father's harps and the wife of his best friend,' Hugh shrugged.

'Oh.'

'And if I ever get my hands on him, I'll skin him alive,' Hugh barked.

'Why?' Edward asked.

'It was my youngest brother's wife he ran off with.'

'That must have been a shock,' Denis commiserated.

'It was.' Hugh shook his head. 'I had money on Thomas Donehey's daughter being the one he would talk into running away with him. I lost two pounds on that wager.'

'Did the lad, young Terence, did he take after the mother or the father?' the old harper inquired.

'He took after anything in a skirt,' Hugh quipped. 'Which I suppose is to say he took after his father.'

Denis nodded. 'I see. And was your master ever tempted to stray from his good wife at all?'

'He was not,' Hugh said with certainty. 'But he would have been sorely tempted if he'd had the use of his eyes.'

'How so?'

'Did you ever meet Miss Stella?' the old distiller asked his friend.

'I never knew a woman by that name,' Denis told him, shaking his head, 'except by dint of reputation.'

'Then I certainly have a tale for you,' Hugh grinned. 'I often felt a great sympathy for my master's blindness until I realised it had saved him a great deal of trouble.'

'Well, tell your story, man.'

Hugh was just opening his mouth to speak when he froze and turned his head sharply. 'What's that?' he gasped.

'What?' Edward asked.

'Voices.'

A few moments later the young rebel heard the noise of footsteps approaching the door to the cottage and then there was a loud knock which rattled the windowpane. Edward's heart skipped a beat and he stood up anxiously.

'Open up in the name of the King!' a deep voice demanded.

'Jesus, it's the redcoats!' Edward cried. 'They'll have me for certain if I don't get out.'

'Whisht and be silent, you foolish boy!' Hugh hissed under his breath. 'It is too late for you to make any escape. You are betrothed to Mhairgead, remember? Keep your damn dim-witted mouth shut. Let me do the talking and all will be well.'

Edward sat down again and reached for his cup. As he did so Mhairgead stood up, and in an instant she had landed in his lap. He gasped in surprise and she landed a kiss upon his cheek.

'What are you doing to the boy, child?' Hugh snapped, hearing Edward's protest.

'Sitting on my future husband's lap, Grandfather.'

'Go and open the door to the soldiers,' the old man told her tersely. 'There'll be plenty of time for that sort of thing when you've tied the knot. And not a moment before!' he added with a hint of a threat.

Mhairgead struggled to stand up, brushed her skirt down and went to the door. No sooner had she unlatched it than a redcoat in a ridiculously tall hat kicked it open, levelled his musket at her and pulled back the hammer, ready to fire.

There was a loud noise outside. Mhairgead stepped back just as Daniel came flying into the room to land in the middle of the floor. His face was bloody and his coat torn.

'Dan!' Mhairgead screamed. 'What have they done to you?'

A smartly dressed officer in a bright scarlet coat entered the cottage, removing his hat so he wouldn't knock it off his head as he passed under the low lintel. He was followed by three other soldiers who held readied muskets. These three redcoats had to duck their heads as they passed through the door to keep their tall headgear in place.

'Is this the Connor household?' the officer inquired with just a hint of disgust in his voice. He touched a lace handkerchief to his long nose as he spoke.

'It is,' Hugh replied, without turning his face from the fire. 'And who in the Devil's name are you?' he asked calmly.

'I am Lieutenant William Moss, grenadier company, second foot guards.'

'That is a long introduction,' the distiller smiled. 'Your mother must have had quite an imagination. Couldn't she have simply called you William?'

'Very amusing,' Moss replied without emotion.

'Will you have a drink?' Hugh offered.

'Is it whiskey?' the lieutenant inquired.

'The finest.'

'I will. Thank you.'

'Mhairgead, get the man a cup,' Hugh told his grand-daughter.

'Daniel's been hurt!' the young woman objected. 'They've beaten him.'

'He was breaking curfew,' the officer declared coldly. 'He's lucky I didn't decide to hang him on the spot.' He looked contemptuously around the room. 'I may hang him yet if the mood takes me,' the redcoat announced.

'Get the fine English officer a cup,' Hugh repeated through clenched teeth. Mhairgead reluctantly left Daniel's side to do as she was bid.

Edward shifted uneasily in his seat but stared steadily into the fire without looking up. The officer took his whiskey, sniffed it and then sipped the liquor, scanning the cottage as he did so.

'Now I ask myself,' Moss went on, savouring the taste of the spirit, 'what would a young fellow like Daniel be doing abroad in the countryside after midnight?'

The lieutenant did not give anyone a chance to answer. 'My guess is that either he was out visiting a lover,' Moss went on, 'or he was dealing in illicit whiskey. On the other hand, however, he could have been out attempting to perpetrate some devilish crime against the Crown. Perhaps he and his as yet unnamed compatriots were intending to shoot down another officer in cold blood or smuggle arms to the rebels.'

'It's that young Bridie, isn't it?' Hugh bellowed. The old man had still not turned around.

Daniel grunted, shaking his head as Mhairgead tried to wipe the blood from his forehead.

'You should be ashamed of yourself!' the distiller shrieked in outrage.

Edward swallowed his whiskey in one gulp and placed the vessel down on his lap, gripping it with tight fingers.

'You're a married man with children of your own and Bridie is but a girl of twenty. You have brought shame on this household. You are no grandson of mine. Get out and sleep with the cows this night! And pray that your good wife is foolish enough to want you back tomorrow.'

'Grandfather,' Daniel began.

'Don't give me any bloody excuses, Daniel Connor McHugh!' the distiller cut in. 'It is time you mended your ways or found another parish in which to dwell.'

'Grandfather,' Daniel repeated. 'They found the still.'

'What?'

'These soldiers discovered me up at the still on the hillside.'

'Jesus!' Hugh gasped. 'Not the still! The one on the side of Geoghan's hill?'

'Yes,' Daniel mumbled. 'They have broken it up and confiscated all the barrels and jugs.'

'The full ones?'

'Yes, Grandfather.'

'My soldiers will certainly appreciate the generous donation of all that whiskey,' the lieutenant smiled.

'What do you mean?' the old man asked.

'Hugh Connor,' the lieutenant interrupted, 'do you know something of this illegal distilling operation your grandson is running?'

'I do,' Hugh admitted sheepishly.

'Look at me when you address me!' the officer shouted, unexpectedly losing his temper and tossing his cup across the room. It bounced off the floor and broke against the far wall.

'I wish I could,' Hugh answered when all was quiet. Then he turned to face the soldiers, deliberately twitching his jaw a little as he did so and revealing his empty eye sockets for the first time.

There was a collective gasp from the three private soldiers.

'You're blind!' Moss stammered.

'I can well understand why they made you an officer,' Hugh nodded. 'You'll be a captain in no time if you keep those wits about you. Fetch the gentleman another whiskey, Mhairgead.'

The young woman brought a fresh cup and the officer drank down the contents in one swig.

'I am also blind.' Denis turned to the soldiers and rolled his sightless eyes around in their sockets. 'So I hope you will forgive me if I do not look directly at you when I reply to your questions.'

The lieutenant raised an eyebrow but did not say anything. When he had regained his composure he handed the cup back to Mhairgead.

'I have reason to believe,' Moss began, 'that a substantial smuggling operation is being conducted hereabouts. And this collection of cottages would seem to be the centre of it. Avoidance of the Crown's excise on liquor is a crime punishable by hanging or worse.'

'What is worse than hanging?' Denis inquired.

'Transportation to Botany Bay,' the officer replied with a certain degree of satisfaction.

'We are poor folk,' Hugh said, 'the whiskey is our only comfort in times of sickness.'

'I see,' Moss replied. 'Are you trying to tell me that the vast quantity of spirit my soldiers discovered was for the consumption of you four gentlemen and this young woman alone?'

'Daniel's wife and children also take a drop,' Hugh explained. 'Whenever they have the cough. And there are two other lads younger than Dan.'

'There was enough whiskey to keep my whole company happy for a month!' the officer exclaimed.

At that moment Lieutenant Moss suddenly noticed Edward for the first time. 'You there!' he demanded. 'What's your name?'

'This is James Ferguson,' Hugh cut in, 'a merchant of Dublin town. He is engaged to marry my grand-daughter Mhairgead.'

Edward did not look up.

'I suppose you're blind too,' Moss laughed.

'As a matter of fact,' the distiller began.

'I am,' Edward finished, turning around as he rolled his eyes back into his head and licked his lips grotesquely.

'Sergeant!' the officer called out.

'Yes, sir?' came the reply from outside.

'What was the name of that rebel we're searching for? The one who shot D'Arcy.'

'Edward Sutler of Dublin, sir!' the sergeant bellowed as he stood to attention at the door.

'Was the rebel blind?'

'I do not recall with certitude any description which mentioned the fugitive suffering the aforesaid affliction, sir!'

The lieutenant thought for a second. 'Is that a yes or a no, sergeant?'

'The rebel was not blind, sir!'

Moss turned to Edward. 'Do you know this fellow called Sutler?'

'I do,' Edward answered in a slur and Hugh began to feel very uneasy. 'John Shuckle was an old friend of my father's. Of course he's been dead for twenty years or more now.'

'Not John Shuckle, you idiot,' the officer cried, putting a hand to his forehead in exasperation. 'Edward Sutler.'

'I don't think he was a saddler,' Edward replied. 'He was a chimneysweep as I recall.'

'You'll have to excuse the boy,' Hugh explained, putting an index finger to his temple. 'He's a little slow since the sickness took him.'

Suddenly the lieutenant was struck by the fact that three men in the same household were blind.

'There's something very strange going on here,' Moss observed, dropping the handkerchief from his nose. 'Sergeant, turn this cottage upside down. I have a feeling there is more to these folk than meets the eye.'

'Yes, sir!' the sergeant bellowed.

Moss put a hand to his ear and winced. 'I am just standing next to you,' the lieutenant told the soldier. 'There is no need to scream.'

'Yes, sir,' the sergeant replied in a more subdued tone. 'Sorry, sir.'

'Well get on with it!'

'Yes, sir.'

The sergeant went straight to Mhairgead's bed and stuck the point of his bayonet into the mattress several times.

'I have never heard of a family where three out of four of the menfolk were blinded,' the officer said to himself, thinking aloud. 'It is most peculiar.'

'Smallpox,' Denis chimed in. 'It was the smallpox that came upon us last year and blinded me. That is to say, I was the first to fall with the affliction, then Hugh here, and finally just two months ago poor young James fell foul of the plague. He was struck down on the same day as he asked our Mhairgead to marry him, as it happened.'

'Smallpox?' Moss asked with just a hint of panic in his voice. He put the lace handkerchief to his mouth again. 'This house has been touched by the pox?'

His soldiers were already retreating to the door. The sergeant stopped prodding with his bayonet.

'Do not fear, lieutenant,' Hugh sighed. 'No-one has died

under this roof yet. We've just been blinded. As long as you do not eat or drink anything in the house, you have very little chance of contracting the affliction. Isn't that right, Daniel?'

The red-haired man was lying back in Mhairgead's arms groaning. There was a small amount of froth at the corner of his mouth.

'I can hear the angels again, Grandfather,' Daniel murmured.

The officer blinked several times, spat out the contents of his mouth, looked toward his sergeant in horror and then turned on his heel.

'I can see I am wasting my time here,' Moss stammered as he made for the door. 'Your whiskey is confiscated and you can take that as a warning. In future I will be much harsher if I catch you distilling again. I bid you all goodnight.'

And then the smartly dressed officer was gone. He was quickly followed by his sergeant and the three soldiers, all of whom knocked their tall hats off on the low lintel in their rush to get out of the door.

Hugh, Denis, Mhairgead and Edward stayed perfectly still until they were certain the redcoats were out of earshot. Daniel crept up to the window to keep watch.

After a long while the red-haired man could restrain himself no longer. He began to giggle with his hand over his mouth and after a minute or so he was rolling around the floor, laughing wildly.

'How in the name of holy Hell did the English ever win themselves an empire,' Hugh cried, 'if that is the best their officers can do?'

'Did you see that fellow's expression when Denis told him about the pox?' Edward grinned.

'No, I didn't,' Hugh answered. 'I am blind, remember?'

'So you are,' the rebel recalled. 'But I wish you could have seen the blood drain from his face.'

'I could hear his stomach turning and that was enough,' Denis laughed.

'Are you all right, Daniel?' Hugh asked.

'They gave me a bloody good beating,' the red-haired man

replied. 'But nothing broken. Only bruises and a few cuts. I'll be mended in a day or so.'

'But the whiskey still!' Edward remembered in dismay. 'They smashed the still and stole the liquor.'

All of a sudden everyone in the room began to laugh louder and harder. Tears were running down Mhairgead's cheeks.

'I don't understand what's so funny,' Edward said, looking from one to another in confusion.

'It wasn't our still,' Daniel replied breathlessly. 'It was Michael Geoghan's. I went up to recover a debt from him but old Michael wasn't anywhere about. The soldiers arrived just as I was about to come home.'

'Mister Geoghan was once our fiercest competitor,' Hugh hiccoughed. 'A fine gentleman but well known for spiking his whiskey with tainted cordials, if you take my meaning.'

'I don't,' Edward frowned.

'In other words,' Daniel explained, 'Michael used the cheapest ingredients available. His last batch gave everyone who supped it a severe and debilitating case of the galloping bowels. To fill his orders poor Michael was forced to purchase several barrels of our fine liquor.'

'The barrels and jugs which the redcoats confiscated,' Hugh revealed, 'were Michael's tainted stock, which I am sure he fully intended to destroy.'

'But he must not have had time to finish the job,' Daniel interrupted.

'We have struck a blow for liberty!' Denis shrieked with laughter. 'The foot guards will be confined to barracks for days, I'll wager.'

Mhairgead was pouring out drinks again and they all laughed until their guts ached.

'Now you have earned yourself a place in the family, young Edward,' Hugh declared. 'And you can go back to Dublin and tell your rebel friends how three blind men incapacitated a whole company of English grenadiers without once leaving the safety of their fireside.'

'I am honoured,' Edward replied, raising his cup, 'to be considered worthy of your kinfolk.'

'You'll have to marry Mhairgead now,' Denis observed. 'To make an honest woman of her. For she has as much as consented to be your bride.'

'I can't get married,' the young rebel dismissed, sure the old harper was having a joke with him. 'There's too much work to be done for the cause of liberty.'

'Now I remember the story I was about to tell,' Hugh exclaimed, slapping his thigh.

'Oh God,' Denis sighed.

'I was about to relate the tale of Miss Stella. A woman whose lover was reluctant to marry her.'

Daniel sat down by the hearthstone and Mhairgead fetched a bowl of water to bathe the cuts on his face. She poured him a generous cupful of whiskey, then took up a wet cloth, but her brother told him to let him be. He drank the cup down and began to carefully wipe the remaining blood off his face.

Mhairgead returned to her stool behind Edward.

'Hadn't I better go out and keep watch for the redcoats?' the rebel asked.

'They will not be back tonight,' Denis assured him. 'They have twenty gallons or more of bad whiskey to take care of.'

'Take your ease, Master Edward,' Hugh soothed him, 'and I'll tell my story.'

The old man lit his pipe again, blew out the smoke and started speaking.

'It was in the same year Father Fogarty was killed by that coachman from County Cork. You remember the murdering scoundrel. He was a tall fellow and as broad as an ox.'

'He was,' Denis nodded. 'I saw them tie the noose around his neck after the magistrate had brought a guilty verdict on him. And I thought to myself that he was so long in the knee that his feet would touch the ground when the cart was pulled away from beneath him.'

'If you thought that, then you were right, sure enough,' Hugh agreed, 'there he stood, on the tips of his toes, strangling slowly for all to see. The coachman died badly. It was terrible. The whole thing took nearly an hour.'

'But he butchered a clergyman. Father Fogarty was a fine priest,' Denis cut in. 'And every man who saw the fellow hang that day knew there was a greater justice at work there than the King's.'

'It was that same year,' Hugh said, realising he was straying from his story, 'my master and I first met the good Mister Swift.'

Denis coughed and held out his wooden cup. Mhairgead leaned forward and carefully refilled the vessel.

Edward sat forward. 'This is a tale about Dean Swift?' he asked.

'It is if anyone will let me tell it,' Hugh huffed. 'First the redcoats. Now endless questions. I'll never get started with all these persistent interruptions.' He drew on his pipe indignantly.

'The gentle Mister Swift was living in Dublin at the time,' the old man continued. 'Master Carolan was acquainted with Doctor Delany who I had served as coachman before entering service with Master Carolan. He was not a medical doctor, mind you, old Delany. He was a Professor of Oratory at Trinity College.'

'What does that mean?' Denis asked.

'He could talk the beak off a blackbird, or the corsets off a whole convent, if he so desired. Give Delany a subject and he could speak about it with eloquence for hours without a break. And he often did. Even if he knew nothing about the subject he was expounding upon.'

'Do the English make a man a doctor just for being able to talk?' the old harper questioned.

'They do,' Hugh confirmed.

'Jesus and why are there not any Irish doctors of the fine speech?' Denis asked. 'For surely our own people are known for their talent with words.'

'The English are a jealous race,' Hugh told his friend. 'They would never allow a Catholic into such an important position. And anyway, before long every man, woman and child from Dublin to Dingle would be claiming the title and it would become utterly worthless.'

'You are right there, professor,' Denis smiled.

'In any case it was the habit of the good doctor to visit Mister Swift twice a week to partake in the pleasure of poetry. One day Delany proposed that Carolan and his humble servant, Hugh the Freckled,' the old man placed his right hand on his chest, 'accompany him to one of these evening meetings.'

'You dined with Dean Jonathan Swift?' Edward gasped, almost, but not quite, believing it.

'In Mister Swift's house there was not often much dining but there was always a sufficiency and more of wining,' Hugh replied. 'The fruits of Bacchus were abundant in that cottage and the gentlemen who attended these literary evenings reclined in the comforting arms of the gracious god of the grape. Do you take my meaning correct?'

'They were all drunkards?' Edward offered.

'Tosspots all,' Denis confirmed.

'They drank from dusk until dawn most nights,' Hugh nodded. 'My master was not known for his shyness with the liquor himself, so after that first evening we were invited back again the next week. In time Carolan's music became as important to that gathering as was spice to their stew or the cup for their claret. Swift often said of my master, *Est homo qui potest bibere.*'

'And what language is that?' the old harper asked.

'It is Latin,' Hugh replied. 'Have you never been to mass?'

'Of course I have,' Denis countered, 'but I never listen to what is said. What does it mean?'

'It means,' Hugh paused, 'Jesus, that boy can drink!' the old distiller laughed loudly and Edward smiled at the broad translation of the phrase.

'Anyway,' Hugh went on, 'Mister Swift was writing a book at that time about a man who is shipwrecked and washed up on a beach in a land where tiny Faeries live. I know for a fact that Master Carolan spoke to him of his own experiences with the Good People to help him research his book.'

'And what did the dean say when Carolan told him his tale of the Faeries?' Edward quizzed.

'The good clergyman that he was, he never took the story seriously,' Hugh admitted, 'and, ever after, the master was reluctant to speak of his adventures among the Faerie folk. But Mister Swift loved Carolan's harping and my master was fond of the clergyman.

'Carolan composed a verse for Mister Swift. "The tender young love of a fair slender girl,"' he quoted. '"The devotion of a fine strong man, the mother's doting on her child, have gone on since time began. But the greatest love, the love of all loves, even greater than that of a mother, is the all-consuming passionate love of one bloody drunk for another."'

Hugh chortled with delight and then went on with his tale.

'One night as my master and I were leaving the house of Mister Swift a woman approached us both. And what a gorgeous woman she was indeed. Hair like the threads of a spider's web with the dew upon it. And eyes that would melt a solid stone. She wore a scent about her, a sweet perfume that filled the air.'

'Who was she?' Denis asked.

'I'll tell you if you stop interrupting me,' Hugh retorted. 'Well, Master Carolan and I were hardly able to stand, so full we were of whiskey. But her tears and sobbing threw the veil of drunkenness from off our heads. And the master asked most humbly how we could help to ease her sorrow.'

'Who was that woman?' Denis insisted. 'I have not heard this part of the tale.'

'Her name was Stella,' Hugh answered and Edward's ears pricked up. The young rebel recalled hearing unkind gossip about a friendship the dean had had with a woman of that name. A woman who had followed the dean from England and bought a house in Dublin just to be by his side.

'She was said by a few men to be secretly married to the kind Mister Swift,' the old distiller said, 'and I would believe that for she knew such things about him as would not be proper for any woman but a wife to know.'

'What did she want?' Edward asked impatiently. 'What was she doing waiting around outside the dean's house in the middle of the night? Was she really married to him? Why was she crying?'

'I heard tell,' Hugh stated, 'that the two of them were indeed married but that Mister Swift had insisted they live apart for he thought it would improve his chances of being elevated to the bishopric when the time came. I also heard of another woman named Vanessa who died of a broken heart when she heard the rumours of Mister Swift's marriage.'

'The ladies loved him, that's for certain,' Denis cut in. 'Many tales attest to his alluring ways.'

'And if the women loved him,' Hugh added, 'he was just as passionate about them in return.'

'So what were you saying about Stella?' Edward pressed.

'All I know for certain,' Hugh said, 'is that this woman, Stella, was in a terrible state of distress, moaning and crying that Mister Swift was drinking himself to death. And that soon, she feared, he would expire from his indulgence in whiskey. Her love for him was such, she told us, that she would do anything to stop him dying from the drink.'

'Why would the lady tell you such things?' the young rebel shot back suspiciously, his eyes narrowing.

'She had it in her mind to cure the man of his indulgence,' Hugh snapped. 'And she wanted our help in attaining that cure.'

'What help could you possibly be to a man who wished to forsake the whiskey?' Denis stuttered in shock. 'By God, Hugh of the Freckled Face, that would be like asking the Devil himself to lend a hand converting the savage nations to the Cross. It would be a foolish act by anyone's standards.'

'It was a challenge,' Hugh admitted, 'but that was in the days before I established myself in the noble trade of distilling. And to see this woman weep was too painful a burden for either of us to bear. It was pitiful to behold. She was very pretty. Very pretty, you understand.'

Hugh sighed deeply at the memory.

'And Mister Swift, you understand, he was already quite mad from the whiskey. It was a terrible shame to think of this poor lass devoted to a man who had almost completely lost his wits.'

'I heard that he suffered an affliction of the mind in his later years,' Edward conceded.

'It started in his earlier years,' the distiller confirmed, 'and became worse as time went on, until the man was little more than a gibbering mass of literary quotations.'

Hugh drew on his pipe but it had gone out. He waited patiently for Mhairgead to put a burning twig to the tobacco. Once it was lit he went on.

'As I was saying, thank God the master had no eyes or he would have surely been damned for adultery. I was sorely tempted by Miss Stella's beguiling ways myself. How could we refuse anything she asked of us?'

'What did she want you to do?' Edward was intensely interested now.

'It was her observation that each night after all Mister Swift's friends, the Reverend Mister Jackson, George Rochefort, Doctor Walonsley and Doctor Delany, had departed for their homes, Mister Swift would fall into a terrible melancholy state. Some nights he would lose all his wits until the sun rose next morning. Often he fell down just within his own door and woke there many hours later.'

Hugh sipped his whiskey and drew in on his pipe.

'It was to his own good fortune, they say, that Mister Swift never suffered the aftereffects of the whiskey when he woke from such a slumber. Every morning he would simply wash his face, eat a little bread and then go straight back to work as if nothing had disturbed the pattern of his life. Sometimes he was forgetful, I'll grant you, but he was never sick.'

'I wish that had been my lot,' Denis complained. 'But I am

cursed to suffer for my indulgence every morning. My head aches and my stomach grumbles and the warmth of the sunlight on my skin is enough to make me fall down groaning.'

'And you fart like a fat cow,' Hugh added. 'But Mister Swift was not prone to any of those maladies. He was never afflicted in any way, apart from the occasional instance when he lost his wits a little in the morning.'

The old distiller took some more smoke.

'One night I witnessed this myself. The good Mister Swift was standing by the fire reciting some new verse he had concocted when he suddenly fainted and nothing anyone could do would bring him to his senses.'

'Who would have thought it of such a pious man as he?' Edward exclaimed.

'It's the pious ones who are the most trouble,' Denis chuckled.

'Miss Stella,' the old distiller continued, 'asked us to come up with a means to deal with this unfortunate state of affairs. I believe the only hours when she had any peace in the good man's company were the early morning of each day and she grieved every moment her true love was incapacitated.'

'So if they were not married, they must have been lovers?' Edward asked, his mouth open.

'Indeed,' Hugh replied, 'but who am I to judge my fellow man for his indiscretions? They were the best of friends and that is better than most men can ask for in a companion.'

'Or most women,' Mhairgead interrupted. Then she smiled sweetly at Edward and went outside to fetch another jug of liquor.

'Anyway,' Hugh went on, 'Carolan told the lady that he knew of a cure for the whiskey but that it was a dangerous and sometimes fatal medicine. Miss Stella cried that she would risk anything to save the man she loved. And so they contrived a plan to fool Mister Swift by seeding the tiniest beginnings of doubts into his head.'

'How so?' Edward frowned.

'At the next poetical gathering Master Carolan and myself

waited behind after all the other guests had gone. In due course Mister Swift, unable to keep up with our drinking, fell into a deep sleep from which we could not stir him. When we were sure he would not wake up, we carried him to bed. The master slipped off Mister Swift's boots and replaced them with a pair of Miss Stella's shoes, which she had kindly loaned to us for the occasion.'

Hugh stopped for a second and considered. 'It is true that her feet were nearly as large as Mister Swift's himself, but that is not to doubt her beauty. She was a diamond among the pebbles.'

'I don't see the point of doing that,' Edward interrupted.

'What do you mean?'

'Why did you put her shoes on the dean?'

'The next morning, you see,' Hugh explained, 'Mister Swift awoke, and his mind being refreshed, the first thing he did was to look down at his feet. And what mystery met his eyes? His own boots were gone and in their place a pair of women's shoes. He doubtless thought it was some joke his friends had played on him. And I suppose he likely had a laugh to himself for he could remember nothing of the previous evening.'

'How could putting a woman's shoes on him cure a man of drunkenness?' Denis asked, shaking his head.

'It was not the shoes that cured him,' the old distiller laughed. 'Be patient till the end of the tale.'

Hugh drew on his pipe again.

'The next time his friends gathered,' he said, blowing out smoke as he spoke, 'Mister Swift expected they would tell him the tale of the shoes, have a snigger at his expense and the whole incident would be explained. But no-one mentioned it of course. For only myself, Carolan and Stella knew of the ruse. In the end poor Mister Swift did not dare say anything himself for fear of how he had come to be in that state. That night Master Carolan and I left early so as not to arouse the good man's suspicions. As soon as the house was quiet we crept back in. Then we went about putting the next part of the scheme into effect.

'We found Mister Swift asleep across the doorstep and took him to bed again. And all the time there was no more than a snore passed his lips and he had no idea of what was happening. When the man was laid on his back upon the bed, Miss Stella did a thing so shameful I still feel my cheeks burn even now with the thought of it.'

'What did she do?' Denis whispered and if his eyes had been able they would have sparkled with mischief.

'She produced a pair of long black women's stockings with fine Belgian lace stitched about the tops and she held them out for us. Then she commanded us to remove Mister Swift's trousers and replace them with the very items she had in her hand. That done, we went home.'

'What on earth were you doing?' Edward exclaimed.

'Master Carolan and Miss Stella had devised this plan and they did not let me in on it,' the old distiller explained. Then he took another mouthful of liquor and swallowed it with obvious enjoyment.

'Bless me, but the next morning Mister Swift awoke in uncommonly good spirits but it was one of those occasions when his mind was not working as well as it should. I knew his serving man quite well and had the story from the fellow's own mouth. The servant noticed his master's strange apparel but was too shocked or polite to say anything.'

'Swift didn't notice he was wearing stockings?' Denis asked in disbelief.

'The poor man did not,' Hugh confirmed. 'His wits were addled by alcohol, and though he was not physically ill, the man's mind was playing tricks on him. And to compound the problem he often went to work in the morning dressed in his nightshirt or whatever clothes he had slept in.

'The serving man told us that Mister Swift arose, went to his toilet and had tea at the table in his study without noticing the nature of his attire. Then the clergyman began work on a sermon without for a moment realising his predicament. At one o'clock a lady parishioner arrived to arrange a baptism for her grandson. Mister Swift stood up from his seat to greet her and only then did he notice the draught blowing around his shirt tails.'

Denis giggled wickedly. 'That's a good cure if ever I heard one.'

'The lady parishioner was so shocked she departed immediately and never returned to that church again while Mister Swift was in attendance. And the gentleman himself, pale as a ghost, went back to bed for the rest of the day, after removing the offending articles of clothing of course.'

Hugh took another mouthful of whiskey and smiled in delight. 'The next time we all gathered together Mister Swift was very reluctant to take a drink. I am sure the seeds of worry were planted fruitful in his mind by that time. It was all I could do to keep my face straight when I saw the furrows in his brow. For by this time I had worked out what my master intended to do.

'Anyway, after a little persuasive talk from his friends, Mister Swift was convinced to indulge himself more fully and soon he was as drunk as the rest of them. Poor fellow. It would have been better if he had never touched the bottle again. But the wisest men have a touch of the fool about them, so they say.

'By the time we departed, both Mister Swift and Doctor Delany were almost senseless with drink. An hour later my master and I returned with Miss Stella. The doctor was asleep on a long low seat by the window, snoring like a hog. Mister Swift had curled up by the fire.'

'What did you have in store for him this time?' Edward gasped.

'A full gown and a beautiful wig that had belonged to Stella's mother. The old lady had been a tall woman who frequented the court of King James in happier times.'

'My God,' Denis cried, 'that Stella was an evil woman if ever there was one! I wish I had got to know her.'

'I can only imagine the scene at the house next morning,' Hugh went on, barely containing his amusement. 'Doctor Delany was a discreet man and he never said anything that came

to my ears about the incident. But it is a fact that he was ever
after careful not to be left alone in the room with Mister Swift.
And he was always at pains to advise the good clergyman whenever he considered too much liquor had been consumed. Mister
Swift's serving man was there of course and he could never
finish relating the tale without breaking into fits of laughter.'

'And did the dean stop drinking?' Edward asked.

'After that night he did not touch a drop for three full
months. The poetry evenings were cancelled, of course, and
Mister Swift rarely indulged himself in a drink more than once
a month for the rest of his life after that,' Hugh said proudly,
'which I believe was a great comfort to Miss Stella in her later
years.'

Hugh took some more smoke.

'And Master Carolan and I got ten pounds for our trouble,
which bought us four dozen jugs of the purest liquor. That kept
us merry and well fed for many a night. Sad we were that Mister
Swift could not share the whiskey with us.'

'What must the poor bugger have thought?' Denis guffawed.
'And what a woman she was! That's exactly the type of female
I would have married if I'd had the chance.'

'Are you referring to Miss Stella or to Mister Swift?' Hugh
wanted to know and both old men fell about in wild drunken
laughter.

Edward sat back smiling. He suddenly realised he didn't care
whether any of Hugh's stories were pure invention or not. In
fact he was beginning to prefer to believe there was a good deal
of truth in them.

'And so why didn't you chase after the wicked Miss Stella,
Hugh Connor of the Freckled Face?' Denis laughed.

'I would have done so,' the old man admitted, 'if only I had
thought I had a chance of winning her affection. But she was
besotted with Mister Swift and would look on no other man.
Although I reckon she might have fallen for my master. They
got on uncommonly well those two. They had the same sense
of wit, if you understand me.'

'Did you know your Katie at that time?' Denis asked.

'No,' Hugh answered. 'I had not met her. But it was not long after that our paths crossed.'

'Who is Katie?' Edward inquired.

'Katie is the name of my dear departed and much-mourned-for wife,' the old distiller explained. 'May she rest in eternal peace. We met under extraordinary circumstances and if it had not been for my master we would never have been married at all. So I have him to thank for that.'

Mhairgead came back into the room with a fresh jug of whiskey and went around pouring out the contents.

'You haven't told this tale for a long while, Grandfather,' she commented gently.

'I have been unable to speak of it,' Hugh admitted, 'so affected have I been by the loss of my own true love.'

He drank down a cupful of his own spirit and then Mhairgead filled his cup again.

'But I will tell you the story now,' he declared, 'for it is a good tale.'

ELEVEN

In the driving rain the mare tucked her head down to stop the droplets stinging her eyes. The man astride her back pulled his coat over his head and huddled down close to her neck.

Out in front Hugh the Freckled led the mount and carried the seal-skin harp case over his shoulder, striving all the while to stay as dry as possible.

'My fingers are frozen,' he grumbled, but his master did not acknowledge the complaint. 'I said I am soaked through to the skin,' the servant went on more loudly. 'My body is like a piece of ice. And it is so dark I cannot see the road.'

'Be quiet,' Turlough mumbled. 'Do you think I would be able to see it better? How can I sleep if you continue moaning about every little thing?'

'That's it!' the servant hissed, throwing down the reins. 'You find your own way to the ferry. I'm sick to death of leading this scraggy mare across the country in all weathers and at all times of the night. You can look after yourself from here on in.'

'It's not that far,' Turlough protested. 'An hour or two at the most. There may even be a ferry closer by than we thought.'

'I don't care. I think it's high time I was sat upon that horse instead of you. My shoes have holes in them and the mud is seeping in between my toes. And I haven't had a drop since we left the last village. A man could perish in these bitter conditions.'

'Indeed,' the harper smiled. 'I must confess I am a little dry myself.'

As if to mock this comment the rain intensified. The water dripped off the harper's chin and down into his shirt and he wiped it away with one hand.

'I smell a hearth fire,' Turlough told his servant.

Hugh looked to the road ahead. 'I don't smell anything but another trick to keep me walking,' he hissed as he wiped the water off his face. 'There may be a small settlement a bit further on,' the servant conceded, 'but it can't be the village we were hoping to reach this evening. We've only been walking a few hours.'

'If you were not such a late riser,' Turlough shrugged, 'we would be inside a warm cottage by now, seated by the fire with a cup in our hands.'

'If you were not always insistent on drinking our hosts out of their whiskey,' Hugh countered, 'I might not have needed to sleep until afternoon.'

'You are right,' the harper agreed. 'I will never force you to have another drink again as long as I live.'

Hugh mumbled an expletive under his breath.

'There's no need for that sort of language,' Turlough admonished. 'It's plain you've been wasting your time mingling with drunkards again. You always talk like that when you've been carousing with the wrong folk.'

Another colourful expression leapt to Hugh's mind but he did not give voice to it.

'Let's ride on to those buildings and beg lodging for the night,' Turlough suggested.

'You are riding,' the servant corrected him. 'I am walking ankle deep in mud.'

'The longer we stand here arguing the point, the colder and wetter we'll get.'

'Very well,' Hugh sighed. 'But if I die of the cold tonight, it will be on your conscience.'

'Calm down,' the harper told him with a hint of reprimand.

'I can always find myself another servant if the task is no longer to your liking.'

'Well,' Hugh replied, unsure whether or not he was being threatened, 'I don't think there's many men would undertake such employment.'

'Perhaps not. Can we make a move then?'

Hugh grumbled again and turned to start walking. But he had not led the mare more than a few paces when the muddy road erupted in blazing light. All of a sudden there seemed to be torches everywhere and Hugh, his eyes used to the half-light of evening, was temporarily blinded.

The servant heard a sword ring as it was drawn from its scabbard.

'Stand your ground!' a voice bellowed.

'Mother of God!' Hugh cried. 'Renegades!'

He let loose the reins and flung his arms about wildly in an impotent attempt to fend off the attackers.

'We have nothing worth taking!' he screamed. 'Have mercy on us! We are but poor travellers. And my master is a good man with no gold to his name.'

'Hugh,' Turlough reprimanded.

'Leave us to continue our journey in peace,' the servant pleaded.

'Hugh!' the harper shouted.

The servant stopped and turned to face his master.

'I have a notion that these gentlemen are not brigands,' the harper told him. 'They surely would have murdered us by now if they were. I have a feeling they have come to guide us to their village.'

Hugh looked about him again and noticed the wry smiles on the faces of the gathered strangers. 'It would not be the first time I had fought off a band of outlaws in my master's defence,' he warned them. 'I am not afraid of any of you, you know.'

'Come in by the fire,' a rather fat, bald man told him. 'You can tell us all about your adventures once we are out of the rain.' He stepped up to Hugh and picked the reins up from the mud. He was slightly shorter than Hugh but he had an air of authority about him.

'You go on,' the man said. 'I'll lead the horse.'

'That's my job!' Hugh protested as the stranger put a hand on his shoulder.

'Go on, my son. There's cabbage and bacon at my house and you are welcome to it.'

'And whiskey?' Hugh asked.

The stranger stepped closer and his cloak blew open in the wind. He was wearing the collar of a Roman Catholic cleric. 'Are you a son of the true faith?'

'I am,' the servant answered, though it occurred to him that he was not the most obedient son.

'My name is Dunleavy. Father Dunleavy,' the priest introduced himself. 'And I am always happy to share a drink with men who profess the true religion of Ireland. I have a drop of brandy if you'll take it with me.'

'That would be fine,' the servant gulped.

The priest stared at Hugh with steel grey eyes, scrutinising him carefully. 'Are you certain you are not Protestants?' he barked.

'Certain,' the servant replied and Hugh felt the question chill him deeper than even the cold and the rain.

'Have you come by way of that village on the other side of the lough?'

'No.' Hugh shook his head vehemently.

'Good,' the priest said. 'We don't allow their kind or those who fraternise with them into our homes.'

With that Dunleavy pulled on the reins and stepped out in the direction of his house, half a dozen men following close behind. Hugh trudged on in their wake, wondering what manner of place this could be. He had never heard of a village where groups of armed men routinely trudged about on stormy nights on the off-chance they might encounter stray Protestants.

It was not long before the party came to a large, very plain stone house with a thatched roof and wooden shutters instead of glass for windows. The priest tied the harper's horse to a post and helped Turlough down.

'You are welcome to stay the night here,' Dunleavy offered.

Though the priest's tone was severe, Turlough nodded and smiled. 'Thank you, father. We might have frozen to death on the road tonight if it had not been for you.'

'Where were you making for?'

'Sligo,' Turlough answered. 'But tonight we had hoped to cross the lough.'

'Sligo town is the seat of all evil,' the priest flared. 'I cannot think why you would want to go there. I have heard that Protestants are allowed to walk freely about the streets, corrupting the faithful with their licentious ways.'

'Then you obviously know a lot more about the place than I do,' Turlough replied in as polite a manner as he could muster.

'With an early start tomorrow,' the priest informed him, 'you may well come to the other side of the lough in a day or so.' Then he opened the door and led the harper into the hall.

'A day or so!' Hugh exclaimed, following on after them. 'We were hoping to take a boat across. Surely that is not nearly as far as the journey around the shore.'

'It is just over a mile and a half to the village on the other bank,' Dunleavy said, ushering the two men to seats close by the fire. 'But it may as well be as far as China, for no folk from this settlement ever travel there. Nor will any of us suffer to take our boats past the middle of the lough.'

Hugh opened his mouth to ask why but before he could make a sound one of the village men pushed through the hall door.

'I have stabled the horse, father.'

'Very well, Padraic. Goodnight to you.'

'Will the gentleman not be playing for us then, father?' the man asked, eyeing the harp case.

'I have not asked him, Padraic.'

'I would be happy to play some tunes for your folk,' Turlough offered. 'I am sorry I didn't speak up earlier. It has been a long day.'

'Let them have some food and drink,' Dunleavy told the man. 'Come back in an hour or so and we'll see how it is with him.'

'Yes, father.' And with that the man was gone.

'I have not introduced myself,' the harper began.

'There is no need,' Dunleavy answered. 'Your fame precedes you, Turlough O'Carolan. I was once a frequent visitor to the MacDermot household where your father was blacksmith. Mrs MacDermot is very proud of you. I have heard all about your adventures. There have been many compliments placed at your feet.'

'My patrons have been very kind.'

'You spend too much time in the company of foreigners and heretics,' the priest snorted.

'Some of my patrons are English and Scots,' Turlough admitted. 'As for their religious persuasion, I do not make it a habit to inquire into the consciences of my fellow men. That is a priest's profession.'

'I am shocked that you flout your disloyalty to King James,' Dunleavy spat.

'King James is no longer our monarch,' the harper countered. 'Even his young son, James the Pretender, makes no open claim to the throne. And folk say they are both quite mad.'

'That is not true!' the priest hissed. 'I have met young James myself. He is a fine lad with a good heart. He will be a great king one day. His son Charlie is a true Scot and a sworn Catholic.'

'The last rebellion failed before it even began,' Hugh cut in. 'It would take the hand of God Himself to remove the Germans from the throne. And I have a feeling that there are few folk who would stand the risk of showing any loyalty to the Stewart cause. They hang Jacobites in London.'

The priest frowned and then turned toward the kitchen.

'Katie!' he bellowed. 'We have guests. Bring them supper and some brandy.'

From somewhere at the rear of the house came a muffled woman's voice. The priest assumed she had heard him and went on.

'You have spent a great deal of time among the heathen in Dublin, haven't you?' he scowled. 'I fear you have both been corrupted by the Protestant scourge.'

'I have met men who were on the battlefield of the Boyne,' Hugh told him. 'Loyal and true to their Catholic king they were. But he did not extend the same loyalty to them. He fled the field before the fight was ended. James forfeited the crown through cowardice. If he or his son were brought back to the throne, there wouldn't be many old soldiers who'd raise a cheer.'

'Those were dark days,' Dunleavy conceded. 'Many folk did things which they later regretted. In the heat of battle a man is prone to make mistakes.'

'Even young Lord Mayo curses the ill luck that brought King James to the palace,' Turlough added. 'And well I remember his father, the old lord, as being a staunch supporter of the Jacobite cause.'

'The Scots Protestants and the English have destroyed our country,' Dunleavy asserted.

'They have done no more evil than the Catholic chieftains and kings did in a thousand years of bitter rivalry,' the harper replied. 'And many of the Scots speak the same language as we do. It is only the matter of faith which divides us.'

'They have been led astray from the Church by the hand of Satan,' the priest said coldly. 'There is no redemption for any of them unless they embrace the Holy Mother Church. They are outlaws in God's kingdom.'

'Their only crime is that they do not pay tithes to Rome,' Turlough argued.

'Some crimes can never be forgiven.' Dunleavy frowned at his guest.

'I'll bear that in mind should I ever find myself seated in your confessional,' Turlough smiled, trying to lighten the atmosphere.

'I have been witness to the work of the heretics,' the old priest declared, his voice full of bitterness. 'I saw the army of King

William on the rampage. I watched helpless as women were raped, their children beaten, their husbands hanged, their houses burned and their livestock plundered. I cannot forgive the heretics their cruelty, for they showed no respect for their fellow human beings or for God's law.'

'And yet you said yourself,' Turlough reminded him, 'that in the heat of battle a man is liable to make mistakes.'

'This was no military engagement!' Dunleavy spat. 'A month after the Battle of the Boyne Duke William's army passed by the lough. His soldiers were foraging for food when they came to our village and burned it to the ground.'

'Did their officers not restrain them?' Hugh asked.

'Their officers were the ringleaders,' the priest shot back. 'And a preacher called Edmund Black. Black was the day he came to our settlement. May he roast over the eternal fires of Hell. And a curse on the folk who live in the village of Buntrane across the lough. For they saw the flames of our burning houses and did not lift a finger to save life or property.'

'That is why your people will not row us across the water?' Hugh asked.

'There used to be a lot of traffic between the two villages,' Dunleavy told them. 'In the days before Duke William there were many occasions when both communities came together to celebrate the harvest or share our bounty. Our folk are well known for their fine fishing nets. The folk of Buntrane are praised for their skill at building fine curraghs which are suited to conditions on the lough. We shared our craftsmanship and kept famine at bay when times were hard in the rest of Ireland.'

'So no-one came from Buntrane to lend a hand?'

'No-one,' the priest confirmed.

'Has anyone from this village ever inquired as to why?' Turlough asked.

'The preacher called Black visited Buntrane the day before the attack and warned them not to interfere or they would be the next to suffer. Most of the folk in that settlement are Protestants so they did as they were told.'

'They must have been very frightened,' the harper said. 'Surely that could have had something to do with why they stayed away.'

'They deserted their neighbours in time of need,' Dunleavy hissed. 'But within a few weeks they were repaid for their treachery.'

'What do you mean?' Hugh asked, feeling the hairs rise on the back of his neck at this tale.

'A month later the remnants of the great army of King James came by this way, travelling toward the garrison town of Limerick. When we told them what had taken place, the King's officers decided to visit the same fate on the village of Buntrane as had been inflicted upon us. Buntrane was razed to the ground and the menfolk enlisted forcibly into the army. We saw the fires that night and our folk felt comforted in witnessing God's justice.'

'That does not sound very just to me,' Turlough noted. 'None of your folk came to the aid of the people of Buntrane.'

'An eye for an eye,' the priest said.

'Do unto others,' Turlough countered quickly.

'The wages of sin is death,' Dunleavy spat.

'Love thy neighbour as thyself.'

'The ways of the heathen are the ways of Satan.'

'Are they not deserving of any compassion?' the harper demanded.

'They do not deserve anything more than our contempt.'

'So it has been thirty years or more since there was any contact between the two villages?' Hugh calculated.

'That is true,' Dunleavy nodded.

'So poor travellers like ourselves have to journey all the way around the lake to pick up the road on the other side?'

'There are not many travellers these days,' Dunleavy laughed.

'I'm not surprised,' Turlough retorted. 'The welcome is subdued to say the least. And it is very inconvenient to have to go all the way around the lough when a boat could cut through the water in no time at all. This foolishness adds two days to

our journey. Is there nothing that can be done? I cannot pay
you very well but I would be eternally grateful if you could find
a way to get us across the lough.'

'That is out of the question,' Dunleavy snapped. 'No-one
travels over the lough. No-one!'

The harper sighed and his servant echoed the sentiment as he
settled down on a bench by the fire. Just as Hugh was shaking
the water off his coat, a young woman with short dark hair entered
the room carrying an earthenware jug and three wooden cups.

'Will you have a drop of brandy, gentlemen?' the priest asked.
'My brother sends it over from France.'

'From France!' Turlough exclaimed, his face lighting up.
'That may make amends for an otherwise disappointing day. I
will indeed take a drop. French brandy is a rare treat in these
times. What do you say, Hugh?'

There was no answer. Hugh was staring off into space with
a strange expression of delight on his face, but Turlough could
not see that of course.

'Hugh?' the harper said again. 'Are you there?'

'I am,' the servant muttered with disinterest.

'Are you sick, man?' the harper whispered, leaning across,
but there was no reply.

Father Dunleavy looked up and followed Hugh's gaze. The
servant was transfixed by the young woman who had brought
in the brandy. And the old priest did not like the attention his
maid was receiving. His eyes narrowed.

'This is Katie,' the priest said sternly. 'She is an orphan and
lives under my care.' There was a hint of a threat in his voice
which woke Hugh from his reverie.

'Since when does the Church allow a priest to keep a young
girl who can't be more than nineteen years in his house?' the
servant asked.

'I'm twenty-one,' Katie cut in. 'And I choose to live here with
Father Dunleavy of my own free will. He helped me look after
my parents when I could no longer care for them alone. They
both died of the cough three years ago.'

'Be careful, young man,' Dunleavy snarled, staring at Hugh. 'I can see what you are thinking. It is written in your eyes.' Then he turned to the girl. 'Go and fetch us some dinner, child. We are all soaked to the bone and in need of nourishment.'

She nodded silently and left the room, pausing for a moment to lean against the doorway and look back in Hugh's direction. When he noticed she was staring at him he blushed and dropped his eyes to the fire. Dunleavy half closed his eyelids and the corners of his mouth twitched.

As soon as Katie was gone the priest stood up and crossed the room. He handed a cup to Turlough and then went to where Hugh was sitting. Dunleavy put a hand on the servant's shoulder and spoke in a deep, menacing tone.

'Any man who lays a finger on that child will have to deal with me,' the priest warned. 'Drive her from your thoughts for she is promised to the convent. I should have sent her away long ago but I have grown used to her ways.'

'You mean that you would have no-one to clean and cook for you if she took the veil?' Hugh replied dryly.

'Hold your tongue!' the priest snapped. 'I know what sort of men travel the countryside playing music for a living. I have seen enough of your kind to recognise you as a corrupter of young women. You are a thief of virtue, a pilferer of purity.'

'That's a bit harsh,' Turlough interrupted.

'The world is a harsh place,' Dunleavy answered, not removing his hand from Hugh's shoulder. 'Trust no-one. Scrutinise everyone. Watch your property. Guard your morals. Choose carefully those with whom you break bread or share a drink. Better to be alone in the wilderness than to fall in with thieves, fornicators and liars.'

'And what about joy?' Turlough protested. 'What about music? Laughter? Love? Is there no room for those things in this world of yours?'

'There is but one love that is worthy,' the priest answered, eyes straying toward the heavens. 'The pure love of Christ, who died that we may live. Anything else is a dim reflection of the holy light of God's affection. Any joy, laughter and music that do not stem from that holy love are empty by comparison. Anything not devoted to God is the work of the Devil.'

'That's fine for a priest,' Turlough said. 'You have renounced the world of the flesh. But what of your flock? You surely can't expect them to live up to your ideal of holy love?'

'The people of this village have suffered from the brutality of the English,' Dunleavy told him, 'but they understand that this was God's punishment for their sins. The destruction of the town was a valuable lesson for all of us.'

'What sins could a fisherman possibly commit that would bring about the burning of his home and the murder of his loved ones?'

'You are a blind harper,' the priest smiled condescendingly. 'What would you know of theology? Have you never wondered what crime you may have committed that caused God to take your eyesight?'

'If I had not been blinded,' Turlough laughed, 'I would have spent a lifetime working in the fields, scratching a living for my family from the clay of the earth. My belly would have been empty more often than not and I would not likely have travelled further than the next parish in my whole life. As I see it, my blindness is the greatest blessing that could have been bestowed upon me. It is no punishment.'

Dunleavy's mouth dropped open in amazement.

'The loss of my sight has humbled me,' the harper went on. 'I had to learn to live all over again. The simplest daily tasks became mountains which had to be climbed. I had to rely on my ears and my hands to find my way around.'

'God took your eyesight to teach you humility,' the priest spat.

Turlough sat back in his chair and sighed. 'The world of music was opened to me when my eyes were dulled by the Galar-breac. And music is more precious than anything else in the whole of creation. Music comes directly from God. It is His gift to all His people. In music there is joy, laughter, love and every other emotion distilled into a fine liquor, like this rare brandy, so that the flavour lingers on the palate long after the melodies have ceased.'

The harper sipped his brandy.

'If my sight were offered to me now, I would not have it back. It has no value to me. I am who I am because I have struggled to overcome a terrible hardship and I have turned the results of that hardship to my advantage.'

'Music is the work of the Devil,' the priest stated angrily, sitting down again in his own chair by the fire. 'I can see the loss of your eyes has blinded you to more than the material world. You have been blinded to the world of the soul as well.'

'If that is how you feel, you probably won't be wanting a tune from me tonight,' the harper snapped.

'I won't,' Dunleavy replied. 'But the poor folk of this village have few pleasures. Their lives are hard and they have little excuse for light-hearted behaviour. Would you deny them your gift?'

Turlough shrugged. 'As soon as I have had a bite to eat I will play for them. But I must be leaving first thing in the morning. Is there no possibility that my servant and I could take a boat to the other side of the lough?'

'None. And don't even bother asking any of the fishermen. They will give you the same answer.'

'Then let my servant borrow a boat,' the harper suggested, 'and row across to the other village. If your people will not take me, then the folk of Buntrane might send a boat across.'

'They will not!' the priest hissed. 'If they would not come in our time of need, what makes you think they will come because you beckon them? You may be a renowned musician, famous and well travelled, but those sort of people do not lift a finger to help anyone else. They would not aid you.'

'And pray tell me,' Turlough scowled, 'how are your two villages any different?'

'We have right on our side. The righteous are above the ways of the world.'

The harper shook his head in disbelief just as Katie entered the room carrying a tray of steaming food. There was a mound of boiled cabbage on each of the three pewter plates, garlanded with thin strips of bacon and some wild thyme. The aroma filled the room but Hugh did not notice the grumbling of his own stomach. His eyes were fixed on the young maidservant.

Dunleavy frowned deeply. 'But to satisfy you,' he hissed, realising that he would have to act quickly to keep these two young people apart, 'I will arrange for your servant to take a boat across to the other side tonight as soon as he has finished eating. He can return in the morning at first light.'

Hugh opened his mouth to protest but before he could speak Turlough clapped his hands together. 'Grand! At last I am hearing sensible talk.'

He turned his head to address Hugh. 'Hurry along now and eat your meal. I want to be able to leave at dawn and it is up to you to arrange it.'

Katie placed a pewter plate in Hugh's lap and the two of them stared at each other with wide eyes full of longing.

'Hugh!' Turlough repeated. 'Have you gone deaf? A fine pair we'd make. I would not be able to see the harp and you would not be able to hear it.'

Katie handed out the other two plates in silence. Hugh did not dare speak and the priest was fuming. Then the girl was gone back to the kitchen.

'What the Devil is going on here?' the harper mumbled

'You have brought the Devil into my house with you,' Dunleavy replied in a soft but menacing voice. 'And if I do not keep him in check, he will plunder the treasures of this village.'

'What are you talking about?' Turlough frowned but did not waste any more time trying to work out what was going on. The aroma of bacon and cabbage had woken his empty stomach from sleep. He scraped the spoon that Katie had placed in his hand around the edge of the plate until he felt that it was full of food.

Why was it that priests always went on and on about the Devil? he asked himself as he took a mouthful of food. They never shut up about him. They were obsessed with Satan. The best of them went about dressed in mournful black, drank heavily and gambled profusely.

The harper chewed his cabbage thoughtfully. Surely they realised that whenever they condemned anything that was even slightly enjoyable, folk naturally concluded that God was harsh, cruel, vengeful and petty. Turlough was beginning to believe that priests were just trying to give God a bad name. They were the ones in league with the Devil. And one day people were going to wake up to that fact.

The harper finished chewing his mouthful of cabbage and bacon and then leaned over toward Hugh. 'I want to talk to you before you leave for the other village,' he told his servant. 'Do you understand?'

'Yes, yes. I'm not a simpleton, you know,' Hugh snapped and then continued with his meal. The cabbage was salty but it was fresh and there was a little pepper sprinkled on the top. The bacon was thinly sliced and very lean. But it was tough like leather. As Hugh slowly chewed he stared at Dunleavy with contempt.

A thought struck him.

Hugh leaned over to look at his master's meal. There was no pepper on the top of the harper's cabbage. He cast a glance at the priest's plate and there was no pepper on his cabbage either. Katie must be giving him a signal in lavishing the expensive spice on him.

The pepper proved it. She wanted him for her own. And he determined that she should have him.

As soon as he finished his meal Hugh got up to take his plate to the kitchen.

'Leave that here,' the priest barked, seeing through the ploy immediately. Then Dunleavy put his own plate down and made for the kitchen door.

'Katie!' he called. 'Go and fetch Padraic. I have a favour to ask him.'

'I will, father,' came the muffled reply.

The priest smiled with self-satisfaction and sat down, his hands resting on his knees, to wait. He did not take his eyes off Hugh until Padraic arrived. Even then it was only long enough to acknowledge his neighbour's presence.

'I want you to give this man one of our curraghs,' the priest told Padraic. 'He is going to row across to Buntrane tonight.'

'Buntrane?' the man frowned. Then his eyes widened in wonder. 'What business has he with them?'

'He and his kind deal with the enemy every day of their lives,' the priest explained. 'Better one of them should fly into that nest of poisonous vipers than one of our own people.'

'How do I know I will see my boat again?'

'If the folk over there were foolish enough to steal it, Mister Carolan would surely compensate you in full,' Dunleavy assured him. 'Wouldn't you, Mister Carolan?'

'From what you've told me, the boats are of a much better make in Buntrane,' Turlough retorted. 'I can't see why they would want to steal one of yours.'

'The Devil works in mysterious ways.'

'There you go again,' the harper protested, shaking his head. 'On and on about the Devil. I have never visited a place where I felt the presence of the Devil so strongly as I do here in this little village far from the evils of the world.'

'You are right,' Dunleavy told him, raising his eyes to the ceiling. 'Satan often takes his sport in paradise. He was even in the Garden of Eden to tempt Eve with the pleasures of the flesh. The weakness of woman is always the downfall of man.' The priest flashed his eyes at Hugh.

'What are you talking about?' Turlough asked.

'Nakedness!' the priest hissed. 'Fornication! Adultery. The evils of woman. Beware, young man, or the carnal lust that burns in all females will inflame your soul and destroy it! If you give in to wanton desire, you will end your life a shrivelled shadow of the man you once were.'

Padraic put his hands over his ears and gasped in horror. Hugh let his jaw drop open in disbelief and then he belched.

'You had better be on your way,' the harper told his servant. 'I don't think this fellow is happy with you at all.'

Hugh grunted the affirmative and stood up to go. As he was passing Turlough's chair the harper grabbed his sleeve.

'I don't care how you do it,' he whispered. 'More than one night in this place and I will be murdering that man. I want to leave tomorrow morning and I want to avoid the journey around the lough at all costs. See to it.'

'Yes, master,' Hugh replied, rolling his eyes.

'And forget about that girl.'

'What do you mean?' the servant asked innocently.

'I know you well enough, Hugh of the Freckled Face,' Turlough told him. 'I know what you're like when you're after courting a woman. You go silent and you stay that way until you've had your will of her.'

'This one's different,' Hugh protested.

'Has she got two heads?'

'No,' the servant snapped. Then he sighed, 'The sun shines out of her blue eyes, flecked with gold they are. And her skin is white like the lily. Her lips are as red as the rose and her cheeks—'

'That's enough!' the harper stopped him. 'Why must the youth of today fritter away their lives listening to popular music? I am sure it affects your wits. Don't you know any songs about real women?'

'I don't know what you mean,' Hugh answered, a little confused.

'Never mind pretending to be innocent. If you have any notion of getting your grubby hands on that girl, you can forget it. While I am paying you I demand a certain standard of behaviour.'

'I haven't seen a penny from you in weeks,' Hugh reminded his master dryly.

'I would have paid you if I had been able,' Turlough argued. 'But you know as well as I do how bad things have been.'

'Don't start,' Hugh warned him. 'I've heard it all before. Why don't we go back to entertaining the lords and ladies? We used to do quite well from them.'

'Maybe you are right,' the harper conceded. 'I could teach the sons and daughters of the aristocracy again. But that has nothing to do with the issue of this girl. You will leave her alone. Do you understand?'

There was a short pause.

'I do,' Hugh acknowledged. Then he went to fetch his master's harp and laid it at Turlough's feet.

'Good,' the harper said, reaching out to touch the harp bag. 'Now run along and get yourself over to Buntrane. I'll see you in the morning just after dawn.'

'What if they want to be paid for the crossing?'

'Tell them I'll play for them in the evening.'

Hugh shrugged his shoulders and followed Padraic out into the pouring rain.

Turlough played that night for the people of Dunleavy's little hamlet in the house of Padraic the fisherman. There was not much whiskey to be had for the village folk were poor. So it was an early night. And in any case, as it came close to twelve o'clock the priest interrupted their revelry and ordered everyone to bed.

'It is not seemly for honest working folk to be out drinking and carousing after the midnight hour,' Dunleavy told them. 'Go to your homes and thank God for the gift he has sent you. And pray for the soul of Turlough O'Carolan who is going to journey to the Devil's own country tomorrow. He intends to travel directly across the lough to Buntrane.'

There were hums of shock and expressions of horror from the fisherfolk. A few looked at Turlough with a new-found respect, but most simply shook their heads and pronounced the harper a fool.

'You'll play for our mass in the morning, of course,' Dunleavy went on, addressing his guest.

'I was hoping to leave just after dawn.'

'There will be a fog across the lough in the morning. You will not be able to travel until it lifts.'

'How do you know there will be a fog?'

'I have lived here, man and boy, at the side of this lough. I know when there will be a fog as sure as any of the fishermen. And when there is an early morning fog we gather in the church to say the mass until the way becomes clear and the curraghs can set out again.'

'If there's a fog at dawn I would prefer to sleep soundly without disturbance,' Turlough stated.

'Would you insult your hosts who have fed you and welcomed you into their bosom?'

The harper sighed, realising that on this point the priest was probably right. It would be rude to sleep in while everyone else in the village was sitting in the church.

'Very well,' Turlough gave in. 'I will see you at morning mass.'

'I will arrange for you to be woken,' Dunleavy smiled. 'Now it is time for rest. You will have my bed tonight. I will sleep in the church. Padraic will take you home. Goodnight.'

'Goodnight, father,' Turlough replied.

'Where would we be without that man?' Padraic asked when the priest had left the room.

'Regularly drunk and able to dance to your heart's content in all likelihood,' the harper mumbled.

'Then we must be all the more thankful,' the man replied seriously and Turlough shook his head in profound disbelief. Then he took the fisherman's hand and was led back to Dunleavy's house.

It was still dark and the world was silent when Turlough felt himself being shaken from sleep.

'Master Carolan,' a soft voice urged, 'it is time for mass. The rain has stopped and the fog has come in.'

'Who's that?' the harper asked.

'Katie,' came the reply. 'Father Dunleavy sent me to get you out of your bed.'

Turlough sighed heavily and rolled over, covering his head with the blankets to muffle all sound.

'I'll be along presently,' he assured her.

'Father Dunleavy told me to make sure you arose,' she said. 'Your serving man has returned from Buntrane.'

Turlough was instantly awake and sitting up. 'Hugh is back?'

'Is that his name?' she asked, her voice softening to a breathy sigh.

'Now listen here, young lass,' the harper began, 'leave him alone. That boy will bring you nothing but grief. He's a womaniser and a drunkard with no sense at all in his head. Why, he has a girl in every town from here to Tory Isle and likely as many illegitimate children running around as red-haired and freckled as their lazy father. Find yourself a good man from hereabouts and be kind to yourself.'

There was a loud clang as something heavy hit the floor.

'Here's your chamber pot,' Hugh cut in, then added, 'I'll know where to come when I need a character reference.'

Turlough blushed furiously.

'I have just come back through a thick fog for your sake,' Hugh told his master. 'I risked life and limb and got a drenching into the bargain. And you speak about me as if I had spent my youthful years robbing the Dublin mail coach, seducing innocent girls and leaving them with child.'

'I am sorry, Hugh,' the harper hastened to apologise. 'I had no idea you were in the room.'

'Obviously,' the servant grunted, shaking his head, then he went on to relate his news. 'The fishermen from Buntrane will meet us in the middle of the lough in an hour. That is, if we should have the good fortune to find them in this rolling fog. I could not convince them to come all the way across. There must be something in the water of that lough that drives men mad, for the fishermen of Buntrane are just as bloody-minded as old Dunleavy.'

'Well done!' Turlough exclaimed, climbing out of bed and searching for his breeches. 'I knew I could rely on you, good man that you are.'

'Oh shut up and get dressed,' Hugh muttered.

Katie averted her eyes, looking to the floor so as not to see the harper undressed.

'Master,' she began, 'would I be able to come along with you and young Hugh to Sligo?'

'Most certainly not, dear child,' the harper answered as he felt around the room for his clothes. 'We are travellers by trade. You would not like our lifestyle. It is a hard and hungry road. It is better that you stay here and marry a good man who will be able to feed you and your children when you are blessed with them.'

'There are no young men in this village. All the males are married or sworn to the Church.'

'The right fellow will come along, do not fear,' Turlough assured her. The harper was still looking for his breeches.

'They're all like Father Dunleavy,' she sighed. 'All of them. Their idea of a wild evening is to stay up after midnight in the winter to put another slab of turf on the fire. Even then they end up confessing it.'

'I'm sure they're not all that bad,' the harper scoffed.

'Last year Padraic got drunk the night before the feast of Saint Brendan and slept through mass next morning,' she countered. 'Ever since then they've called him Padraic the Miscreant. He's never lived it down. His brother left the village when he was sixteen and went to sea. When he returned last year no-one would speak to him.'

'Why not?'

'Father Dunleavy said that all sailors are infected with the scourge of the Devil because they visit heathen lands and fornicate with pagan women.'

'That old bugger seems to have a fascination with fornication,' Turlough noted. 'Any priest who could condemn a man for having a good time must be a little strange himself. There is something mean-minded about it. Isn't the world a bad enough place, full of misery and hard work? What's wrong with having fun? Didn't God give us these gifts to take our minds off the hardship and drudgery of life?'

Then Turlough stopped what he was doing and stood perfectly still. 'Where are my breeches?'

Hugh bent over and picked them up off the chair where they were hanging. Then he casually handed them to his master.

'Thank you,' the harper mumbled and began climbing into them.

'Master Carolan,' Hugh began, 'I have been in your employ for ten years now.'

'Nine years, ten months and thirteen days,' Turlough corrected him.

'Ten years or close enough,' Hugh repeated, trying to keep to the point. 'I would like to have myself a wife and a home of my own, just as you have. Have you ever thought of how I might feel whenever you return to the bosom of your family? I have no-one in the world.'

Turlough stopped what he was doing. 'Mary is a good woman,' the harper admitted, nodding his head. 'And the children are quite adorable.'

'I wish to marry Katie,' Hugh declared. 'And I'd like your permission to do so.'

'I'll think about it,' Turlough replied.

Hugh smiled broadly. The harper sat down on the end of the bed for a moment with his hand on his chin. He breathed in deeply and then out again. After a few moments he abruptly stood up.

'Well, I've thought about it,' he stated, buttoning his breeches. 'No, Hugh, we can't take the girl. And that's an end to it.'

'But, master—'

'I said no,' the harper insisted, 'and I meant it. If this girl comes along with us, we will never hear the end of it. You can't even imagine the trouble it would cause us. Now go out and get the boat ready. I'll be along presently. You'll find yourself a nice girl in Sligo and you'll forget young Katie in a few days.'

Hugh gritted his teeth in frustration, then turned around and stormed out of the room.

'Please, Master Carolan,' the girl begged.

'Be patient, child,' the harper told her. 'All things come to those who wait. You may yet have your wish and be set free from this mean little village. Now go and tell Dunleavy I am ready to depart.'

As Turlough finished getting dressed the priest burst in on him.

'You will have to wait until after mass,' Dunleavy told him. 'None of my folk will go out with you in this fog.'

'I am in a hurry,' Turlough stated clearly. 'It is bad enough that I am going to have to change boats in the middle of the lough. Your stubbornness is costing me valuable time. I have had enough of your hospitality, such as it is, and would like to leave this place as soon as possible. I'll ask Padraic to row out with us and return with the curragh when we have met the fishermen from Buntrane.'

'You will wait here until after the mass.'

Turlough frowned and decided to change tack.

'I was dining with the Bishop of Armagh last month,' he told the priest. 'A good man.'

'I know him well,' Dunleavy snarled. 'He is not fit to hold the office.'

'Nevertheless I think him to be a good man,' the harper went on. 'He was telling me about a priest in a little village in Donegal who was so harsh toward his parishioners that the good bishop had to remove him. I believe the offending clergyman was sent on a voyage to the West Indies and is now ministering to the savages.'

'Worthy work,' Dunleavy hummed.

'Yes,' the harper agreed. 'A brave man to daily face and overcome such temptations in the service of the Church.'

'What do you mean?'

'The natives in that part of the world do not wear any clothes, I am told,' Turlough said with no expression on his face. 'The weather is too hot and they like to take their pleasure in the open fields whenever the whim strikes them.'

'Jesus wept!' Dunleavy exclaimed and hastily crossed himself.

'That priest is assured of a place in Heaven for choosing to live amongst the naked heathen.'

'Naked?' the priest repeated hoarsely.

'I would find it extremely difficult to restrain myself, personally,' the harper confided. 'But then I am not sworn to celibacy as you are.'

'Are you threatening me?' Dunleavy asked with the slightest hint of a nervous quiver in his voice.

'I don't know what you mean,' Turlough said innocently. 'But I will certainly mention you to the bishop the next time I dine with him. In fact I will recommend that he come and visit your little community to see for himself what a stern hand can achieve in a small settlement.'

'That fornicator?' the priest fumed. 'Here in my village?'

'Yes. Maybe it is what the place needs,' the harper sighed thoughtfully. 'A new broom. Perhaps a fresh-faced priest lately ordained to be your curate. Or perhaps you could do with a spell in foreign climes to put a new edge to your faith. I am told the weather is unusually warm in the Bahamas.'

He leaned in close to the priest. 'And I believe the Indian women are incomparably beautiful. Dark skinned. With long curly hair and shapely limbs as luscious as the fruit upon the trees. Their bosoms are smooth and round and crowned with the most exquisite . . .' Turlough pinched his index finger and thumb together.

'Enough!' the priest cried, putting a hand to his mouth in horror.

There was silence for a few seconds and then Dunleavy spoke again. 'Go! I'll be glad to be rid of you. How dare you try to tempt me!'

'Tempt you?' the harper asked in a wounded tone. 'I was just telling you about the sultry women of the Indies. Women who have no morals whatsoever. Women who spend their nights in glorious orgies of unbridled—'

'Padraic!' the priest called out before the harper had a chance to finish. 'Padraic. I want you to take Carolan and his servant out to meet the fishermen of Buntrane.'

'But, father,' the man protested, 'what about the mass?'

'You can say mass with me tonight,' the priest barked to cover the shake in his voice. 'Now take this man out of my sight before he says something that I will regret.'

'Thank you, father,' Turlough smiled. 'I am grateful for your change of heart.'

'Leave us in peace,' Dunleavy breathed, mopping his brow with his handkerchief.

'You would have been popular in the West Indies, father,' the harper couldn't resist. 'I am told that men who are slightly over-weight and lacking a full head of hair are much sought after by the young girls of that country.'

'Shut up!' the priest shrieked and then he pushed past the harper and made for the church.

Turlough smiled then shouldered his harp and waited for Padraic to lead him down to the lough.

Once they were at the water's edge Hugh took the harp and placed it beside the saddle and their bags in the little cowhide boat.

'Watch where you place your feet,' Padraic told them. 'One false step and you'll put a hole in the hide and we'll go straight to the bottom.'

Hugh led the harper to his seat and handed him the reins of the horse which was already standing knee-deep in the water.

'Hold on to her, master, until I have my seat,' the servant advised. 'It is a short swim but she is not used to more than a walking pace. She will certainly tire quickly, so I'll have to keep an eye on her.'

In a few minutes they had set out from the shore through the clearing fog. Hugh stared back longingly at Katie who waved to him from the pebble beach until Dunleavy came to drag her away to mass.

Padraic stood at the stern of the curragh, his long oar rhythmically pushing the craft through the water toward the middle of the lough. All was perfectly quiet apart from the gentle splashing of the oar.

Once in a while the fisherman looked back toward the shore, and as soon as he was certain the fog had closed enough and they were out of sight, he retrieved a leather flask from his pocket. Carefully he removed the cork and took a long draught of the liquor.

The fisherman passed the flask to Hugh who drank deeply. The servant then handed it on to Turlough. The three men smiled, sharing the joy of Padraic's indiscretion as the whiskey warmed them.

'Old Father Dunleavy's never been out on the lough before midday,' the fisherman told them. 'He has no idea how cold and damp it gets. I don't tell him how I keep warm.' Padraic touched a finger to his nose.

'Don't worry,' Hugh assured him. 'We won't let on about your little secret.'

'I knew I could rely on you gentlemen,' the fisherman grinned. 'Now, Mister Carolan, tell me more about the West Indies. I overheard you speaking with the father about it earlier and I was thinking it would be just the place for a stout fellow like me. Do you think I could join a ship in Dublin that might visit these exotic lands?'

Turlough laughed and proceeded to invent a wonderful tale of young maidens driven by their insatiable lust to unimaginable acts of ecstasy.

Before long Hugh spotted a lantern light glowing in the fog and he pointed it out to Padraic. The fisherman nodded silently and turned the delicate craft toward the light. The mare followed on, swimming hard to keep up. Padraic noticed she was tiring so he slowed his pace a little.

Within a short while they settled alongside a much wider and longer vessel of far superior build. Two men sat in the large curragh, scowling at Padraic. The fisherman did not return their gaze. He did not even glance at them.

Hugh passed the reins over to one of the men from Buntrane and then began transferring the saddle, harp and other items from their baggage. At last he too climbed over into the other boat and held out a hand for his master.

Padraic helped the harper to the side of the boat and then placed the blind man's hands upon the gunwale in readiness for him to step over.

Turlough smiled as he lifted one leg into the other boat, brushing Hugh's hand away as if to say that he needed no assistance.

'It is going to be a beautiful day today,' the harper stated, slurring his speech slightly from the effects of the alcohol. 'I hope Father Dunleavy can forgive me for missing his mass but I could not have stayed another minute in his company.'

The harper lifted his nose to the sky and sniffed loudly. 'Yes, it'll be a glorious day, I can smell it in the air.'

Then he half turned to where he thought the fisherman was sitting. 'By God that was a fine drop, Padraic,' he hummed. 'A fine drop.'

Then, without any struggle or panic whatsoever, the harper clumsily pushed the large curragh away from him with his foot. Then he slipped calmly over the side of Padraic's curragh into the deep black waters of the lough with hardly a splash.

TWELVE

In less time than it takes to draw a breath Turlough's head had disappeared completely from sight. All four men in the boats were left dumbstruck, blinking in shock.

'Mother of God!' Hugh exclaimed. 'How did that happen?'

'He missed the side of the boat!' Padraic cried out in distress.

'Well don't just stand there. Do something!' Hugh shrieked.

'I can't swim,' Padraic panicked.

'He'll drown!' the servant cried. 'He's as blind as a mole and he's never been above his waist in water in his life before.'

In a second Hugh had pulled off his coat and shirt. Then, still searching for some sign of his master, he dived headfirst into the water and disappeared from view.

On both boats there was a strained silence which dragged on for long seconds until Hugh broke the surface, gasping and spitting for breath.

'Oh Jesus!' he rasped. 'I can't find him.'

At that very instant the water churned up beside him and the harper, coughing and spluttering, grasped Hugh about the shoulders, dragging his loyal servant back down.

'Grab him!' Hugh called out, struggling to keep his own head above water.

One of the men from Buntrane reached down into the lough and snatched the harper by his coat. With a great heave he pulled Turlough up into the curragh like a full net groaning with a heavy load of fish.

The Buntrane man laid the harper on his back at the bottom of the boat and then went to help Hugh. In moments the servant was beside his master, desperately seeking for signs of consciousness.

'It's all my fault,' Padraic muttered to himself as the Buntrane boatmen turned their curragh round and began to make for their own village. 'If I had not given him a whiskey he might have had his wits about him. I have shamed my village. Well am I named Padraic the Miscreant. May God forgive me.'

The poor man sat in his curragh in that spot for a long time before he finally gathered the courage to put his oar to the water and set out for home again. He was already framing the words of his confession, certain that the wrath of Father Dunleavy would be terrible.

By this time the curragh from Buntrane had run up onto the pebbled shore on the opposite side of the lough. One of the fishermen handed the reins of the horse to a young lad waiting on the shore, while his comrade lifted Turlough out of the boat and carried him up the narrow stretch of stony beach.

Hugh followed after, shouldering the harp in its seal-skin case.

'I'll never forgive myself if he passes away,' the servant told himself. 'I should have been watching out for him.'

The whole village started to stir as the news spread through the settlement. Folk came out from their cottages to watch as the fisherman carried the bedraggled blind man past their houses.

After what seemed to Hugh to be a long while they came to a large wooden cottage with a freshly thatched roof. The front door swung open as they approached. In seconds Turlough was laid on a straw bed by the fire and the fisherman who had carried him was gone.

'Is this the great Turlough O'Carolan?' a voice asked from a dark corner of the room as two old women began stripping the sodden clothes from the harper.

'It is,' Hugh answered. 'I hope we got him out of the water in time.'

'Those bastards,' the stranger declared.

'What bastards?' the servant asked, confused. He turned around to try and see who was speaking to him.

'Those bastards from Ballynew,' the stranger hissed. 'I have never known them to treat travellers with any kindness, but to push a man overboard because he would not attend the Roman mass is unforgivable.'

'That's not exactly what happened,' Hugh started to say, but the man ignored him.

'You see, ladies?' he addressed the old women who were now wrapping the harper in blankets. 'That is typical of papists. They don't even look after their own. In this village he will receive the full benefits of Christian charity. We do not turn strangers away. Not even travelling musicians.'

The ladies hummed in agreement and went on with their task.

'I don't think you understand—' Hugh interrupted but he did not get the chance to finish his sentence.

'Don't you worry, young lad,' the stranger told him as he stepped into the light and placed a hand firmly on his shoulder in very much the same manner as Father Dunleavy had the previous evening.

'We will take care of your master and when he has passed away, as all flesh must, we will give him a Christian burial.'

Hugh's jaw dropped open. 'He's not dead yet!'

The tall thin man before him had deep blue eyes set in darkened eye sockets, the result, no doubt, of too much reading and writing late into the night. His skin was pallid and his hair was cut very short. It was grey with tiny dark streaks.

'My name is Harris,' the stranger declared, offering his hand, 'Reverend Harris. And what would your name be?'

'I am Hugh the Freckled, servant to Master Carolan.'

'You are the man who came here last night?'

'Yes.'

'You are a brave and loyal servant,' Harris told him, 'to have risked your very life for that of your master.'

'I couldn't let him drown,' Hugh nodded modestly.

'No,' the minister said, shaking his head, 'I mean by coming over here to arrange his escape from that den of popish evil that calls itself Ballynew.'

'Escape?' Hugh muttered.

'I can see that you are a Protestant at heart and I welcome you,' the stranger said, embracing Hugh as if he were a long-lost brother. 'I will see to it that you are well fed,' Harris assured him. 'Though I suppose you will not want to eat while your master lies here dying.'

'Dying?'

'Oh yes,' the minister nodded. 'I have seen this a hundred times before. The half-drowned may seem to be well enough when dragged from the lough. But the waters rarely surrender a life they have once held in their devilish grasp.'

Harris held out his hand and slowly clenched his fingers as if he were strangling some small animal. The minister's eyes lit with a fiery passion.

'The master is still breathing,' Hugh noted.

'He won't be for long. Rest assured.'

Hugh opened his mouth but thought better of what he was about to say. 'Look, I think I would prefer to tend to him myself,' the servant offered instead. 'There's no need to bother yourselves. I have often cared for the master in times of sickness.'

Harris held up his hand in protest but before he could speak, a feeble voice cried, 'Hugh?'

In a flash the loyal servant had pushed past the reverend and was kneeling at his master's side.

'What happened, Hugh?' Turlough whispered.

The servant grasped his master's hand and held it tight.

'I should have been watching after you,' Hugh began, the emotion catching in his throat. 'I let you slip from the boat and you almost drowned.'

'You mustn't blame yourself,' Turlough said, patting his

servant on the hand indulgently. 'It is the will of God that I should pass away now in this place.'

The harper paused for a second, obviously trying to think clearly. 'By the way, where are we?'

'Buntrane,' the minister said solemnly.

'Buntrane,' Hugh repeated.

'I see,' Turlough sighed. 'It is God's will that I should set out on my last journey here in the village of Buntrane. I am feeling very weak, you know. Will I be mourned, do you think?'

'You are the greatest harper Ireland has ever known,' Hugh said, fighting back the tears. 'Folk will come here to this place to see the spot where you passed away, just as they go to the shrines of the saints to pray.'

'There'll be no popish talk in this house,' Harris spat. 'I know you have suffered in your flight from Ballynew, Master Carolan, but this is no time for popery of any kind. I'll not have you talking about saints and suchlike in front of these two fine upstanding widows whose sons died fighting the evil agents of Rome and the Catholic conspiracy to dominate the Protestant Kingdom of Ireland.'

Turlough grabbed Hugh's hand. 'What did he say?'

'He doesn't like talk of saints.' The servant shrugged.

'All the folk of this village profess the one true faith,' the minister declared. 'We do not need a pope to order our lives for us. We are proud and free in our religion. And anyone who deviates from our laws is strictly and savagely dealt with.'

'I can feel my strength failing, Hugh,' the harper whispered hoarsely. 'Fetch me a priest. It is time to make my peace with God.'

'I will comfort you,' Harris soothed. 'I will lead you on toward the light of the eternal paradise of Christ.'

'Then hear my confession, father,' Turlough began.

'I am not a father,' the reverend replied sharply. 'And I do not hear confession. There is none of that Roman nonsense in Buntrane.'

'I'll go and get Father Dunleavy,' Hugh said.

'You will not!' the reverend screeched. 'I will not have that pagan in my house, in my village or even on my side of the lough.'

'You wouldn't let me die unshriven of my sins, would you?' the harper asked in a soft, weak voice.

'You will be the better for it after you are gone, believe me,' Harris told him. 'No man should have to answer for his sins to anyone but God in His glorious seat of heavenly judgment. If you have led a blameless life, you have nothing to worry about.'

'I always feared this would happen,' Turlough sobbed gently. 'That I would not have the chance to make my peace.'

Hugh stood up and took the reverend by the sleeve.

'For God's sake, man,' he pleaded. 'My master is dying. Grant him the courtesy of his own beliefs. Do not deny his soul the comfort it seeks.'

'There is nothing I can do,' Harris replied coldly. 'As the leader of this community I cannot allow the agents of Rome into our midst lest they should corrupt our young people with their ways. Your master must face God in the next few hours and I will do what I can to prepare him for that. But I will not countenance any priest from Ballynew muttering his maledictions and spreading his holy water all about the place.'

'Will you write a letter for me then?' Turlough coughed. 'I wish to let my friends know what befell me in my last hours.'

'That I will gladly do,' the reverend said, clapping his hands with glee. 'I have a very neat hand, you know.'

Hugh frowned at the man and took up his position at his master's side.

In a few moments the minister returned with a quill, ink, paper and a portable writing desk which he laid across his knees.

'Now, who would you like me to write to?' Harris asked excitedly.

'The Dean of Saint Patrick's, Dublin,' Turlough told him. 'Jonathan Swift.'

'The Dean of Saint Patrick's, Dublin,' Harris repeated slowly as he wrote the words down. 'Jonathan Swift.'

Then the reverend looked at what he had written and raised his eyebrows. 'Are you acquainted with the dean?'

'We often dine with Mister Swift when we are in Dublin,' Hugh told the minister.

'I see,' Harris beamed. 'What an honour to meet you then, Master Carolan. I had no idea you were friends with Dean Swift. I do hope you will mention me in this letter.'

'I will,' Turlough said coldly. 'The letter begins, Dear Jonathan.'

'Dear Jonathan,' Harris hummed. 'My goodness. On first-name terms with the Dean of Saint Patrick's, are we?'

'Dear Jonathan,' the harper repeated. 'You will have, no doubt by now, received the news of my untimely death in the village of Buntrane.'

'Yes, yes,' the reverend muttered, scratching away frantically with the quill.

'First of all I would ask you to find it in your heart to forgive ...' Turlough paused. 'What did you say your name was?'

'Reverend Harris,' the minister replied quickly.

'To forgive Reverend Harris,' the harper went on, 'for his appalling lack of compassion. If it had not been for him I would have died a happy man and gone to my eternal rest with an easy conscience.'

The reverend went on writing but his expression changed slightly as he scratched the words. The tiniest wisp of a cloud crept over his face.

'With an easy conscience,' Harris repeated uncomfortably, reading the last words aloud.

'I know it is your way to punish such men severely, especially clergymen who hold their own views in high esteem and close their minds to the rest of humanity,' Turlough continued. 'But it would grieve my spirit to think of this man suffering for his sins in some Godforsaken parish in the jungles of the West Indies.'

'The West Indies?' Harris asked.

'Didn't you hear what happened to Reverend Thomas of Blackrock?' Turlough asked.

'No,' the minister replied nervously. 'What happened to him?'

'You haven't heard the tale of his voyage to the West Indies?'

'No.' Harris looked up with an expression of genuine worry.

'It won't happen to you,' the harper assured him. 'That's why I'm sending this letter to Jonathan. He'll lose his temper with you, that's for certain. And what a mighty temper he has. But in six months or so he'll recall you home to your own parish.'

'From the West Indies?' Harris gulped.

'You know what they say about the colonies in the Bahamas,' Turlough smiled.

'No,' the reverend muttered, 'what do they say?'

'Bring me some water, will you, Hugh?' the harper mumbled.

'I'll be back in a minute,' the servant replied and leapt up from his place to go and find the village well.

Hugh was terribly worried about his master. They had travelled together for years and truly he did not know what he would do without him. He could hardly believe his master was now on his deathbed composing a last letter to his friends.

In a few minutes Hugh returned bearing a pewter jug full of fresh water. As soon as he opened the door Harris stood up and faced him.

'There isn't a moment to lose,' the reverend insisted, tearing up the letter he had been writing. 'You must take the best curragh in the village and go to fetch Father Dunleavy this instant.'

'What?' Hugh asked in bewilderment.

'Don't stand there mumbling!' the minister shrieked. 'Your master is close to death. If you don't leave this very instant he will have no chance to make amends for his sinful ways. And it will be all your fault.'

Hugh put the jug down and rushed over to Turlough.

'Go now, Hugh,' the harper sighed. 'And God speed.'

'Jesus and all the saints,' the servant cried and in the next instant he was at the door making his way back to the water's edge. He jumped in the first boat he found and, struggling with the oar, set out across the lough, determined to bring the priest back and fulfil his master's dying wish.

An hour later he stood panting on the shore of Ballynew pleading with Father Dunleavy to come back to Buntrane with him.

'I will not go into that cursed place,' the priest declared flatly. 'Not even if Saint Brigid herself were to command me.'

'Would you let him die unshriven?' Hugh argued. 'Amongst the Protestants?'

'That is his own doing,' Dunleavy answered, shaking his head. 'I warned him not to go there. I told him of the dangers. But would he listen? No. He was too proud. And now he is being punished for his pride.'

Hugh covered his eyes with both hands, trying desperately to think of some way to persuade the priest to change his mind. Suddenly it came to him.

'The folk of Buntrane are saying,' he told Dunleavy, 'that the master was pushed into the water because he refused to attend your morning mass.'

'What?' the priest bellowed. 'Where did they get that idea? What did you tell them?'

'Father?' a timid voice spoke up and both men turned to see who it was.

There stood Padraic with his head bowed and his broad-brimmed hat in his hands.

'Father, I think there is something you ought to know,' the fisherman said sheepishly.

'What's that?'

'It is my fault that Master Carolan fell into the lough.'

'How so?'

'I take a flask of whiskey out with me on damp, misty mornings,' the fisherman admitted, 'just to stave off the weather, mind you. I swear Master Carolan only took a drop.'

'Jesus!' Dunleavy hissed.

'You would not like the Bishop of Armagh to find out that one of your folk caused the death of Turlough O'Carolan, would you?' Hugh whispered. 'And that afterwards you refused the great harper the last rites?'

'I'll be ready in a minute,' Dunleavy sighed in resignation. 'Padraic, go and get your boat ready!'

'Yes, father.'

'And we will certainly be discussing this later in private. Do you understand?'

'I do, father.'

'Thank God,' Hugh whispered to himself with a glance skyward.

As they were stepping into the boat Katie came running up to Padraic and pushed her way past to sit down by Father Dunleavy. She threw a small bundle down at Hugh's feet and winked at him.

'Go home, child,' the priest commanded. 'Buntrane is no place for an innocent such as yourself.'

'Did it cross your mind that the harper might not in fact be dying?' she countered.

'What are you talking about?'

'He might simply have caught a chill. What if he dies of neglect?' she said. 'Do you trust the women of Buntrane to nurse him as well as they would one of their own?'

Dunleavy thought for a moment. He did not want her to come along but he did not want it said that Carolan died because the priest of Ballynew had not provided good care for him in his time of need.

'Very well,' Dunleavy conceded, feeling as though matters were beginning to get beyond his control. 'But what is in the bundle?'

'Herbs and simples to soothe the man,' she replied innocently.

Padraic pushed the boat out and it sat low in the water with the weight of four people. The going was slow because the fisherman did not want to risk capsizing the delicate craft and because he was towing the boat Hugh had brought from Buntrane.

By the time they reached the other shore there was a small group waiting for them.

'He's taken a turn for the worse!' one man shouted out as they pulled close to shore.

'He may have already gone by the time you reach the house,' another added.

'Oh God,' Hugh prayed under his breath, 'let the master live. I know I haven't been the best of servants but I vow I will change my ways if you'll just grant him his life. It was all my fault. I promise I'll look after him much better in future.'

As they got out of the boat at the water's edge Katie grabbed Hugh's hand and whispered to him, 'I hope Master Carolan recovers, but if he does not there will be no-one to tell you that you can't be married.'

Hugh looked at her, the shock showing clearly on his face, but she had already turned away and was walking up the beach.

'Jesus in Heaven,' Hugh mumbled to himself, 'I don't want to lose the master, but I don't want to lose her either!'

By the time they reached the house where Turlough was laid out, the whole village had gathered outside the door. Most folk hissed or uttered heartfelt curses under their breaths at the sight of the Roman priest.

Dunleavy ignored their hostility, holding his head high and gripping his missal in both hands to ward off their ill-wishes. But the priest was sweating, his brow beaded with perspiration.

As Hugh ducked his head to enter the cottage he noticed the place was much darker than when he had left it. Black cloths were hung over the windows and candles burned in each corner of the room.

The two old women who had helped Turlough out of his wet clothes were kneeling at the foot of the cot where he was laid. They mumbled the psalms in lowered voices.

'I am Reverend Harris,' the minister informed his new guests as he stepped into the light of a candle.

The priest nodded, frowning. 'My name is Father Dunleavy.'

'Have you come to see your handiwork?' Harris asked with a cynical smirk.

'I had nothing to do with this accident,' Dunleavy protested angrily. 'What you have heard is a wicked rumour.'

'Are you presuming to tell me that my people are liars?'

'Only if you are calling my folk murderers.'

'Gentlemen!' Turlough coughed and both men turned to face him. 'I wish you would save this argument until my body has grown cold. I would rather not hear it.'

'You have arrived just in time,' Harris said coldly, not taking his eyes off the dying man. 'He is not long for this world.'

'I came as quickly as I could,' Dunleavy answered defensively.

'Well you had better get about your work then,' Harris told him sternly.

Neither man noticed that the harper's breathing was becoming more and more strained.

'Your superstitious nonsense will be tolerated in the village on this occasion,' the reverend went on, 'but do not think you can make a habit of it. I am only allowing this out of Christian charity to an ignorant wretch who knows no better.'

'How dare you call the sacraments of the Holy Mother Church superstitious nonsense!' Dunleavy fumed.

Turlough gasped loudly, opening his mouth as if to speak but seemingly unable to make a sound. Suddenly he was perfectly still, his hand clutching at the covers. But everyone was listening intently to the battle of words between the two clergymen.

'The sacraments are founded upon the rock of Saint Peter and the wisdom of Saint Paul,' the priest declared. 'If you are going to profane the rites of the Roman faith with your heretical doctrines, please do it in a place where I cannot hear you. I did not come here to be humiliated. I came to do my Christian duty. Now I really would like to get on with my work, if you don't mind.'

'Very well,' Harris sighed with a wave of his hand. 'I will not interfere.'

'The harper has stopped breathing,' one of the old women cut in. 'He's dead.'

The priest and the minister caught each other's eye guiltily.

Had they not gone on with their petty fight, the last rites might have been performed in time. But in an instant both men's eyes hardened. It was plain that each was blaming the other for Turlough's unshriven death.

'I wasted my time coming here,' Dunleavy stated coldly as Hugh pushed past him to kneel by his master's body. 'I knew it was foolish to come on this journey.'

'If your pride had allowed you to come sooner, you would have been some comfort to the man,' Harris replied. 'As it is, he saw you arrive and likely fretted in anguish that you tarried about your task. The upset was what probably killed him.'

Hugh was weeping by this stage, holding Turlough's hand and kissing it.

'Great harper,' the servant whispered, 'forgive me. I came back as quickly as I could.'

'If your Protestant ways hadn't already poisoned him, he would still be with us,' Dunleavy observed.

'Papist lackey of Rome,' Harris whispered.

'Immoral heretic,' Dunleavy retorted.

'Hypocrite.'

'Fornicator.'

'Shut up!' Hugh cried, getting to his feet in a rage. The room went suddenly quiet. No-one dared speak. Both clergymen coughed to show their disgust at being addressed in such a manner.

'A great man has passed away in this house,' the servant sobbed bitterly, 'and you still can't forget your petty grievances, not even for a moment out of respect for the dead. As far as I can see, the both of you are selfish, small-minded men with no care at all for the feelings of your parishioners. You drone on and on about what is good and right but you are too frightened of one another to stand in the same room together without making jibes at each other's expense.'

Dunleavy raised a hand and opened his mouth to speak but Hugh wasn't going to let him.

'Don't interrupt me!' the servant shouted. 'I have had to

listen to the both of you go on and on about how bloody right you are. Well you're both wrong. You're both to blame for my master's death. If you had acted like Christians, your two villages would have had regular traffic between them and my master would not have had to change boats in midstream.'

'That's hardly—' Harris cut in.

'I told you to shut up, you sanctimonious, conceited little man!' Hugh was really losing his temper now. Then he turned to Dunleavy, pointing a finger.

'Don't smile. You're just as bad.' Hugh took a breath. 'Well, now you'll be sorry for what you've done. The whole country will know the story of Master Carolan's death and the two men whose simple-minded intolerance brought about his passing long before his time.'

'You are distraught,' Dunleavy soothed, not making eye contact. 'Perhaps you should take a rest and consider carefully all that you have said.'

'Yes, my son,' Harris concurred. 'Your grief has got the better of you. You have been up most of the night. You are tired.'

'I will not rest,' Hugh vowed, 'until every man, woman and child in Ireland knows what happened here. And the first people I will be telling are the Dean of Saint Patrick's and the Bishop of Armagh.'

Both clergymen held up their hands in horror, silently begging the man to calm down. But Hugh was livid.

'Don't try to placate me, you pair of unforgivable rogues. I wouldn't trust either of you with an empty collection plate. Manipulative rascals, that's what you are.'

'Hugh?' a weak voice groaned. 'What time is it?'

The priest frowned. The minister put a hand to his mouth. Hugh blinked.

Then all three men looked down at the body of the harper in astonishment.

'Hugh? Are you there?'

The servant knelt by his master again and clutched his hand, not daring to speak.

'What time is it?' the harper repeated hoarsely.

'Nearly noon,' Hugh replied, tears running down his cheeks in relief that his master was still breathing.

'Then it's not too early for a whiskey, is it?'

The servant stopped sobbing suddenly and scrutinised his master's face. The colour had returned and he certainly did not seem to be at death's door. In that moment Hugh had a strange feeling that all was not what it seemed. He shook his head, banishing the thought as uncharitable.

'What is he after?' Dunleavy asked. 'Is he ready for the extreme unction?'

'Or a word or two of prayer?' Harris added.

'He's asking for whiskey,' Hugh replied without taking his eyes off the harper. Both clergymen raised their eyebrows in unison.

'Then he shall have whiskey,' Harris announced. 'The best that Buntrane can provide.' And the reverend scurried to the door to order the liquor to be brought in.

'How are you feeling?' Hugh asked his master.

'I'll be much better when I've had a drink, thank you,' Turlough replied politely, and without any evidence of discomfort at all. 'I've just had a lovely sleep,' he added.

Hugh scowled.

'Here it is,' Harris declared as he brought a cup of home-made spirit. 'Perhaps you should administer the whiskey to your master,' he suggested as he handed it to Hugh.

The servant nodded, taking the cup carefully so as not to spill the contents.

'Before I take my last drink,' Turlough rasped, 'I have a favour to ask of you two clergymen.'

The priest looked to the minister and the minister looked to the priest.

'What manner of favour would you ask?' the reverend ventured nervously.

'Come closer and I'll tell you. My voice is weak. I am fading fast.'

The two men knelt down on either side of Hugh and each held one of Turlough's hands.

'I have led a life of extravagance,' the harper admitted. 'I have indulged my love of music, my taste for whiskey and my relentless pursuit of pretty women.'

Both clergymen coughed and looked away.

'Is this your confession, my son?' Dunleavy asked solemnly.

'In a manner of speaking it is,' Turlough told him. 'It grieves me to think that I should leave this world in such unfortunate circumstances.'

'As it does all of us,' Harris agreed, closing his eyes and folding his hands in front of him.

'Good, then you agree that something must be done urgently about this terrible state of affairs.'

The clergymen frowned.

'It would be a burden on my soul if I left this world and my death were the cause of more bitter fighting between the gentle folk of Ballynew and the good people of Buntrane.'

No-one dared interrupt; the clergymen were beginning to see where this speech was headed.

'I know that each of you will blame the other for the manner of my death,' Turlough went on weakly. 'And so I ask that you reconcile to one another and bring your communities together in the common bond of friendship and co-operation.'

Dunleavy took a sharp breath through his teeth. For once he was completely lost for words. Harris put a hand to his cheek in horror at the suggestion.

'Master Carolan,' the priest began, 'these people are Protestants!'

'The folk of Ballynew are papists,' Harris shot back.

'And yet in times past both villages shared their knowledge to the benefit of all.'

'That was a long time ago,' Dunleavy laughed.

'A long, long time ago,' Harris echoed.

Hugh tried not to smile. He did not want the clergymen see his amusement.

'Imagine the adulation you would both receive from your people if the fishermen began to take a large enough catch for everyone. There would be no more poverty in your villages and perhaps excess fish to sell at market.'

The clergymen scowled and Hugh looked from one to the other, noticing for the first time how similar their features seemed. It must be years of frowning, he told himself.

'My soul would sing,' the harper continued, 'to know that with my dying breath I had healed a rift that could have carried on for generations.'

'What you ask is impossible,' Dunleavy stated emphatically. 'Our people are sworn enemies. It would take a miracle to convince them to change the ways of thirty years.'

'Perhaps it would,' Turlough sighed with resignation. 'But then stranger things have been known to occur.'

The harper took Hugh's hand as he turned on his side to address him. 'Loyal servant and bearer of my harp,' he began. 'You have witnessed what these two men have had to say about my simple request?'

'I have, master.'

'Then I charge you to go to the Bishop of Armagh and tell him this whole tale from beginning to end. And when you have visited the bishop I want you to go to the house of our esteemed friend the Dean of Saint Patrick's and tell the story to him.'

'Yes, master.'

Turlough let go of Hugh and sought out the clergymen's hands again.

'If the old broom won't do the job,' he informed them, 'perhaps a new broom will. If my dying wish is not enacted by you both here and now while I still have breath in me, then there is nothing more certain but that my friends in Dublin and Armagh will see my desire fulfilled. And believe me, my loyal patrons will not let your refusal go unpunished. The West Indies is much in need of men of the cloth.'

Both men gasped and glanced at each other.

'You are threatening us,' Dunleavy objected indignantly.

'It is no idle threat,' the harper assured him.

'What do you want us to do?' Harris asked under his breath, not wishing his people to hear him discuss something so unthinkable.

'Shake hands publicly and pledge to work together in future regardless of religious differences.'

'Out of the question!' the minister snapped, keeping his voice low.

'You are surely having a joke with us,' the priest echoed.

'I am not,' Turlough told them in a serious tone. 'Not only will you both be blamed for my death because you would not co-operate, but you will be shown up for the self-absorbed opportunists you really are.'

'How dare you say such a thing in my house?' Harris gasped.

'I am shocked at your lack of respect for your good host,' the priest chimed in. 'He has sheltered you in your time of need and this is how you repay his good nature.'

'Shake hands or face the consequences. Hugh could be in Dublin in no more than a few days. In a little less time a messenger could be sent back here from Dean Swift's residence. Before I am even cold in my grave you could both be on your way to the wild forests of the Bahamas.'

'And what if we agree to your strange request?' Harris asked.

'Hugh will remain silent on this matter forever after.'

The servant nodded to signify that he would, indeed, say nothing.

'Your man would also have to commend us to our superiors for our good judgment,' Dunleavy hissed, chancing his arm. 'And let them know that we behaved in a seemly manner. And that this whole affair was a regrettable accident.'

Turlough breathed in slowly, considering the proposition.

'Very well,' he agreed finally. 'I can see the sense in that. As long as your two villages go on working together in peace, I will be happy. Hugh, did you hear all of that?'

'I did, master.'

'Good.'

The harper squeezed the fingers of the two clergymen. 'Now, gentlemen, all that remains is for you both to make your pledges of peace to one another. It would be best if you did so now before I expire.'

Dunleavy cast a distasteful glance at Harris who shook his head in disgust.

'Now, gentlemen. If you please.'

The two men slowly stood to their full heights and grasped one another in an unwilling handshake.

'I pledge to work together with the people of Ballynew,' Harris whispered almost inaudibly.

'And I pledge to work with the folk of Buntrane,' Dunleavy muttered.

'That is fine, gentlemen,' the harper beamed, 'but now I want some witnesses to hear your pledge. One independent observer from each village.'

'You can't be serious!' the priest hissed. 'This will be the end of us. No-one will take us seriously ever again.'

'Because you have preached against each other for so long?' Turlough asked. 'And if you were to change your mind, it would prove just how wrong you were all along?'

The two men fell silent but not from guilt. They were fuming.

'Is there anyone here from Ballynew?' the harper asked in a strained voice.

'Katie came across with us,' Hugh told him.

'Go and fetch her,' the harper said. 'My two kind nurses will bear witness for Buntrane. Won't you, ladies?'

The two old women at his feet suddenly stopped their prayers and looked up.

'What's that?' asked one.

'I said, you'll witness an important agreement for me, won't you?'

'Oh yes!' the other nodded with a look of utter surprise on her face. 'We thought you were dead.'

'A few folk had that impression,' Hugh muttered, making for the door.

In a couple of minutes Hugh returned with Katie on his arm. He led her in to stand behind the two old ladies sitting at Turlough's feet.

'In front of these witnesses you must make your pledge, gentlemen,' the harper insisted.

Harris turned to face Katie and the old women and then waited for the priest to follow suit.

But Dunleavy stayed put. For a second it seemed he would not go through with the pledge. Then the priest's expression suddenly softened and he reluctantly held out a hand to the minister.

The two old enemies shook hands and made their pledges of friendship, each gripping the other as hard as he could and speaking through gritted teeth.

'Give me that whiskey,' Turlough asked Hugh. 'I am mighty thirsty.'

The harper sipped the liquor until the two clergymen had finished speaking and then he put the cup on the floor beside him.

'Gentlemen,' Turlough began, 'it warms my heart that you have reconciled with such good grace. I am so warmed by it, in fact, that I am feeling much better all of a sudden.'

The harper threw the covers off and sprang up from the cot dressed only in his long woollen underwear. The two old ladies shrieked with embarrassment even though they had been the ones to undress him.

'It's a miracle!' Turlough cried. 'I am healed! I have been brought back from the dead by the blessings of these two men of God! Hearing their pledge, the Angel of Death was frightened off and the Devil kept at bay. Hurrah!'

Harris and Dunleavy looked at each other skeptically. But before either of them could protest that they had been tricked, the two old ladies at the end of the bed had leapt up as well. Then the two old souls ran outside to proclaim the wondrous news.

'He was dead!' they both cried in ecstasy. 'But Harris and

Dunleavy brought him back to life by pledging to work as brothers from this day forth. After today there will be no enmity with the folk of Ballynew. God has ordained it.'

Katie smiled. Hugh shook his head slowly while the two clergymen struggled to contain their rage. Now that the miracle had been declared and the cause of it, there was no backing down from their pledges. They would be bound to their promises by their people's belief in their joint power to heal the sick, indeed to bring the dead back to life.

'It's a miracle,' Dunleavy whispered, casting his glance skyward and crossing himself.

'So it is,' Harris agreed, his eyes also staring toward the rafters as if some angelic messenger was seated on the roof beams looking down.

'You are a shrewd man, Master Carolan,' the priest stated.

'Thank you, father. I was afraid you wouldn't take the bait for a while there.'

Then the harper started searching for his clothes. Hugh brought him a dry shirt and breeches and a pair of stockings from their baggage.

'I'd guess it to be about half-past midday,' Turlough said to Hugh.

'About that.'

'If we leave now, we might get as far as Duncastle by this evening.'

'True enough,' Hugh agreed.

'Then let's be off.'

'You're a good man, master,' Hugh told him.

'Nonsense,' the harper mumbled. 'If ever I have to travel this way again, I'll be damned if I am going to change boats in the middle of the lough or ride an extra two days around the shore. My motives were purely selfish.'

'You put the fear of God into me,' Hugh said with a slight reprimand in his voice.

'I am sorry. But I had to teach those two a lesson and I didn't have time to explain what I intended to do. I must admit I thought the game was up when that old woman pronounced me dead. Thank God you piped up or I wouldn't have had a chance of tricking those two dour clergymen.'

'But don't you think it was rather dangerous,' Hugh cut in, 'to dive off the boat into the depths of the lough like that? Didn't you consider the risks?'

'I didn't dive off the boat intentionally, Hugh,' Turlough confided. 'I was so drunk that I lost my balance and fell off. It was only later I came up with the idea of turning that misfortune to some good.'

'I was worried half to death!'

'I was a little worried myself,' the harper laughed. 'But it was all in good fun really.'

Turlough beckoned his servant to come a little closer so he would not be overheard. 'Did Katie come across thinking she would be able to have you all to herself after I was gone?'

Hugh blushed deeply and, not for the first time, was glad of his master's blindness. 'She came out of concern for your health, master,' he lied.

'And if I had died, would you have gone off with her?'

'Yes,' Hugh admitted, hanging his head. 'I suppose I would.'

'I was in love with a woman once,' Turlough began. 'There was a time when I would have done anything for her. But she scorned me because of the lowliness of my birth. Now that I am renowned, now that I am welcomed in the great houses of Ireland and sit at table with lords and ladies, bishops and colonels, Bridget wishes she could have me back.'

'I don't quite see your point, master.'

'Make sure this Katie loves you for yourself,' Turlough advised. 'Not for what you do or who you know. Make sure you let her see the real you and that she is content with what she sees.'

'I will, master,' Hugh promised.

'Then I can't see the sense in trying to keep the two of you apart,' the harper decided. 'If she still wants to come with us, I will welcome her.'

Hugh's face lit up with joy. 'Thank you, master,' he hummed, taking the harper's hand and squeezing it tightly in gratitude.

'But only as far as Dublin, mind you,' Turlough added. 'After that she would be well advised to stay out of our journeys.'

'Indeed, master,' Hugh beamed. 'Indeed.'

Old Hugh the distiller smiled at the memory as he stretched his legs out before the fire.

'And that is how I met my wife Katie,' he told Edward. 'A fine woman who stayed by me until her passing only a few short years ago.'

'And did the two villages keep the peace?' Edward asked.

'They did,' Hugh affirmed. 'They are prosperous places known for their hospitality and the fine ferry that plies its way across the lough. Carolan's ferry it is called, after my master because he nearly drowned from the lack of it.'

'And what happened to the two clergymen?'

'Harris died not long after,' Hugh sighed. 'But he was replaced by a good man who kept the peace as agreed. Dunleavy, on the other hand, lived to a great age and at the end of his life, I am told, took ship to the West Indies and was never heard of again.'

'But was it right to trick them that way?' Edward wondered.

'My master used to say that any trick is justified if it gets you what you want. He reckoned that was the way of the Faerie folk. They had taught him that as long as you don't hurt anyone in the process, it is fine to use whatever means you may to achieve your ends.'

'But that is immoral!' the young rebel protested.

'Perhaps it is,' Hugh conceded. 'But it is the way of the world. Perhaps that is why some folk despise the Faeries for they often put a glamour about themselves. But everyone bends the truth to some extent or for some reason. Any man who says otherwise is a liar.'

'Do you really believe that?'

'The kings, ministers and generals think nothing of using subterfuge when it is to their advantage,' Hugh reminded his guest. 'Even the humble horse-trader makes use of trickery from time to time. Priests lie habitually and the entire English empire is built on the practice. Indeed if I hadn't done some tricking of my own, you wouldn't be sitting here listening to my stories, would you? You'd be rotting in a Dublin gaol or hanging from the gibbet at the behest of Lieutenant Moss.'

'You're a great trickster if ever there was one,' Denis chuckled. 'And so was your master.'

'He was that,' the old distiller agreed. 'And a man of incomparable wit. It was the gift of the Faeries that he was to be blessed forever with a quick mind and a sharp tongue.'

'I am dying of the thirst,' Denis informed his host. 'Is there not another drop in the house?'

'Mhairgead?' Hugh called out and in a moment his granddaughter was up at the table uncorking a large earthenware jug.

'Is this what you're after?' she asked, pouring the contents into the two men's cups.

'You are an angel come down to earth, young girl,' Denis told her.

'I am not a young girl any longer,' she laughed. 'I am a woman.' She looked Edward directly in the eye and raised one eyebrow. The young rebel blushed deeply and looked away.

'You are that,' Hugh told her as she poured some more drink for Edward.

Mhairgead put the jug back down on the table and moved closer to the young man, placing a hand upon his shoulder.

'Don't you think she is a fine specimen of womanhood, my lad?' her grandfather asked proudly.

Mhairgead's smile widened as her hand snaked down the young man's arm, across his chest and into his lap. The two old men sipped away at their whiskey contentedly, quite unaware of what was happening.

'She's quite remarkable,' Edward stuttered nervously, spilling his whiskey.

'You are a gentleman,' Hugh told him as the young woman removed her hand and crossed over to the door.

Edward mopped his brow with the sleeve of his shirt. 'I really think I should be going to bed now,' he stammered.

'What's that?' Hugh exclaimed. 'To bed? And I have just come to the best part of the story.'

'I am feeling tired,' the young rebel said. 'Can't it wait for another time?'

'There may not be another time,' Denis confided.

'What do you mean?'

'I am a hundred years old,' Hugh reminded his guest. 'My days are numbered. I will not always be around to tell these tales. And if you miss out on them, I guarantee you will regret it in times to come.'

Edward dropped his head and thought about that for a second.

'I'll ask Mhairgead to fetch you another cup,' Hugh offered.

'No!' Edward cried, forgetting himself for a moment. 'No,' he repeated in a more subdued tone. 'I'll be fine for the moment, if you don't mind.'

Denis leaned over to his old friend and whispered just loud enough that Edward could hear, 'He can't hold his liquor.'

'Why aren't you married?' old Hugh asked Edward bluntly.

'I am only young,' the rebel replied cautiously.

'Do you like women?'

'Of course I like women,' Edward shot back.

'More than anything else?'

'Yes,' he replied. Then he thought about his answer. 'That is to say, I haven't tried anything else.'

'Then why aren't you married?' Hugh pressed.

'I was too busy with my studies,' the young man explained defensively. 'And then I became involved in the fight for Ireland's liberty.'

'I suppose you don't meet many pretty girls in that line of work,' Denis nodded.

'I suppose not,' Hugh sighed. 'That could explain it.'

'What are you trying to say?' Edward asked suspiciously.

'It is high time you found yourself a good woman,' Hugh told him. 'Get a wife and you won't have the time or the inclination for shooting English soldiers in the head. Your every breath will have to be accounted for. I can't imagine a good wife letting her husband go out in the middle of the night to murder redcoats.'

The distiller turned to Edward.

'Find yourself a good wife, young lad,' Hugh advised. 'And if that doesn't keep you from roving around at night on rebel business, nothing will.'

'Your master and his missus were very close,' Denis sighed. 'When they were together at all.'

'They were a loving couple,' Hugh agreed, 'they were. But she surely must have guessed some of the things her husband and I got up to. Harmless mischief really it was. I reckon she just turned a blind eye and enjoyed their times together. Which they did. No-one gave a grander party than the Carolans and no-one ever had a better laugh than those two together.'

'And if they were wanting to be alone in the evening, they would make a terrible noise about their business,' he sniggered. 'You might as well have slept out in the snow for there was no resting in the same house when they were at it.'

'At it?' Edward smiled. 'At what?'

'What?' Hugh asked.

'At what?' Edward repeated.

'At *it*,' the old man said slowly. 'At *it*!'

The young rebel looked around the room. Mhairgead and Daniel were giggling behind their hands like two little children.

'What is he talking about?' Edward mouthed the words silently.

Mhairgead held up her hands. She curled her left index finger over and touched her thumb, then she took her right index finger and inserted it several times in the hole formed by her other hand.

Edward blushed immediately and his gaze dropped to the floor.

'You need a good woman, young fellow,' Hugh sighed.

Mhairgead and Daniel broke out laughing again and Hugh could not go on with his story because they were making so much noise. He sipped his whiskey and allowed himself to get lost for a while in his reflections. Gradually the smile fell from his face and he dropped his head. Mhairgead noticed the change and stopped laughing, placing a smoking pipe in his hand. Hugh took a deep draught.

'I was there the night Mary passed over, you know,' he muttered and it was plain to Edward that the old man was back there, reliving the scene.

'There was hardly any light in the room,' the old man began. 'I remember the master and I rode three days without pause so we would make it to her in time. And it was evening when we got there. It was so dark in that room.'

He sighed.

'And I thought to myself that I could hardly see the poor woman's face and shouldn't they light more candles so the master could see her one last time. Then I realised that my master had not looked on the woman he loved, his best friend, in over forty years. And even then he had only got a glimpse of her through the veil of his sickness.'

The old man put his pipe in his mouth again and Mhairgead went back to sit on the stool behind Edward and listen.

'She was terribly tired,' Hugh continued, trying to smile. 'And she would come and go between sleep and waking. But when Mary understood that her husband was with her she made up her mind to take her leave while he was present. She told him that she had waited for him as long as she could and had been nearly ready to give up the fight when he arrived.'

Hugh took another puff of his pipe.

'Carolan blessed her for waiting. For it would have broken his heart if she had already passed over when he arrived. Then they held each other's hands for a long while and he touched her sleeve. And then he said four words to her. "That sleeve is white." She held his hand tighter. I watched her.'

The old man took a mouthful of whiskey to cover his emotions.

'I was there in the room with them, you mind. And she said a few words to him. "It is as white as the new snow," she said. "It is as white as shining silver," she said. "It is as white as the light." And then she died. The air just passed out of her in a long sigh. And then she was looking to the roof beams with empty eyes and smiling and I thought to myself, she saw the light. The white light, you understand. The light of the Angel of the Lord come to take her away.'

Hugh coughed and wiped his nose.

'But the thing is, you see,' he whispered, barely containing his emotion, 'her dress was black. The sleeve was black. But my master had never guessed the colour wrong before. He always knew the shade. She didn't want him to think that he had guessed wrong. She knew it was a special bond they had and she did not want to sever it. That is true love if ever I saw it.'

'And what of the tune?' Denis asked gently after a moment's silence.

'He played the most beautiful melody for her after she was gone,' Hugh said. 'I only ever heard him play it once or twice again afterwards. He called it The Song for the Separation of Soul and Body.'

'Not long after her death he sold the house, as I recall,' Denis said.

'Indeed,' Hugh confirmed. 'The tiny cottage that had been a gift to them from Lord Inchinquin. My master sold it. And he never stayed in one place more than a few days after that. And sometimes his useless son would come travelling with him, but mostly that lad was to be found sleeping in some ditch or some strange woman's bed.'

Old Hugh took another draw of smoke from his pipe and sat up straight again. 'My master's heart was forever broken after that and he himself passed on but five years later.'

Mhairgead wiped the tears from her eyes and hid her face in the folds of her sleeves.

'After her wake and the funeral,' Hugh remembered, 'there never passed a night when my master would not drink less than a jug of whiskey. Even I couldn't keep up with him. He drank and drank until he would fall over senseless. And then in time he began drinking first thing in the morning when he woke up. And then at midday. And then at dinner as well, so that he drank more than he ate and I was not being paid. All my wages were going on his whiskey.'

'So what did you do?' Edward asked.

'I solved the problem after a fashion,' Hugh smiled. 'But without solving the problem at all really.'

'How was that?' Edward was confused.

'I came up with a plan,' Hugh went on, 'contrived so that Carolan would not spend all his money on whiskey and leave me to fend for myself. I had a wife and three children to feed at the time.'

The old man put down his pipe and tapped out the ashes onto the flagstone at his feet.

'My master was a very bright man,' Hugh explained. 'I knew it would be no easy matter to fool him. So I had to think a long while before the answer came to me. A daring plan. And wasn't I stupid enough to think it would work?'

'What did you do?' Edward laughed.

'I'll tell you if you'll let me get a word in,' the old man snapped. 'First of all I spoke with Doctor Delany and Mister Swift. McCabe was helping Delany at the college at the time; translations as I recall. Of course both men were only too happy to help me with my strategy, especially Mister Swift who had a special interest in my master's drinking habits.'

'Why was that?' the young rebel asked.

'Do you never listen?' Hugh sighed. 'Because it was my master's idea that cured Mister Swift of the drink himself, and by that time all of Dublin knew the truth of it so there was no keeping the story from the good reverend. Anyway, Mister Swift contrived to be with Doctor Delany at the coffee house where David Murphy went each day to meet his friends. Those fellows used to sit there all day sipping that filthy black brew.'

He held out his cup for more whiskey and Daniel filled it.

'I don't know what young people see in coffee. It tastes like the leavings of the whiskey vat and it is twice as deadly. I saw many a young life wasted away by the evil beans of Africa. If only its poor victims had known what a ghastly herb the coffee is, they would never have embarked on lives of utter enslavement to it. It destroys folks' lives,' he warned, 'you mark my words. I know men who have spent their last shilling on it and starved to death afterwards. They say it completely demolishes the mental faculties.'

'You don't touch the stuff!' Denis exclaimed.

'Of course I don't,' Hugh snapped.

'Then what is your excuse?'

'Be quiet,' the old distiller demanded, 'I am telling a story now. Where was I?'

The distiller thought for a moment and then clapped his hands. 'Now I remember ... So the two of them, Delany and Swift, were sitting in the coffee house when Murphy and his boys came in. And the doctor says aloud that Master Carolan reckons there is no man as good a harper as himself in all of Ireland. And Swift says he heard that Carolan will take any wager from any man who thinks he is the better musician.'

Old Hugh picked up the whiskey cup again and took a sip.

'And so David Murphy hears this talk and he says that Carolan is too big for his boots and he should be careful what he says. And Doctor Delany encourages him and says he should place a wager on that. But Mister Swift says he thinks Carolan is the best musician in Ireland and this upsets Murphy.'

Hugh giggled to himself.

'Well, Murphy says he knows a far better musician. And we all knew he would say that for he had a high opinion of himself. And Delany says to him, "If you think you know a better man, you must challenge Turlough O'Carolan to a match of skills." Murphy says he will and the three of us sat back to wait and see how that came out.

'Well, a few days later, Murphy stops my master in the street and tells him he is not worthy to be called a musician at all and would he care to wager otherwise. Carolan still had a poor leaning to Murphy so he laughed at the man and took up the challenge.'

'And?'

'Be patient,' the old distiller hissed, 'I will have a drink.'

He did so and then went back to his story.

'They shook hands. That was the only time my master and Murphy ever touched each other without drawing blood, as I remember. But then Murphy told Carolan the wager was to be a fine white Connemara pony and a cow. Well my master smiled and not to be outdone bet his harp and his horse as well.'

'An expensive wager,' Denis declared.

'It gets better,' Hugh went on. 'Then Murphy said he'd bet a new coat to replace the one Carolan had torn at their last meeting. And so my master replied that he was so confident of winning he would wager his servant. That was when I stepped in to stop the foolishness and put the next part of my plan into action.'

'How did you feel about being wagered?' Edward laughed.

'Uncomfortable,' Hugh admitted. 'So I had to be more thorough after that. I decided that I could not leave anything to chance. Doctor Delany introduced me to a physician, a certain Doctor Stafford, who agreed to help me with what I had to do.'

Old Hugh took a deep breath and then he smiled broadly at the memory and his own cleverness.

'One morning, not long after, I woke the master and says to him, you have a strange colour about you today. I must bring the doctor. And he told me that he felt fine and would feel even better after a few whiskeys to wash out his mouth with. I gave him the whiskey but I sent for the doctor.'

'What colour was he?' Edward asked, puzzled.

'He wasn't any colour at all!' Hugh explained. 'That is to say, he was the same colour as you or I. But I had told him his skin was a yellow tinge. And the first thing the doctor said when he got into the room was, "My God but that's the yellowest skin I ever saw in my life. You should be a dead man!"'

The old distiller laughed.

'And then Carolan sat up and was worried,' he said with glee. 'The doctor told him there was to be no contest with David Murphy as he was not fit for it since he had the whiskey jaundice. And the master asked what that was and the doctor told him that when a man has consumed too much liquor his skin turns yellow and his fingers freeze up and won't move. And that if Carolan wanted to win his wager with Murphy, he would have to stop drinking that very day, that very minute. Or his fingers would stop moving and there wasn't a doctor in all Ireland would be able to set them to rights.'

'Did he stop?' the young rebel cut in.

'It would have been cruel to make him stop completely for he drank more than he ate,' Hugh chortled. 'So the doctor wrote him a receipt which said he was to take only three cups of whiskey a day and then only in the evening after dinner. On Sundays he was allowed four. The master stayed in bed a week and then he was back to his old ways, though eventually, after the contest, I did receive a month's wages.'

'And what of the competition?' Edward remembered.

'Well, it was an evening only six weeks later,' Hugh explained, 'that was set for the great competition. A few days before, the master got the shakes and Doctor Stafford was sent for. The doctor told my master that Mister Swift's health had declined in a similar fashion in the last week. They both had contracted a new discovered disease that had originated in London.'

'What was it called?'

'Stafford called it the Nerves,' the old man said. 'Master Carolan had a bad case of the Nerves. Men died of it then and still do. And the poor doctor thought he might have been partly responsible for the condition for he had taken away the one thing that still gave the master any pleasure in his life since his wife died. And that is one of the chief causes of the Nerves, you know,' Hugh confided. 'Taking away the one thing a man cherishes to do most in his own time.'

'So what did the doctor do?'

'Full of remorse he wrote a new prescription and this receipt increased the dose of whiskey to a maximum of half a bottle and no more per evening enjoyed in convivial company. And my master was so happy he composed a lovely melody which he named after Doctor Stafford. He called it Planxty Stafford, but it is known as Carolan's Receipt these days.'

'What does that word mean?' Edward inquired. 'I don't have any Irish.'

'Do you mean planxty?'

'I do.'

'That is not an Irish word,' Hugh told him. 'It is a word my master invented. He was always coming up with new words and it was a mark of his genius. He told me that the speech of the Faerie people contained many such strange expressions and he was always trying to imitate their language.'

Hugh stopped and took another sip.

'I never doubted the truth of that for a moment,' the distiller declared, 'and neither should you. A planxty was always a melody dedicated to one of his patrons. And before he would perform a planxty, the master would yell the word to get everyone's attention and then announce the person for whom he was about to play.'

'And what of the competition with David Murphy?' Edward reminded his host.

'The competition,' Hugh giggled. 'That was a fine night if ever there was. And I was thinking the whole night, will I be bound into slavery with David Murphy for the rest of my life. And all because I was fool enough to want to be paid my wages and not lose them to my master's desire for whiskey. I wouldn't have minded so much if I had been doing some of the drinking myself.'

'Get on with it,' Denis grumbled.

'I will if you would stop interrupting me,' Hugh barked.

'I wasn't interrupting you. You were interrupting yourself,' the old harper pointed out.

'It fell about the start of winter,' the old distiller recalled, turning his head toward Edward. 'I remember this well because it was bitterly cold and Mister Swift had to sit in a large chair covered with blankets. He suffered from aching bones in the cold weather. And he could hardly move that night, what with the terrible onset of the Nerves.'

'I love the winter,' Denis sighed nostalgically. 'There is no feeling so sweet as to be curled up in bed with a fire at your feet and your arm around a woman's slender waist.'

'Now you *are* interrupting me,' the old distiller snarled.

'I am,' Denis admitted and then he put his nose in his cup and was silent.

THIRTEEN

Two figures in large riding coats huddled under the stone-capped gate to Doctor Delany's house. The rain was pelting down and this was the only shelter anywhere around. The two men looked into each other's eyes and both were quietly thankful to be a little dry.

Abruptly the wind picked up and started to blow rain hard into their faces. The great flat stone across the top of the gate had ceased to afford them any shelter.

'Let's get inside, Hugh,' Cathair McCabe yelled. 'He'll be back in time. We don't need to worry. Turlough O'Carolan would never miss an opportunity like this.'

'What if he's run off to England or America?' And then a terrible thought struck Hugh and he had to lean against the gate pillar to steady his nerves. 'What if he's gone off to the West Indies?'

Suddenly this seemed the most likely possibility to the servant and he started to shake with fear.

'What is it, man?' McCabe shouted. 'What's the matter?'

'Master Carolan has run off to the West Indies!' Hugh replied, trying to speak above the wind.

'What are you talking about?' McCabe frowned.

At that very second a large dark form appeared on the road and both men stepped out from their shelter. Though the rain threw up a mist, they could soon make out the distinctive shape of Turlough's old draughthorse.

'It's him!' McCabe cried, running out to greet the harper.

'*Deo gratias!*' Hugh sighed, looking to Heaven as he made the sign of the cross. That little duty done, he ran out after McCabe to make sure it was indeed Carolan.

At least it wasn't snowing yet, the servant told himself, but he could tell from the bite in the air and the colour of the clouds blowing in that there would be snow soon enough.

By the time Hugh reached his master he was already soaked to the skin and his broad-brimmed felt hat hung down over his face. McCabe looked at Hugh with terror in his eyes.

'I can't seem to wake him!' McCabe yelled. Just then the wind picked up into a gale.

'Dead drunk,' Hugh muttered but McCabe did not have to hear those words to know what the servant was thinking.

'Let's get him inside the house!' McCabe cried at the top of his voice. Hugh was already dragging his master from the mare's back.

Carrying Turlough between them by the shoulders and dragging his feet, they finally got the harper into the hall of Delany's house. No sooner had they shut the door than the wind dropped and the rain ceased.

Hugh rolled his eyes to the ceiling.

They sat the harper down on a chair and McCabe slapped his friend's face.

'It's all right!' the harper grunted. 'I'm awake.'

'No, you're not,' Hugh replied. 'You're completely gone.'

'I am in full possession of my mental faculties,' Turlough struggled to say three times.

'You are not,' the servant argued. 'I'll bet you can't stand up on your own.'

'I can.'

'I'll wager you can't.'

'A jug of whiskey.'

'Done.'

Turlough flexed his whole body bit by bit and then moved his arms so that his elbows were supporting him. The harper dragged his feet closer to the chair. And then he breathed out, collapsing back down in the wooden seat.

'I told you that you were not awake,' Hugh laughed. 'You owe me a jug of whiskey.'

'My body may be in some doubt,' Turlough conceded, 'but my mental faculties are fully possessed. And I promise I will honour all my debts to you, as and when the need should occasion me. And anyway, if I was asleep I wouldn't be sitting here arguing with you about whether I was awake.'

'Jesus,' Hugh groaned. 'The competition is this evening. We'll never sober him up in time.'

'Calm down,' McCabe smiled. 'He's been worse than this before and still managed to perform.'

'It's all right for you,' Hugh pointed out. 'If Carolan loses the wager, I'll be handed over to Murphy as a spoil of war.'

'Did it ever cross your mind that you could leave Carolan's employ if he loses? Do you realise you don't have to accept Murphy as your new master?'

'I couldn't do that,' Hugh shook his head in all seriousness. 'I am a very loyal person. If my master tells me to do something, I do it. No questions asked.'

'Then what are you complaining about?'

'I don't want to work for Murphy!'

McCabe rolled his eyes. 'You're not the entire wager. There was more as I recall. There was a fine Connemara pony, a cow, a harp, a draughthorse and a fine coat listed before you in the stakes.'

'Are you insulting me?'

'Not at all,' McCabe protested with a smile. 'Carolan kept the best till last when he struck the wager.'

'I kept the best till last, I did,' the harper murmured.

'Let's get him upstairs and into bed for a little while to sleep it off,' McCabe strained as he lifted Turlough's arm over his shoulder and dragged the harper to his feet.

'Cathair!' Carolan cried.

'I am here,' McCabe replied.

Turlough turned his head around from left to right, frantically searching. 'I can't see you!' the harper shrieked in terror.

'You're blind, Turlough.'

'Oh yes. So I am. Thank you for reminding me.'

Then he cried out again and tried to push McCabe away.

'What's wrong now?' Cathair snapped in frustration.

'Cathair! The world is topsy-turvy,' Turlough declared. 'A chair is supposed to help me rest when my feet are weary. And this one is trying to drag me up the stairs.'

'Be quiet,' McCabe smiled. 'We are going to take you to your nice comfortable bed where you can sleep for a while.'

'I don't want to sleep!' Carolan whined. 'I want to go out and get drunk and find myself a lovely girl with bright shining eyes, a sharp wit and a nice backside.' He held his hands out in front of him and felt the imaginary bottom.

'Shut up, Turlough,' McCabe insisted, 'there's a good lad.'

The three of them began their climb up the wide grand staircase which led to the upper floors of the great house. They were no further than halfway up when a door near the top opened and Murphy emerged from a drawing room, accompanied by another gentleman. Both men were dressed in the latest fashions. Wide skirts on their coats. Deep pockets. Large coloured wigs. And of course a fine white powder applied to the face to hide any wrinkles.

'Be quiet now, master,' Hugh whispered. 'David Murphy will be passing us on the stair.'

'David Murphy!' Turlough grunted. 'What do I care about him? He has the morals of a mermaid and the mind of a mussel. His hands are like the claws of a crab and he's as slippery as a fish.'

Turlough tugged at McCabe's sleeve. 'I am quite hungry. Is it Friday?'

'It is,' McCabe replied.

'Bless me but I could murder a plate of seafood right now,'

the harper smiled. 'Isn't it wonderful being a Catholic? Fish every Friday. I have never understood why anyone would want to be a Protestant. If you were brought up that way and you knew no better, perhaps it might not seem so bad. But any pope who orders his flock to eat seafood at least once a week is going to stay popular for a long time, that's what I say.'

His speech was interrupted as Murphy and his male companion approached. McCabe prodded Turlough in the ribs to quiet him and the harper fell forward straight into Murphy's arms.

Turlough stayed like that for a few seconds, propped up by a shocked David Murphy. Gradually the harper moved his hands around until they found their way to the other man's face. The skin had a strange texture. Turlough sniffed his fingers and smelled greasepaint. Straightaway he tried to stand up.

'I am terribly sorry, sir,' the harper bowed. 'I had no idea you were a woman.' He realised that the statement hadn't come out exactly as he would have wished but it was too late to do anything about it now so he shrugged.

'I am not a woman!' Murphy replied in a high-pitched whine.

Turlough detected a slight Italian accent and a strange effeminate quality to the man's speech. He raised his eyebrows. 'Are you absolutely certain?' he asked as his brows collapsed into a frown.

'Of course I am.'

'Where have I heard your voice before?'

'It's Murphy,' McCabe whispered.

'Murphy!' the harper exclaimed. 'Jesus. You're wearing a woman's paint on your face.'

'It is the fashion in London,' Murphy explained condescendingly. 'Just as it is at the Italian courts.'

'Italian!' Turlough coughed. 'They say all the Italians are fat with large teeth, spindly legs and bad breath. Why would they bother painting their faces unless they were exceptionally ugly on top of all that?'

'I would like to present,' David Murphy smiled maliciously, 'Signor Francesco Geminiani.'

'Sir,' Turlough bowed in the wrong direction. 'I have been pleasured to meet you.'

Geminiani looked the harper up and down with a scowl.

'Signor Geminiani is a violinist,' Murphy went on. 'He is teaching me to play his instrument. Apparently I have a natural gift for horsehair and resin. The signor has also kindly consented to represent me in the wager we have arranged for tonight.'

'Represent you?' Hugh cut in. 'You are playing against the master, aren't you?'

'Indeed not!' Murphy gasped in mock surprise. 'No-one said anything about me playing against Carolan. I simply bet your master that he was not the best musician living in Ireland. I think I have found the best.'

'But he's Italian,' the servant pointed out.

'But as you will observe from the steady intake of his breath,' Murphy smiled, touching the top of his walking cane to the signor's lower abdomen, 'he is living in Ireland.'

'Has he got large teeth?' Turlough cut in.

'Be quiet!' McCabe told the harper.

Turlough sat down heavily on the step.

'That is against the rules,' Cathair went on.

'What rules?' Murphy smirked. 'I don't recall any mention of rules.'

'Then how is the competition to be decided?' McCabe asked.

'The better musician will be the one whom the audience appreciates most. He will be the one who plays the most intricate and beautiful melodies. He will be the one who can imitate the style of others easily.'

'That is not fair,' McCabe protested. 'The signor has spent a lifetime perfecting his craft. He can read and write.'

'He is educated,' Murphy agreed. 'Are we to hold that against him?'

'I cannot see how this can be resolved,' McCabe breathed, seeing an opportunity to withdraw from the competition without any loss of honour. 'Before there is any contest we must first agree on how it will be run.'

'You make the rules,' Murphy laughed. 'If you are so worried about losing, then go ahead and you set the tasks yourself. And let the audience decide. I am still confident that Signor Geminiani will be proved the better musician. Under any conditions.'

Murphy grinned. He was certain he had already won the bet. Geminiani was one of the most popular musicians of the day. He performed all the most beautiful melodies from Italy and France. Carolan and Hugh had often heard other musicians attempt to imitate Geminiani and his mentor Signor Corelli.

'You had better sober him up,' Murphy suggested. 'I would be disappointed if he defaulted the bet because he was too drunk to sit beside the harp.'

'He'll be there,' Hugh assured Murphy.

'And tomorrow you will be working for me,' Murphy reminded the servant, 'so it would be wise of you to speak to me with some deference.'

Hugh thought for a few seconds. Then he bowed his head slightly. 'Yes, sir,' he said courteously.

'Until this evening, gentlemen.' Murphy bowed and moved on down the wide stairway, snaking his arm through that of Signor Geminiani.

'That's it,' Hugh gasped. 'I'm finished. That fop will work me to death just because I used to be in Carolan's employ.'

'There still may be a way Turlough can win this competition,' McCabe reassured the servant. 'We just have to think of it. In the meantime we had better give the great harper some rest so he is in good form for this evening.'

With that the two men dragged Turlough to the top of the stairs and placed him in bed. Then Hugh sat by the door and Cathair at the bedside to make sure the harper didn't go wandering off looking for more whiskey.

McCabe was silent for a long while, lost in his own thoughts. He was struggling desperately to come up with an idea that might save his friend from embarrassment at the hands of Murphy.

Suddenly Turlough sat up and looked around the room.

'I want a cup,' he cried.

'You'll get nothing till after the competition tonight,' Hugh told him tersely. 'I am in fear of being signed into servitude in the house of David Murphy and here you are drunk to senselessness.'

'I just went out for a breath of fresh air and to take the morning dew,' Turlough protested.

'Noon is too late for the morning dew,' Hugh snapped.

'Now that depends on who's distilling it,' the harper smiled slyly, touching his nose with the tip of his finger.

'The doctor said you were not to drink before dinnertime,' Hugh rebuked him.

'Doctor Stafford is a stupid old bugger who can't cure his own flatulence.'

'Are you feeling better?' McCabe asked.

'My head is spinning and my stomach is fit to burst,' Turlough replied. 'But I will be much recovered after a drop of whiskey.'

'I think it might be best that you leave off the whiskey for a spell,' McCabe suggested.

'I tried that,' the harper sighed, 'when Doctor Stafford told me it was killing my fingers. But I felt worse than when I was drinking a few jugs a day.'

'This evening,' Hugh said slowly, hoping that some of what he said might sink into his master's head, 'you are to play your harp for all your assembled friends and patrons. Then Signor Geminiani will play. Afterwards the assembly will decide which of you is the better musician. And if you do not perform well, you will lose your harp, your horse and me.'

'I won't lose,' the harper assured his servant. 'I'm not bad at the strings, even if I say so myself. Wider than the mighty heavens above is my fame. The power of my fingers is unmatched. Nobody will ever be found to better me.'

'You're drunk.'

'I am not!' Turlough snapped back. 'If I was drunk I wouldn't be talking to you. I would be asleep.' Then he thought for a second. 'Haven't we had this conversation before?'

'Many times,' Hugh grunted. 'But the stakes were never so high.'

'I don't know what you are complaining about,' Turlough laughed. 'I am a fine player. The music will not desert me.'

'I wish you would take this seriously,' his servant hissed.

'I'll wager you a month's wages,' the harper said, 'that I play better than the Italian.'

'You haven't paid me in three months!' Hugh exclaimed. 'What happened to all the money you should have saved when you cut down on the drink on doctor's orders?'

'Times have been hard,' Turlough began. 'Since the coming of the English there has been nothing but death and destruction. It's terribly difficult for a harper to make a living. Not much fun playing funerals all the time.'

'Shut up!' Hugh barked. 'I have heard that little speech too many times in the last ten years. I have a family to support and a drinking habit of my own to nurture. You do not treat me very well sometimes.'

'Then you will be glad to move to Murphy's household where I am told the whiskey flows freely and there are beautiful women, and men apparently, at every hand.'

'Why do you think I have stayed with you?' Hugh asked. 'Do you think I enjoy being underpaid? Do you imagine I relish following you round in the rain, wheeling you home after a night out and coaxing you back to the waking world each morning?'

'I have no idea,' Turlough mumbled. 'Perhaps you do enjoy looking after me. If you didn't, you wouldn't have stayed around.'

'That's it,' Hugh declared. 'If you are not going to make some effort to sober up and do your duty to me, I will leave your employ forthwith.'

'You can't do that, Hugh.'

'Why?'

'I can't afford to pay you off at the moment. Times have been tough and I have no money in my purse. Ever since the coming of the English . . .'

'I don't want to hear it!' Hugh bellowed.

'Very well,' Turlough conceded. 'I will make every effort to win the wager this evening. If I had known that you had such little faith in me I would not have kept you in my employ for these many years past.'

'Folk are gathering in the next hour,' McCabe told the harper. 'Would you like to get dressed?'

'Very well,' Turlough shrugged. 'But I can play just as well without fine clothes. Indeed I would dearly love to play just once without any clothes on at all. Do you think I'd win the competition if I played the harp naked?'

Then a recollection struck him and he didn't wait to hear an answer. 'Was Murphy wearing a woman's make-up?' he asked Cathair under his breath. 'Just as the quality do in Dublin?'

'He was,' McCabe confirmed.

'Jesus. He's a man of sixty-five years of age,' Turlough exclaimed. 'Some people never know when to slow down and surrender their youth.'

'That is too true,' Hugh said under his breath.

'Do you think,' the harper went on, 'that Murphy and that Italian fellow Geminiani are a little too close?'

'What do you mean?' McCabe asked.

'Do you think,' Turlough inquired, trying to find another way of putting his question without it seeming indelicate. 'Do you think they share a seat at the harpsichord?'

'Perhaps,' McCabe frowned, not really understanding the question.

'Do you think they play duets in the middle of the night when no-one else is around?'

'Maybe,' Cathair ventured.

'He means to ask,' Hugh cut in, 'do you think Murphy handles the signor's bow on occasion and that Geminiani perhaps plucks at Murphy's wires with too much familiarity?'

McCabe blushed. 'I never thought of that.'

'I suspect it may be the case,' Turlough sighed. 'All those years he spent as a young man at the French court. I am sure it was the French corrupted him. But then I suppose Murphy is no better or worse than Father Augustus who spent his days in the arms of any young lad who would have him. And Augustus went on to become a cardinal. Indeed he could be the pope now for all I know.'

'Perhaps that is why Bridget fell out with Murphy,' Hugh suggested.

'That would be it,' the harper said, clapping his hands. 'Poor old Bridget. That must have been a terrible blow to her. Here she was, following the fellow around all her life, just as I might have followed her around if I hadn't found my dear departed Mary.'

Turlough paused to think on his wife for a moment.

'And Murphy was probably the only man Bridget ever truly loved,' he went on. 'He was everything she looked for in a man. Everything I am not. He was elegant, witty, educated, fashionable ...'

'But not the slightest bit interested in women at all,' Hugh sighed.

'Poor Bridget,' Turlough breathed, echoing his servant's sigh.

'I have heard,' McCabe said, 'that Bridget has taken to attending the pilgrimages and lives in a convent most of the year.'

'She would be sixty-two herself,' Turlough calculated quickly. 'She must be readying herself to meet her maker. I hope I see her again. She was exceptionally beautiful as a young girl, you know.

'She had a slender neck,' Turlough whispered to himself, 'and skin like fine porcelain. And her hair was just like strands of pure gold. I loved her for her beauty when I was a lad,' the harper admitted. 'And perhaps in a strange way I love her still, even though there was no woman for me but my Mary.'

'You just contradicted yourself,' his servant pointed out.

'And you would be contradicting yourself too,' the harper told him, 'if you had spent as much time in the stables with that young Bridget as I did.

'I have composed three airs for her. The first was a sad,

mournful piece which reflected the state of my poor broken youthful heart. The second was a melody which spoke of my respect for her and my acceptance that she and I would never be as one. The third was composed after my mind began to clear of its infatuation and I saw her for the woman she really is. That air was full of disappointment too.'

The harper coughed and belched. 'Bridget Cruise has been a source of constant sorrow for me throughout my life. Even now I cannot think of her without regret.'

'Perhaps a little of that pilgrimage business would not harm you either,' Hugh suggested. 'You are an old man.'

'I am that,' Turlough said smiling. 'A pilgrimage couldn't harm me at all,' he agreed, warming to the idea. 'We will talk about it later. But now it is definitely time for me to get dressed.'

The harper stood up and McCabe thought his friend must have sobered up considerably for they could understand what he was saying without any trouble. So Cathair went to the travelling cases and brought out Turlough's fine green coat.

Ever since Squire Crilly gave him his first dark green coat, the harper had continued to wear that colour. And he was easily recognised for it. This latest coat, the finest Turlough had ever owned, was made for him by a tailor in Dublin. The harper had paid for the clothes with a melody dedicated to the tailor.

When he had first heard about this, McCabe had not been able to understand why a tailor would gladly give a suit of clothes in exchange for a tune. Then one day he realised how much social stature one of the harper's compositions bestowed upon such a man. Carolan usually only composed for the wealthy and the well born. To have a tune named for him made the tailor a member of an exclusive club. And membership of that club meant that his business expanded rapidly. The tailor had so many orders from gentlemen desperate to move in the same social circles as himself that he had to hire staff. The next thing he knew he had a very good premises and enough work to last him the rest of his life.

It was then Cathair had realised the tailor got a good bargain.

It took Hugh and Cathair only twenty minutes to get the harper into a presentable condition. When Turlough was dressed they led him down the wide staircase toward the ballroom where the servants were running around making last-minute preparations for the banquet.

'Everyone we know will be here,' McCabe told Turlough. 'Delany invited the young Lord Inchinquin, Dean Swift, Loftus Jones and his brother the squire, James Betagh, Morgan Magan, Squire Sheehan and his wife, the Power family and of course Mrs MacDermot and her husband who has just returned from France.'

'It will be a gathering of old friends,' Turlough hummed.

'And old enemies,' Hugh reminded his master.

'An old enemy is simply one you haven't dealt with properly,' the harper quipped. 'And what of Bridget? Will she be here?'

'No,' McCabe replied. 'She will not see Murphy any more and shuns all contact with society in case she should have to deal politely with the fellow.'

'I wonder what the truth of it is.'

'We will probably never know,' Cathair shrugged.

'Can you not drive her from your mind for a minute?' Hugh asked.

'She put a spell on me, my friend,' Turlough told his servant. 'I will not forget her even beyond the grave. And yet I'd gladly give all my times with Bridget Cruise for one moment with Mary my wife.'

'Don't speak like that,' Hugh rebuked him. 'What will I do for a living if you drop dead?'

'I am sure you would be able to find something to keep you occupied,' the harper smiled.

At that very moment a small chamber orchestra began playing in the ballroom and Turlough dragged his companions toward the source of the music.

'They must be preparing for their performance this evening,' the harper beamed. 'And they are playing Corelli. I love Corelli's music. It makes my heart sing.'

'That is Signor Geminiani's ensemble,' Cathair told Turlough. 'They travel all around Europe with their master, performing the works of Corelli, Vivaldi and Geminiani himself.'

'They are very good,' Turlough whispered and then he hummed along with the melody. 'I know this piece,' he enthused, echoing a phrase to himself. 'What a grand evening it will be.'

'Let us go into the sitting room and await the other guests,' McCabe suggested. 'There you can tune the harp without distraction and perhaps play a few pieces for the first folk to arrive.'

'God knows you will need every scrap of goodwill you can muster,' Hugh sighed.

'You worry too much,' the harper scoffed. 'And where is my harp?'

'Up in the room,' the servant told him.

'Well go and get it!' Turlough demanded. 'How can I tune the harp if it is at the other end of the house?'

'I am not going to let you out of my sight, Turlough O'Carolan,' Hugh replied with a laugh. 'I didn't just get off the boat from England, you know. I am well aware what you are about.'

'I am sure I don't know what you mean!' the harper replied in an injured tone.

'The moment my back is turned you will find yourself some whiskey and gorge yourself on it.'

'You have a vivid imagination, Hugh Connor,' the harper said in a serious tone. 'Do you think I would do such a thing and risk your future happiness?'

Hugh raised one eyebrow and thought for a second. 'Yes,' he replied.

'I'll watch him,' McCabe assured the servant. 'Just don't be gone too long.'

'Very well,' Hugh gave in. 'I will be no more than five minutes.'

'Right then,' the harper answered, clapping his hands together, 'see you when you get back.'

And with that Hugh made his way as quickly as he could to the stairs while McCabe led the harper into the sitting room.

'I am worried about Hugh,' Turlough confided to Cathair. 'He's always charging about concerned about something. He has to learn to relax. If he's not careful, his heart will give in on him. You mark my words.'

McCabe shook his head but did not reply.

Inside the sitting room there were already guests milling around, taking claret from fine crystal glasses. It was the European fashion to drink claret before dinner. A few of the guests were tasting Italian delicacies the doctor's cooks had prepared to mark the occasion.

Young Mrs Elizabeth Power and her husband were the first to greet the harper and his friend. They moved on after a short conversation and then McCabe led the harper over to pay his respects to Dean Swift.

The dean was seated in a large chair surrounded by cushions. His servant was standing close behind. The dean's legs were bandaged and strapped together and he was pulling strands of wool from his blanket.

Swift looked up as Turlough and Cathair approached.

'You are looking the worse for wear, my lad,' Swift grunted.

'And you are sounding the worse, Mister Swift,' Turlough replied. 'I heard that you have been unwell.'

'I was at the club two months ago,' Swift explained, speaking excitedly, his words tumbling over one another in the rush to get out of his mouth. 'I was reciting poems for my followers when I was overcome by a fit. I can't remember much of anything at all about the convulsion. But last Thursday my butler made me a creamy leek soup. He is a Welshman, you know.'

'I am,' the butler confirmed.

'And he told me,' Swift went on, 'that in Wales anyone who shows the slightest symptom of violent convulsions or lunacy is given leek soup straightaway. You see, if the disease is caught before the malady spreads to the lower parts of the brain, the leek soup cures it every time. Then I had a lovely sleep. But I can't remember anything before the afternoon at the club.'

The dean shifted in his seat and shook his head as if he was throwing off a spider web caught in his hair. Then he put his hand to the side of his mouth so that no-one else would hear. 'I know you from somewhere, don't I?' he asked Turlough.

'Me?' the harper replied.

'Yes, you.'

'I am Turlough O'Carolan.'

'No,' Swift muttered. 'Carolan is a young man with a full head of hair and a hundred ladies chasing him. You are not he. You are wrinkled and bald.'

In an instant the dean's mood changed and he sat back comfortably and smiled. 'I hope you will come to tea, Turlough, the next time you are in Dublin. It is a long time since we spent the nights together drinking with Delany and the others. If only Stella were about the place to see us now.'

He thought for a second. 'Where is Stella? She popped out to fetch some flowers for the sickroom and I haven't seen her since.'

'Miss Stella passed on five years ago,' Turlough stuttered, shocked that this could have slipped the dean's mind.

'Of course she did,' Swift replied, slapping his thigh as the memory returned. 'Did she bring the flowers then?' he asked his butler.

Before the servant had a chance to answer, Dean Swift had turned his attention back to Carolan. 'So, Turlough, here we both are at the nether end of our days. We've had good lives, haven't we? You are a fine musician and I am a famous author. And Stella has gone off to fetch some flowers. I used to wear her clothes, you know.'

Turlough coughed. McCabe raised his eyebrows.

'I beg your pardon?' the harper said.

'Here we are at the nether end of our days,' Swift frowned. 'What did you think I said?'

'I thought you said,' Cathair cut in, 'that you used to wear Miss Stella's clothes.'

'Did I say that?' the dean asked in horror, putting a hand to his mouth. 'Then perhaps it is true. Perhaps I really did wear her clothes. The rumours have some foundation.'

'I am sure I am wrong,' McCabe assured the old man. 'I am a little hard of hearing.'

'Are you?' Swift inquired.

'What?' Cathair strained. 'I'm sorry, you'll have to speak up.'

'Are you?' Swift asked at the top of his voice.

'Am I what?' McCabe answered, raising his own voice to match it.

'A little deaf?'

'Yes,' McCabe nodded. 'I am. You'll have to speak up.'

Then Cathair put out a hand to touch Turlough's sleeve, hoping the harper would be able to get him out of this predicament. But Turlough had gone.

'Where is he?'

'What's that?' Swift said as loud as he could.

'Where is Turlough?' McCabe asked again.

'The harper?'

'Yes.'

'I haven't seen him in years,' the dean sighed. 'Why don't you ask Stella. She'll be home soon. She's just gone out to fetch some flowers.'

Then the dean turned his attention back to picking at the strands of wool at the edge of his blanket.

McCabe looked at Swift for a second and as he watched, the old writer fell suddenly into a deep sleep. McCabe was so fascinated by the way the dean simply shut his eyes and dropped off that, for a moment at least, he utterly forgot about Turlough.

Then there was a tug at his sleeve. Cathair turned around to see Hugh standing with his hands on his hips and frowning.

'He got away from you, didn't he?'

McCabe nodded sheepishly. 'I don't know how it happened,' he shrugged, scanning the room.

'I knew I should have stayed down here with the two of

you,' the servant complained. 'Now we'll have a job finding him.'

'Surely he won't have gone far,' McCabe soothed. 'I mean, he is blind after all.'

'Where there is whiskey,' Hugh told Cathair, 'there will be Turlough O'Carolan, last of the great harpers and Chief Musician of Ireland.'

They searched the sitting room quickly. But the harper was not there. They searched the hall and the ballroom to no avail. Then McCabe went into the kitchens and Hugh went out into the garden. But both men returned to the hall without locating Turlough at all.

'How did it happen?' Hugh asked in exasperation.

'I was talking to Dean Swift,' Cathair explained, 'and I suppose I was distracted. One minute Turlough was there and the next he was gone.'

'I think I know where he might be,' Hugh smiled and made his way quickly back into the sitting room. He went straight to the corner of the room where Swift was still seated. When he got there he leaned over the top of the chair to see if his master was hiding behind it.

McCabe saw the servant reach over to retrieve something and in a second Hugh was standing with an empty whiskey jug in his hand.

'He has been here,' the servant declared solemnly. 'How else did this get behind Mister Swift's chair?'

'Then he could still be in the room,' McCabe reasoned.

The two of them went over to the long table where exotic Italian delicacies were laid out on white tablecloths. Hugh tasted one of the pastries.

'It has liquor in it,' he declared. 'The master will not be far away.'

McCabe looked under the table at one end and Hugh at the other. And there, seated on the floor in the middle, was Turlough, calmly chewing a pastry whilst simultaneously holding a jug of whiskey to his mouth.

'Master!' Hugh whispered. 'Come along, it is time for your recital.'

'Leave me alone,' the harper hissed. 'Can't you see I'm happy?'

'Come out now,' McCabe soothed. 'It is time for your performance. You would not want to let people down, would you? Some folk have travelled many miles to be here tonight.'

'I will come out,' Turlough replied. 'I am just a little shocked at the strange manner of Mister Swift. I had no idea his condition had deteriorated so much. I just need a drink.'

'Where did you find two jugs of raw whiskey in a sitting room full of the well-to-do?' Cathair asked.

'Doctor Delany always has a few jugs secreted throughout the house,' Turlough explained. 'They're not much trouble to track down, even for a blind man, if you know the way old Delany thinks.'

'Are you ready to play the harp?'

'I suppose so,' Turlough grumbled and then crawled out from under the table, much to the consternation of the gathered guests, none of whom had noticed him slip under it.

Hugh unpacked the harp, set it at his master's feet and the harper began to play. First Turlough performed some of his popular pieces, then he played a few melodies only certain educated individuals in the room would recognise. Tunes from the ancient days. Then he played his dances. And then his planxtys.

At last Turlough played SheeBeg SheeMor, the first tune he had ever composed. And when he finished that melody the room broke out into applause. The harper stood up and took a bow. He was slapped on the shoulders from all sides and congratulated. Laughter filled the room and not for the first time Turlough thanked his guardian angel that he had been blinded and led off on this life of music.

'If I had to go through the whole of my life again,' the harper shouted, 'I would do so gladly and I would not change a thing!'

'I am happy to hear it,' a familiar voice cut in through the cheers.

'It is Mrs Sheehan!' Turlough cried. 'I beg you all to be quiet! The gracious Queen of the Faeries is with us tonight.'

Mrs Sheehan giggled behind her hand, seemingly embarrassed by the comment.

'This is the woman for whom I composed the melody which I named The Faerie Queen. And that is one of my strongest tunes.'

'If that is a strong melody,' David Murphy cut in, affecting an Italian accent, 'then Heaven help you in this contest.'

Turlough leaned over to McCabe. 'Didn't Murphy use to speak with a French accent?' he whispered.

'That was years ago. Italian is all the fashion these days,' Cathair explained.

The audience fell silent, feeling the tension rise between these two men who had been rivals, first of all for the same woman and then later for the patronage of the noble houses of Ireland.

'Signor Geminiani is ready to perform in the ballroom,' Murphy announced grandly.

The audience began to move slowly out of the sitting room, gossiping all the way.

'Good luck, Turlough,' Mrs Sheehan wished him as she passed by.

'Thank you, Your Majesty,' the harper bowed, touching his lips to her fingers.

'You're laying it on a bit thick, aren't you?' Hugh hissed when she was out of earshot.

'Don't you dare say anything about the Queen of the Faeries for I am sworn to uphold her name!' Turlough threatened.

'Calm down,' McCabe intervened. 'Let's go to the door of the ballroom to listen to the ensemble.'

'Very well,' the harper agreed and took Cathair's hand. Hugh brought the harp along behind.

Two violas, two cellos and a sweetly tuned viola da gamba struck up the opening phrase to one of Turlough's favourite pieces. A concerto composed by the renowned Italian violinist, Arcangelo Corelli. Then, as the intensity of the music increased, the signor began to draw the notes from his own instrument. His violin had a piercing clarity and he played with unearthly grace.

Turlough was enraptured. He stood on the tips of his toes with his hands clasped in front of him. He sighed and hummed. McCabe glanced at his friend and saw the joy in that old face.

The music came to an end and the signor bowed. The audience applauded wildly, calling for more, and Geminiani acquiesced, giving hurried instructions to his ensemble. The viola da gamba struck up a chord and its sympathetic strings hummed like a human voice. Then the violas and cellos joined the droning chorus until finally Signor Geminiani drew his bow across the strings. Cathair's mouth dropped open in surprise when he heard the first notes. Turlough squeezed his friend's hand and smiled as broadly as he ever had.

Signor Geminiani's violin was singing the melody of SheeBeg SheeMor. Hugh gasped when he recognised the tune and he searched silently through the gathering, eager to witness the look on Murphy's face. But Murphy was nowhere to be seen.

The audience were enchanted. Overwhelmed. Spellbound.

Turlough whispered something to his servant and Hugh slipped the harp out of its case. In a few moments Hugh lifted his master's harp onto his shoulder and carried it over to where Geminiani stood. The violinist bowed as he played and then Turlough walked out to take a seat beside the signor.

In a flash Turlough was checking the tuning against the other instruments. And then, as the ensemble played through the melody one last time, the harper joined the other musicians. The assembled listeners were entranced.

Before the music had even stopped, Doctor Delany was cheering wildly. Folk swarmed over the musicians, patting them on the back and wishing them well. Turlough sat throughout all this mayhem serene and peaceful until the tumult died down and the audience began to quiet themselves.

'Tonight,' Delany began, addressing all his guests, 'we have heard two great musicians perform. And tomorrow night I can promise you more of the same. In the presence of such wondrous music, how can we even think of a contest between these two men?'

The guests showed they agreed by calling and applauding. All except for one man who pushed his way through the crowd.

'There is a small matter of the wager which Carolan and I made,' Murphy spoke up. 'A winner must be declared or the prize is forfeit to me.'

'Each is as brilliant as the other,' Delany reasoned. 'How can any man judge one man to be the more skilled?'

'Composition,' Turlough replied. 'That is the real test of a musician. Composition.'

'Is this really necessary?' Delany whispered to Murphy with a frown.

'It is.'

'Very well,' the doctor announced, raising his voice, 'this is my judgment as the host of the contest. The two musicians have one night and a day to compose an original piece which must extol the virtue and character of their chosen instrument. The compositions will be heard tomorrow evening.'

'A concerto?' the signor asked.

'Indeed it could be called that,' Delany replied.

'I cannot do it,' the violinist declared. 'It is an almost impossible task.'

'I will do it,' Turlough cut in. 'And what is more, I will compose a concerto in the Italian style. I will have a harp concerto for you tomorrow evening that could have been composed by Corelli himself, if he had been born an Irishman.'

'If you are so confident, Signor Carolan, then I will also try,' Geminiani countered. Then the Italian leaned in close to the harper and whispered to him. 'I had hoped to put an end to this silly wager by playing your piece,' the violinist explained. 'It was Doctor Delany's idea.'

'There is no stopping Murphy,' the harper shrugged. 'He must have a clear winner.'

'Can you really compose a concerto overnight?' the signor asked.

'I can.'

Geminiani held up his hand to silence the audience. 'I will concede defeat in this matter if,' he declared, 'Turlough O'Carolan performs his concerto tomorrow evening for the assembled guests. If he cannot, I will make an attempt the following night.'

This suggestion was met with general approval and then Doctor Delany stepped forward again, held up his hands and cried, 'So be it! Tomorrow evening the wager will be settled. And now we have a grand dinner waiting to welcome Signor Geminiani.'

The Italian stepped forward and bowed slightly to the guests. Everyone in the room returned his bow politely. Then Doctor Delany ushered him from the ballroom. The guests followed, filing out in twos and threes into the banquet hall to take part in the feast.

Turlough, McCabe and Hugh remained behind to pack the harp and have a few quiet words alone.

'Wasn't that a treat?' Turlough clapped his hands.

'How did he learn the tune?' McCabe asked, amazed.

'He told me that Squire Reynolds taught it to Delany years ago. Delany played it on the harpsichord for Geminiani,' the harper replied. 'Then the signor wrote parts for the other instruments.'

'Squire Reynolds!' McCabe laughed. 'May he rest in peace. So he enjoyed that piece after all.'

'He must have,' Turlough beamed, 'even though he never would have said so when he was alive.'

'Can you do it?' the servant asked, changing the subject.

'Do what?'

'Compose a piece in the style of Corelli by tomorrow evening?'

'You should know better than to ask that question, Hugh,' the harper reproached. 'I have a method for composing which never fails. If I go to sleep thinking about the melody I want and the person it is dedicated to, I will wake up in a few hours and have the tune in my head. Then it is simply a case of committing the notes to memory. By the next morning I am playing the new composition with confidence.'

'That is a rare gift, Turlough,' Cathair said. 'I have never heard of anyone else who has such a talent.'

'I have been blessed,' the harper agreed. 'And to ensure I do a good job of the composition, I am going to eat well and retire early this evening.'

'A wise plan,' Hugh enthused, eager that his master should have a night of creative rest. He tied the straps on the harp case and hoisted it onto his shoulder. Then the three of them joined the rest of the company at dinner.

Turlough went to bed before midnight while the other guests were still dancing, singing and drinking.

'Hugh?' the harper addressed his servant as the man was leaving his room.

'Yes, master.'

'Would you like to come on a pilgrimage with me?'

'Where were you thinking of going?'

'Lough Derg. Saint Patrick's Purgatory.'

'That is a vigil throughout the night, isn't it?'

'It is.'

'I will come along with you. It would do both our immortal souls good to spend a day without food, whiskey and rest.'

'If I had not been blinded,' Turlough told him, 'there would have been many days I had gone without any comfort at all. It is a strange thing that my eyes were taken from me and yet I have had a better life than if I had been able to see the world.'

'That is what I love about life,' Hugh nodded. 'The miracles. The things that don't make sense when you think about them but can't be ignored.'

'You are right,' Turlough agreed and then he laid his head down to sleep and begin composing. Hugh shut the door and returned to the festivities.

Turlough lay comfortably in bed for what seemed ages. But

he could not sleep. He could not concentrate on the composition. He could not think about music or Corelli or David Murphy's wager. The harper's thoughts were far away in the past in the days before he had been blinded.

He recalled the faces of all the folk he had known. His father, long dead; Mrs MacDermot, a young woman of twenty-seven with a baby daughter and a household to run while her husband was off serving King James. Squire MacDermot was a young man when Turlough last saw him. Squire Crilly who had passed away twenty years earlier under mysterious circumstances without leaving an heir. Turlough had heard that Dublin Castle took Crilly's estate at his death. They gave it to a Protestant who cut down the sacred grove on the hill for firewood and sowed the hurling field with oats.

Bridget Cruise was one of the few folk he knew of his own age, one of the few who had survived the wars, the plagues and the deprivations of the last fifty years. Turlough had long since ceased being bitter about losing her. It would have been impossible for the two of them to have had any life together.

'It was only youthful foolishness that made me think otherwise,' he told himself under his breath. 'Young love is but infatuation. True love is friendship.'

He recalled her face; the face of an eighteen-year-old, fresh and clear like a portrait miniature.

Then Turlough thought of David Murphy, the arrogant young harper who had come to the MacDermot household with Lord Mayo. Murphy had grown into a haughty man without a lord to follow around. Young Lord Mayo did not like him at all and the harper thought it was with good reason. But Turlough recognised that if David Murphy had not been at the MacDermot house that evening all those years ago, his own life would likely have taken a completely different turn.

Bridget Cruise and David Murphy had been a source of great pain to him, but they were each in their own way partly responsible for the events which had led him to his life's path.

At last the harper began to feel drowsy and his thoughts

drifted away into the realm of the Faerie hurling match he had played as a lad. Then he heard Mrs Sheehan's voice in his head.

'You must compose a concerto,' she reminded him. 'Sleep now and journey to the land of dreams.'

In the next instant the old man was breathing heavily, enveloped in slumber.

In his dreams Turlough was never blind. To the sleep-traveller in him, sightlessness was an annoying consequence of living in the material world. In the Otherworld of dream visions anything was possible.

So it was that Turlough suddenly became aware of himself, a young man in a coat that was too big for him. He was standing on the shore of a lake, looking out to an island. He glanced down at his feet and saw the water washing over the pebbles. He yawned and stretched as if waking from a long slumber.

'I am at the edge of the lough,' he whispered to himself. 'My eyes have life again,' he marvelled. 'I can see the rocks and the light on the water and the toes of my boots.'

On the island across the lough there were stone buildings and a chapel bell which sounded the midday angelus. There was no breeze. The water was perfectly still, mirrorlike.

When the bells had finished sounding out like the dying tones of his harp wires, Turlough could hear the cries of gulls and crows in the distance. And then he caught the dimmest echo of a melody crossing the lough on the breeze.

'I must get to that island,' he told himself in his thoughts and no sooner had the notion come to him than a large curragh came into shore and the boatman hailed him.

'Do you remember me?' the man cried. 'It's Padraic!'

Turlough smiled and took a seat in front of the fisherman.

'You are not as ugly as I imagined you to be,' the harper confided.

'Everything is better than you imagine in this place,' Padraic laughed.

'You have a fine curragh,' Turlough remarked.

'It is a finer one than the curragh you fell out of,' the fisherman agreed. 'Did you ever learn to swim?'

'I did not.'

'Stay in your seat then, for Heaven's sake,' Padraic giggled. 'We'll be there soon enough.'

'Where are you taking me?'

'To the music,' the fisherman replied.

And sure enough, as they approached the island the strains of the tune became stronger. Turlough listened with joy as the notes of the harp filled the air like a swarm of humming bees.

'Step ashore,' Padraic told him as the curragh miraculously dragged itself up high and dry onto the stony beach. 'And I'll be waiting for you here when you have gathered in the music you wish to take with you.'

'What do you mean?'

'You can take with you as much music as you can carry in your head,' the boatman smiled.

'I wish I had brought my harp with me,' Turlough replied. 'Then I would have been able to play each tune once and remember it the better.'

'It would do you no good,' Padraic shook his head. 'There are no musical instruments allowed in this place. That is the rule. Nor can you take the instruments you find here away with you when you go. Only memories are permitted to be taken back to your world. And sometimes they are not allowed either.'

Turlough nodded to show he understood and then made his way up the narrow beach toward the church in the centre of the island. He could clearly hear the music was coming from within this building. All else was perfectly silent. There were no birds and the breeze touched the trees silently.

The harper walked right up to the double doors of the building and pushed at them. But they would not move an inch. So he put his ear to the timber to try and hear every gorgeous note. As he did so the doors opened inwards to reveal a beautiful and unexpected scene.

The floor of the church seemed to be overgrown with vines and ivy and every kind of vegetation. Where the pillars should have been to support the roof there were trees of enormous size.

'It is like being in a grand forest,' Turlough muttered in his sleep. 'A forest within the church.'

This was like no building he had ever seen in his life before. Where the altar should have been there was a stone with a spring of water erupting from it. Sunlight streamed in through gaps in the trees, lighting his way.

Somewhere deep inside the building the sweet music played on under the fingers of an experienced harper. As much as Turlough was awed by the strange scene, he now wanted desperately to find the invisible musician.

'I must learn that tune,' the dreamer told himself.

Turlough climbed over the twisting roots and knotted vines, making his way toward the altar. At the foot of the stone he bent down at the spring to take a drink.

'Never taste the drink of the Faeries or eat of their food,' he heard Squire Crilly say in his memory but Turlough had no fear.

'Let them take me,' the harper declared as he cupped the crystal-clear icy water into his mouth. Instantly his thirst was slaked and he felt refreshed.

At that moment the music intensified. Now the harper was completely consumed with the desire to find this musician. At first he thought the sounds must be coming from beneath the floor of the church and he looked carefully at the spot where the spring water disappeared under the flagstones.

'Perhaps the melody is coming from the crypt,' he told himself.

But as he spoke he somehow knew this was not the source of the music. He listened carefully and discerned that the golden notes seemed to be emanating from somewhere high in the roof of this strange structure.

The harper scanned the treetops where Gothic arches should have been. There were bright birds in the branches, the like of which he had never seen before. And strange fruits which begged to be plucked and eaten.

'It won't hurt just to taste one of the fruits,' he told himself as the music dropped away. In moments he was clambering up the nearest tree to reach into the low branches. The harper plucked a bright red fruit the same shape as a pear but three times as large, and then slipped down to the floor again with his prize.

The skin of the fruit was like velvet and Turlough cut into it with his long fingernails. The flesh oozed a milky juice as he peeled away the skin. Inside the fruit was the same colour as fresh cream.

The harper felt his mouth watering. He recalled the warnings not to eat of the food of this place but he could not restrain himself. Closing his eyes he took a bite.

Instantly his mouth was tingling with sweetness. The juice ran down over his chin and the soft flesh of the strange red fruit melted in his mouth. When he was finished he sucked the core of the fruit until there was no flesh left upon it at all and only a few dark seeds clung to the stem.

Turlough lay back satisfied, his belly full. And he would have fallen asleep there and then if the music had not returned just at that moment to grab his attention again.

The harper noticed unearthly songlike calls floating down from the treetops. He had not noticed them earlier and he wondered if the strange fruit had given him the gift of hearing all the treasures of this cathedral.

Unexpectedly the dreamer caught a scent in the air. A fresh earthy odour that reminded him of rain.

No sooner had that thought crossed his mind than the first drops fell on his face. In moments there was a heavy shower. The harper sat down on a tree root, opened his mouth and laughed for the joy and wonder of such a thing as his clothes were drenched. Then, as suddenly as it had come, the rain stopped and the air was clean and sparkling like a spring morning.

Turlough stood up and looked about him. There were two huge carved wooden chairs before him on either side of the altar which somehow he hadn't noticed earlier. Each one was decked with sprigs of holly and ivy. The red berries were so bright and enticing he thought that he would pick a few to take home with him. Then he remembered Padraic's warning that only memories could be taken from this place. He felt guilty for having eaten the red fruit.

Turlough brushed his hands over the berries and the carved chairs and as he did so a great light illuminated the space behind them. Turlough suddenly noticed a chapel leading off the cathedral a little beyond the altar. Bright shafts of sunlight were pouring through the stone archway which led to this chapel.

The harper made his way to the arch and stood under it, awe-struck. Before him was a great stained-glass window glowing with gold and ruby red, emerald green and the deepest ocean blue.

There was no picture of any saint or scene from the gospels worked into this window. The design was intricate and difficult to decipher. There were birds not unlike those living in the main part of the church. And there were unknown fruits and flowers all about the edges. At last Turlough made out the branch of a massive tree and he realised then that this window represented the church itself.

The light shone down onto a small grassy knoll at the foot of the window. In the bright rays of light Turlough saw an old man sitting with a harp resting against his shoulders.

And the old harper was playing the wondrous tune that had drawn Turlough to this island in the first place. The dreaming harper felt his heart leap as if he had seen some great friend he had not met in years.

He crossed the distance to the old man very quickly but stood for a long while listening so as not to break the musician's flow. The melody was even more lovely than it had been earlier.

The tinkling upper notes of the harp vibrated like bells in the clear air and the bass reverberated through the floor, shaking the grass in time with the tune. Turlough struggled to remember every phrase of the melody. He knew this would be the only gift he would be allowed to take back with him.

For a second the thought crossed the dreamer's mind that he really did not want to leave this place. He had never seen such a wondrous and beautiful building. This was the most peaceful, restful, joyous cathedral on earth, he thought to himself. But then he recalled that he probably wasn't on earth at all.

As if in answer to his racing mind the old man ceased his playing.

'You will have time enough for the rest you have been seeking when your work is done,' the old man smiled. 'But I do understand your impatience.'

Turlough looked into the man's face and immediately noticed that his eyes were empty. He was blind.

'I may not have my eyes,' the stranger said, hearing the dreaming harper's thoughts again, 'but I have other faculties which compensate for the lack of sight. Anyway, you haven't got all day to be standing around listening to me prattle on. You have a tune to learn before you return to the world you still inhabit.'

'Do you mean the tune you have been playing?' Turlough asked.

'Indeed.'

'What is the name of it?'

'Carolan's Concerto,' the old man chortled. 'It is a gift to you from your patrons.'

'Which patrons?' the dreaming harper inquired, confused.

'The ones who granted your wish,' the stranger declared. 'Have you no memory of the hurling match and the king and queen?'

'Of course I remember,' the dreamer frowned. 'But sometimes I question whether it was a dream vision brought on by the smallpox.'

'Like this vision?' the old man asked. 'This dream you are having now? Is this not real enough for you?'

'It is real but it is not,' Turlough protested.

'You ate the fruit,' the old man said, shaking a finger at the dreamer. 'Now you are doomed to return here one day and help to tend the garden.'

'Gladly,' the dreamer sighed, his eyes straying toward the roof again.

'Now, you must listen to this piece carefully,' the old man scolded him. 'It is a difficult melody to pluck out on the wires and you will have to practise for the better part of the morrow if you want to get it right. Believe me, it will be worth your effort if you can learn it well.'

Turlough crossed his legs, sat in the grass at the harper's feet and listened with his very soul to the tune being played for him. He could not tell how long he sat there. He knew instinctively that time did not matter in this place. The only things that were important in this dreaming world were the experiences and the insights gained.

'Do you have it?' the old man asked without stopping the flow of his tune.

'I think so,' Turlough told him.

'That is not good enough!' the man berated him. 'Do you have it?'

'I do,' the dreaming harper replied and in the instant he spoke the harp music ceased and the old man disappeared.

'Who are you?' Turlough cried. 'What is your name?'

'You know me well enough,' the old man's voice came to him. 'Too well, perhaps.'

The dreaming man stood up, heartbroken that he had not spoken further with the old man.

Turlough turned to leave, still humming the melody, anxious not to let it slip away from him for a second. He made his way as quickly as he could to the front door of the church and down toward the beach.

Padraic was waiting for him. 'I see you have a tune,' the fisherman noted.

'I do, and a fine melody it is,' the harper said as he climbed into the boat.

'Hold on tight to it,' Padraic advised, 'or it will be washed overboard. The waters are always unsettled on the journey back and many a hard-won treasure has been lost forever in the murky blackness of the lough.'

Suddenly the curragh moved out from the shore by itself and then it turned around in the water. Turlough sat in the front of the boat, splashed by the waves from the blunt prow of the vessel. He looked back to the shore and noticed a small crowd of people waving to him from the stony beach.

'Goodbye, Turlough,' one man cried. 'Come back soon.'

'Squire Crilly,' the dreaming harper muttered in disbelief. And then he took a closer look at the other faces in the group.

He recognised Doctor Lindsay but there were a host of others whose faces were completely unfamiliar to him. Nevertheless he felt he must know them in some way.

'Who are they?' he asked Padraic.

'You should know better than to ask questions, Master Carolan,' the fisherman rebuked him. 'But I will tell you if you cannot guess.'

'They are the souls of my departed friends,' Turlough realised. 'And the reason I do not recognise some of them is that I never laid eyes on many of them in my whole life.'

'You have it.'

'Is Mary there?' the harper asked.

'I shouldn't be indulging you,' Padraic whispered, 'but she is there. Look. The woman on the very end dressed all in white.'

'Mary!' Turlough cried out as he stood up. 'Mary!'

'Sit down and be still, will you?' the fisherman cried. 'I wouldn't want to be tossed into this lough if I were you, for there would be no returning to the surface again if you did so. And if you are not careful, you'll drop that tune overboard and it will be gone forever.'

'I'm sorry,' Turlough mumbled, his attention focused on the woman who stood waving to him. 'Will I see her again?'

'Bless me,' Padraic hissed, losing his patience, 'of course you will! Now that's enough of your questions.

'Here,' Padraic offered a little leather-covered bottle. 'Since you have eaten the fruit and sipped the waters in the temple, a mouthful of this won't hurt you.'

Turlough slipped the cork out of the bottle and took a mouthful of the liquor. It burned his throat like whiskey but it tasted like the sweet juice of the red fruit.

'What is it?' the dreamer asked, handing the bottle back to Padraic.

'Be quiet with your questions,' the fisherman grumbled, straining at the oar. 'I must concentrate if we are to make our way through this storm.'

'What storm?'

No sooner had Turlough posed this question than the sky darkened. Lightning lit the horizon briefly and there was a deep roll of thunder which shook the boat.

'You keep your mind to your melody,' the fisherman yelled over the noise of the falling rain. 'Don't let go of it for your life and pay no heed to this storm. It is my duty to get you home and I will do the best I can to fulfil that obligation. But I cannot do so with you jumping about like that.'

Waves washed into the currach, soaking Turlough to the skin. Another question burned the dreaming harper's curiosity. But he dared not ask it for Padraic was looking at him sternly now as if he knew what was on his mind. So he held his tongue and stared back longingly at the island, humming his tune under his breath all the while. When they were nearly at the other shore the rain ceased but a silver sheet of it obscured the island from view. The waters around the currach were calm and so Turlough asked his question.

'Who was the old man?'

'You know the rules,' Padraic replied quietly. 'No questions. It is impolite.'

'I don't care about the bloody rules and, from memory, neither do you.'

Padraic smiled. 'In that case I will tell you the answer without giving away the secret.'

Turlough frowned, not understanding what the fisherman meant.

'If you could look in the mirror you would know him,' Padraic said, and the words were no sooner out of his mouth than the curragh struck the pebbled beach on the other side. The harper stood up at the bow and looked at the rolling hills in the distance, no more than a glance. And when he turned back to Padraic, the fisherman was gone without a trace. The boat was empty.

Turlough stood there with the tune ringing in his head and in that instant a hand took his as he stepped out of the boat. It was the hand of a young woman and when Turlough looked into her face he knew her immediately.

'Bridget!' he cried in surprise.

'Step up quickly from that boat,' she told him. 'There are others waiting.'

'Are you going to take that journey?' the harper asked her.

'One day soon,' she replied without taking her eyes from the sheet of rain which blanketed the island. The harper realised that her eyes were full of longing, just as his had been before he set out in the curragh.

'Will I meet you again?' the dreamer asked.

'Turlough O'Carolan,' she said with a merry laugh as her eyes met his at last. And then she melted into the air as if she had never been. But her words echoed on, and in the next instant the harper was lying on his back. He grunted with frustration.

McCabe was shaking him.

'Turlough,' Cathair said, 'it is time to get up.'

'Have you got your tune?' Hugh asked anxiously as he readied his master's clothes.

'I have got it,' the harper replied. 'Will you fetch me my harp?'

Hugh did as he was asked and when the instrument was unwrapped the servant lay it down at Carolan's feet so the harper could lean the top of it into his shoulder. Tentatively Turlough touched a few of the wires until he found the starting note.

Then he launched into the piece, stopping here and there to

correct himself or relearn a difficult phrase. McCabe sat on a couch in the corner and listened, astounded at his friend's skill.

'Where does such music come from?' Cathair asked aloud.

'It dwells in the realm of dreams,' Turlough informed him. 'On a holy island where all the folk we have ever known wait for the day when we will join them again. It is to be found in the depths of the sanctuary, behind the altar, among the sacred grove of trees which hold up the roof of the world. On the other side of the lough. In the Chapel of Grassy Knoll.'

His friend looked at the harper, trying to decipher that strange description.

'The ancient Greeks had a name for such inspiration,' Cathair recalled. 'Anyone who had travelled in the dream world and brought back a gift was said to have worshipped at the high altar of the Soporific Temple of Aesclepius.'

'Aesclepius?' Hugh asked, repeating the name with difficulty.

'The god of dreams,' Cathair explained, 'and the Otherworld.'

'That is where I have been then,' Turlough agreed. 'The Soporific Temple of Aesclepius.'

The harper played on, perfecting the melody.

'The tune flows out of you as easily as water from a spring,' McCabe noted.

'But the melody did not originate with me,' Turlough pointed out as he stopped playing. 'Any man who claims to be the composer of any music is a liar or a braggart. It comes from another realm and it links us to that strange world like a magical cord. We return to the temple in our dreams to receive rest, nourishment and guidance. And sometimes we are allowed to take away a gift. A memory of our voyage to the Otherworld.'

'Of all the wonderful tunes you have played in your life,' McCabe frowned, 'are you saying none of them are really yours at all?'

'I cannot own a piece of music any more than I can put a thought in my pocket or measure a recollection on a set of scales.'

'I don't understand.'

Turlough sighed. 'Music is the purest form of speech. It is the sticky sap of emotion. It is the preserved spice of love and war. It is the beginning and end of all grieving. It is the essence of all feelings. I do not know exactly where the music comes from but I know that I am only an instrument, just as is the harp, through which the spell of music flows. And I am at my happiest when it is flowing free, unrestricted by regret, guilt or fear.'

'That is the tune you will play tonight?' Hugh asked.

'If I am allowed time to practise it,' Turlough snapped.

'We'll leave you,' McCabe said tactfully, rising from the couch.

'I'll get you your breakfast, once I've dressed you,' his servant offered.

'I can sit here in my underwear playing for a while before I will begin to feel the chill,' the harper replied. 'Fetch me a jug.'

'Turlough,' McCabe soothed, 'it would be best if you had some solid food.'

'That is such an unappealing expression,' Turlough scowled, curling up his lip. 'Solid and food in the same sentence makes me think of a sickbed. I am not that old yet that I can't decide what's good for me.'

He sat still for a second but Hugh did not move.

'Whiskey!' he cried at the top of his lungs. 'Get me a jug of whiskey! Or I'll shout the house down.'

'All right,' Hugh replied. 'Calm down. If it's whiskey you want you'll get it. Who am I to judge your drinking habits? I have never travelled to the temple on the island you describe. If the liquor helps you get there and back, then drink it until your toes turn up, I say.'

'I'll take your advice,' Turlough smiled slyly, seeing he had got his way.

Hugh went off to fetch the whiskey and Cathair waited a few moments to listen at the door. When the servant returned the two of them left the master in peace to practise.

FOURTEEN

That evening Turlough O'Carolan entered the ballroom dressed in his dark green coat and led by his friend Cathair McCabe. The harper was greeted by Signor Geminiani and Doctor Delany, and in front of the assembled guests he announced that his concerto was the most satisfying piece he had ever composed.

'I will take you on a journey to that Otherworld I have visited in dreams,' the harper told them. 'To a place where music is the brightest of jewels and melodies are valued higher than any gold.'

Turlough paused, wondering whether there was anyone in the ballroom it was so silent.

'Listen to my music and you will know that I have been given a gift more valuable to me than mere eyesight,' he continued. 'And blindness was a small price to pay in exchange for it.'

Turlough sat down at the harp, strummed a few chords and conjured the scene of the cathedral in his mind. He recalled the twisting boughs that were its pillars and the many birds and fruits that were nestled in the branches of the trees. He imagined he tasted the water from the altar stream again and that he was sitting at the feet of the old harper, listening intently to his melody.

And when he heard the gorgeous tune flowing clearly in his

head, Turlough O'Carolan put his fingers to the wires and began to play. The harper started slowly, as was his custom, and when he reached the end of the first phrase he launched into a lively melody which had the audience gasping in delight and amazement.

Turlough's fingers tripped delicately over the wires as he brought all his concentration to bear, conjuring the cathedral clearly in his mind. Every sound, every sight, every aroma returned to him as clearly as if he were there. When he recalled the strange red fruit he had eaten, he allowed the melody to become more playful. His fingers found new patterns in the tune which satisfied his yearning for the sweet succulent flesh.

Then he recalled the journey back from the island and the struggle he had had not to let the melody fall overboard. Turlough remembered Padraic's face, a face he had never looked on in life, and the row of folk who stood on the shore to wave him off. And at last the harper brought to mind his meeting with Bridget on the shore.

With this vivid before him, Turlough O'Carolan ended the first public performance of his concerto. And before the last notes had died away the audience were on their feet, stamping wildly like a mad crowd, calling for more and praising him until he thought the roof would fall in from the noise.

Signor Geminiani was the first to reach his side.

'I cannot think of competing with your genius, Signor Carolan,' he cried above the rapturous applause. 'Truly you are the Chief Musician of Ireland.'

'Thank you,' Turlough muttered, quite overwhelmed by the reaction.

Doctor Delany came and took the harper's hand and shook it until Turlough leaned in close to him. 'Who is it would squeeze my fingers until they fell off?' he asked.

'It is Delany,' the doctor replied. 'Congratulations, Turlough. That was magnificent.'

'Congratulations,' Mrs MacDermot added, taking his hand. 'There seem to be a few more folk here tonight than there were last night,' the harper commented. 'Either that or your guests are extremely noisy.'

'Twice as many people at least,' Mrs MacDermot told him. 'There was not enough space in the ballroom for everyone so there are folk standing in the hall and some sitting on the floor at your feet.'

'How is it so many people came to hear me play?'

'When the word got around Dublin,' Delany laughed, 'that the great Turlough O'Carolan would be performing his concerto for the harp, the whole town turned up at my gates begging to be allowed in to listen.'

At that the doctor whispered to the harper to stand up as he brought the audience to silence by raising his hands in the air.

It was a short while before the crowd had settled and then when all was quiet Signor Geminiani stepped forward.

'Tonight a wager was lost,' he began. 'I concede that there is no better musician living in Ireland than Turlough O'Carolan, master of the Irish harp.'

There was more rapturous applause and wild cheering.

Geminiani put his hands in the air for silence. 'I would like to invite the good signor to visit my home in Italy, to play before the Doge of Venice who is one of my honourable patrons.'

'I would be happy to oblige,' Turlough replied quickly, bowing low to the Italian.

Delany stepped forward and spoke before the crowd got too enthusiastic again. 'For some years,' he began, 'we have been accustomed to referring to Turlough O'Carolan as the Chief Musician of Ireland. But this is no official rank and there is no appointment which coincides with the honour.'

Delany paused.

'I have been told that the King reserves the right to endow worthy individuals with knighthoods,' the doctor went on after a moment. 'After careful consideration my compatriots and myself decided not to approach His Majesty to request a formal recognition of Turlough's genius. Carolan has held the title already for many years because he is a generous, good-natured, convivial and charming musician of the highest standing.'

The audience applauded again but Delany spoke over the top of them.

'Kings are merely born to their rank. It takes no special talent to become a monarch. But great musicians must have passion, talent and in most cases a degree of genius. No king could ever compare to Turlough O'Carolan and so it would not be fitting to have a king's honour given to him. He is the Chief Musician of Ireland by popular acclaim.'

The audience stood up, cheering, hooting and calling, and Turlough bowed deeply.

'I can truly say,' the harper said in reply, 'that I have often wondered what it would be like to look on the faces of those who have heard my music. But tonight I do not wish I could see you all. Your voices and applause are more precious to me than a hundred pairs of eyes or a thousand honours from a thousand kings.'

Then Turlough O'Carolan stepped down from the stage and was ushered to the dining room for dinner with a select group of guests. As McCabe led him out of the ballroom a woman's hand brushed the harper's and he heard a voice at his ear.

'Congratulations, my friend,' the woman said and then she was gone.

'That was Bridget!' Turlough exclaimed.

'I did not see her,' Cathair replied. 'I did not even know she was here tonight.'

'I'll swear it was her,' Turlough declared.

'I cannot see her,' McCabe answered. 'Are you sure?'

'Absolutely certain,' the harper answered. 'Is Murphy here tonight?'

'He is not,' Cathair told his friend. 'He is conspicuous by his absence. Doctor Delany had a seat put aside for him in the front row, but a message came to say David Murphy had been taken ill. He did not want to be shown up publicly as he was last night.'

'I just hope he honours his debt,' Turlough laughed. 'I went to a lot of trouble to win it.'

Murphy was renowned for his bragging and he was an acknowledged liar with it, but he always honoured his debts. The next morning, as Hugh and Turlough were preparing to set out for the north of the country, they found a fine white Connemara pony and a speckled brown cow waiting for them in the courtyard. Laid over the pony's rump was a fine green coat lined with silk which Hugh handed to Turlough to try on for size. It was, of course, several sizes too big for him, which gave Turlough a laugh.

Signor Geminiani waved them off as they departed. 'I will play the Carolan's Concerto when I return home,' he promised. 'So that folk in Italy may know of the great Irish composer Turlough O'Carolan.'

The harper was very happy to hear that.

'Imagine that,' he told his servant, 'all these years I have been an admirer of Corelli and Vivaldi and now my tunes will be played in the country of their birth.'

Hugh smiled broadly, overjoyed that he had not ended up in service to David Murphy. And he was well pleased that he could carry the harp over his shoulder while he sat astride a young Connemara pony. But it was the cow that pleased Hugh most.

'We shall have fresh milk every morning for our breakfast,' he told his master.

Not long after they had travelled beyond the town and were amongst the fields again, Turlough declared, 'I would like to make for Saint Patrick's Purgatory, Hugh.'

'It will take us some days to come to Lough Derg.'

'How many?'

'Two or three, depending on how long we tarry at each house along the way.'

'Then let us not tarry,' Turlough replied. 'I have a feeling that I must get there quickly without wasting any time at all.'

'Do you have a premonition of your death?' Hugh asked, becoming worried at this change in his master.

'No,' the harper laughed, 'I just have a strong feeling that I should make the pilgrimage at least once in my life and that now is the best time. I want to thank God for the gift of the concerto. And I want to show Him I am still humbled by the great gifts I have received.'

'Was it God gave the gift to you?'

'God made everything,' Turlough said thoughtfully, 'so I suppose that means he made the melody of my concerto, even though I am sure any priest would condemn my vision as the work of the Devil.'

'The Devil may be evil,' Hugh laughed, 'but, by Jesus, he works hard.'

'You can't fault him on that,' Turlough agreed.

'And so it wasn't the goodwill of the Faeries,' the servant asked, 'that brought the concerto to you?'

'It may have been,' the harper mused, 'but weren't the Good People also made by the hand of God?'

'If God made everything,' Hugh replied, beginning to understand Turlough's reasoning, 'then I suppose it follows He also made the Faeries. Everything has the mark of the hand of God.'

'Why are priests so worried about the Good People then?' the harper asked himself. 'I have never been able to work out why the clergy are so hostile to the old beliefs.'

'Because folk worshipped the Faeries in the days before Saint Patrick came to bless us with the true religion,' Hugh asserted.

'But folk worship the Faeries still,' Turlough reasoned, 'despite the teachings of the Church.'

'Hold your tongue, master,' the servant gasped. 'I'll not hear blasphemy come from your mouth at your age. Isn't it time you started choosing your words more carefully? I mean to say, none of us is getting any younger and the Almighty may call us to His eternal home at any moment.'

'The Faerie Folk are the most beautiful of all God's creatures,' Turlough went on, ignoring the warning. 'They are gentle and musical. They are compassionate and wealthy beyond our modest imagining. And they are immortal. What man or woman does not dream of acquiring at least a few of those attributes at some time in their life? I can understand why folk would worship them.'

'And yet the Faeries are capable of great evil,' Hugh pointed out.

'I have heard that,' the harper nodded, 'though I have never seen any evidence of it, unless David Murphy was a prodigy of the Dark Faeries. And what matter in any case, for there is good and bad in all things and in all people. Even the best of us has our weaknesses. And I don't doubt there is good and bad among the Faerie kind as well.

'We will go Saint Patrick's Purgatory,' Turlough decided. 'I have made my mind up. Tonight we will take our rest at the last house before sunset and then we will ride on without stopping to the shores of Lough Derg.'

Hugh sighed and grumbled under his breath. There was nothing he disliked more than riding through the night. But he knew that when the harper got an idea into his head there was no stopping him.

'Once we get there,' Hugh told his master, deciding that he should make some protest, 'we must take a ferry to the island. And we must have fasted the day before. Then there is a full day and night of prayer and the stations of the cross. The deprivations are not easy, not even for the younger pilgrims. If you expect the journey to be hard, the pilgrimage will certainly be far more difficult.'

'If it was easy, it would not benefit the soul,' Turlough shrugged.

'There is no whiskey.'

'I guessed that,' the harper snapped. 'I can do without it for a day or two if it is going to benefit my immortal soul.'

'Master, may I ask you a question?' Hugh ventured.

'You just have,' the harper retorted, tiring of all the talk.

'You have never professed a deep belief in the teachings of the Church,' the servant stated. 'What has brought about this change? Why the sudden desire to go to a Catholic shrine and perform rituals which you don't really have any faith in?'

'I do have faith, Hugh,' Turlough smiled. 'That is where you are wrong. It is just a different kind of faith from most people. I have known enough priests, reverends and other clergy in my life to realise they also have all had their doubts about their faith at some point. I am coming to the age when a man thinks on his death. If there is an afterlife, I want to be ready for it. I can only hope it is not full of God-bothering ranters who won't let you dance on Sunday for fear it will inspire you to acts of evil.'

Turlough went silent for a while and then he heaved a deep sigh. 'There is something about that island, Saint Patrick's Purgatory, that is calling me. I know I must go there. Ask me all these questions after we have performed our pilgrimage.'

They stayed with a farmer and his family that night and the next morning set out again, but they did not come to the shores of Lough Derg until dawn of the day after. Hugh unpacked the horses at the little cottage known as Ferry House. This was the place where the boatman waited for his passengers to assemble before rowing across to the island.

Once the pony and mare were seen to and the baggage unpacked, Hugh excused himself.

'I must take some rest if I am to have any hope of surviving the rigours of the pilgrimage,' he told his master.

'I'll make my way down to the shores of the lough,' Turlough told him. 'Don't worry about me, I'll find my way back when it is time to journey on.'

Hugh made a protest but his heart wasn't in it. He lay down on the floor of the house, closed his eyes and immediately fell asleep.

When he awoke his master was prodding him with a stick.

'It is time to get up,' Turlough urged him. 'I can hear voices out on the lough.'

Sure enough, when Hugh looked out across the water, he could see a boatload of pilgrims making its way to shore.

'We'll wait here,' the servant said. 'There are clouds gathering and I would not want to be outdoors when the rain comes.'

'Describe it to me,' the harper begged, tugging gently on the other man's sleeve. 'Tell me what the lough looks like and the island too.'

'The water is remarkably calm in parts,' Hugh began, 'but as the weather moves across it the surface becomes very rough. There are sheets of rain around the island but I can make out a church and some other buildings. And there is a small group of people standing on the other shore waiting.'

Hugh felt the harper's grip tighten and he looked down at Turlough's hand. The knuckles were white.

'What else do you see?' his master whispered.

'There are gulls and crows in the air. There is a boat coming over the water toward us. It is a wide curragh similar to those we saw at Buntrane.'

By this time the boat had struck the pebbled shore and folk were already jumping out to wade ankle deep through the water toward the road. A few of the passengers helped to drag the boat up beyond the reach of the lapping waves.

An old priest struggled up to the cottage, a walking stick supporting him. He held out his hand in greeting as all the pilgrims dispersed to return to their homes.

'My name is Father John,' the aged priest told them. 'It is my duty to see that pilgrims understand what is required of them before they undertake the journey to the Purgatory.'

'I am Hugh Connor,' the servant replied, 'and this is Turlough O'Carolan, my master.'

'I see that you are afflicted with the blindness,' the priest told Turlough.

'I wish I could see that,' the harper answered quickly.

'But then you wouldn't be blind,' Father John replied and the words were out of his mouth before he understood the man was joking with him.

'I may have no eyes but I plainly see that you are a priest who lives a sheltered life in a closed community,' Turlough quipped.

'You see well enough for a blind man,' the priest mumbled as he recorded their names in the register. 'Have you fasted?'

'We have,' both men answered in unison.

'Are you well prepared for the days of religious observance which lie before you?'

'We are.'

'Then proceed to the boat and may God bless you on your journey,' Father John told them.

Hugh picked up the seal-skin harp case and put it over his shoulder.

'What is in that bag?' the priest asked.

'It is my harp,' Turlough replied.

'There is a strict rule that no musical instruments are to be taken onto the island,' Father John informed him. 'I will keep it here while you are gone. I will not be returning to the island for three days.'

'That is his harp,' Hugh cut in. 'Thirty years of war with the English and another twenty of famine couldn't part him from it. The destruction of the old nobility and the arrival of the new aristocracy could not keep him from that instrument for even a moment. The best fiddle player in the Christian world could not convince Turlough O'Carolan to lay down the harp. How can you ask him to do so?'

'That is the rule,' the priest answered blankly. 'I don't make the rules, I just follow them. You may leave it in the corner by the chair. No harm will come to it.'

'Do you know who this man is?' Hugh fumed.

'You have said his name is Turlough O'Carolan,' Father John replied with a frown, 'I have just written it down.'

'He is the greatest harper alive,' the servant blustered.

'Well, I have never heard of him,' the priest shrugged.

'Where have you been for the past fifty years?'

'Out on that Godforsaken island,' Father John snapped. 'And I intend to have a few days here in peace and quiet on my own. I won't have the abbot sending you back because you have broken the rules. Once your boat has pulled away, I wish to have no disturbances. I have earned this rest and no-one is going to take it away from me.'

'It is all right, Hugh,' Turlough interrupted. 'I am nearing the end of my life. I will soon make another pilgrimage. And I will not be able to take the harp with me there either. Let the priest have his rest. We will entrust him with our horses and my harp.'

'Bless you, stranger,' Father John muttered. 'Now kindly let me be. I have a great deal of nothing to catch up on and it simply won't wait another minute.'

Turlough grinned and let himself be led to the boat. As he stepped on board he leaned close to the boatman.

'What's your name?' he whispered.

The boatman smiled.

'Michael,' the stranger answered.

Turlough shrugged and settled down at the front of the vessel. Within a short time ten more pilgrims had arrived and the boat set off.

Hugh and Turlough spent their two nights on the island fasting and praying. It was a great trial for Hugh for he was exhausted from the journey. But Turlough meekly sat the vigil, said the stations, stayed out in the pouring rain by the stone cross to pray and then hardly slept at all when the observances were complete.

On the morning of the third day the two of them stepped into the boat again and set off back across Lough Derg to Ferry House.

'Did you find what you came in search of?' Hugh asked his master.

'I am not sure,' Turlough admitted. 'But I am glad I came. It has settled my soul.'

At that moment the wind whipped up and the spray struck the harper in the face. He wiped the water from his chin and laughed. Hugh could see that his master was truly at ease and he'd had no help from the whiskey to feel that way.

The boat pulled up onto the shore again and everyone but Turlough disembarked as a new group of pilgrims made their way down to the curragh. The harper stood up in his seat at the prow and offered his hand to help his fellow pilgrims on board.

A woman pushed past all the other waiting folk, held out her hand and grasped his. At that instant Turlough's face went pale.

'Are you ill, master?' Hugh cried from the shore, seeing that something was obviously wrong.

'That is the hand of Bridget Cruise,' the harper declared.

'God bless you, Turlough,' she replied. 'How did you know it was me?'

'I will always know the hand I once worshipped,' the harper replied. 'Will you help me to my harp? I have a last tune for you.'

'I will,' Bridget said and together with Hugh they brought him to the edge of the pebbles where the grass grew.

Turlough sat down to wait for Hugh to bring the harp. While he waited Bridget sat with him, holding his hands and rubbing them to get the blood circulating. Folk were still gathering to take their places on the boat, but Bridget was in no mood to rush away just yet.

'We are both old,' she sighed, looking out across the lough.

'We may not meet again in this life,' Turlough added.

'It was my father that caused me to go to Dublin,' Bridget said. 'If he hadn't filled my head with foolish tales of the riches to be had there, I never would have left you.'

'But if I hadn't yearned for you so, I would never have taken up the harp,' Turlough soothed, stroking the back of her hand.

'Can you ever forgive me for believing that David Murphy and his kind would offer me more from life than you?'

'I forgive you,' Turlough assured her with a laugh. 'I forgave you many years ago. I thank you with all my heart and I thank Murphy too. For if it had not been for you both, I would never have taken up music.'

'Perhaps you would never have been blinded if I had been there to care for you.'

'Perhaps,' Turlough conceded. 'But the girl who nursed me

was the finest woman I ever knew. And now I am only waiting to fall into the care of my darling Mary again. If it had not been for my foolish wish, I would never have met her. Nor would I have had the life I was gifted with.'

'What foolish wish?' Bridget asked.

'I wished to become the best harper in the land so that I might have a chance to win back your love,' the harper admitted, and though it had all happened many years ago, he found himself blushing.

'I always loved you, Turlough,' Bridget told him as she leaned back to tidy the silk ribbon which held his long hair in place. 'I was just too young to know the value of real love. I threw it away like a soiled handkerchief. That was my loss.'

'And mine, I think,' the harper agreed as he bent forward to let her brush the strands of hair together.

'We will never know how things might have turned out,' she said at last and at that moment Hugh placed the harp down beside his master. Turlough wrapped an arm about the instrument and hugged it into his shoulder.

'If I only had a farthing for every time I wished you would hold me like that,' Bridget whispered. Then she kissed the harper on the cheek, got to her feet and made her way to the boat.

Turlough said no word of farewell. His mouth would not do his bidding. But he quickly tuned the harp and began to play the fourth and final melody he had composed for Bridget Cruise. And as the boat pulled out from the pebbled beach the notes drifted across the water to her and her eyes were full of tears at their last parting.

Old Hugh the distiller, former servant to the famous Turlough O'Carolan, sat back in his seat and smiled. He drew in another fill of tobacco smoke and raised his whiskey cup to his lips.

'Quite a little miracle it was to meet Bridget Cruise in that place at that time,' Hugh told his listeners. 'I have often suspected that my master spent the entire pilgrimage praying to meet Bridget just once more and this was the answer to his supplications.'

'Did they ever meet afterwards?' Mhairgead asked.

'They did not,' the old man answered. 'For she passed away on the island three days later.'

'And what happened to David Murphy?' Edward inquired.

'In time young Lord Mayo forgave him his indiscretions, and Murphy ended his days in a fine house, surrounded by admirers. But he took to the drink in the last year of his life and, being unaccustomed to it, I believe it drove him quickly to his death.'

'And were you paid more regularly after all that?' Denis asked.

'I was for a while,' the old distiller replied. 'But in time my master returned to his hard-drinking ways and I had to take more drastic steps to secure my income.'

'What did you do?' Edward wanted to know.

'I learned to distil the whiskey myself,' old Hugh explained, 'so that at least my master would not squander his income and I might see some wages from him on occasion. In time my liquor became famous and now the secret of it is the basis of a family business.'

Daniel coughed and downed the cup of whiskey he was holding.

'And you don't think it was the drink that killed Carolan?' the red-haired man asked.

'It was not!' Hugh snapped. 'My whiskey was a great comfort to him. And it was the last thing he tasted on this earth.'

'That is exactly what I meant,' Daniel noted with a raised eyebrow.

'Turlough O'Carolan lived to the great age of sixty-eight years,' the old distiller told his grandson. 'That was an incredible feat for his time. Only Cathair McCabe and Mrs MacDermot, of all the people who were about his own age, survived him. You do not realise because times are much easier now, but in those days death was a regular visitor.'

Hugh took a draught of his whiskey.

'Children had little hope of living to become adults,' the distiller went on. 'There was war and famine such as Ireland has never known before or since.'

'And may she never know it again,' Denis added.

'Indeed,' Hugh agreed wholeheartedly. 'And my master was composing tunes right up to the very last, you know.'

'Was he really?' Edward asked, impressed.

'He was,' the old man confirmed. 'And his last melody was his greatest, for it was a strange thing, not of this world.'

'Are you going to tell us about it?' the old harper asked, settling down in his chair.

'I will, if you would listen,' Hugh replied and Mhairgead went around filling pipes and cups while her grandfather made ready to launch into the next part of the tale.

The coach lurched into the courtyard as the driver called encouragement to his horses. This brought the MacDermots's butler to the kitchen door to see what the noise was all about.

The serving man squinted and then his eyes opened wide in surprise.

Seconds later William O'Flynn ran out of the kitchen on his long spindly legs to meet the coach. The old servant had not expected guests at the house today so he was quite flustered at the sudden appearance of this vehicle.

Snow had fallen quite heavily during the night, blanketing the yard in white, and there were patches of ice in between the cobbles. The servant was very careful where he placed his feet. He did not want to slip over and bring embarrassment to the household.

William's mind was on his duty. Mrs MacDermot had a reputation for hospitality that had to be upheld. O'Flynn stopped at the edge of the cobblestones, breathing steam from the exertion of his run. He looked hard at the dark green doors of the coach edged with yellow, struggling to remember which lord or lady favoured these colours.

After a moment William realised this was the livery of young Squire Reynolds. O'Flynn straightened his cuffs where they protruded under his butler's coat. He took a deep breath and strode confidently over to where he guessed the vehicle would stop.

Years of practice had perfected his skill at judging a coachman. So it was with a graceful ease that O'Flynn grasped the handle of the coach door, turned and pulled it open in a single flowing motion just as the vehicle came to a halt. In a second the butler had folded down the wooden steps beneath the door.

Then he waited with a hand held out to help the passengers disembark.

But no-one moved. Nothing stirred. And when William looked inside the coach he could hardly believe his eyes. Seated in the corner, fast asleep, was an old man, nearly bald but with long strands of hair tied behind his head in a black ribbon.

The old man was dressed in a fine dark green coat and breeches; his belt buckles were of shining silver; his stockings of the finest cotton. His skin was deathly pale and his forehead beaded with fine drops of perspiration.

But William O'Flynn would have recognised the man anywhere.

'Master Carolan!' the butler exclaimed after a few seconds.

The old harper stirred from his sleep and cocked his head in the direction of the old serving man. 'William?' he said in a feeble voice. 'William, is that you? Are you still with us?'

'I am, Master Carolan. Welcome to Ballyfarnon.'

'I am afraid this may be my last visit,' Turlough coughed. 'I have been taken very ill this time. And this is the coldest March I can remember.'

'The weather will not break,' William agreed. 'It may as well be the dark days of January for all the snow and ice we've had.'

Hugh climbed down from his seat beside the coachman and stood by the butler with the harp case slung over his shoulder.

'How are you feeling now, master?' his loyal servant asked

him, brushing the snowflakes from his own coat as he spoke and rubbing his hands together inside his leather gloves.

'Much better,' Turlough lied with a smile in his voice to hide the truth from the other two men.

'Is her ladyship about?' Hugh asked William.

'I'll go and fetch her to you,' the butler replied, turning on his heel. He had barely crossed the distance when the kitchen door opened and an old woman appeared, leaning on the arm of a much younger girl.

The lady wrapped a shawl about her shoulders and then held her hands tightly in front of her against the cold. The young girl held an arm about the old woman to stop her shaking with the cold.

'Who is it, William?' the woman called out in a voice weak with age but still full of authority.

'It is Master Carolan, my lady,' the butler reported and the old woman's eyes lit up as if the years had dropped away from her and she was young again.

'Turlough?' she cried in delight and she pushed the young girl at her side away. With surprising agility Mrs MacDermot was off across the courtyard, making for the coach, and her young companion was left standing at the kitchen door for a few seconds in bewilderment.

The girl gasped as she realised the ground was icy and treacherous. Then she was off after Mrs MacDermot like a greyhound after the hare.

Suddenly the old lady's back was straight, there was a spring in her step and a broad smile on her face. Her eyes shone like the old days when the house was full of guests and the music went on until the rising of the sun.

When Mrs MacDermot came to the door of the coach, Hugh stepped respectfully back so she could get a good view of his master. She leaned against the vehicle for a few seconds to catch her breath and then peered inside, her eyes adjusting to the darkness of the interior. Then her face suddenly dropped and the joy was replaced by lines of deep concern.

'Turlough?' she said again. 'Mother of God, you look like you could do with a whiskey.'

'There's time enough for that,' the harper replied.

'There's never enough time for that,' Hugh replied under his breath and Mrs MacDermot scowled.

'Leave him be with your foolishness,' she told Hugh. 'Can't you see the state he is in?'

The harper sat up. 'It's all right,' he smiled. 'Don't chastise Hugh. He has been very good to me and I have been glad of his company all these years. I don't blame him for being tired of my ways. He has had to bring me home drunk on many's the night and he is entitled to a little sarcasm.'

The harper leaned forward to cough and his whole body shook with the effort. It was a damp cough. It came from the chest and not from the throat. It was the kind of cough that often took young children and old folk to their graves in the depth of winter.

'How long have you had that?' the old woman pressed, understanding that the situation must be very serious. 'When did this illness come upon you?'

'In November,' Hugh answered for his master. 'That is why we could not be here for Christmas. The master was in bed at Delany's straining to breathe. I thought he was going to leave us then.'

'I wasn't going to die at Delany's,' Turlough scoffed. 'And risk being buried in Dublin? And I wasn't going to pass on without composing one last piece of music.'

'We'll get you into a nice warm bed with a fire at your feet,' Mrs MacDermot told him. 'And I'll send for the doctor.'

She turned to the girl standing at her elbow. 'Go inside and tell the cook to brew up some willowbark. That will ease the cough a little.'

The girl stood there, weighing up her duty to the old lady and the order she had been given.

'I was commanded to stay by your side at all times,' the girl said meekly.

'Do as you are told!' Mrs MacDermot insisted, raising her voice to show her temper was straining. 'I have been walking across this icy courtyard for more years than I care to remember. I know the pitfalls and the bad patches because I fell on my backside many times when I was your age. I am not likely to do it now.'

The girl curtsied and ran off to the kitchen without raising another objection.

Mrs MacDermot turned back to the harper. 'It does my soul good to see you again, Turlough,' she sighed, taking him by the hands. 'I count myself lucky to be able to call you my friend.'

'I have returned,' Turlough wheezed, 'after all the adventures I've been through, to spend my last days in peace in the house where I received my first learning and my first horse. I have come to show my gratitude for your generosity and your gentle heart which launched me on a grand adventure.'

The old woman squeezed his hands tightly. They were icy cold. Mrs MacDermot no longer made any attempt to restrain her tears but they fell silently. She was determined the harper would not know how upset she was.

'Come inside, Turlough,' she told him in her best motherly tone. 'And I'll have William fetch you a whiskey.'

The harper sat forward and, helped by the old butler, got out of the coach. Then the lady and the harper walked slowly arm in arm, each supporting the other on the way back into the house. O'Flynn and Hugh hovered around behind them in case either showed any sign of stumbling.

Once they were in the kitchen, Mrs MacDermot sat Turlough down by the fire. Then his favourite cup, the largest one in the house, was filled with the finest whiskey and brought to him.

'I have been travelling to the homes of my patrons,' Turlough told her as he sipped his liquor, 'and I have been playing the tune I have composed as my own elegy. I have called it Slan le Ceol, The Farewell to Music. I only wish Cathair could have heard it from my own hands.'

'Cathair McCabe is tutoring the Prince,' Mrs MacDermot

reminded him. 'I will send word to France to tell him of your illness.'

'I wanted my dear friend by my side at the last,' Turlough sighed, 'but I am proud that he is teaching Prince Charlie to play the harp.'

'I would dearly love to hear your composition,' the old woman told him, touching a hand to his shoulder. 'But first you must have some tea made from willowbark. It will soothe your lungs and ease the pain.'

A cup of steaming liquid was set down in front of the harper.

'Are you there, Hugh?'

'I am,' the servant answered.

'Will you deal with that tea?'

'I will,' Hugh replied, rolling his eyes. And then he poured the liquor into the tea, swirled it about and tipped the whole mixture back into Turlough's whiskey cup.

'That should do it,' Hugh told him. 'Have a taste and see what you think.'

The harper put his lips to the cup and winced, but he drank the whole lot down quickly.

'It's the only way I can get him to drink tea,' Hugh explained. 'He doesn't like the taste of any waters that are not flavoured with a touch of whiskey.'

'I am not sure that willowbark is entirely beneficial when taken in that manner,' Mrs MacDermot smiled, raising her eyebrows in amusement. 'But if it means you are getting even a little benefit from the herb, then I suppose I will have to accept it.'

'I will play the new melody for you the moment my fingers have warmed up and I can feel them again,' Turlough declared. 'They are already beginning to tingle so it should not be long.'

'There is no need to hurry, my friend,' the old lady assured him. 'You are welcome to stay here as long as you wish.'

'I would wish to stay here for the rest of eternity then. But alas, I fear it will not be long,' the harper sighed and coughed again, bringing looks of concern to all who heard it.

'I can barely stay awake for a few hours each day,' Turlough admitted. 'So the sooner I play this tune for you the better.'

'Very well,' Mrs MacDermot said. 'I will have William light the fire in the music room.'

'The room with all the mirrors?' Turlough asked with a waver in his voice.

'You have a good memory, Turlough.'

'I would rather not play in that room, if you don't mind,' the harper told the old lady.

'Why not?'

'It's the mirrors,' he replied. 'They make me feel nervous. I don't like the idea of all those disembodied figures watching me. I cannot even consider that room packed with people. The notion gives me goosebumps and sets my teeth to chattering.'

'You are blind, Turlough,' Mrs MacDermot laughed. 'How could the mirrors possibly make you feel uncomfortable?'

'It is not the mirrors,' the harper insisted. 'It is the thought of all those reflections that upsets me.'

'Very well, then,' the lady smiled. 'To suit you I will have my late husband's library heated and we will listen to your composition there.'

'Thank you, my lady,' the harper answered with some relief.

'As long as the idea of sharing a room with over six hundred books does not bother you at all,' she ventured.

'I haven't read a word for fifty years,' he told her, 'not since the blindness came upon me. I haven't even thought about books for longer than I can remember. That room will do very nicely.'

'Good,' the old lady said, clapping her hands together. 'Then I will go to prepare things. Have you eaten?'

'There was a good breakfast laid out at Squire Reynolds's house,' Hugh told her, 'but the master ate sparingly.'

'Of course he did,' the lady replied. 'He is ill. I will have the cook prepare some nourishing soup which will not tax his digestion.'

'You can talk to me, you know,' Turlough complained. 'I am

not dead yet. I am still in the room and breathing.'

'I am sorry,' the lady offered, realising how rude she'd been. Then she stood up and called for William to go and light the fire in the library. After a short while she followed the butler to supervise the preparations.

The very moment Mrs MacDermot had left the room Hugh leaned in close to his master.

'Is it true that the music room makes you feel uncomfortable?' the servant asked.

'I shake like a leaf in the breeze when I'm seated in there. I always have. Ever since the first time I played there when I was a lad.'

'Why?'

'I have a notion,' Turlough explained, 'that I am reminded of the playing field of the Faeries the night of the hurling match. There were hundreds of souls hovering about before the game and it makes my bones turn to jelly to recall it.'

'Do other rooms affect you in a similar manner?'

'Some do,' Turlough confirmed.

'What about the Nature Room at the house of old Squire Reynolds?' Hugh pressed. 'Did you ever feel uncomfortable there at all?'

'Do you mean the small chamber where the gentlemen used to gather after dinner to listen to my music?'

'That's the one,' the servant confirmed.

'I had no particular feelings about that chamber at all,' the harper replied with a frown. 'Other than the fact that there was never enough air circulating when the doors were closed. I can't think why Reynolds chose a room with no windows in which to listen to me play.'

Then Turlough thought for a few moments. 'Why was it called the Nature Room?'

'That is where the squire kept his collection of studies,' the servant whispered with a mischievous giggle.

'Studies?'

'Nudes.'

'Jesus wept!' the harper exclaimed. 'Paintings of women? Naked?'

'Yes,' Hugh admitted. 'All over the walls. Every inch of space was dedicated to portrayals of women in their natural state.'

'I wish I had known that,' the harper sighed, shaking his head in disappointment. 'It would have made my visits much more interesting.'

'You would not have been able to see the paintings, master,' the servant laughed.

'But I could have imagined them,' Turlough explained with a grin.

Then the harper frowned. 'I always thought the gentlemen were so silent out of respect for my playing, and all the time they were sitting staring at the walls! That's why they were so quiet.'

'I must admit it was difficult to concentrate on the music at times,' Hugh conceded.

'Mother of God,' Turlough said sadly. 'Why didn't anyone tell me?'

'The squire thought you might inadvertently mention the paintings in front of his wife,' Hugh explained, 'so he decided not to tell you at all.'

'Mrs Reynolds didn't know about her husband's collection of studies?'

'She did not,' Hugh smiled.

'So taking me up to the room was just an excuse for all those gentlemen to escape their womenfolk?' the harper gasped in genuine shock. 'And to gaze on the forms of ladies other than their own dear wives?'

'That's right,' the servant replied, wishing he had mentioned this before.

'So every man in that room was unfaithful to his spouse,' Turlough laughed.

'In a manner of speaking,' the servant replied, hurt at the accusation. 'Were you never unfaithful yourself?'

'I was tempted,' Turlough admitted. 'Many times I was tempted. But I stayed loyal to my Mary throughout the years of our marriage.'

'And before you were married?' Hugh asked. 'I'll wager you were a bit of a lad for the ladies.'

'Do you remember that young bull Lord Inchinquin kept out on an island in the middle of a lake for a year?' Turlough asked.

'He put it there to keep the animal away from the cows for a time,' Hugh recalled, 'until the bull reached maturity.'

'Do you remember what that bull did when he was reunited with the cows?'

Hugh thought for a moment, blushed and then smiled broadly. 'I do.'

'I was like that bull among the cows until Mary taught me some sense,' the harper declared. 'I suppose I will see her again soon,' he added with a smile.

At that moment William the butler came back into the kitchen. 'Her ladyship has asked me to show you into the library,' he announced. 'Are you ready?'

'I am,' the harper replied, making the effort to stand. As soon as he was on his feet another coughing fit came upon him and he doubled up in pain. Hugh put an arm around his master to comfort him as best he could.

He had seen Turlough ill many times before. The Galar-breac had left the harper with a weak constitution. But the servant had never witnessed his master suffering this much.

When the fit passed, Turlough stood up straight and struggled to regulate his breathing. Some minutes passed before he put a hand on Hugh's shoulder.

'Let us go,' the harper wheezed, 'before my body gives up its ghost once and for all.'

'You have a way to go before that happens,' Hugh told him, trying to keep his master's spirits up.

'I don't think so,' the harper replied solemnly. 'When the Angel of Death comes calling, you recognise his summons.

Especially if you have been fending off his advances for nearly seventy years.'

O'Flynn took Turlough's arm and Hugh followed on behind them bearing the harp in its seal-skin bag. The library was upstairs but it was close to the bedroom which the maids were preparing for the old harper.

'Things can't be too bad in the MacDermot house then,' Turlough commented when they were halfway up the staircase.

'What do you mean?' O'Flynn asked.

'I'll swear there are twice as many steps here as there were when I was a lad,' the harper replied.

Hugh and the butler laughed but the harper saved his breath for the climb.

At last they came to the top of the stairs and then made directly for the library. Turlough was led to a deeply cushioned chair and the harp was placed at his feet. He leaned into the instrument, caressing the curve of the top and then running his fingers down the thick forepillar, gently touching the carved decorations.

'I will miss the harp,' he told his listeners. 'My instruments have been almost as loyal to me as my servant Hugh Connor, the man known as the Freckled Face.'

Hugh blushed and stepped back to stand by the door to listen.

The household servants were gathering to hear the performance and a few pushed past Hugh in their excitement to find a place to sit. There were not enough chairs so most of them stood around the back wall.

The rumour had passed around the house that the master was gravely ill. Many of the serving staff were by now aware this might be the last time Turlough O'Carolan touched the harp in this life.

'I have sent for Doctor Stafford,' Mrs MacDermot whispered, touching Turlough's shoulder on her way to her seat. 'And Doctor Duigenan will be here this evening. He is my own physician. Do not give up hope yet. This may just be a passing malady.'

'My whole life could be called a passing malady, my lady,'

the harper answered with a little laugh. 'But soon enough I will have this cloud of blindness lifted from me and that thought alone gives me great joy.'

The old lady brushed a tender hand across his forehead and then she went to her seat. The moment she was gone, Turlough ran his fingers tentatively over the wires and then took the little tuning key out of his pocket. Then, with a deft skill, he brought the notes into harmony, carefully adjusting a wire here and there until they sang in a sweet voice together.

Hugh thought then that even though his master's body was slow and tired, his mind was as sharp as ever.

Finally Turlough leaned back in his chair, satisfied with the sound of his instrument. He took a deep breath and placed his hands close to the strings. Then the harper stroked the wires with the tips of his fingers, gently at first, bringing his melody to life with a tenderness that enticed sighs of wonder from his listeners.

The tune began in a plaintive manner, slow and deep. It was a strange air, even to the ears of Hugh. The servant had heard his master play many different pieces to appeal to a wide variety of tastes, Protestant and Catholic, rich and poor; old aristocracy and newly created lords from Scotland and England.

The servant realised, suddenly, that this was one of the few pieces the harper had composed purely for his own pleasure rather than that of his audience. The melody was evocative of the ancient music, the bass notes resounding like great drones and the higher notes delicately dancing with subdued mirth, striving to break out into a merry jig.

Suddenly the tune changed as the harper began the second measure. The melody was now a bright cheerful echo of the opening phrases played in the upper register. At the end of this lively interlude the tune faded a little, slowed, and the master harper reintroduced the first theme.

Now the composition was so mournful that it was all Hugh could do to keep the tears from running down his face. With this tune, he understood, Carolan was truly saying farewell to his life of music, his adventures and his dear friends. And Hugh knew that with this man's passing a whole tradition would likely fade away. Turlough's son had taken up the harp but his playing was unremarkable and his compositions were empty echoes of the master's melodies.

There were perhaps thirty harpers left in the whole of Ireland, scratching an existence from their performances, most barely surviving at all. Wealthy patrons no longer welcomed such travelling musicians; they were more interested in the new music from the Continent. Men like Signor Geminiani were in great demand. The musical fashions of Italy and France had overtaken the tradition of the roving bard. And the poorer folk, which was most of the Irish-speaking population, could offer little more than a meal and a bed for the harpers. So most of the musicians dressed shabbily and looked like beggars.

Turlough O'Carolan had been exceptionally lucky. He had been born at a time when the old order was on the brink of extinction. The harper had been astute enough to realise that the influx of foreigners would bring a change in musical tastes. And so Carolan had adapted to the change.

His patrons and friends, such as Cathair McCabe, had introduced him to a wide circle of folk who became his followers. Turlough was never without a warm bed, a good meal and a glass of the finest.

The master had incorporated aspects of the art music from Italy into his compositions, while retaining a flavour, a hint, of the great Irish music that had been his inspiration and the foundation of his craft. Most of the other harpers had stubbornly refused to play the new music and that was their downfall.

But this last melody, The Farewell to Music, was a purely Irish air. It was haunting and captivating. It could have been composed in the far-off ancient days when harpers truly were accorded the same status as kings.

And in that instant Hugh realised something he had never thought of before. He cast his mind back to the competition between Geminiani and his master. To Hugh there was simply no doubt that Carolan was the finer player. For even though the harper did not embellish his melodies in the same way as the violinist, he was able to enter into the tunes in a way that other musicians could not.

Carolan did not just perform his compositions. He became them. The master was able, perhaps through years of practice, or maybe through a God-given gift, to bring all his emotions to bear in a melody. His dances were the merriest. His laments were heart rending. His tributes to patrons were revealing portraits of the individuals they were dedicated to.

At that moment Turlough slowed the pace of his tune a little and allowed the bass strings to ring over the melody instead of stopping them with the tips of his fingers. This gave an ethereal quality to the melody, a ghostly resonance.

Hugh closed his eyes and easily imagined he was hearing a snippet of the Faerie music. He wondered if his master had heard this tune on a Faerie hill and had remembered it with the intention of performing the piece as his own epitaph.

Just then the tune ended and the harp strings rang out for the last time under the fingers of Turlough O'Carolan. The harper waited until his instrument was perfectly silent. He did not dampen the strings. He wanted to enjoy every last echo humming from his beloved harp.

'I have travelled far,' the harper said in a quiet tone so that his listeners had to lean forward to hear him, 'to come back to this place where it all began. I have a full belly, fine friends and I have led a life untroubled by the strife that has brought ruin to our country and taken the lives of most of my childhood friends. The harp has been my purpose. Music has been my offering to God. And now I offer up my soul to Him in thanks for the precious gifts I have received.'

Turlough paused for a moment, finding it difficult to breathe, but whether it was because of the sickness or an outpouring of emotion, none but he knew.

'Now it is over,' the great harper said finally.

No-one applauded. No-one dared speak or make any sound

at all. It was Mrs MacDermot who moved first and as soon as she stood up the servants went about their business, filing out of the room. Many of them cast a last long glance at this man who was known and welcomed the length and breadth of Ireland.

'I will see you to your bed,' William said softly at the harper's ear. 'You are to have the room you took from me when I was a butler's assistant all those years ago.'

Turlough nodded and pushed the harp forward. As always Hugh was there to take the instrument from him. The servant packed the instrument away in its seal-skin bag as he had done for years.

'I hope you have taught that melody to one of your students,' Mrs MacDermot commented.

'Charles O'Connor, the friend of Doctor Delany, has it,' the harper assured her. 'And he will ensure it is not forgotten. He was putting it down on paper when I left him so that each note would stay in the place I allotted to it and not stray under the fingers of a musician with a poor memory.'

'I am relieved to hear that,' the lady breathed. 'It would be a tragedy indeed if your last and greatest work had been lost to future generations.'

'It is a fine tune,' Turlough agreed, 'and now I am not sure the concerto was my best composition after all. Did I tell you how I dreamed that tune?'

'You did,' the lady replied.

'I thought for a long time that the old harper who taught it to me in my dream was a Faerie or even an angel come to earth to grant me a gift. But now I understand that the old blind man in the vision was myself.'

'Yourself?' Mrs MacDermot asked.

'I haven't seen my own reflection in fifty years,' he told her. 'And so I can't even guess what I might look like now. I still imagine sometimes that I am eighteen years old, even though I know my head is almost completely bald and my stomach rather large. In the dream I did not recognise myself.'

'You are still a handsome man,' she told him.

'I am not,' the harper chortled, 'and I'll thank you not to waste your flattery on me. I have had more than my fair share of fine compliments in this life. And I know that flattery leads to vanity. Heaven help me if I should end up like David Murphy. And at my age!'

Then the harper made the effort to stand and leaned on O'Flynn.

'Padraic, the boatman, told me in my dream,' Turlough stated, recalling his conversation with the fisherman, 'that if I could have looked in the mirror I would have recognised the old man who taught me the concerto. It was myself. There is no other explanation. The music was always flowing through me. It was always looking for a way to travel from the Otherworld into this one which we inhabit. I have been the ferry and the music was my passenger.'

The harper leaned heavily on the butler and coughed a little.

'The Queen of the Faeries,' Turlough went on, 'and her husband—'

'Consort,' Mrs MacDermot corrected him and the harper smiled to think that the old lady might have known the truth about the Sheehans all these years.

'Her consort,' Turlough amended. 'Those two were my patrons as much as you were. I have been well taken care of by those who had faith in me.'

Turlough began coughing again and he gripped Mrs Mac-Dermot's hand tightly as the convulsions rolled over him.

'Now I see you must rest,' the old lady told him. 'We will have plenty of time to talk in the coming days. Do not fear.'

'I pray that we do,' the harper replied, struggling to breathe.

Turlough O'Carolan did not wake again until late the next day. The doctors examined him and told Mrs MacDermot that, regretfully, there was nothing to be done.

Hugh did not leave his master's side for an instant, not even when the old harper was asleep.

'I want to be with him,' the servant told William O'Flynn, 'when the time comes.'

And so the MacDermot household waited a vigil at the harper's side. Two days passed. Then a third. Turlough slept most of the time and whenever he awoke he was fed a little soup and given a whiskey to still the pain of his suffering. For even in his sleep the harper's body was racked with hacking coughs. Then, unexpectedly, on the evening of his sixth day in bed, he woke up feeling much better.

'The cough has left me now,' he told Hugh, 'but I will not live through the night.'

'Nonsense,' the servant replied. 'It's clear you're on the mend. You'll be up and about in a few days, sitting at the harp and drinking like the old days.'

'Mary used to tell me that I should play the harp as much as possible in this life,' Turlough sighed, 'because the place where I am going afterwards does not have any harps at all.'

Hugh laughed half-heartedly at the joke. He did not want to show how worried he was but he did not feel very mirthful either. And he did not want to admit to himself that his master was leaving. It was as if he were clinging to Turlough's hand, begging him not to go.

'I am looking forward to seeing Mary again,' the harper confided. 'For on the island there is no blindness.'

Turlough reached out and took Hugh's hand, holding it tightly.

'I want you to tell me something,' the master said. 'And I want to hear nothing but the truth from you. Do you swear?'

'I swear.'

'Was I a good harper?'

'What are you talking about?' Hugh gasped. 'There was never a greater harper in all of Ireland.'

'How do you know?'

'I have listened to you play these many years,' the servant

soothed. 'And I have heard almost every other harper in the land perform. Your music and your harping have no equal.'

William O'Flynn came into the room at that moment.

'Ireland is in mourning indeed,' he informed them. 'For I have just heard that David Murphy passed away but a week ago at his house in Dublin.'

'Ireland mourned for the foolish man when he was alive,' Hugh frowned. 'I can't see her wasting much energy on him now that he's gone.'

'I have heard there was a grand farewell party for him,' William said. 'It lasted throughout the night.'

'Folk will take any excuse for a drink and a stomach full of sweetbreads,' Hugh quipped.

'He was not a bad man,' Turlough interrupted and Hugh's eyebrows raised at this change in his master. 'David Murphy was conceited, selfish, silly and unequalled in his snobbery,' the old harper went on. 'But I wouldn't say he was a bad man. Everyone has their faults.'

'Well some folk must have regarded him highly,' O'Flynn cut in. 'His wake lasted until dawn.'

'Is that the sign of a good harper?' Turlough asked. 'Can it be measured by the duration of the wake?'

'It is the sign of a well-loved person,' Hugh answered. 'I suppose David Murphy must have had some admirers. But it's just as likely his friends were enthusiastically clearing out Murphy's cellar.'

'Glad I am that I don't have a cellar then,' Turlough laughed. 'If there is a wake, it'll be because folk are sincere in their mourning.'

'Your music will live on long after you have gone,' Hugh told his master.

'Do you think so?'

'I am certain,' the servant replied. 'I will carry the concerto in my mind for the rest of my life and that means it will live on.'

'So if Murphy's wake lasted through the night,' the harper continued, 'how long do you think they'll wake me?'

'That depends.' William had a mischievous tone in his voice. 'A poor harper might not be missed at all and the wake might be a subdued affair with a few close friends. Over by midnight.' The butler snapped his fingers.

'A moderately good harper could expect that his friends and acquaintances would sit with the body through the dark hours until sunrise, though there might not be enough food, drink and tobacco to last them their vigil.'

'A very good harper,' Hugh went on, picking up the train of thought, 'could expect an all-night party such as the one Murphy received.'

'A great harper,' William stated, 'would certainly still have a few friends dancing around the coffin at midmorning the next day.'

'Make sure there is plenty of whiskey, Hugh,' Turlough told his servant.

'There will be. I have just finished distilling a large batch which I hoped would see us through the spring.'

'I will need it to see me to the other side,' the harper sighed and his mouth dropped open.

A short while passed and Hugh thought his master must be asleep again. He was just about to rise when Turlough spoke.

'William?' he whispered with failing strength. 'Are you there?'

'I am,' the old butler replied softly.

'Will you fetch me a last drop of whiskey?'

'I have it here in your favourite cup,' came the reply.

'The liquor and I have been close friends for such a long while,' Turlough told him, 'it would be a terrible shame for me to go on my way without one last kiss.'

O'Flynn held the cup to Turlough's lips and the old harper tasted a drop of it on his tongue and then he fell asleep again. And a short while later, with his friends present, Turlough O'Carolan, Chief Musician of Ireland, passed away from this world into the next.

FIFTEEN

Edward sipped his cup of whiskey and looked hard at old Hugh Connor, the former servant of the great Carolan.

'And how long did his wake last?' the young man asked.

'Four days,' Hugh answered proudly. 'Four days of solid drinking, dancing and merry-making. Six thousand people came to his funeral on the fourth day and there was never a greater gathering of harpers and nobility ever after again in the whole of Ireland. A hundred clergy sent him off and the tears flowed freely for a week afterwards.'

'He was well loved,' Denis nodded. 'And that was a grand party. That was where Hugh and I first became firm friends, for the wake turned into a great festival of harping. Every harper in the country came to pay their last respects.'

'This old bugger and I knew each other before that, of course,' Hugh explained, gesturing toward Denis. 'But it was at the funeral I decided to become the harp-bearer of Denis Hempson.'

'You carried his harp, just as you had done for Carolan?'

'I did,' the old distiller confirmed. 'But I had no heart for travelling any more. I left Denis after a year and took up my distilling with serious dedication.'

'And praise be to God that you did,' Denis said. 'For you were always getting me lost out in the countryside. I don't know how Carolan put up with you and your sightless eyes.'

'I was not blind in those days,' Hugh protested.

'That is a matter of opinion,' Denis replied.

'I like to think that my master took the boat across to his island,' Hugh sighed. 'And that waiting for him on the other side was Mary and all his friends who had passed away during his long life. I like to think that his last thoughts were of that dream world where he learned the concerto. And I like to think that I will visit him there one day.'

'You're too young to be talking that way, Hugh Connor,' Denis rebuked his friend. 'Folk like ourselves do not die young. We are too fond of a drink, a party and a bit of mischief.'

'And yet in my mind I can imagine Turlough O'Carolan playing at the hurling amongst the Faerie kind,' Hugh grinned. 'For in that place everyone is young, healthy and happy. I can see him dancing with the Faerie Queen and with Mary. I know he is still playing his music for those who will listen. For he ate of the red Faerie fruit and he drank deep from the spring at the foot of the altar.'

The old distiller breathed deeply and put the whiskey cup to his mouth. When he had taken a sip he said, 'Will you not play me the Concerto now, Denis?'

'It was a good tale,' the old harper conceded. 'But I am too tired just now. You should have asked me earlier.'

'I did ask you earlier and you told me you would play it later,' Hugh pointed out.

'Now there's a contradiction,' Denis agreed, nodding. 'For at this present moment it is too late to be performing the Concerto. Playing the harp is all about a good sense of timing.'

'I'll give you a good sense of timing,' Hugh snapped, 'you old drunkard. Sucking the whiskey out of my cups like a lord and nothing to give back for the pleasure of a fine drop.'

'I will play the Concerto,' Denis protested. 'I have given my word. But not tonight. I don't feel well enough prepared just now.'

'What more bloody preparation do you need?'

'A good night's sleep,' the old harper yawned. 'It must be close to three in the morning.'

Daniel took a watch from his pocket and looked at the face.

'It is three-thirty,' he groaned. 'I have to be up at six to take a delivery of barley for the next distilling.'

'Off to bed with you then,' Hugh demanded. 'I don't want you being late for that appointment. The whole year's supply depends upon it.'

'Yes, Grandfather,' Daniel replied with a tone of resignation and then he got up to guide Denis back to his lodgings.

'Goodnight, Hugh,' Denis wished his host as he was making for the door.

'You'll play it for me tomorrow, won't you?'

'In all likelihood I will,' the old harper answered. 'For I feel a burst òf inspiration coming on and that is always a good sign. Goodnight, Master Edward,' Denis ended and then Daniel led the old man out of the house and down to the village.

'A man in Dublin offered me twenty pounds,' Hugh told Edward, 'if I would relate that tale to him from beginning to end.'

'And did he believe all of it?'

'Don't be rude!' Hugh barked. 'Every word of it was true as far as I know. For I had a great part of it from the master's own lips.

'This fellow from Dublin was a scholar at Trinity,' Hugh went on. 'He told me he could not write down anything in his book that wasn't already well documented.'

'And so most of your story was useless to him,' Edward realised.

'Indeed,' Hugh replied, 'since few folk in my master's day could read. So not much was recorded in books. I had a little reading but then I travelled with the most famous harper in history. I was his guide. So I had to learn some words. Those few tales of Carolan's life that were written down have been lost in the wars or the upheavals.'

'You cannot prove a word of your story?'

'That is correct,' Hugh admitted. 'So the gentleman from

Trinity would not pay me twenty pounds, though I suspect he used the stories anyway.'

'I suspect he did,' Edward nodded and then he placed a hand on Hugh's shoulder. 'I believe you,' he said sincerely.

'Do you?' Hugh answered in surprise.

'I do. It is too fanciful a tale to be an invention. And even if there are moments when credibility is thinly spread, it is a good story.' Edward found himself smiling broadly. He wondered if perhaps there was more truth to Hugh's tales than he had thought possible.

'Perhaps you'll write it down some day,' the old distiller pressed.

'I might.'

'It would be a greater service you would be doing for Ireland than running about shooting redcoats in the back of the head.'

'You may be right,' Edward conceded. 'You may be right.'

'I am off to bed,' Hugh sighed. 'I am exhausted from all these tales.'

'Goodnight,' Edward wished him.

'I am glad I decided you were too dangerous to be let loose on the world,' Hugh told his guest.

'Is that what you decided?' Edward laughed.

'I did. I was afraid that you would draw attention to my own unlawful activities. And so I thought to keep you here as surety against discovery. But now I can see that it was fate brought you to this house. And I am glad to have made your acquaintance.'

'I have been very glad to make yours also,' Edward replied with sincerity. All of a sudden he had a yearning to stay here and live in peace, listening to stories every night. The cause of liberty seemed empty somehow after a few nights with Hugh.

'I suppose you will be going in the morning?'

'If that is all right with you,' the rebel ventured.

'As you wish, young master,' Hugh shrugged. 'I would not wish to hold you against your will. But I do believe I will miss you.'

Hugh stood up.

'If ever you should decide,' the old man whispered, 'to invest some of your father's money in the whiskey distillation business, I hope you will not hesitate to contact me.'

'If I were to consider such a move,' Edward promised, 'it is to you I would come for advice.'

Then the rebel remembered something. 'What of the ninety pounds?'

'Which ninety pounds are you speaking of?'

'The money you and Seamus and your friends lost,' Edward reminded him, 'through my rash action in killing D'Arcy.'

'You weren't considering reneging on the agreement, were you?' Hugh stammered in shock.

'No indeed.'

'Then send the money down to us from Dublin,' Hugh sighed. 'Don't worry. I know where you live and my friends in the town would not let you board a ship to escape the country without settling the debt.'

'I see,' the rebel smiled.

'You are a fine lad, Edward,' the distiller told him, 'but business is business.'

Hugh found his way to the door and waited there for Mhairgead to return after checking the horses for the night.

'My grand-daughter has an eye for you,' the old distiller confided. 'And I think the two of you would make a good match. She is still young, though she has two children. And though I know you have your heart set on a rebel's life, if you should decide to remain here you could call this house your home. And you'd be as safe from the English as you would be in New York.'

'And what would you be asking in return for the guarantee of my safety?' Edward smiled. He had learned one or two things about Hugh from listening to his tale.

'You have wounded me, Master Edward,' Hugh sputtered. 'I am almost speechless.'

'Almost, but not quite, I'll wager,' the young man laughed.

'Daniel cannot run the distilling alone, and his two younger brothers have no mind to help him. They have their own plans. And I am sure that with your father's contacts in Dublin we could expand our business to the town itself. No more waiting half a year for country folk to settle their accounts. We could deal with the quality houses and the taverns of Dublin. With the loss of Major D'Arcy my income is severely compromised.'

Hugh thought for a moment, then decided to say what was on his mind.

'And with your contacts among the rebels,' the old distiller said under his breath, 'we could make a few pennies from selling arms. And be helping the cause at the same time.'

'I'll think about it,' Edward conceded, not giving anything away.

'I would be happy to arrange for the payment of your debt to the local people to be spread out over a longer period,' Hugh offered.

'I would have to consider your proposal more carefully,' Edward hesitated, beginning to feel nervous about being trapped in this place for the rest of his life. 'I can't give you an answer tonight. What of the revolution? I can't simply leave my comrades to fight on without me, can I?'

'I don't see why not,' Hugh laughed. 'The revolution was doing fine before you came along. I don't doubt that the rebels will still carry on with it after you have forsaken them.'

'I don't know if I can forsake them.'

'I have seen half a dozen rebellions in my short life,' the old man said, shaking his head. 'Not one of them achieved anything but the senseless slaughter of the flower of Irish youth. King James never came back to us as he promised. His son made a feeble attempt to return. His grandson Charlie was chased about the Scottish highlands disguised as a woman. I believe the Stewarts have had their chance. Now we must live with their successors.'

'Ireland could be free of all kings,' Edward insisted. 'The Americans have no monarch. They have a congress.'

'Nonsense,' Hugh dismissed. 'If there are no kings to keep

order, and for folk to respect, the world would lapse into confusion, war and famine.'

'That's what Ireland has suffered for a hundred years under an English king,' the young man pointed out.

'I would rather suffer hardship under a poor king than under a committee of faceless men who call themselves a parliament. For at least when there is a king the people have one man to focus their anger upon. Every rogue in a parliament blames the next fellow. No-one takes responsibility. And the disgruntled people soon give up any hope of having their voices heard.'

Edward smiled at that notion. 'But the whole point of the American Republic is to give the ordinary man a voice. In America popular sentiment rules the government.'

'The ordinary man doesn't want a voice,' Hugh laughed. 'He wants food in his belly, a roof over his head and a good woman in his bed at the end of the day. Show me a government that offers those comforts and I'll show you a government that has won the popular sentiment.'

Mhairgead coughed as she entered the room and she took Hugh by the arm.

'I'll take you to your cottage now, Grandfather,' she said.

'Very well,' the old man replied, making sure he had his pipe in his pocket. 'I must be well drunk tonight!' he exclaimed. 'I haven't felt this light on my feet for years.'

'Come along. It is nearly sunrise and I have a full working day to put in tomorrow,' Mhairgead scolded. 'It is all right for you. You can lie about until you have the inclination to rise. I have to be up to get the breakfasts ready, bake the bread and draw the well.'

'I'm moving as fast as I can, woman!'

'Will you still be awake when I get back?' Mhairgead asked Edward.

'I might be,' the rebel answered cautiously.

'I won't be long,' she told him.

'Right then,' the young man replied and put his nose in his whiskey cup, feeling slightly uncomfortable.

A few minutes later, when she had led her grandfather out to his own cottage and settled him in bed, Mhairgead returned. She walked straight up to Edward. Then, taking a handful of his hair gently, she tilted his head back and placed her lips on his.

The young man dropped his cup and struggled briefly but without conviction. And when he felt her hands caressing his face, he succumbed at last.

'Do you think we should be doing this in your grandfather's house?' Edward asked as Mhairgead straddled his lap.

'Didn't you hear him?' she giggled. 'All he can think about is us getting married and you taking a stake in the distilling.'

'What would he say if he walked in on us now?' Edward inquired, a hint of fear in his voice.

'Nothing,' she replied. 'He would just strangle you without a word.'

Edward sat back in shock and then caught the mischievous glint in Mhairgead's eye. She was beautiful, he had to admit. And she knew what she wanted from life. He blushed again, realising he had been deeply attracted to her from the first moment he had laid eyes on her. There was an air about Mhairgead too that must have been passed down to her through Hugh. A sense of the joy of life; the humour to be found in it through all the struggles. A sense of liberty.

'He'd have to catch me first,' he declared. 'And if the whole English army can't find me, I doubt that an old man with no eyes will be able to get his hands around my rebel throat.'

The two of them laughed together and fell back into an embrace. And there they stayed, talking, teasing and giggling until the sun rose and the room was bathed in the blue light of early morning.

It was almost noon when old Hugh made his way into the house with the aid of his stick to guide him. Because of the lateness of the hour he expected to find Edward sitting by the fire sipping broth. But when the old man had found his own familiar chair he could not sense the young man's presence in the room at all.

It crossed his mind that the young rebel had decided to leave after all. Straightaway his heart began to race at the missed opportunity.

'Edward?' he called out. But there was no answer.

'Edward, are you about at all?'

A few seconds later there was a loud groan and the sound of a man yawning noisily.

The old distiller turned in his seat, a frown on his face, as he tried to discern where the sounds had originated. He turned his head in the direction of the bed that had been made up for his guest. But the noise was not coming from there.

Then Hugh heard a pair of bare feet hit the floorboards and the old man's blood began immediately to boil.

The distiller knew this house like he knew no other place on earth. Every part of the floor had its own distinct sound. Every board, every roof beam reflected noises in its own peculiar way. By Hugh's reckoning the young rebel had just rolled out of Mhairgead's bed.

'Where are you, Edward?' he inquired, trying to disguise the rage that was bubbling up inside him.

'I am over here,' the young man answered. 'Good morning to you.'

'It is after noon,' Hugh spat.

'Is it?'

'Is it, indeed?' the old distiller cried, standing up and shaking his stick in Edward's direction. 'What are you doing sleeping in Mhairgead's bed?'

Edward did not answer.

'Did you hear me?' the old man shouted. 'What were you doing sleeping in my grand-daughter's bed?'

'I wasn't,' Edward lied.

'You can't fool me,' Hugh shrieked. 'You have defiled my darling Mhairgead's honour!'

The old man crossed the floor, holding his stick high and knocking the table aside in his fury.

'I invited you into this house and gave you the best of whiskey, food and storytelling and this is how you treat me! You seduce my innocent grandchild under my own roof!'

'I didn't seduce her,' Edward protested. 'She was the one—'

'And you are not even man enough to admit that it was your doing!' the old distiller bellowed. 'Daniel, come here this minute! I want you to teach this lad a lesson.'

Edward muttered an obscenity, realising that he was in real trouble now. If Daniel took offence, all hell would likely break loose. The rebel buttoned his breeches and bent down to put on his shoes as the old man stormed across the room. Edward was just pulling his second shoe on when he heard a sound beside him on the bed.

It was Hugh's stick thudding into the bedclothes.

'I'll kill you myself!' Hugh cried. 'You thief of a maiden's honour!'

'Mhairgead is no maid,' Edward pointed out indignantly. 'She has two children.'

'Would you insult her dignity as well? You treacherous little Dubliner! I'll have you drowned in a vat of your own urine for this. To think I wasted two nights of tales and all that whiskey on you. And what for? So that you could sleep with my precious Mhairgead and steal her priceless maidenhead.'

'She has two children,' Edward reminded the old man emphatically, but no sooner had he spoken than the walking stick found its mark, cracking him across the back of the head. The young man was stunned for a moment, then he ducked for cover, crawling as fast as he could across the floor to get out of Hugh's reach.

'Hugh,' Edward said soothingly. 'It is not my fault.'

'There you are!' the old man exclaimed as soon as the rebel had spoken. 'I'll kill you!'

'Hugh!' the young man shrieked as the old distiller made a lunge at him with the stick.

'This is partly your doing,' Edward reasoned and at that comment Hugh stopped to think.

'How could this possibly be my doing?'

'You were encouraging her to find a good husband,' Edward reminded him. 'And you kept telling me what a fine wife she would make.'

'I wanted you to marry her,' Hugh shouted, 'not make love to her!'

Edward frowned but thought it wise not to point out the contradiction inherent in that statement.

The old man whirled his stick around his head again, knocking all the cups off the table. 'I'll murder you with my own two hands,' the old man vowed. 'You will not escape me, you vagabond!'

While the cups were still scattering across the floor both Daniel and Mhairgead burst into the room to see what the fuss was all about.

'What's the matter here?' the grandson asked.

'I'll tell you what the matter is,' Hugh snarled. 'This fine fellow who has been drinking our whiskey and sharing our fireside has seduced your sister Mhairgead.'

'What are you talking about?' the red-haired man laughed, shaking his head.

'When he rose just now,' Hugh told him, 'he slipped out of Mhairgead's bed.'

'Is this true?' Daniel asked Edward in a threatening tone.

'It is,' Mhairgead cut in defiantly before the young rebel had a chance to answer, crossing the floor to stand by him.

'What do you think you are doing?' Daniel stuttered. 'To sleep with a guest in your grandfather's house.'

'You slept with your wife in that bed in the next room long before you were both married,' she reminded her brother. 'I know because her moans kept me up all night.'

'What the Devil?' Hugh stammered in shock. 'Have you turned this house into a den of seething passion? My own grandchildren sleeping with all sorts under my own roof?'

'She isn't all sorts,' Daniel replied, 'Bridie is my wife.'

'But she wasn't when you first slept with her,' the old man countered.

'No,' the red-haired man admitted.

'Then you can't judge me, Daniel Connor McHugh,' Mhairgead stated confidently.

'Will you shut up!' Daniel hissed at his sister.

'You dare not rebuke me, brother,' she smiled. 'For you are as guilty of this sin as I am. And I have only done this once. You also had young Kathleen and her sister Moira.'

'At the same time?' Hugh gasped, leaning heavily on his stick.

'No, Grandfather,' Daniel reassured him. 'It was on two different nights.'

Then Hugh's grandson put a hand to his forehead and closed his eyes.

The old distiller stood with his mouth wide open, absolutely speechless.

'Jesus,' Daniel moaned. 'I should have kept my mouth shut.

'Shouldn't you sit down, Grandfather,' he suggested, adopting a calmer tone.

'How did I not know of this?' the old man asked under his breath. 'My dear innocent grandchildren mating like rabbits under my own roof and I had no idea.'

Hugh shook his head and leaned back toward his chair. Daniel hurried over and grabbed him so he would not fall over.

'Take your hands off of me, you philanderer!' the old distiller spat.

'I don't understand,' Hugh muttered. 'Where did I go wrong?'

'Are you trying to tell me you never spent a wild night with a pretty girl?' Daniel frowned.

'Never under her grandfather's own roof!' the old man shrieked. 'And I never spent the night with two sisters!'

'It was on two separate nights, Grandfather,' Daniel reminded him. 'I never managed—'

Daniel closed his eyes again and stopped speaking. The room fell silent as each person finished the red-haired man's sentence in their own imagination. Mhairgead stifled a giggle. Edward shook his head.

'Mother of God,' Hugh whispered to himself. 'Saint Bridget and all the Holy Hosts of Heaven. I can hardly believe my poor old ears.'

'Sit down, Grandfather,' Daniel said softly, hoping to appease the old man's anger.

'Did you know about this?' Hugh asked his grandson.

'Do you mean Mhairgead and Edward?'

'Of course I mean Mhairgead and Edward!' the old man bellowed.

'I had an idea that something might come of it,' Daniel admitted.

'Now they'll never be married and Mhairgead will be an old spinster,' Hugh moaned.

'What are you talking about?' his grand-daughter laughed.

'Now that he's had his will of you, he will surely not marry you. That's the way with young men. Especially rebels.'

'Don't be ridiculous,' Mhairgead scoffed. 'Would you buy a horse without riding it round the field once?'

Edward raised his eyebrows.

'You don't need to sleep with a horse to be able to discern whether or not it will bear your weight,' Hugh snapped.

At that very moment Denis came in through the door led by Finbar, Daniel's youngest brother.

'God bless all here,' the old harper wished them.

'Be quiet, you old fool!' Hugh shouted.

'I know how you feel,' the old harper commiserated, touching a hand to his forehead. 'I woke with a powerful head-throb myself this morning. I am not as young as I used to be.'

'I have just caught my grand-daughter sleeping with this young rascal,' Hugh fumed.

'Sleeping were they?' Denis asked. 'And what's the harm in that?'

'They were doing a damn sight more than just dozing off.'

'And you caught them at it?'

'Not at it,' Hugh admitted. 'Mhairgead was outside and he was in her bed.'

'She's a wise girl to have taken that precaution with a young man,' Denis nodded.

'What are you talking about?' the old distiller raged.

'They couldn't have been up to much,' the harper concluded, 'if he was in here and she was outside. Do you have a drop for an old man with a sore head?'

'My grand-daughter's honour has been compromised!'

'Are you feeling well?' Denis asked his old friend. 'Do you think a drink would help you sort things out in your mind.'

'Don't speak to me like that, you dottery old bugger!' Hugh yelled. 'I'm not mad. I heard the floorboards under Mhairgead's bed creak just as Edward was rising from slumber.'

'The floorboards?' the old harper repeated, trying to work out what his friend was on about.

'Don't you see?' Hugh sighed with exasperation. 'He must have spent the night with her.'

'Are you trying to tell me,' Denis frowned, 'that you recognise the very creaking of the floorboards near Mhairgead's bed.'

'That is true enough,' Hugh responded with a nod of his head.

'You couldn't tell the difference between the sound of a floorboard and the noise of a flour mill,' the old harper laughed.

Hugh turned red but, unaware of his friend's change in colour, Denis went cheerfully on, spurred to some personal reminiscence.

'My cousin worked in a flour mill when I was a lad. My young brother and I would take his dinner to him whenever he worked through the night. Terrible work it was too. He would come home caked with the white powder and weevils in his hair.'

'Will you shut up about your bloody cousin!' Hugh yelled.

'There's no call for such rudeness,' the harper admonished as he found his chair by the fire. 'I came to give you a tune, not to become embroiled in your imaginative ramblings.'

'I heard the flour mills creak!' Hugh screamed.

'The floorboards,' Edward piped up.

'What?' the old man snapped, cocking his head in the young man's direction. 'What did you say?'

'You heard the *floorboards* creak.'

'I know I bloody well heard them creak! Why do you think I'm so upset?' Hugh bellowed, really losing his temper now. 'You stay out of this! It is none of your bloody business.'

Edward put a hand to his forehead, wishing he had not said anything.

Hugh rounded on his grand-daughter. 'I should have known you would turn out like this. Your mother couldn't keep her hands off anything in breeches. My poor son nearly died of grief at some of the things his wife got up to.'

'How dare you speak of my mother like that!' Mhairgead cried. 'She was a fine upstanding woman who reared me properly and had a hard lonely life while my father was away at sea for years at a time.'

'My son only went away to sea because of the terrible things she did to him,' Hugh spat back. 'She must have been from Dublin. Everyone knows the folk of that city are licentious and driven to sin. The proof of that is skulking somewhere in this very house.'

'Ah, Dublin. What a place,' Denis sighed nostalgically but everyone ignored him.

'My mother was a Kelly!' Mhairgead snapped. 'She was of pure Irish stock. She didn't have a drop of Dublin blood in her veins.'

'I think you'll find the Kellys were Normans,' Edward interjected.

'What?' Mhairgead asked, distracted for a moment.

'The Kellys aren't actually Irish at all if you trace their family tree back far enough,' the rebel repeated. 'They came over with the Norman invasions hundreds of years ago.'

'Shut up!' Hugh and Mhairgead yelled in perfect unison and then they turned their attention back to their argument.

Edward sighed and sat down on the edge of the bed.

'Wait a minute,' Denis cut in. 'It doesn't really matter.'

'I wish you people would stay out of our family discourses,' Hugh bellowed.

'Are they going to be married?' the old harper asked.

'What?'

'That is what you wanted all along, wasn't it?'

'Yes, of course it is,' Hugh hissed.

'Well why don't you ask them?' Denis said softly.

Hugh took a few deep breaths as he considered this suggestion. Then he turned to where Mhairgead was standing. She said nothing so he addressed Edward.

'Well, young fellow, now that you have partaken of my grand-daughter's gracious gifts, are you willing to wed her?'

'I am,' Edward answered without any hesitation.

'You are?' Hugh was momentarily caught off guard.

'I am.'

'There you are,' Denis chuckled. 'All settled. Now, can we have a whiskey to celebrate?'

'Why didn't you tell me?' Hugh asked, his voice full of suspicion.

'You wouldn't give me a chance,' Edward protested.

'Very well then,' Hugh said as he thought about this latest development. It took him but a few seconds to adjust to the situation and then he blew the air out of his mouth and grunted.

'I am glad you have come to your senses at last,' he told Edward. 'I was afraid I would have to beat some charity into you. It soothes my heart to think that you and Daniel will take over the family business in my place once I have passed on to my spiritual reward.'

'We're off to America,' Mhairgead interrupted.

'You're what?' Hugh gasped.

'We're going to America to help raise an army to liberate Ireland from the oppressive English invaders,' she said.

'You're talking like that young rebel now,' the old distiller cried, his face reddening again. 'Has this whole house gone mad?'

'I can't just sit back and calmly watch my people suffer under the yoke of the foreigners,' Mhairgead explained.

'I don't believe I am hearing this,' Hugh muttered. 'And what of your children?'

'Daniel and his wife are going to care for them until we return,' she told him defiantly.

'I forbid it!' the old man declared. 'I forbid you to go off and marry this stupid young adventurer. How will you live? He won't be able to support you. He hasn't even got the sense to know when he's had enough to drink!'

'I am in love with him,' Mhairgead declared.

'I don't care one whit for all your talk of love. I will not have my grand-daughter married to a rebel. I won't have you risking your life in politics. It is no pastime for a young woman. Or a decent man for that matter.'

'But you buy arms from crooked English majors and sell them to the rebels,' Edward pointed out. 'You are already involved in politics.'

'That is an entirely different matter,' the old man snapped. 'That is business. May the saints preserve us if ever politics should become a business. Where would we be then? The two do not mix. They are a dangerous combination.'

'Where do you think these arms are bound?' Edward asked. 'They are going to end up in the hands of rebels.'

'I make a good return on those arms. I do not ask what they are to be used for. And I do not deal in gunpowder or shot. The weapons are useless without ammunition and powder.'

'But in that case aren't you just taking advantage of the rebels?'

'Don't let him fool you,' Denis smiled. 'That old man was one of the heroes of forty-five.'

'What?' Edward exclaimed.

'He went off to Scotland to fight for Bonnie Prince Charlie,' the old harper laughed, 'in seventeen forty-five. He was nearly sixty years of age at the time. And he's been an ardent rebel ever since. Seamus Kelly will tell you that and so would Major D'Arcy if he had the breath in him to speak.'

'That is enough!' Hugh bellowed and his face turned bright red again. 'I am not a bloody rebel! And I will not be berated in my own house!'

Edward opened his mouth to speak, 'Can you—'

'Shut up!' Hugh cut in. 'How do you think you were fed for the last two days? It was only the money I earned delivering those muskets that put food on the table. I risk my life for this family and this is the thanks I get.'

'You didn't risk your life,' Daniel piped up. 'I was the one who went out to meet the major and take the wagonload off him. Finbar and Francis came with me. As I recall, you didn't lift a finger to help.'

'I have provided you with a steady income through my many acquaintances in the military,' Hugh scolded him. 'And you should be grateful.'

'Don't you think you should sit down and have a drop of whiskey?' Denis suggested. 'You are just working yourself into a state.'

'I am not working myself into a state!' Hugh screamed at the top of his lungs. The words emptied out of him with such force that he stood for a few seconds gasping to breathe.

Suddenly the old man's face paled and he staggered a little, reaching out with his stick to find his chair. In a second it seemed as if he was choking but he managed to gain control again and pointed his stick across the room.

'You knew all about this,' Hugh said to Daniel. 'You knew all along they were going off to America and you said nothing.'

'It was only this morning that Mhairgead discussed the children with me,' Daniel countered.

'Under my own roof,' the old man coughed and he was suddenly so weak he had to lean heavily on his stick.

'Grandfather!' Mhairgead cried out as she ran to his side. 'Are you all right?'

Hugh sat down in his chair by the fire, shaking visibly.

'It is the shock,' he managed to say in between coughs. 'It is all too much for me to bear.'

Daniel narrowed his eyes, suspecting this was one of Hugh's ploys.

'You are an old man,' Denis pointed out. 'I wouldn't be surprised if this proved to be your last little tantrum. Sean Farrell went that way when he discovered his old cow at it with a Protestant's bull in the neighbouring field. It stopped his heart dead to think his fine beast, the one he had fed the best hay for years, could go and turn to the Presbyterians for physical solace.'

Hugh lifted his stick as if he were going to strike at the old harper but the hand that held it suddenly went limp. The walking stick clattered to the floor. Hugh closed his eyes and groaned. Then he was silent.

Edward frowned and crossed the room to kneel beside the old man.

'He's still breathing,' the young rebel announced. 'He's just fainted. We'd best get him to bed.'

'Pretty young women, politics and muskets,' Denis said, shaking his head. 'A lethal combination.'

'Would you like a whiskey?' Daniel offered.

'That would be grand,' the harper replied. 'Just a small one. The sun has not yet set and I don't want to be rushing into anything.'

'As you wish, Denis.'

'Daniel,' Edward said insistently, 'your grandfather may be dying. How can you be so unconcerned?'

'Oh, that's the third time he's lost his colour and fainted since Christmas,' the red-haired man replied.

'Six times last year,' Denis recalled. 'He usually gets his way from it. But we don't take much notice of him any more.'

'It's different this time,' Mhairgead interrupted. 'I think he really is quite ill. His skin has gone cold and he is breathing shallow. And look at the colour in his face.'

Daniel came over and touched the old man on the forehead.

'Oh sweet Jesus!' he whispered after a few seconds and then he ran for the door.

'Francis!' he bellowed. 'Go and fetch Doctor Morrisey. Grandfather has taken a turn. And then go and get Father Anthony. Quick as you can.'

Francis called back to say he understood and then he was off.

'Let's get him into my room,' Daniel said as he returned to stand beside the old man. 'My wife and I have the most comfortable bed in the house and the room will afford him some privacy. She and the children can sleep in Grandfather's cottage tonight.'

With that Edward and Daniel lifted Hugh together and carried him carefully to the room where Daniel and his wife slept. They laid the old man down and Mhairgead pulled the covers up around his shoulders. Then the three of them waited at his side until the doctor arrived.

When Morrisey came in to examine the old man, Daniel and Mhairgead stayed with their grandfather and Edward went to sit with the old harper.

'This is all my fault,' the young rebel muttered under his breath.

'Don't be ridiculous,' the old harper laughed, almost choking on his whiskey. 'The man is a hundred years old. He couldn't last forever. If you hadn't come along, some other disaster would have struck us to be sure.'

Edward frowned a little at this then took a sip of whiskey.

'That old bugger has had a good life,' Denis went on. 'Not a moral one, mind you. But a bloody good one. I shall probably miss him.

'One thing's for certain,' Denis grinned. 'It'll be a bloody fine wake.'

'Four days?' Edward asked with a smile.

'It would take a dozen stout men a week to do the slightest damage to the contents of the secret cellar,' Denis told him.

At that moment Daniel opened the bedroom door and walked down the hall into the main room.

'What's the news?' Edward asked, rising from his chair.

'It is not good,' Daniel began in a subdued voice. 'Morrisey says that Grandfather will not last through the night. He has had a shock and it has affected him badly.'

Denis crossed himself solemnly and Edward sank back down into his seat. Just as he settled there was a knock at the door and Daniel went to see who it was. At the same time Doctor Morrisey entered the main room of the cottage, putting his coat on and speaking to Mhairgead.

'Keep him warm and give him plenty of whiskey,' the doctor was telling her. 'There's not much else can be done for him. If he wasn't a hundred years old I wouldn't be concerned about him. Feisty old bugger. But I fear his time is short.'

'Thank you, doctor,' she replied as Daniel let the priest in. The two gentlemen saluted each other with a slight nod of the head as their eyes met.

'Are you following me around today, Horan?' the doctor asked.

'It seems you are making an awful lot of work for me,' the priest answered.

'Not I,' Morrisey smiled. 'This is all the work of God.'

The young priest tried to smile at the quip but he suspected that Morrisey was not a good Catholic and the jibe was meant in earnest.

'I am Hugh Connor's grandson,' Daniel said, offering a hand to the priest. 'We were expecting Father Anthony.'

'My name is Horan,' the young priest replied, taking the offered hand. 'Father Anthony has been struck down with a most mysterious malady and cannot attend to your grandfather. So he sent me instead.'

'A sudden illness?' the red-haired man repeated, shaking his head. 'What brought that on?'

'The father was fine this morning when we did our rounds,' the priest explained, mystified, 'but no sooner had your brother Francis brought us the news of your grandfather's fit than Father Anthony had a little turn of his own. I had to help him home or I would have been here much sooner.'

'Will you have a whiskey, father?' Daniel offered as the door closed behind the doctor.

'I don't drink,' the priest replied quickly. 'I have never touched the stuff in my life and I do not feel the need to start now.'

'What the Hell sort of a priest are you then?' Denis inquired.

'I'm a Jesuit,' Horan explained, trying not to smile at the quaintness of these country folk.

'I know many men who joined the Jesuit order specifically for the liquor,' the harper frowned.

'I'm not one of them,' the priest gently asserted.

'Then why did you join the priesthood?' Denis asked, suspicion in his voice.

'There are many reasons one takes the cloth,' Father Horan said after a moment's thought. 'I felt called to the life of the Spirit and the service of the Almighty Father. I was inspired by the rigorous denial of the flesh which was preached by our Redeemer and Saint Paul. I have always been an admirer of the sacred martyrs.'

'Jesus and all the saints,' the harper muttered under his breath. 'There is a raving God-botherer in Hugh Connor's house. I never thought I'd see the day. I'm sure I don't believe it.' With that Denis swallowed his cup of whiskey and held it out for more.

'Is there something the matter?' Horan asked. 'Do you object to a Jesuit performing the last rites? I could ask another priest to hear the man's confession if you don't think he would appreciate my presence. Father Anthony would have come but—'

'I know,' the old harper smiled, 'he took a bad turn when he heard Hugh was on his deathbed.'

'There is always Father Murphy from the next parish,' Horan suggested. 'I would be happy to send for him.'

'Oh no, father,' Denis hummed. 'You are bloody perfect. Old Hugh will love you. Take my word for it.'

'Where is the poor man then?' the priest inquired. 'I had better see to him as soon as possible.'

'I'll show you to the room, father,' Daniel said as he poured another drink for Denis.

'One last question, father,' the harper cut in.

'Yes, my son?'

'How long have you been ordained?'

'Three weeks.'

'And how many times have you heard the last confession and given the extreme unction?'

'Once,' the priest admitted. 'This morning at the house of one of Morrisey's patients. I assisted Father Anthony at the side of a Mrs Feeney.'

'She was an old woman who had almost lost the power of speech,' Denis sighed.

'That's her,' Horan said.

'I'll wager she told you a riveting tale of her life in the Turkish harem?'

'No,' the priest replied in confusion.

'Did she not tell you of the time she was ravished by a sultan and his entire bodyguard in a single afternoon?'

'Are we speaking of the same woman?' the priest asked, blushing.

'She lived in a cottage not far from the old mill and she had a collection of Turkish silks hanging all about the place?'

'Yes,' Horan recalled, 'the house was hung with silks from the East. I thought they were exotic but I never guessed . . .' The priest stopped speaking when he noticed the broad grin on the harper's face.

'I think you might be having a joke with me,' Father Horan smiled, wagging his finger.

Denis smiled on, ignorant of the gesture. 'I might be,' he replied, mimicking Horan's tone. 'Or I might not. But you'll never know if Kitty Feeney didn't tell you.'

'It took all her energy to tell us her few insignificant sins,' Horan went on, a little flustered. 'The effort to unburden her soul drained the last life from her, I think.'

'Good luck with Hugh Connor then, father,' Denis wished the priest.

'Thank you,' Father Horan replied and then he followed Daniel through to the room where Hugh lay.

'That priest is the answer to all of Hugh's prayers,' the harper whispered to Edward.

'What are you talking about?'

'You'll see,' Denis grinned. 'You'll see.'

Daniel soon came back out to sit in Hugh's seat by the fire. 'Have you any of that Virginia left about you?' he asked Edward.

The young man found his tobacco pouch and handed it over.

'I suppose it is up to me now,' the red-haired man whispered as he stuffed his pipe. 'The first thing I'll have to organise is the wake. Then I'll be wanting to be rid of all that bloody whiskey.'

'Rid of it!' Denis hissed.

'I don't want to be dealing in arms and home-made liquor,' Daniel told him. 'I want to run this land like a farm should be run. Instead of jugs, barrels and muskets buried in every field, I am going to plant crops. I have no mind to be ending my days in Botany Bay with chains about my ankles and the lash across my back like my father.'

'You are making a terrible mistake,' Denis warned him. 'If Hugh could hear you now, it would surely cure him. He would cling to life just so you wouldn't get your way. What of the family tradition?'

'My father and my eldest brother are pursuing that tradition,' Daniel replied, 'in the penal colony of New South Wales. The distilling is ended for this family. From now on we'll be doing honest work. I have a mind to plant potatoes, barley and oats. And perhaps run a few cows.'

'You will be cursed by your descendants, Daniel Connor McHugh,' the harper sighed. 'Cursed to an eternity in the depths of Hell itself for giving up the family tradition of making the whiskey.'

'It wasn't such a long tradition,' Daniel smiled, sucking in the smoke from his pipe. 'Grandfather was the first to take it up.'

'But his whiskey is the finest in the land,' Denis protested.

'If you knew what went into it, you wouldn't say that,' the red-haired man declared.

The blood drained from the old harper's face.

'Barley,' Denis guessed tentatively. 'I know it's made from barley. And I am sure there are some spices in it as well.'

'It's no use, old man,' Daniel laughed. 'It's a family secret. I'll never tell.'

Denis huffed, unhappy at being the butt of any joke.

The priest was a long while with Hugh and the house fell silent while the holy man did his work. Mhairgead put some whiskey in the kettle to heat, thinking that it would not be long before her grandfather's spirit departed. She told Edward it was only fitting they drink warm whiskey to mark Hugh's passing, but the young rebel did not want to show his ignorance so he didn't dare ask why.

Then, just as the sun was setting, she brought out a freshly baked loaf of coarse brown bread from the oven and broke it with her hands.

'There'll be no knives in this house tonight,' she said and everyone nodded in agreement, though once again Edward had no idea why.

The four of them had just finished their bread when they heard the door to Daniel's room open. After a few seconds it closed again and everyone could hear Father Horan saying a prayer to himself in Latin.

'Fill a new cup with whiskey,' Denis ordered.

'What for?' Mhairgead asked.

'Just do as you're told. You'll soon find out,' the harper told her.

So Mhairgead found a clean cup and filled it with liquor.

'Take it, Edward,' Denis commanded, 'and stand by the hall ready for when the priest comes out.'

'Horan told us he doesn't touch the stuff,' the young man protested.

'Stop with your foolish talk and do as I say,' the old harper snapped. So Edward took the cup and stood waiting for the priest to appear.

Horan moved slowly into the room and stood for a few moments beside Edward. He cast his eyes about the dimly lit space and put a hand to his mouth to touch his lip. He was pale and drawn and he had obviously shed more than a few tears.

'Is he gone?' Mhairgead asked finally when she realised no-one else was going to broach the subject.

'Your grandfather is still with us,' the priest mumbled and then he saw the cup of whiskey in Edward's hand and he gazed longingly at it.

The young rebel passed the cup to him and Father Horan drank it down quickly. Then he stood for a few seconds looking to the ceiling before he handed the empty vessel back.

'Forgive me, Father,' he whispered to himself as he made the sign of the cross.

'Is something the matter?' Edward asked.

'Nothing that another drink won't cure,' the priest smiled weakly.

'No man is immune to the allure of whiskey,' Denis sniggered. 'And never trust a fellow who claims he is,' he advised to anyone who would hear him.

'Are you all right?' Mhairgead asked.

'When I took my holy orders I knew there would be many challenges set before me,' the priest began, 'but I never dreamed I would have to listen to such a confession as that which I have just heard.'

The priest took himself to Edward's seat by the fire and dropped down onto it as he was handed another cup.

'I am going to have to seek confession myself after some of the things I heard this afternoon,' Horan admitted. And then he downed the second whiskey as quickly as the first. Almost immediately he held out his cup again.

'I'll get a fresh jug,' Daniel offered.

'Do that,' Horan said, 'for I am to stay here tonight until he is gone. It is his wish that I should read his will before his body grows cold and before he has been washed.'

'Now you can call yourself a priest,' Denis told him. 'Any man who could sit through that fellow's confession and come out of it with only a thirst for whiskey is bound for the bishopric.'

The harper raised his cup. 'To your health, Bishop Horan,' he toasted.

'I don't believe we've been introduced,' the priest said, turning to focus on the old man.

'I am Denis Hempson, the harper.'

'Oh sweet Jesus!' Horan exclaimed, eyes widening in horror. 'I know too much about your life to be raising a toast with you!'

'What did that old bugger tell you?'

'Oh God,' the priest sobbed, making the sign of the cross again, 'now I am going to have to hear your confession as well. Will there be no end to it?'

Father Horan closed his eyes and covered them with his hands. He stayed like that sobbing for a long while and ignoring the harper's pleas to tell him what was wrong.

'I'll murder that old mischief-maker,' Denis vowed. 'I'll bloody well murder him.'

'You'll have to hurry,' Daniel whispered as Denis stood up.

'I wonder what other little tricks he has in store for us?' the old harper grinned.

'Where are you going?' Mhairgead asked him.

'I'm off to play the dying man a few notes on the harp,' Denis explained, 'to soothe his soul into the afterlife. There is nothing so calming for a doomed soul as the sound of the harp strumming softly.'

He leaned on his stick and turned around. 'Take me in, will you, Daniel?'

'I will, Denis,' the red-haired man replied, 'but not a word about my plans. Do you hear?'

'What sort of a man do you think I am?' the harper retorted. 'He has been a good friend to me and I would not dream of spoiling his last few hours upon this earth. Let him find out halfway to purgatory. By that time it will be too late for him to come back and give any of us a hard time.'

Daniel breathed a sigh of relief as he lifted the harp case and took Denis by the elbow.

The two old men must have had a lot to talk about for Denis was gone for a long while. Occasionally the strains of a harp tune would float out by the fire to entice those who were seated around waiting. After a long time Daniel thought to get up and see how Hugh was feeling and he came back leading Denis by the arm.

'I have not had enough to drink!' the old man yelled back over his shoulder. 'What is your bloody hurry? I told you it is a challenging tune to play. I'll be back in a while to perform it for you.'

Edward could hear the muffled protests of old Hugh but he couldn't make out exactly what was being said. Denis sat down in his place by the fire and as soon as he was settled and had a drink in his hand, Edward leaned over.

'The Concerto?' the young rebel asked.

'What else would it be?' Denis snapped. 'It is a very difficult piece for me to play because I don't like it at all. I have to love a melody if I am going to do it justice.'

'He's dying, Denis,' Edward reminded the old man.

'He is lucky to have anyone to play for him at all,' the old harper retorted. 'There won't be anyone to play for me when I cross over. I have a vision of myself lying on my back in my bed with the harp stretched out beside me. And I'll have to play myself out of the world. It is hard to be the last of your kind.'

'You're not the last harper, surely?' Edward exclaimed.

'I will be if I live as long as is my intention,' came the reply.

'Do you think it might be wise to go in and have a word with the old bugger yourself?'

'I thought I'd better let him be,' Edward hesitated.

'Well he asked after you. So you had better go and make your peace with him.'

Edward drained his cup and decided Denis was right. It would be best to try and smooth over any trouble between them. After all, the old man might be dead by the morning.

Edward poured Father Horan another drink, put a splash more in the old harper's cup and then made his way into the room.

As he opened the door he saw the old man lying in the narrow bed with his arms folded in front of him. The light of a single candle lit the table at the bedside where there was a whiskey jug and an empty cup.

'I was wondering how long you'd be, Edward,' Hugh muttered as the young man pulled the little wooden door shut behind him.

'How did you know it was me?'

'I sent for you,' the old man replied. 'Who else would it be?'

Edward shrugged.

'I came to apologise to you,' the young rebel said.

'It is about time too,' Hugh replied.

'You are right.'

The old man frowned with suspicion. 'Don't you go thinking that I am going to help you settle your debts, young fellow. If that is your plan, in coming here to speak with me, to pretend you are full of remorse, well, it won't work.'

'I am full of remorse,' Edward protested. 'I am not pretending.'

'Don't interrupt me,' the old distiller hissed. 'I have lived in the country long enough to know the scent of a fox when I smell it. The offer of helping to pay off your debts over time was made on the condition that you and Mhairgead remain here and help Daniel.'

Hugh thought for a moment.

'I suppose you expect to get a share of the inheritance,' the old distiller grunted, tossing his head back, 'now that you're family.'

'I don't want your money,' Edward said softly. 'I just came in to say I am sorry and to thank you for saving me from the redcoats.'

'Think nothing of it,' Hugh snapped. 'I would have done the same for a decent man.'

'Look, I could stay on for a while and help Daniel, if you like,' the young rebel offered. 'It will surely take Mhairgead and I a while to secure a passage to America. And this is a much safer place to stay than Dublin.'

'I will not arrange for your debts to be forgiven unless I have an assurance that you will stay here permanently,' Hugh stated obstinately.

Then the old man coughed to clear his throat.

'Fetch me a cup of whiskey will you?'

Edward leaned over to the table to pour a cup from the earthenware jug. Then he carefully placed it at Hugh's lips and the old man drank deeply.

'That is the purest drop of whiskey I ever made,' Hugh smiled. 'I am getting better at it day by day.'

'We can all be thankful, then, that you have lived so long,' Edward rejoined.

'That's enough of your smart comments, my lad,' the old man said, trying to discern whether there was an insult hidden in the remark. 'You are getting altogether too familiar for my liking,' he grumbled.

'Tell me more about your master,' Edward cut in to divert Hugh from another bout of scolding.

'What do you want to know?' the old man replied sullenly.

'Everything you told me about the Faeries,' Edward asked, 'do you really believe it?'

'There is another world,' Hugh explained with conviction. 'Close by this one, perhaps between this world and the next. I have heard the priests call that place purgatory but I do not think it is a place of punishment. It is a land of merriment where the whiskey flows free, the music never ceases and our departed friends dance the evenings away in uninterrupted bliss.'

'Where is it?'

'I cannot tell you,' the old man sighed with regret. 'But my master reckoned that he often visited that country in his dreams and returned with some great composition or other that he had learned there. It may be the dreaming country where our souls go when we fall asleep.'

Hugh breathed deeply and shifted uncomfortably. Then he gasped and put a hand to his chest to still the pain.

'Perhaps,' he went on in a weak, strained voice, 'we all gather in that place in the night to learn skills and meet other like-minded spirits. Have you never had the feeling that you have met someone before but you can't for the life of you remember where?'

'On many occasions,' Edward admitted. 'I often wonder whether or not we have all lived at other times or if our spirits are simply reborn into new bodies at the end of each life.'

'That seems rather far-fetched,' Hugh scoffed. 'I prefer to believe in my own idea of purgatory, if you don't mind. Why would anyone choose to come back to this world of their own volition?'

'Perhaps we don't have a choice in the matter,' Edward suggested. 'Maybe that is the way of nature.'

'Did you come in here to comfort me or are you here for some other reason?' Hugh grunted. 'I have already spoken with the doctor and the priest and neither of them inspired me to feel very good at all. This conversation is beginning to make me feel nervous. I mean to say, I am about to embark on a little journey myself and I imagine it will be a rather vexing experience. I wouldn't like to think I'll be back here in a hurry, thank you very much.'

'Father Horan was in here a long time,' Edward offered, changing the subject.

'Poor man,' Hugh sniggered. 'I heard him muttering to

himself during my confession and I swear he was babbling a lot of nonsense.'

'I saw his face after he emerged from the room,' the young rebel smiled. 'Whatever did you tell him?'

The old distiller crossed himself and placed his palms together in front of him. 'Forgive me, father, for I have sinned,' Hugh began, mimicking his own speech to the priest. 'It has been seventy-six years, four months and twelve days since my last confession.'

The old man laughed and then he began coughing. It took a few minutes for the fit to pass. Edward sat patiently, waiting for Hugh to settle.

'I had a lot to catch up on,' the old man admitted. 'And once I got started I remembered a lot of things that hadn't crossed my mind in many years. I passed my youth in wickedness, I surely did,' he said, shaking his head.

'Horan looked like he'd seen a glimpse of Hell,' Edward whispered.

'One man's Hell is another man's Heaven,' the old man wheezed and then he tried to sit upright. Edward helped him raise himself on the straw pillow.

'I want you to take care of young Mhairgead,' Hugh said sternly. 'Her mother's father was a good friend of mine and I promised I'd see her well protected while he was away fighting in the French army.'

'I promise I will look after her.'

'Think again about this journey to America,' the old man pleaded. 'There is a fortune to be made here with the whiskey distilling. I hate to think of poor Daniel doing all the work alone. And you have your acquaintances in Dublin. You could make a pretty penny from them, I'll wager.'

Edward did not answer.

'I have never killed a man as you have,' Hugh conceded, 'though if I had, it certainly would have been Denis Hempson,' he added, 'and I do not understand why you would choose to go off to live in the wild forests of the Americas. You will not escape the deed by running away from it. It worries me that you may carry this murder on your conscience for the rest of your life.'

'I have thought about all you have said,' Edward replied. 'I have lived the few moments of the shooting over a hundred times in my head. I am not a hero. I was scared witless as I marched up to the major and pulled the trigger. But I felt I had to prove myself to my comrades. To give them hope. To make us feel like we had achieved something.'

'A man is dead,' Hugh sighed. He coughed again painfully before he went on. 'And his children have lost their father. And as it turns out, he was one of the few redcoats who might have offered your cause any sympathy. How will you make restitution for all that?'

'I don't know,' the young man admitted. 'But I am sure now that I was wrong to take that course of action.' Edward covered his eyes with one hand, silently berating himself for his foolish deed.

'It is true that Major D'Arcy was a cold-blooded and cruel man,' the old distiller said softly. 'I am sure he killed a few fellows himself in the thick of battle or in the course of his duties. But he was a good father to his children and a loving husband to his wife. His friends admired him and the soldiers respected him. And in the end he was beginning to soften to the world.'

'What are you trying to say?'

'I know for a fact that Major D'Arcy regretted some of the things he did in his life,' Hugh went on. 'He told me as much over a barrel of particularly fine whiskey I had been keeping for Christmas. We all make mistakes when we are young. And some of us continue to make them as we grow older, but there is no sense in berating yourself for the blunders. It is better to learn what you can from them and strengthen your resolve so that you never make the same mistakes again.'

'I suppose you are right.'

'D'Arcy had come to that realisation, you know,' the old man informed his guest. 'He had decided to make amends for all his wrongdoing. That is why he patronised so many poor folk. And it suited his sense of justice that the army spent lavishly on Irish whiskey.'

'And that the garrison's arms were redistributed to the rebels?'

'Indeed,' Hugh nodded. 'That was D'Arcy's doing entirely. I was just the middleman in the transaction.'

Hugh laughed a little. 'It is rather unfortunate that you chose that particular officer as the first target for your rebellion.'

'It was, wasn't it,' the young man breathed.

'I hope you will make amends, Edward,' Hugh told the rebel. 'I hope you will go to your grave with a light heart and a clear conscience. For that is what I intend to do.'

Old Hugh coughed a little and reached out to take the young man's hand.

'My master had a gift,' the old man wheezed. 'Carolan was loved, admired and cherished by all who knew him, except David Murphy who loved no-one but himself. The master found his gift by cruel chance. But the very misfortune that robbed him of his sight bestowed upon him an unequalled ability to make music which touched the souls of his listeners.'

Hugh coughed again and squeezed Edward's hand.

'I saw him perform many times, you know. I watched folk drift off into the Otherworld with his music. I myself sometimes found I was transported to another place by the melodies. He never complained about the blindness. He never once openly regretted the life he had been given. And though I am sure he was as wicked a sinner as any man alive, he passed over with a smile on his face and joy in his heart.'

Suddenly Hugh began coughing violently. The old man sat forward as the spasm engulfed him and Edward put an arm around his shoulders to soothe him. In a few moments the fit passed and Hugh leaned back again on his pillow. But his face was terribly pale and his breathing was shallow.

'I will be going to worship at the Soporific Temple of Aesclepius soon,' Hugh muttered weakly.

'What's that?' Edward asked. 'Is there anything I can get you?'

'Pour me a cup,' the old man mumbled, coming back to his senses.

Edward picked up the jug to pour a whiskey but there was only enough for half a cup.

'Did you drink that whole jug of liquor?' the young man asked.

'It was that bloody priest,' Hugh smiled weakly. 'I couldn't keep him away from it.'

'That explains why Horan was so pale when he came to the fire,' Edward said to himself. 'After a jug of that stuff he was lucky to be able to find his feet on the end of his legs.'

Just at that moment Daniel opened the door.

'Is everything all right?' the red-haired man asked. 'I thought I heard Grandfather coughing.'

'You could fill this jug for him,' Edward suggested, passing the vessel over.

Daniel looked inside the jug, raised his eyebrows and shrugged. 'Is he starting the wake without us?' he asked.

'Is that you, Grandson?' Hugh whispered.

'It is,' the red-haired man replied.

'Fetch me a whiskey quick, will you, lad? I'll die if I don't get a drink.'

'You had better leave us some,' Daniel warned. 'We can't send you off properly if there isn't a drop in the house.'

'Whisht with you,' the old man smiled. 'Just do as you're told.'

Daniel shook his head and left the room. The old man settled back in his pillow and breathed loudly.

He had no sooner settled than he abruptly sat forward again as if he was in some pain. Edward instinctively reached out and took the old man's hand to comfort him.

'Are you there?' Hugh suddenly cried out.

'I am,' Edward replied.

'Did you fetch me a drink?'

Edward looked at the half cup of whiskey he had drained from the jug.

'There is a drop here in this cup,' the young man replied. 'Do you want it?'

'Quickly,' Hugh moaned softly, 'there isn't much time.'

Edward lifted the cup to the old man's lips and Hugh took a sip of the liquor. Then he leaned back on his pillow again and sighed deeply with satisfaction.

'Thank you, Grandson,' Hugh breathed. 'Now all will be well.'

'It's Edward,' the young man told him.

'What's Edward?' Hugh frowned.

'I am Edward. I am not your grandson yet. Mhairgead and I are still to be married.'

The old man tried to sit up, reaching out wildly to find the cup again.

'Jesus!' he cried. 'It wasn't supposed to be you.'

Edward did not have a clue what the old man was talking about. He thought Hugh must be raving or had simply lost all sense of where he was.

Daniel opened the door, saw what was happening and put the jug down on the table. Then he tried to calm his grandfather.

'What's the matter?' the red-haired man asked. 'Calm yourself.' Then he turned to Edward. 'What happened while I was gone?'

'He asked for a cup of whiskey so I gave him what was left from that last jug.'

Daniel sniffed the cup and winced as if he smelled something bad.

'There does not seem to be anything wrong with the liquor,' he stated confidently. 'It smells as awful as ever.'

'Is that you, Daniel?' Hugh gasped.

'It is, Grandfather.'

'Pour me a whiskey, will you?'

'You've had enough for the time being,' Daniel soothed. 'Now it is time for you to rest.'

'I can't yet!'

'You must.'

'You don't understand,' Hugh protested. 'It wasn't meant to be him.'

'Who, Grandfather?'

'The rebel,' the old man sighed, breathing easier and slower. 'It was meant to be you.'

Daniel shook his head, cast a glance at Edward and then took his grandfather's hand as the old man slipped into unconsciousness. The young rebel dared not move. He did not know what he had done to upset Hugh, but he didn't want to attract any more attention to himself by leaving the old man's side.

Gradually Hugh's breath slowed and, as Daniel and Edward watched, the life ebbed out of the old man. After only a few minutes his breathing ceased altogether and Hugh Connor was still.

'Go and fetch Father Horan,' Daniel said in a low voice. 'It is ended now. He is at peace.'

SIXTEEN

Edward left the room as quietly as he could. In a few minutes he returned with Father Horan. Mhairgead, tears streaming down her face, came in a little while after, leading Denis and carrying his harp for him.

The priest blessed the body, checked three times that the old man was not breathing and then took a piece of paper from his coat pocket.

'I am bound by my promise,' Father Horan began, slurring his words slightly, 'to proclaim the will and the final wishes of Hugh Connor Esquire lately deceased.'

'Can't it wait?' Mhairgead whispered.

'This is what he wanted,' the priest explained. 'Who am I to disrespect the wishes of the recently departed?'

'If you don't do as he asked,' Denis muttered, 'the old bugger will come back and give you a piece of his mind.'

Father Horan's face turned even paler and he leaned against the bedside table.

'I wouldn't want that,' he said sombrely and then he crossed himself again just to put his mind at ease.

'I wouldn't put it past him,' Daniel declared. 'So get on with it and then we can all have a drink.'

The priest unfolded his spectacles and perched them precariously on the end of his nose. Edward was surprised to see such a young man wearing reading glasses. He thought they made him look incredibly silly.

Father Horan coughed to clear his throat.

'This third day of July in the year of our Blessed Lord, one thousand seven hundred and eighty-eight, conveyed in the hand of Father Horan, parish priest.'

'That's today!' Daniel whispered. 'That's why you were so long in here with him.'

'Believe me,' Horan hissed, 'the dictating of the will was a minor matter compared to the confession.' The priest glanced at the full jug of whiskey on the table.

'You can drink your fill when you've read the document,' Daniel told the clergyman.

'Very well,' Horan agreed and turned his attention back to the piece of paper in his hands. 'I, Hugh Connor, one hundred years of age, renowned distiller, rebel, confidant of His Highness Prince Charles Edward Stewart and former travelling companion to the great Carolan—'

'Prince Charles Edward Stewart?' Edward repeated in confusion, not sure whether he had heard correctly. 'Did Hugh know Bonnie Prince Charlie?'

'Jesus,' Denis groaned, 'you don't know how lucky you are the old bugger didn't live long enough to tell you that one. What a bloody tale!'

'Be quiet,' Mhairgead told the old harper, squeezing his arm hard.

Denis winced in disgust.

'... travelling companion to the great Carolan,' the priest repeated, 'do hereby bequeath to my dear friend Denis Hempson two small paintings which were gifts from the late Squire Reynolds. I know that if he were able to see them he would surely appreciate the subject matter.'

'The old bastard,' Denis whispered to himself.

'All my other goods and possessions, my entire fortune of four thousand pounds which is buried with my mother in the churchyard of Kilronan ...'

The priest had to stop for a moment to rub his eyes. He lifted his spectacles off his nose and breathed heavily. He was obviously distracted by the thought of Hugh's mother nursing four thousand pounds in gold in her arms as she lay in her coffin. The priest looked to the ceiling as if he was staring intently at something in the rafters.

It occurred to Edward that there might be muskets concealed in the roof, but when he looked up the rafters were bare and he breathed easier. When Mhairgead and Daniel noticed both men were staring at the roof, they too raised their eyes.

'Why have you stopped?' Denis asked.

Father Horan shook himself from his private thoughts and Mhairgead poured him a drop of whiskey.

'Take this, father,' she told him. 'It will still your nerves.'

'Thank you,' the priest replied and he downed the cup in one gulp. Then, breathing deeply, he forced his eyes down to the paper again.

'. . . my two stills,' Horan continued, picking up where he had left off, 'the one on the mountain and the one in the old mill, my annual income of two hundred pounds, my four cottages, two horses, three carts, sixteen goats and the carcass of my recently departed cow, Philomena, go to the man who poured me my last drink. As God and Father Horan are my witnesses, may a curse come upon any man, woman or clergy who dismisses my wishes.'

'His last drink?' Daniel asked, disbelieving.

'I . . . I gave him his last drink,' Edward stuttered in shock. Then he realised what Hugh had been muttering about just before he passed away.

'It wasn't supposed to be me,' the rebel said. 'Hugh intended Daniel to serve him his last whiskey. I just happened to be here. It was a mistake.'

'You conniving little Dublin dreg!' the red-haired man hissed.

'I had no idea what the old man wanted,' Edward protested. 'It was an honest mistake.'

'You ferret,' Daniel cursed menacingly. 'I have been putting up with that old man's complaining, his foul temper, his manipulating ways and his bad whiskey—'

'Not to mention his endless tales and his tiresome practical jokes,' Denis cut in.

'I have put up with him all these years,' Daniel went on, ignoring the harper's interruption, 'just to be cheated out of my inheritance at the very last?'

'By rights everything should have gone to your father,' the priest explained. 'But since he is,' Horan chose his words carefully, 'biding his time in another part of the world, it is unlikely that the bequest would be of any use to him. So I would imagine the old man intended you to take possession of his worldly goods. It is obviously a simple mistake.'

'The mistake I made was in not turning this little weasel over to the redcoats and in failing to collect the reward on his head,' Daniel fumed. 'Indeed that is still the best plan I can think of.'

'Daniel,' Edward reasoned, 'I don't want the money.'

'Yes you do!' Mhairgead cut in. 'We're off to America, remember? That money will come in very handy.'

Edward glanced at Daniel. There was murder in the man's eyes.

'I don't want the money,' Edward repeated. 'I don't want the still, the horses, the goats or anything. You can have it all, Daniel. The lot. Just let Mhairgead and myself leave in peace.'

Daniel was about to open his mouth to accept the offer when Father Horan interrupted.

'I am terribly sorry,' the priest said, attempting to stand to his full height without leaning on the table, 'but I cannot allow that.'

'What?' Daniel bellowed.

'Your grandfather was very specific,' Horan told him. 'He told me that no matter what happened as a result of the reading of this will, no matter what arguments came of it or what terrible fights erupted, I was to stand firm on his wishes and see they were executed to the letter. I gave him my solemn promise.'

'But he didn't know this was going to happen,' Edward protested. 'It was an accident.'

'It is God's will,' the priest insisted. 'I gave my word as a Jesuit and I am going to stand by it.'

Horan made a sweeping gesture with both arms, almost losing his balance as he did so. 'Edward,' the priest declared, 'all this is yours.'

'Except the two paintings which were a gift from Squire Reynolds,' Denis interrupted.

'All except the paintings,' Horan confirmed. He carefully removed his spectacles, placed them in the inside pocket of his coat and smiled, satisfied that he had done his duty. As he did so his eyes rolled back in his head, his body swayed and his knees gave way. He collapsed at the side of the bed, rolling off the end to fall with a heavy thud face first onto the floor.

All of them, except Denis of course, watched the priest faint, but no-one made a move to touch him.

'You won't get any of it,' Daniel snarled, turning his attention back to Edward.

'I don't want any of it,' the young rebel repeated.

'Yes you do!' Mhairgead hissed, punching her husband-to-be in the arm.

Suddenly all three of them heard giggles. They turned to Denis. The old harper was leaning up against the door, struggling to stifle his amusement.

'What is so funny?' Daniel demanded to know.

'It was his last little joke,' the old harper sniggered. 'He thought Daniel would surely serve him his last drink and the rest of us would go on wondering what would have happened if we had poured that whiskey. It was supposed to settle all arguments but it didn't turn out quite as he expected it.'

The old harper bent over, put his hands to his mouth and attempted to stop laughing.

'The best years of my life I wasted tending to that old bugger,' Daniel snarled, 'and what have I got to show for it?'

'Daniel,' Edward soothed, 'we all know he intended for you to inherit everything. I don't care what the priest says. You should take the lot and forget that I ever interfered. I really didn't intend to.'

The red-haired man let out a low growl.

'This is not the time to be discussing such matters,' Denis advised. 'Have a drink and a pipe. Sleep on it and in the morning it will all be clear. An answer will present itself.'

'He's right,' Mhairgead agreed. 'Tonight we should be mourning our loss and remembering our dear departed grandfather. We'll discuss the inheritance once he's buried.'

She took her brother by the arm and led him out to the fire as Denis sat down by his harp. Edward turned to go, then he noticed the harper was preparing to pay his last respects, so he stopped at the door to listen.

The melody was slow and mournful and it put Edward in mind of the passing of his own grandfather who had led an honest life as a merchant in Dublin. At that moment the young rebel decided to take Hugh's advice. And then a solution to the problem caused by the will presented itself to him.

He decided it would be best to think carefully about how he presented his idea to Daniel and he resolved not to broach the subject until the morning. He went out to the fire where Mhairgead was cradling Daniel in her lap. The great tall man who was usually so strong and subdued was crying like a little baby.

Mhairgead looked up at Edward and smiled the way she had the first time he had set eyes on her. The young rebel sat down beside the two of them to stare at the fire, to listen to the lament and drink some of old Hugh's whiskey.

When Father Horan opened his eyes the room was very dark. The young priest struggled to roll over onto his back and then he lay still for a long while. He breathed deeply, trying to remember where he was and how he got there. But no answers came to mind.

Horan's mouth was dry and his tongue swollen. His teeth felt like they had grown little hairs which tickled the inside of his lips. But it was his head that was giving him the most pain. At the back of his skull there was a dull thudding ache which seemed to spread out with each thump until the beating reverberated across his forehead.

'Mother of God,' Horan groaned, rubbing his eyes in the hope of easing the agony.

All of a sudden the priest noticed another rhythmic thumping sound. It was like a whole regiment of redcoats was marching around in his head, beating their drums. The noise slowly built in intensity until Horan could stand it no longer.

With another groan the father sat up. He immediately regretted the hasty move.

'My head!' the priest mumbled. 'I feel like my skull has been used for a cannonball. Where in God's name am I?'

He had no sooner spoken than he felt his stomach turn, full of wind. Horan moaned loudly, farted and then staggered to his feet. The drumming was getting louder by the minute. His head was thudding wildly now and Horan thought his skull would burst with the persistent steady beat.

There were sheets hanging over the only window in the room, blocking out all light. The young priest reached out to drag one of the coverings aside. All of a sudden the room was flooded with light. Horan cried out in anguish, covering his eyes to soothe the searing pain in his head. He turned away from the window and the sheet fell down onto the floor.

It was then Father Horan noticed a silent, motionless form lying upon the bed.

Quietly the young priest approached the figure, careful not to make any sound that might disturb this stranger's slumber. He leaned over to take a look at the face, hoping to recognise the man so he might have a clue as to where he was or what he was doing in this unfamiliar room.

Just then, however, his stomach rumbled noisily and he let out a large belch of air. When the spasm had passed, the priest stood perfectly motionless until he was certain he had not disturbed the sleeping man. He was reassuring himself that there was no movement in the bed when the door to the room swung open and a tall red-haired man came in.

'I see you are awake then, father,' the man said. 'We have been waiting on you.'

'Be quiet,' the priest insisted, pointing to the bed. 'You'll wake him.'

'Not that one, father,' Daniel smiled. 'Not even the offer of ten gallons of free whiskey at Finnegan's would stir him. My grandfather has been dead since last night.'

'Who is he?'

'Hugh Connor.'

'Dead?' the priest asked as he reached out to touch Hugh's hand. The fingers were icy cold and stiff. 'Hugh Connor,' Horan repeated to himself and suddenly a flood of memories came to him.

'Mother of God!' the priest exclaimed, withdrawing his hand swiftly. Then his eyes rolled back into his head once more and he began to faint.

'No you don't, father,' the red-haired man told him as he strode across the room to catch the priest. 'You have a burial to perform this afternoon and there's only a few hours of light left. We've been waiting all day for you to stir.'

'I don't feel very well,' Horan protested as Daniel helped him out to sit by the fire. 'My head is thumping like a dozen drummers have set up residence inside my skull.'

'You'll be much better after a few days' rest and plenty of fresh water to flush your body out,' Daniel advised. 'But for the time being we are in need of your services. You had better gather your wits so you can do your duty.'

'But I want to go to sleep,' the priest complained. 'The floor is moving under me and I feel like a horse has kicked me in the stomach.'

'That will teach you to be intemperate, father,' Daniel told the priest as he sat him down by the fire next to Denis Hempson.

'What are you talking about?' Horan asked, trying to focus

on the red-haired man. 'I never touch a drop. I am as temperate as any other Jesuit.'

'That is exactly what he means,' Denis sniggered.

Father Horan turned in his seat to look at the old harper. He stared for a few moments and then another memory came to him. Suddenly there was a look of horror on his face.

'Oh my Lord!' the priest cried. 'It's you! The harper. I know all about you.'

Then the Jesuit put a hand to his mouth, slid off his seat onto the floor and curled up, sobbing quietly.

'What did that old bugger say about me?' Denis demanded indignantly, but the priest was beyond hearing.

'Why won't those drums stop beating?' Horan cried, thumping his head with the heels of his hands. 'I can't get the noise out of my head!'

'Wait a minute,' Denis told him. 'Be quiet for a moment.'

The priest stopped crying.

'I can hear drums too,' the old harper whispered, and he swallowed another cup of whiskey.

At that instant Mhairgead appeared at the door and Daniel could see by the expression on her face something was terribly wrong.

'Redcoats!' she cried. 'A whole company marching up the road. And Colonel Cumberland is riding out in front.'

'Jesus!' the red-haired man hissed. 'Where's Edward?'

'He went down to the well,' his sister answered breathlessly.

'Well it's too late to warn him now,' Daniel told her. 'Let's hope he's decided to take a wash and won't be back for a while.'

'What will we do?' Mhairgead asked, half frantic.

'Calm down for a start,' her brother told her. 'And act like nothing has happened.'

'Your grandfather just passed over,' Denis reminded them.

Mhairgead and Daniel looked at each other in relief as the answer came to them.

'We're in mourning!' they both said together.

'Whiskey all round,' Daniel told her. 'Break out every jug you can lay your hands on. I'll get the soldiers drinking and hopefully while they're busy you'll get a chance to slip away and warn Edward.'

'Thank you,' Mhairgead said. 'I know you don't think much of him right now but I am grateful for this.'

'Be quiet, girl, or I'll change my mind.'

With that Daniel went to help Horan back into his seat. Then he poured the young priest a drink.

'Now be a good Jesuit,' Daniel said in a patronising tone, 'and stay put. Don't say anything at all, no matter what the soldiers ask you. I'll do the talking.'

'Very well, Daniel,' Horan promised meekly.

'Good fellow,' the red-haired man replied, patting the young priest on the head. 'Watch him, will you, Denis?'

'That won't be easy,' the blind harper quipped, 'but I'll do my best.'

Just as Daniel was sure everything in the house was in order he heard the beating drums outside and decided he could ignore the redcoats no longer. He went to the door and stepped out in the weak afternoon sunshine.

Daniel looked to the sky and reckoned it would be raining in a short while. Then his eyes strayed to the road and they nearly popped out of his head.

An entire company of redcoated soldiers was making their way up to the house in a column. They were led by half a dozen drummers and an officer mounted on a white charger. Daniel instinctively crossed himself.

'May God help you, young Edward,' he whispered as the column wheeled around in front of him and a sergeant called the soldiers to a halt. The drumming ceased suddenly and from inside the house Daniel heard a man's voice.

'Thank God it's stopped!' Father Horan cried.

The officer on the white horse walked his mount down the line of his troops, quickly inspecting them.

'Company!' a sergeant bellowed. 'Order your firelocks!'

The soldiers brought their muskets down from their shoulders to rest them by their sides.

'Company, fix bayonets!' the sergeant commanded.

The soldiers rattled about affixing their long thin bayonets to the ends of their muskets.

'Oh no,' Daniel muttered in shock.

'Sergeant,' the officer on the white horse said calmly, 'make sure the men have their pans properly primed.'

'Yes, sir!'

'And have them draw up in two ranks for volley fire.'

'Yes, sir!'

Then the officer calmly walked his charger over to where Daniel was standing. He dismounted and casually removed his leather gloves as he surveyed the darkening sky. Then he handed his reins to a soldier who led the mount away to a safe position behind the ranks of redcoats.

'Good day, Colonel Cumberland,' the red-haired man offered. 'It's a fine day to be drilling your troops. Thank you for bringing them up here to show us.'

'Daniel,' the colonel replied, avoiding the other man's eyes, 'I have a confession to make.'

Then the officer coughed. 'The truth is, I'm afraid I'm not up here to drill the soldiers,' the colonel admitted. 'I've come on business.'

'I see,' Daniel said. 'What sort of business?'

'Military business on this occasion.'

'Company!' the sergeant commanded. 'Shoulder your firelocks!'

The colonel waited until the soldiers had finished moving.

'It concerns all this rebel activity in the parish,' Cumberland went on.

'Company! Present your firelocks!' the sergeant yelled.

'Rebels, is it?' Daniel asked.

'Yes,' the colonel replied, clearly embarrassed. 'I was wondering if your grandfather was at home?'

'He is,' Daniel answered quickly. 'He is lying on my bed.'

'Taking a rest?'

'You could say that.'

'For volley fire!' the sergeant ordered, 'Company! Pre-sent!'

The soldiers brought their muskets up to their right shoulders, ready to fire.

'May I have a word with Hugh?' the colonel asked.

'You may not,' Daniel replied.

'Please don't make this any more difficult for me than it already is,' Cumberland pleaded. 'I have known Hugh for many years. I grew up listening to Master Carolan's music and your grandfather's wild stories. I was able to overlook Hugh's involvement with the Jacobites all those years ago because he assured me he had settled down to a quiet life. But I am sorry to say he has broken that assurance.'

'Have you come to arrest him?'

'I have.'

'On what charge?'

'Treason. Conspiracy to supply arms to the rebels,' Cumberland told him, 'and the attempted poisoning of the grenadier company of the second foot guards, apparently with tainted whiskey.'

'The entire company?'

'Every mother's son, including a goat which was the company mascot,' the colonel answered, struggling to retain some semblance of dignity.

'Any fatalities?'

'Only the goat.'

'I am relieved to hear that,' Daniel replied, raising his eyebrows.

'I am very sorry to say,' Cumberland went on, getting back to business, 'that the evidence against your grandfather is impeccable.'

'How's that?'

'After D'Arcy's murder,' the officer explained, 'the major's personal diary came into my possession. In this journal D'Arcy detailed his dealings with the rebels. It transpires that the major was a traitor who stole muskets, cannon, pikes and shot belonging to the regiment. He then sold these arms on to the rebels.'

'I see,' Daniel nodded. 'And how is my grandfather implicated?'

'Unfortunately Hugh's name comes up again and again in respect to these illicit transactions. It is apparent that Hugh was a middleman between D'Arcy and the insurrectionists.'

'I heard tell that D'Arcy was murdered by the rebels,' Daniel ventured. 'How could he have been dealing with them?'

'I cannot be certain of all the facts,' the colonel admitted. 'It is possible that D'Arcy made himself a target for the advocates of liberty. But that is no longer any of my concern. I am here to arrest Hugh Connor.'

'So the Crown has finally caught up with Grandfather,' Daniel sighed, shaking his head.

'Believe me,' the colonel told the red-haired man in a sympathetic voice, 'if the facts of his indiscretions were not irrefutable, I would dismiss the charges out of hand. But this is treason we are talking about and I have the proof in writing. Naturally Hugh's past history has also come to light.'

'Past history?'

'His dealings with Charles Edward Stewart in the forty-five rebellion,' the colonel whispered.

'I see.'

'Now,' the officer went on, 'I would appreciate it if you would go inside and ask Hugh to surrender quietly without any fuss. Then I can take him back to the barracks, show him to the brigadier and this nasty business will be resolved quickly. No need for soldiers standing about, pointing loaded muskets at poor crofters' cottages and fixing their bayonets to intimidate the populace. Believe me, Hugh will be treated like a gentleman if he gives himself up.'

'Nothing I could say would bring Grandfather out of the house,' Daniel told the colonel.

'Daniel!' the officer pleaded. 'I don't want to see any blood shed. I only brought these soldiers with me because the brigadier insisted upon it. The last thing I want to do is order these men to remove Hugh from his own home under duress.'

'You'll never take him alive,' the red-haired man replied with just a hint of defiance in his voice.

Cumberland sighed and rubbed his forehead. 'Please don't try to force my hand,' he begged quietly.

'You'll never take him alive,' Daniel repeated, 'because he passed away peacefully last night.'

The colonel looked hard into Daniel's eyes, trying to discern whether the other man was telling the truth.

'Passed away?' the officer asked as the relief started to show on his face.

'Last night,' Daniel nodded. 'The priest was with him and all his family were gathered around.'

'Daniel, I can't tell you how relieved I am to hear that!' Cumberland exclaimed with a smile. Then he thought for a second and shook his head. 'I mean, of course, it would have been a terrible thing for me to have to arrest him,' he explained. 'You have my deepest sympathies.'

'Thank you,' Daniel replied.

'Sergeant!' Cumberland ordered.

'Yes, sir?'

'Have the men stand at their ease.'

'Yes, sir,' the sergeant answered with a frown.

'This business could have been very embarrassing for me,' the colonel admitted. 'If my friendship with your grandfather had come to light, it could have spelled the end of my career. I could have kissed my pension goodbye and looked forward to spending the rest of my days rattling keys in Botany Bay.'

'Quite a stroke of luck then,' Daniel observed dryly.

'A terrible loss of course,' the colonel cut in. 'But your grandfather was blessed with a wonderful sense of timing.'

'And it was just like him to always be thinking of others,' Daniel agreed. 'Will you come in for a drink?'

'Just a quick one,' Cumberland acquiesced. 'I'm supposed to be hunting down this nest of rebels.'

'You're not in a great hurry then?'

'Not really, no.'

Together they turned and walked into the cottage just as Father Horan fell unconscious off his seat onto the floor.

'Colonel Cumberland,' Daniel began, 'I'd like you to meet our new parish priest, Father Horan.'

'The good father heard Hugh's confession last night,' Denis explained. 'And he has not been feeling the best ever since.'

'Perfectly understandable under the circumstances,' the colonel nodded. 'How are you, Denis?'

'I could do with a drink,' the old harper beamed.

'Then we'll have one together,' Cumberland replied, clapping his hands enthusiastically. 'But before we do,' he mumbled, broaching the subject of business once more, 'do you think I might be allowed to look in on Hugh?'

'Of course!' Daniel answered. 'How rude of me! I should have offered earlier. You'll be wanting to verify that he is, in fact, gone?'

'Yes,' the colonel admitted. 'Is he in that room at the end of the hall?'

'He is,' Daniel confirmed. 'Go through. You'll find him on his back.'

'I'll just be a minute,' the officer excused himself and then he made his way out to the bedroom where Hugh was still lying in bed.

When Cumberland returned a few minutes later he took a drink from Daniel and offered a toast. 'To Hugh Connor,' the colonel declared, 'a generous host and a fine distiller. A man who would do anything for his friends. May he rest in peace.'

'Aye,' everyone answered.

Father Horan groaned.

At that moment there was a loud knock at the door.

'Colonel?' a man was calling. 'Colonel, may I have a word?'

Daniel opened the door and the sergeant burst in. Two soldiers followed close behind, dragging Edward between them.

Mhairgead followed after, pleading with the redcoats to let the young man go.

'What is the meaning of this intrusion, sergeant?' the colonel bellowed.

'I've captured the rebel who calls himself Edward Sutler of Dublin,' the sergeant declared proudly. 'And this man,' the soldier pointed at Daniel, 'is his accomplice.'

'What are you talking about?' Cumberland frowned.

Daniel suddenly recognised the sergeant. He was the soldier who had tried to arrest Edward at the stream.

'You shot my grandfather's cow,' Daniel accused. 'Without giving any warning whatsoever.'

'Bloody rebel!' the sergeant replied.

'He's soon to be my husband,' Mhairgead cried, 'don't take him away. I couldn't bear to lose another one to the prison hulks.'

'Are you Edward Sutler of Dublin?' Colonel Cumberland cut in tersely.

'I am,' Edward replied, his voice filled with defiance.

'And did you murder Major D'Arcy?'

'I did.'

'Well,' Cumberland went on, his tone weighted with the seriousness of the situation, 'you are to be congratulated for acting as a loyal subject to rid the kingdom of a notorious traitor.'

The colonel turned to the sergeant. 'Release the gentleman.'

'Colonel?' the sergeant stammered in protest.

'I told you to release him.'

'He's a rebel.'

'And if you don't do as I order,' the colonel advised, 'you may consider yourself a mutineer.'

'Does the army still hang mutineers?' Daniel asked casually.

'By God, yes,' Cumberland assured him and downed his whiskey.

'You may go, sergeant,' the officer ordered. 'And have the company form ranks to march back to barracks. I believe there's a beef stew being prepared for their supper. I wouldn't want it to go cold on them.'

'Yes, sir,' the sergeant replied with a hesitant salute. Then he and the other two soldiers were gone.

Cumberland smacked his lips as he handed his empty cup back to Daniel. 'Well, I suppose I had better be getting back to work.'

'Stay for one more,' Daniel urged.

'No, I mustn't really,' Cumberland declined. 'I do have to sort this rebel business out at some point. Perhaps later in the week we could all have a quiet chat over a jug or two? After the wretched ceremonial of the King's birthday parades are finished with.'

'That would be fine,' Daniel told the officer. 'I'll look forward to it.'

'Very well then,' Cumberland concluded. 'Glad to make your acquaintance, Mister Sutler. Congratulations on your impending marriage. She's a fine girl, our Mhairgead.'

The colonel coughed. 'I do hope you won't mention this unfortunate business to anyone,' he said to Edward. 'And I really can't thank you enough for dealing with D'Arcy so efficiently. Of course I should have been on to him long ago but I never suspected a thing. You've saved me a lot of trouble really. I might never have discovered the major's little scheme but for your shooting him in the head.'

'That's quite all right,' Edward replied, somewhat stunned, as the colonel shook his hand.

'If ever you should consider a career in the army, let me know,' Cumberland went on. 'I believe you'd make a fine soldier. And the regiment is always looking for officers who act on their own initiative.'

'I'll consider your offer carefully,' Edward promised with a rather baffled look on his face.

'Fine,' Cumberland smiled. 'Mhairgead, Denis, Father Horan, Daniel,' the colonel nodded to each in turn, 'I bid you good day.'

As soon as the officer had gone Edward went straight to the table, poured himself a whiskey and sat down heavily on the hearthstone beside the sprawled form of Father Horan. He drained the cup in his hand then turned to face the red-haired man.

'Thank you, Daniel,' he said. 'You didn't have to stand up for me.'

'Don't thank me,' Daniel laughed. 'Thank Grandfather. If he hadn't breathed his last just when he did, you could have found yourself in deep trouble. As it is, Cumberland is more than happy to let the matter of D'Arcy's death be brushed aside.'

The drums began to beat again outside as the company of redcoats marched off.

'Don't we have a funeral to arrange?' Denis reminded everyone.

'If we can wake the priest,' Daniel sighed.

'He's not going to be any use to us,' Mhairgead told her brother. 'Look at him. He must have slept fifteen hours and he's still a mess.'

'I can sympathise,' Edward cut in. 'Poor fool.'

'Throw a bucket of water over him,' Denis suggested.

'He's a priest!' Mhairgead gasped. 'You can't do that to a priest!'

'Don't they ever wash?' the old harper asked.

'Not fully dressed, I imagine,' Edward opined.

'Well he's no use to us like that,' Daniel decided. 'Perhaps we should send out for another one.'

'There's a race meeting today in the next parish,' Denis advised. 'You are bound to find a priest or two there.'

'No, this one will have to do,' Daniel explained. 'There isn't more than a few hours till sundown and there's rain on the horizon. So if we want to bury Grandfather today, we had better see that Father Horan is sober.'

'What do you suggest?' Mhairgead asked.

'Throw a bucket of water over him,' Daniel shrugged, heading outside to fetch a bucket. He was at the door when Finbar and Francis appeared carrying an empty coffin.

'Did you finish the grave?' Daniel asked his brothers.

'It is the finest hole in the ground in the parish,' Finbar told him, looking back over his shoulder. 'Fit for a king. If he were alive he would have nothing but praise for it.'

'If he were alive he wouldn't stand in need of it,' Denis noted dryly as Daniel left to draw the water.

'I'll go and wash the body,' Mhairgead told Edward. 'You look after our future bishop.'

Edward nodded and stood staring at the unconscious priest, not really knowing what to do. Daniel returned shortly and immediately tossed the contents of the bucket over Father Horan. The priest gasped and sat straight up, his hair standing on end.

'Christ in all His majesty,' he screamed, 'what in the name of Lucifer is going on here?'

'Now you are sounding more like a Jesuit,' the old harper said, clapping his hands together, 'invoking the Devil with a passion.'

The priest sat on a chair by the fire and wiped the water from his face. He immediately took a cup from Edward and drank the contents down quickly without the slightest hint of discomfort. Then he calmly held the cup out for more.

'It doesn't take long for the spell to take effect,' Daniel noted and he poured himself another drink while they waited for the body to be prepared.

In due course Mhairgead came out into the main room again and announced that Hugh was ready to be laid in his coffin.

'It is time,' she told them solemnly, 'to make our way up to the hill to bury him.'

'The churchyard is two miles away,' Father Horan complained. 'It is too far. We'll never make it before sunset.'

'We are not going to the churchyard,' Daniel explained. 'It was my grandfather's wish to be buried on the site of his first still. On the very spot where he lost his eyesight all those years ago. It was the last place he looked upon on this earth and so he thought it appropriate that it be his final resting place also.'

'But that is not consecrated ground!' the priest objected.

'Then you will have to consecrate it, won't you?' Daniel told him, a hard edge to his voice.

Father Horan looked into the red-haired man's eyes, gulped and said quickly, 'Very well.' He held out his cup with trembling fingers. 'I will oblige you, if you will oblige me.'

Daniel smiled. 'I have four barrels of that stuff sitting in an underground cellar,' he told Horan. 'And you can have the bloody lot.'

'I can?' Horan asked meekly. The priest screwed up his face and shut his eyes tight as if he were fighting a great internal battle against the demons of temptation.

And losing.

'What are we doing sitting here wagging our chins?' Denis demanded. 'We have one man itching to be buried and another eager to be drowned.'

'I'll take your offer,' Horan accepted finally. 'Not for myself, you understand, but for the comfort of the sick and the infirm. And to help Father Anthony rest at the end of each day.'

'And you'll perform the burial without any further objections?' Daniel asked.

'I'll give you a burial for each barrel if you like,' Father Horan answered and then, realising he had betrayed his eagerness, blushed. 'I mean to say, if ever anyone else in your family needs burying, I would be honoured to perform the rites.'

'That's what I like to hear,' Denis murmured. 'The satisfied sound of a man who loves his work.'

Daniel, Edward, Francis and Finbar lifted Hugh into his coffin, nailed the lid shut tight and carried the burden up to the hill. They were led on by Father Horan and followed by Mhairgead and Denis. The rest of the family, who had been away gathering turf, came after in a ragged procession.

It was a short journey. The grave was within sight of the cottages. And so it was that, after an adventurous life, old Hugh was laid in his grave with a jug of fine whiskey under his arm.

The young priest spoke his words over the coffin, committing the body back to the soil and the soul to a dubious future somewhere between the holy bliss of Heaven and the eternal fires of Hell. When his speech was ended, Father Horan made a slow progression around the assembled family, offering condolences and assurances of God's almighty plan.

As the priest was doing his rounds Denis sat on the ground preparing to play the harp one last time for his old friend. Finbar and Francis began shovelling the clods of earth down into the grave. They were nearly finished when Father Horan made the suggestion that everyone go back to the house for a drink. Mhairgead and Daniel led the way, already heatedly discussing the future.

They had not gone far when the harper struck up a merry tune that had Father Horan looking back to the grave and crossing himself again.

'The very thought of it,' he hissed at Edward who was standing a little away from the graveside, listening to the harper. 'To play a jig at a man's graveside. If that is not blasphemy, I don't know what is.'

'I think old Hugh would appreciate it,' Edward grinned, ignoring the priest. 'You had better get back to the house before Daniel doles out all your whiskey.'

Horan's eyes widened with worry and he was off without another word.

Finbar and Francis were soon done so they made for the house, leaving Edward to wait for Denis.

The young rebel closed his eyes to concentrate on the glorious sounds emanating from the harp. And almost immediately a series of wondrous images came clearly to his mind.

Edward could see an island looming out of a great calm lough. In the centre of the island there was a grey stone cathedral. And along the shoreline Edward thought he could make out a group of people who seemed to be waving to him. Then a great mist rolled in across the lough and suddenly the island was gone, swallowed up by the fog.

As he listened he imagined Hugh dancing a merry jig with his master, and gathered all about were the friends they had made over the years. The two men, harper and servant, bowed to one another and at that very instant Denis finished his lively tune. The last notes rang out clearly across the hillside. Edward opened his eyes, realising he had been given a glimpse of the Otherworld.

Then the young rebel went to help the old harper to his feet.

'I'll carry the harp back to the fireside,' Edward offered.

'Where do you think old Hugh will be sleeping tonight?' Denis asked the young man.

'I don't know,' Edward admitted. 'But I like to think that right this minute he's sitting down on the side of a field in the land of the Good People, watching a hurling match and drinking his fill. I can almost hear that tune, SheeBeg SheeMor, playing as the opponents prepare to do battle.'

The old harper laughed.

'I think of him telling outrageous tales at the fireside to the King of the Faeries and his wife,' the harper giggled.

'She is the queen,' Edward smiled, correcting the old harper. 'He is merely her consort.'

Denis chortled again merrily.

'Are you really off to America then?' the harper asked, suddenly serious.

Edward looked to the ground. 'I have given it some thought,' he began slowly, 'and I reckon I might offer to give Daniel a hand with the farm for a while and see what happens from there. And I would like to write down the story old Hugh told me. I think it would make a good read. And I have a notion that I'd like to learn the noble art of distilling for myself.'

'He would be mighty happy with that, Master Edward,' Denis hummed. 'Mighty happy.'

'Tell me, Denis,' the young man said, changing the subject. 'That was a strange piece to play at a man's graveside, wasn't it? Especially the grave of a dear friend.'

'What do you mean?'

'I have never heard a dance tune played at a funeral before.'

'That wasn't a dance,' Denis smiled as he searched in his pockets for his pipe.

'What was it then?' Edward asked.

'That was Carolan's Concerto.'

Caiseal Mór

The Circle and the Cross
Book One of The Wanderers

A rich historical drama that blends fact and fiction in a sumptuous feast of storytelling.

Imagine that you sit warming yourself by a fire in a tiny settlement lying deep in snow. Sweet peat smoke scents the chill breeze and an old song-maker raises a keening cry for summer's long absence. Here amongst folk who call themselves the Feni was a young lad born and there passed his first years on Earth.

Raised as the son of a blacksmith, Mawn, this very lad, knows little of the world outside his sleepy village.

But Eirinn, his island home, is in turmoil. Black-robed monks have made their way across the tempestuous sea from Rome and have set the people at war with one another.

The High-King and his Druid Council know that they cannot survive the furious might of the Roman Empire so they must find other ways to save their ancient magical traditions from the evils that threaten to engulf them.

For this great task the Council has named a young boy who amongst the Feni was born and there passed his first years on Earth ...

'An immensely satisfying fusion between early Celtic history and fantasy'

Dr Colleen McCullough

Caiseal Mór

The Song of the Earth
Book Two of The Wanderers

Nine seasons have passed since the Druid Council of Eirinn banished the sadistic Christian, Palladius, from its island shores.

But now an even greater force has arrived from Rome in the shape of Patricius, a powerful and fearless bishop who is determined to corrupt the ancient traditions of the Druids to his own ends. Aiding him in his task is a monk whose very name inspires fear and hatred in all Eirinn.

It is nine seasons, too, since Mawn and Sianan began their Druid training. Now they face their greatest test: a journey to the Otherworld. Only if they survive can they partake of the Quicken potion brewed by the Faerie kind, which will make them Wanderers, keepers of the ancient magical ways.

But as they undergo their testing, a fierce confrontation is taking place between Patricius and the High-King of Eirinn. Neither leader wishes for bloodshed but there is one amongst them who is determined to destroy any hope of peace, intent only on violent and bloody revenge.

Caiseal Mór

The Water of Life
Book Three of the Wanderers

High on a grassy hill on the troubled island of Eirinn two young Druids eat the sacred bread of the Faerie folk and drink the holy Water of Life. With this wine and this bread Mawn and Sianan embrace the burden and the blessing of eternal life. They will be Wanderers through the endless years, sent as messengers to future generations to preserve the ancient customs and beliefs of the Druid kind.

With the King and Queen of Munster, and their teacher, Gobann of the Silver Branch, they journey to Alba to help free the Gaels of Dal Araidhe from the savagery of the barbaric Saxons. Old friends, such as Declan, the Christian Abbot of Saint Ninian's, travel with them, as well as old enemies, such as Seginus Gallus, murderer, traitor, renegade priest.

The Saxons are not easily defeated, however. They have made a surprising alliance with a man hated and feared by the people of Eirinn, who brings with him techniques of war that herald victory for the Saxons. A bloody battle is fought on Samhain day and what has been foretold for so many years finally comes to pass. Leaving the Wanderers alone on their endless cycle of the soul ...

EARTHLIGHT

A SELECTED LIST OF FANTASY TITLES
AVAILABLE FROM EARTHLIGHT

THE PRICES SHOWN BELOW WERE CORRECT AT THE TIME OF
GOING TO PRESS. HOWEVER EARTHLIGHT RESERVE THE
RIGHT TO SHOW NEW RETAIL PRICES ON COVERS WHICH MAY
DIFFER FROM THOSE PREVIOUSLY ADVERTISED IN THE TEXT
OR ELSEWHERE.

☐	0 7434 0893 4	Talisker	Miller Lau	£6.99
☐	0 6848 6036 8	Cettika	Robert Holdstock	£16.99
☐	0 6710 2261 X	The Sum Of All Men	David Farland	£6.99
☐	0 7434 0827 6	Brotherhood of the Wolf	David Farland	£6.99
☐	0 6848 6061 9	Wizardborn	David Farland	£10.00
☐	0 6710 1785 3	The Royal Changeling	John Whitbourn	£5.99
☐	0 6710 3300 X	Downs-Lord Dawn	John Whitbourn	£5.99
☐	0 6710 2193 1	Sailing to Sarantium	Guy Gavriel Kay	£6.99
☐	0 7434 0825 X	Lord of Emperors	Guy Gavriel Kay	£6.99
☐	0 6848 6131 3	The Dreamthief's Daughter	Michael Moorcock	£16.99
☐	0 6848 6670 6	Silverheart	Michael Moorcock & Storm Constantine	£16.99
☐	0 6710 2190 7	The Amber Citadel	Freda Warrington	£5.99
☐	0 7484 0826 8	The Sapphire Throne	Harry Turtledove	£5.99
☐	0 6710 2282 2	Into The Darkness	Harry Turtledove	£5.99
☐	0 6710 3305 0	Darkness Descending	Harry Turtledove	£6.99
☐	0 6848 6007 4	Through the Darkness	Harry Turtledove	£10.00
☐	0 6710 2189 3	The Siege of Arrandin	Marcus Herniman	£5.99

All Earthlight titles are available by post from:

Book Service By Post, P.O. Box 29, Douglas, Isle of Man IM99 1BQ

Credit cards accepted. Please telephone 01624 675137,
fax 01624 670923, Internet http://www.bookpost.co.uk or
e-mail: bookshop@enterprise.net for details.

Free postage and packing in the UK. Overseas customers allow
£1 per book (paperbacks) and £3 per book (hardbacks).